Applause for Joe Keenan's

My Lucky Star

"Joe Keenan fills *My Lucky Star* with the kind of zany twists he perfected in *Frasier*." —Raven Snook, *Time Out New York*

"Keenan's comedy is of a high order . . . sophisticated, deliciously camp entertainment." —Kate Saunders, *The Times*

"Part high satire, part *Will & Grace*, and part clue-sniffing Nick, Nora, and Nick." —Emily Gordon, *Newsday*

"When you think page-turner, you probably think of a crime novel or a thriller. Or maybe a juicy tell-all biography. Now take the suspense and gossip and stir in a good splash of laughs. *Voilà!* You have a novel by Joe Keenan. . . . The main attraction is Keenan's seemingly bottomless inkwell of bons mots and witty zingers. . . . Bring on the popcorn!" —John Terauds, *Toronto Star*

"Keenan's command of the written word is as deft as the words he puts in other people's mouths on TV. . . . *My Lucky Star* is a venomously funny autopsy of the hypocrisy and venality of Hollywood . . . the funniest novel of the year." —Ian O'Doherty, *Irish Independent*

"Keenan clearly has been schooled in the Academy of Plot. . . . The novel is fueled by twists and turns, contrivances and coincidences. There's even a car chase." —Debra Weinstein, *Washington Post*

"The Hollywood farce, with its made-up celebrities who are never quite as ridiculous as the real thing, is tricky to pull off. But as a former head writer on *Frasier*, Keenan has the advantage of insider knowledge for this hilarious tale. . . . The manic twists and jibes at modern celebrity are a delight." —Andrea Mullaney, *Scotland on Sunday*

"A delight . . . relentlessly humorous. . . . Although Keenan's side-splitting writing is often compared to P. G. Wodehouse's . . . the wit is incredibly elegant and owes more than a little to Oscar Wilde and Ronald Firbank, with more subtle dashes of the lyric agility of Noel Coward and Cole Porter."　　　　　—Frederik Liljeblad, *Pages*

"An uproarious satire on Hollywood life. *My Lucky Star* is a gift from the gods."　　　　　—Kelly Apter, *The List*

"*My Lucky Star* is madcap, charming, and hilarious. . . . Keenan's in fine form here with both farce and wit."
　　　　　—Marilyn Dahl, *Shelf Awareness*

"Witty, twisted, dry as a martini, and sporting more daringly stylish wrinkles than a Hollywood bad boy's tuxedo after a long night in questionable company, *My Lucky Star* lampoons the very excess in which it gleefully partakes, jumping from the lofty to the low and back again with easy abandon."　　　　　—Kilian Melloy, AfterElton.com

"Joe Keenan's novel has taken him two decades to complete, but it has been worth the wait. It's a feisty, entertaining tale."　　—*Metro London*

"The glamorous Hollywood novel gets a sharp send-up as a smart drawing-room comedy crossed liberally with farce. . . . The witty banter, zany plot twists, and colorful, likable characters (even the dastardly villains) prove a delight for fans of brainy comedy. If the ghost of Noel Coward isn't pleased, Frasier's is."　　　　　—*Booklist*

"A hilarious cast of writers, actors, agents, and hacks collide in vicious, psychotic, backstabbing, and back-scuttling mayhem . . . fart-out-loud funny."
　　　　　—*Lads Mag*

Also by Joe Keenan

Blue Heaven

Putting on the Ritz

My Lucky Star

A Novel

Joe Keenan

BACK BAY BOOKS

LITTLE, BROWN AND COMPANY

NEW YORK   BOSTON   LONDON

Back Bay Books / Little, Brown and Company
Hachette Book Group USA
1271 Avenue of the Americas, New York, NY 10020
Visit our Web site at www.HachetteBookGroupUSA.com

Originally published in hardcover by Little, Brown and Company, January 2006
First Back Bay paperback edition, November 2006

The characters and events in this book are fictitious. Any similarity to real persons, living or dead, is coincidental and not intended by the author.

Library of Congress Cataloging-in-Publication Data
Keenan, Joe.
My lucky star : a novel / Joe Keenan. — 1st ed.
p. cm.
HC ISBN 0-316-06019-4
PB ISBN 0-316-01335-8 / 978-0-316-01335-2
1. Screenwriters — Fiction. 2. Motion picture actors and actresses — Fiction. 3. Hollywood (Los Angeles, Calif.) — Fiction. 4. Authorship — Collaboration — Fiction. 5. Autobiography — Authorship — Fiction. 6. Motion picture industry — Fiction. 7. Closeted gays — Fiction. 8. Ghostwriters — Fiction. 9. Gay men — Fiction. I. Title.
PS3561.E365M9   2006
813'.54 — dc22   2005010882

10   9   8   7   6   5   4   3   2   1

Q-MART

Text design by Meryl Sussman Levavi
Printed in the United States of America

For Chris and David Lloyd

My Lucky Star

One

★

I T IS NEVER A HAPPY MOMENT in the life of a struggling artist when some fresh assault on his fragile dignity compels him finally and painfully to concede that Failure has lost its charm. He has up until this point soldiered bravely along, managing to persuade himself that there's something not merely noble but downright jolly about Struggle, about demeaning temp jobs, day-old baked goods, and pitchers of beer nursed like dying pets into the night. He would, of course, grant that *la vie Bohème* with its myriad deprivations and anxieties was not an unalloyed delight. But whenever its indignities rankled unduly he could console himself with his certainty that Bohemia was not, after all, his permanent address. Oh, no. His present charmingly scruffy existence was a mere preamble to his real life, a larval stage from which he would soon gloriously emerge into the sunshine of success. Its small embarrassments were, if anything, to be prized, not only for their lessons in humility but for the many droll, self-deprecatory anecdotes they would later provide, stories he'd polish and trot out for parties, interviews, and—why be pessimistic?—talk shows.

Then one day he is faced with some final affront, minor perhaps, but so symbolically freighted as to land on him with the force of an inadequately cabled Steinway. He reels, stunned, and dark speculations, long and successfully repressed, rampage through his mind. For the first time he allows himself to wonder if his life twenty years hence will be any different than his present existence. "Of course it will be different," coos the voice in his head. "You'll be old."

From this icy thought a short road leads to panic, and from panic to despair, self-pity, desperation, and, finally, Los Angeles.

MY OWN RUDE EPIPHANY came a year ago last fall shortly after the closing of *Three to Tango*, a larky little comedy I'd written with my good friend and collaborator Claire Simmons. The play had been enthusiastically received in a series of readings, stirring a cautious hope in Claire's heart and extravagant optimism in my own. The production, alas, was doomed from the start, owing chiefly to our producer's decision to present the show in a small basement playhouse that was as damp as Atlantis and harder to find. We tried to persuade him that the show might fare better in a space that felt more like a theater and less like a hideout, but he felt confident that people would find us. People did not. We opened in mid-September and by month's end the play had closed and I was back to my day job, pounding the pavement as an outdoor messenger for the Jackrabbit Courier Service.

You might suppose this experience would have left me a broken and bitter man, but on the day in question my mood was actually pretty chipper. The autumn weather was brisk and lovely. The job, though lacking a certain prestige, allowed me to write much of the day, and I'd just gotten an idea for a new comedy. Best of all, my chum Gilbert, whose consoling presence I'd sorely missed during the deathwatch for my play, was due to return soon from Los Angeles. I'd been slightly miffed at his desertion but couldn't really blame him. His mother, Maddie, had recently snagged herself a rich Hollywood mogul, and Gilbert—who if mooching were an Olympic sport would have his picture on Wheaties boxes—could not resist flying west to bond with the lovebirds poolside. I looked forward to hearing of his romantic exploits, which, if the hints in his e-mails were any indication, would give new life to the phrase "Westward Ho." So buoyant in fact was my mood that I was even coping stoically with the news that a musical penned by the loathsome Marlowe Heppenstall, my nemesis since high school, had opened to unfathomably kind reviews and was looking like a major hit.

By late afternoon the benevolent sunshine had given way to darker skies and a sudden cloudburst forced me to sprint the six blocks to my final destination, a Park Avenue law office. I raced into the building, ascended to the seventeenth floor, and entered a spacious foyer, every mahogany-paneled inch of which bespoke the age and prosperity of the firm. The prim, bespectacled woman at the desk glanced up and fixed me with that look of quizzical disdain legal receptionists have long reserved for dampened members of the messenger class.

I removed from my satchel an envelope addressed to a Mr. Charles O'Donnell and marked PERSONAL. I presented this to the human pince-nez, who gazed right past me and said, "Mr. O'Donnell, this just came for you."

I turned. Walking toward us was an extremely handsome blond fellow about my age, dressed in a flawlessly tailored charcoal pin-striped suit. He had wonderfully broad shoulders though I couldn't say if this was the result of weight training or if it was workout enough just lifting the massive Rolex and chunky gold cuff links that sparkled on his tanned wrists.

Reminding myself, as I need to at such moments, that this was not a movie and the fellow could *see* me, I tried not to stare too blatantly as I handed him the envelope. He took it, barely glancing at me, then did a little double take as though he recognized me but wasn't sure where from. He suddenly looked familiar to me as well. I wondered if we'd shared some fleeting romantic liaison but immediately dismissed this notion as it hinged on the ludicrous premise that I could have slept with such a man then forgotten him. I knew that if we'd dallied even once ten years ago, I'd still be mooning over him and writing maudlin sonnets starting "If love, thou wouldst but phone me once again."

His puzzled look morphed suddenly into a smile of delighted surprise.

"Phil?" he said. "Phil Cavanaugh?"

Light dawned.

"Oh my God! Chuck O'Donnell! How the hell are you?"

"I don't believe this. It's so great to see you!"

We'd been friends back in high school, though only briefly as we'd moved in very different circles. Chuck had been the brightest member of the football-playing, cheerleader-groping set, while I had been a leading light of the sarcastic, underwear-ad-ogling theater crowd. He'd crossed lines once, gamely agreeing to play the braggart warrior Miles Gloriosus in *A Funny Thing Happened on the Way to the Forum* when our own group failed to produce a single nonrisible candidate for the role.

I scrutinized his face, which seemed different, improved in some way.

"You're looking at my nose, right?" he said with a laugh. "I broke it boxing a few times. They kept having to reset it."

"Ah," I said, wondering what it must be like to live so charmed a life that facial injuries only made you handsomer.

"Look at you." I grinned. "Mr. Big Shot Lawyer."

"Not so big, trust me. How 'bout you? Still writing plays?"

"Just did one."

"That's great! How'd it go?"

"Really well," I said. "Big hit."

It was the sort of fib I might have gotten away with had we met at a cocktail party and I was wearing the secondhand yet stylish jacket Gilbert calls my Salvation Armani. The problem was we *weren't* at a cocktail party. We were in the stately foyer of his white-shoe law firm and I was wearing faded jeans, waterlogged Nikes, and a gray polo shirt adorned with my company's logo, a zealous, bucktoothed rabbit in a mauve tracksuit. In short, I was in no position to swank.

Charlie, bless him, managed to say "Great" without a trace of irony, but the receptionist, who'd never liked me, didn't even try to keep her eyebrows in neutral. Mortified, I averted my gaze, which landed on the foyer's large gilt mirror.

I spoke earlier of moments that carry a great symbolic weight. This was unquestionably such a moment. There we stood, Charlie looking straight out of a Barneys catalog and I in my soggy ensemble from the *Grapes of Wrath* Collection. So perfectly did we exemplify our divergent fortunes that we might have been allegorical figures from some medieval morality play, with Charlie starring as Diligence Rewarded and self in the cameo role of Dashed Hopes.

"So," said Charlie as the blood drained from my face, "been in New York long?"

"Since school," I mumbled, searching for a way to say that, while I was enjoying our chat, I should really get going as I'd be needing to burst into tears soon. The receptionist, more eager to rescue Charlie than me, reminded him of an impending meeting.

"Gotta run. But hey, let me know next time you've got a show on."

"You bet."

"My wife loves the theater. In fact that's what you just brought me—tickets for this new musical. Friend of mine couldn't use 'em."

"Ah."

"Maybe you've heard of it?" he said, then smacked his forehead comically. "What am I saying? Of course you have. It's by Marlowe—you know, Marlowe Heppenstall from school? Are you two still in touch?"

WHEN SUCH MOMENTS BEFALL US, we have, of course, two options. We can say "Fiddle-dee-dee" and shrug it off or we can surrender entirely to self-lacerating despair. I chose the latter course and, after walking sixty blocks in the rain to my small, unkempt apartment, settled into a chair with a nice view of the air shaft to contemplate my future.

It did not look bright.

I was twenty-nine. This meant I was still technically a young man, though no longer *young* young, thirty being, as everyone under it knows, the middle age of youth. True middle age was still reasonably distant, though not, as it had once been, unimaginably so.

My career to date had consisted of a frustrating series of near misses. While I'd never had any trouble imagining the ultimate breakthrough, it was now equally easy to picture this dispiriting pattern repeating itself till I woke one day to find I'd become that most poignant figure the theater has to offer, the Struggling Old Playwright.

I'd met my share of them, bloated pasty fellows, doggedly upbeat or surly and embittered, haunting the workshops and readings where their younger brethren gathered. I'd seen them in theater-district bars, cadging drinks while boasting of their latest effort, often a retooling of some earlier work culled from the trunk and reread with a parent's myopic affection.

"Amazing how well it holds up! Why it's more timely now than when I wrote it. Can't believe Playwrights passed on it back then. Just as well though since Streep was too young at the time to play Fiona and she'd be perfect now. Damn, left my wallet home."

There was one especially Falstaffian old gasbag whom Gilbert and I had often observed in our favorite watering hole. Not knowing his name, we'd christened him Milo. In my imagination, which had grown uncontrollably morbid, I pictured him twenty years from now, older, fatter, but still warming the same bar stool. I watched him turn toward the bar's entrance, his blubbery lips parting in a smile of welcome. He patted the stool next to his with a nicotine-stained hand and bid the weary newcomer welcome.

"Philip! We've been wondering where you were. Wouldn't be a proper Friday without you. Sorry I missed your birthday bash at the Ground Round. Any word from MTC on the new one? . . . The philistines! . . . How awkwardly you're holding your glass—the old carpal tunnel acting up again? Well then, here's a bug I'll just put in your ear—you tell Blue Cross they can stuff their job, then come join me behind the necktie counter at Saks! What fun we'll have, discussing our plays and ogling the young ones! I tell you, Philip, the days just fly by!"

This ghastly reverie was mercifully interrupted by the shrill buzz of my intercom. I shambled to the door and asked who it was.

"It's me," said Claire through the crackle of static. "Can I come up?"

I buzzed her in, relieved to have a sympathetic listener to whom I could relate the day's tragic events. You can imagine my chagrin then when she burst melodramatically through the door, her mood apparently even fouler than my own.

"It's over!" she declared hotly, stabbing her umbrella into the orange crate that served as a stand.

"Oh?"

"I mean it this time. He saw her again!"

"He," I knew, referred to her boyfriend, Marco, a very hirsute ceramist Gilbert and I had nicknamed "Hairy Potter." "Her" could have referred to either of his two former girlfriends. Since moving in with Claire he'd vowed to put them both behind him, though when he met one he tended to put her beneath him. Claire did not elaborate. She just removed her raincoat and hurled herself onto my couch, where she sat, arms crossed, awaiting compassion.

I found this quite irksome. I'd assumed that if there was any sympathy to be offered I'd be on the receiving end. To be asked, in my shattered state, to start dishing it out made me feel like a stabbing victim who's just lurched into the emergency room, only to be tossed a pair of scrubs and told to get to work on the burn victims.

"What's with you?" she asked, noting my tetchy expression.

"Sorry. It so happens I've had a pretty vile day myself."

"Oh?" she asked.

There was a note of challenge in her voice, and, hearing it, I decided not to elaborate. A woman whose man has just done her dirty was not likely to care that I'd been seen to bad advantage by an old classmate. I could, of course, have thrown in the stuff about Milo and the necktie counter, but Claire's a logical girl and would only have pointed out that my undistinguished midlife, however sad, was still somewhat theoretical, that her own misfortune had actually *happened* and that this was, perhaps, a useful distinction.

"Never mind. Scotch?"

"Please."

I poured us both stiff shots of Teachers as Claire poured out her tale, which differed little from the others I'd heard since Marco had oiled his way into her heart. Three suspicious hang ups, questions as to recent whereabouts, inept lying, expert grilling, confession, tears, shouting, "Go back to your whore," curtain.

"It's really over this time," she proclaimed. "I mean it."

"Good."

"And don't roll your eyes."

"When did I roll my eyes?"

"Just now. Inwardly. You're enjoying this."

"*Excuse* me?"

"You never liked Marco. You're thrilled to see your low opinion's been borne out."

"Thanks a lot!" I said, miffed. "You think it *pleases* me when Chewbacca mistreats you? You're my friend, for Christ's sake. This upsets me."

A noble sentiment, if not entirely true. There is, I confess, a small mingy part of me that feels, if not quite pleased, not exactly crushed either that, when it comes to men, Claire's instincts are even sorrier than my own. It's not that I wish her ill. It's just that in every other aspect of our lives she's so annoyingly and unquestionably my superior.

She's smarter than me. She speaks four languages to my one and I've stopped even trying to play chess with her, as my odds of winning are the same I'd enjoy in a Czechoslovakian spelling bee. She's a much better person too. She volunteers, writes thank-you notes, and adheres to a code of ethics the average bishop might find uncomfortably lacking in wiggle room. Most unforgivably, she's more talented than me. She composes marvelous music, something I can't do at all, and, when we write plays, tosses off bons mots and plot twists with a facility that leaves me feeling both dazzled and superfluous.

So when she periodically announces that she has, owing to her woeful misjudgment, taken yet another one on the chin from Cupid, my compassion is always leavened by an agreeable dollop of condescension. How nice for a change to be the one who gets to cluck sympathetically while thinking, "Poor dear, when *will* she learn?"

I topped off her glass and let her vent some more. When she'd finished I described my mortifying encounter with Charlie, adding several poignant embellishments.

"How awful for you!" she gasped. "There were actual pigeon droppings on your cap?"

"I had no idea till Charlie pointed it out!"

"How utterly tactless! Almost as bad as Marco. You know what he said when he left?"

"We're on to me now."

"Sorry, go on."

When I'd finished we agreed that our souls required the healing balm that could only be provided by a highly fattening meal sluiced down with a suitably excessive quantity of wine. We were donning our coats, debating the relative merits of Carmine's fettuccine Alfredo and Szechuan West's Double-Fried Chicken Happiness, when my phone rang. I let the machine answer and heard Gilbert's voice bellowing cheerfully from the speaker.

"Hi, Philip, it's me! Are you there? Pick up! That's an order! You may not screen this call!"

Claire shot me a pleading look, but I raised two fingers promising brevity and crossed to the phone as Gilbert continued his wheedling.

"Pick up! I have news, Philip! Amazing news!"

"Hey," I said, "are you back early?"

"No, I'm still in LA."

"When are you coming back?"

"Never!" he said exultantly. "I never want to leave this magical place and neither will you once you're out here."

"What are you talking about?" I asked, confused. "What's this earth-shattering news?"

"He saw Cher at Home Depot," said Claire.

"Tell Claire I heard that. What's she doing there? No date tonight with Hairy Potter?"

"No, they broke up."

"Do you *mind?*" said Claire.

"About time," said Gilbert. "The hair on those shoulders! Like epaulets!"

"Your news?" I prompted.

"I got us a job!"

So intrigued was I by the last and loveliest word of this sentence, i.e., "job," that it took me a moment to register the more ominous one lurking dead center. How could he have gotten "us" a job when there did not, for ample reason, exist any professional entity that could be described this way?

"What do you mean, 'us'?"

"You and me, naturally. Claire too, of course. Can't have her back home mooning over wolf boy while we're off conquering Tinseltown."

"The job's for all *three* of us?"

"Hang up," said Claire, her instinct for self-preservation undulled by the scotch.

"Yes. And for big bucks too. I should think at least fifty apiece."

"Fifty thousand *each?!*" I exclaimed and even Claire's eyes betrayed a wary glimmer of interest. "What is it, a writing job?"

"No, I got us a gig as astronauts. Of course it's a writing job. We're adapting a novel into a screenplay."

"But . . . but *how?*" I sputtered.

"Connections, baby! I'll explain it all when I see you tomorrow. You're booked on the two-thirty flight. American Airlines."

"Tomorrow?!"

"First class, of course!" he assured me, as if that were the issue.

"Tomorrow?"

"Is that a problem?" he asked impatiently.

"Well, it's pretty damned sudden! We're supposed to just drop everything and hop on a plane?"

"What the hell's stopping you?" he said, getting testy.

"Well," I sniffed, "I *do* have a job."

The moment I said it I realized that, while there may have been valid reasons for me to reject such an offer, my standing commitment to trudge through Manhattan delivering parcels to the contemptuous was not the most compelling I might have offered. Gilbert concurred.

"Your JOB?" he shouted incredulously. "Your MESSENGER JOB? Are you *insane?!* For ten years I have listened and pretty damned patiently while you've bitched and moaned about your tragic career. Poor noble Philip, struggling to keep the torch of Molière aloft and no one will give him a break! Now I'm standing here handing you Success on a silver tray with tartar sauce and you're *arguing* with me? I'll only say this once—TAKE THE DAMN JOB! Pass it up and, as God is my witness, I'll write the damn script myself, win an Oscar for it, then spend the rest of my life following you with a sharp knife and a salt-shaker!!"

"All right! Calm down! Did I say we wouldn't come? I just need to talk it over with Claire."

"Talk all you like, just get her out here. And by the way, you're *welcome!*"

"Give me a break, okay? This is all a bit abrupt."

"That's how things happen out here," he said, all cheery again. "It's a very impulsive town. I'm fitting in beautifully. See you at LAX!"

"Don't hang up!"

"I'm late for a date. Your tickets will be at the counter. Bobby arranged it."

"Bobby who?" I asked, but he was gone. I replaced the receiver and turned to Claire, whose face had taken on that stern squinty look it gets whenever Gilbert descends on our playground proffering candy.

"Well! How's that for good news? He's found us a job!"

"I gathered."

"Hollywood, baby!" I said in my best Sgt. Bilko voice. "Our ship has come in!"

"Have you counted the lifeboats?" she replied and exited to the hall.

I locked the door and caught up with her in my building's cramped vestibule-cum-gentleman's lounge. She sailed grimly into the drizzly night and I fell in beside her, wondering how on earth I could coax her onto that plane.

YOU MIGHT SUPPOSE THAT a high-paying Hollywood job would not be a difficult thing to sell to a heartsick lady playwright whose most recent offspring had expired quietly in the cradle. You would only suppose this, however, if you didn't know Gilbert.

Claire knew Gilbert.

And even if she were willing, in the hope of financial gain, to over-look his complete lack of talent, his nonexistent scruples and alto-gether tenuous grasp of reality, there remained still his most unique and troubling feature, i.e., the spectacular, almost supernatural rotten-ness of his luck.

Gilbert's friends and victims have long debated what lies at the root of his uncanny knack for misfortune. Some feel it's karmic pay-back for misdeeds in a previous life in which he must have been, at the very least, a Cossack. Others maintain that a touchy sorceress must have been given the bum's rush at his christening. Whatever the rea-son, bad luck trails Gilbert like some relentless paparazzo. It dogs his footsteps, pops up where least expected, and rains disaster upon him and any hapless confederates he's cajoled along for the ride. Twice in the past Claire had (thanks solely to me) become embroiled in Gilbert's affairs with results ranging from mere humiliation to mortal peril. She was not eager as such to enlist for a third tour of duty, no matter how generous the signing bonus.

I understood her apprehension, feeling more than a shiver of it myself. But, convinced that my alternative was Milo and necktie land, I'd decided to view Gilbert's previous debacles as a mere bad-luck streak that *had,* after all, to end *sometime.*

"I can't believe," I said, as we settled into our favorite booth at Carmine's, "that you're thinking of refusing this."

"I can't believe you're not."

"C'mon! This is exactly what we need! After all we've been through. The timing's perfect!"

"That," said Claire, "is what scares me. It's so typical of Gilbert. He always oils around with these offers just when you're at your most vulnerable. He's like some—"

"Friend in need?"

"Opportunistic infection. And by the way, what's this nonsense about him passing us off as a team? You don't find *that* alarming?" asked Claire, who'd sooner have collaborated with Al Qaeda.

I replied that though a creative partnership with Gilbert was unlikely to prove the maxim that many hands make light the work, his motive for proposing it was obvious. He'd clearly used his formidable powers of persuasion to talk his way into a job, then, fearing himself not up to the task, drafted us as partners. "And a lucky thing for us, considering how bad we are at selling ourselves. Anyway," I added, playing my strongest card, "I can't wait to see the look on Marco's face when he hears you're scaling the heights in Hollywood."

I could see that Claire had not yet viewed the matter from this perspective. Her scowl softened, and a smile, fleeting but unmistakable, played across her lips. As any wronged lover knows, success is the best revenge, and nothing stokes ambition like an unworthy ex begging to be left in the dust.

"He *never* took your career seriously. It's one of the things I hated most about him."

"It really is charming how willing you are to exploit my heartbreak for your own greedy purpose."

"Your heartbreak," I countered, "is half the reason we should go. What better time to take a free trip to Hollywood as guests of a real live mogul! We'll blow town, see LA. We'll party with Gilbert and his mom—whom you *adore*. We'll find out what the job is and if you don't like it you'll fly home. First class! At best it's a job, at worst a vacation, so cut the Cassandra routine and eat fast 'cause we need to pack."

This tough-love approach, abetted by wine and more catty allusions to Marco, eventually won the day. She agreed to join me so long as I understood that she was not committing to anything whatsoever.

Her subsequent references that night to our "glittering new careers" were all made in the droll manner of a governess humoring her delusional charge. But for all her glib ironies I could detect in her quick smiles and flushed cheeks the first reluctant stirrings of hope. I knew that beneath that wry, guarded exterior she burned with the girlish desire to win some small sliver of Hollywood fame, then stab her sweetie in the eye with it.

My own optimism was less guarded and soared higher as the level in the wine bottle descended. I marveled at how my fortunes had rebounded and chided myself for my earlier pessimism. How absurd that a man of my gifts and obviously shining future had allowed himself to wallow in morbid, cravat-themed fantasies.

Swell talk show story though!

MY THOUGHTS WOULD NOT return again to old Milo until a bleak and drizzly afternoon the following February.

Gilbert and I, reeling from the latest in a seemingly endless string of catastrophes, had wandered numbly into the Beverly Hills Neiman Marcus in the preposterous hope that a spot of shopping might cheer us. We discovered a bar on the top floor and agreed that a cocktail might soothe our nerves and quiet the facial tic I'd recently developed.

As I nibbled morosely on my olive, I glanced up and noticed the necktie counter, where a well-dressed man about my age was meticulously arranging the latest merchandise. How cheerful he looked. How content to spend his days among so many pleasing fabrics and designs. How blissfully unencumbered by lawsuits and threats of imminent incarceration.

The song playing over the Muzak system ended, and another began, something old and familiar from *South Pacific.* I couldn't place the title, but hearing it, I felt a sharp, inexplicable pang.

"What's this song?" I asked Gilbert.

He listened a moment.

" 'This Nearly Was Mine.' Why?"

Two

★

I F THERE SHOULD BE AMONG MY readers any underpaid couriers who are contemplating giving notice, I can tell them right now that there's no more agreeable place from which to do so than the first-class compartment of a 767 just after the free champagne's come around.

"Carlos!" I said, ebulliently addressing my foul-tempered supervisor. "Cavanaugh here."

"About fucking time!" replied Carlos, to whom an expletive-free sentence was a pale and juiceless thing. "Where the hell are you?"

I told him, not omitting reference to the champagne. He countered incredibly that if I did not promptly report for duty I could consider myself fired. I assured him that I comprehended the gravity of my situation but could not focus on it fully at the moment as I'd just been handed a menu and couldn't decide whether to have the merlot or cabernet with my steak au poivre.

"Any suggestions?"

He had one, of course, and, after making it, hung up.

As I pocketed my cell Claire nudged me and said, "Looks like the in-flight entertainment's starting early." She directed my attention to a drama unfolding on the other side of the cabin. It involved a dispute between a large disgruntled businessman and an aging Hollywood actress.

When I say she was an aging Hollywood actress, I do so not because I recognized her, for I did not. But everything about her dress and bearing so clearly announced this as her station in life that a child of three, beholding her, would have lisped, "Look, Mommy, an aging Hollywood actwess."

The face was still pretty in a pixieish way with an upturned nose and a pert little chin. She'd traded in her wrinkles for the taut, pink translucence of the frequently pulled and peeled. Her vivid orange hair was teased high in the front, cascading down to a flip at the nape of her neck, giving her that aging cheerleader look familiar to anyone who has spent even two minutes on Rodeo Drive. Her outfit was chic in a retro "cocktails with Ike and Mamie" sort of way. She wore a kelly green travel cape and beneath that a blouse of copper silk with a high neck such as Katharine Hepburn favored in later life. Also deployed on wattle-hiding duty was a flowing red silk scarf. Charm bracelets adorned both wrists, and her ears sparkled with costume diamonds the size of doorknobs. This ensemble was finished by large dark glasses meant to convey the laughable pretense that she desired anonymity.

She was sitting in an aisle seat, scribbling intently in a small notebook and ignoring the many-chinned fellow glaring down at her.

"I said *excuse* me. You're in my seat."

She affected not to hear this and a passing flight attendant asked what the problem was.

"This woman's in my seat and she won't move."

Aging Hollywood Actress looked up and removed her sunglasses, blinking strenuously in an unpersuasive show of surprise.

"I'm sorry, were you addressing me? I get so engrossed when I'm working!"

"I'm sorry," said the attendant after verifying the man's claim, "but this isn't your seat. May I see your boarding pass?"

"There's no point in my showing it to you. It's a mistake. It says I'm supposed to be at the back of the plane."

"Did you purchase a first-class ticket?"

"I didn't purchase it. The producer of the play I was doing—fabulous production, raves everywhere—bought it for me. I'd made it quite clear to him after my horrible flight east that I wanted first class going back. He said he'd see to it, but then the lady at the counter—dreadful woman, I'm filing a complaint—claimed to know nothing about it and stuck me in the back. Can you imagine!"

"I'm sorry, ma'am, but you'll have to return to your original seat."

"Sorry. Quite impossible. I was recognized by the man next to me. He began asking one question after another so I had to get as far away as possible!" She laughed ruefully. "The price of fame!"

"I see," said the attendant, who clearly hadn't an inkling who she was. "Look, I'm sorry for the mix-up—"

"Ah!" said the actress triumphantly. "So you admit there was a mix-up?"

The attendant said she'd instruct her cabin-class neighbor to respect her privacy but she had to return to her seat immediately as she was holding up the flight.

The actress gasped dramatically. "Holding up the flight!" She turned and addressed the whole cabin, hoping to rally support. " 'Holding up the flight,' she says! As though I'm some sort of terrorist! *Me!!*" She gestured to her seatmate, a young Donna Karan–clad woman who'd been staring wretchedly out her window through the whole contretemps. "Perhaps this young lady—or *someone,*" she added, pointedly eyeing the rest of us gawkers, "would be kind enough to change seats with me. I'd be immensely grateful."

This request inspired a sudden cabinwide fascination with the inflight magazine. The actress cast her eyes at the unchivalrous souls around her, shook her head in disgust, and addressed the attendant.

"Send more champagne back to me. It's the least I am owed." And with that she rose and, donning her shades, indignantly withdrew.

There are few things so wounding to a young homosexual's self-esteem as finding himself unable to identify a bejeweled Hollywood actress over seventy, however obscure. Claire too found her vaguely familiar and we bandied names for a moment before turning to the more pressing question of what films we should watch on our personal DVD players.

My savvier readers are no doubt stroking their chins and thinking, "This mystery woman—she'll be back." And of course she will or I'd have left her out entirely. But our bizarre entanglement with Lily Malenfant (for that was her name) was still, like so much else that lay before us, happily beyond our power to imagine. I didn't think about her again for the rest of the flight. I was too busy savoring the wine, the warm mixed nuts, and my frequent and pleasant chats with our handsome steward, who somehow managed to coax from me the news that I was bound for Hollywood and cinematic glory.

GILBERT, TRUE TO FORM, arrived at the terminal ten minutes after we'd retrieved our bags. I didn't recognize him at first. His tan was very deep and his chin now sported a Hollywood hipster goatee. He wore a tight, navy short-sleeve shirt and de rigueur Hollywood sunglasses, a choice I took, incorrectly, to be satiric.

"Darlings!" he cried, embracing us both in a single hug. "Welcome to my town!"

"You've been here three weeks," said Claire.

"Work fast, don't I? Oh, Dimitri!"

A short, stocky man wearing a dark suit and an unfortunate ponytail materialized at our side wheeling a luggage cart.

"Dimitri, these are my dear friends and writing partners, Philip and Claire. Dimitri works for Max."

The chauffeur nodded deferentially and, displaying surprising strength for a wee fatty, hoisted our bags onto the cart. He murmured an order into a scarcely visible headset, then wheeled the cart outside, reaching the curb just as a limousine long enough to bowl in pulled up. An assortment of onlookers stared at it, eager to see what celebrity it had come to fetch or disgorge. Gilbert, never one to waste an opportunity for drama, made us hang back in the terminal till Dimitri had opened the rear door for us. Then, shielding his face, he dashed from the terminal and into the car with a fleetness meant to suggest years of paparazzi dodging. Claire and I, relegated to the role of entourage, rolled our eyes and sauntered behind, passing the rubberneckers just in time to hear a teenage girl say, "No way! Brad Pitt's much cuter—and he's *not gay*."

We settled into the car's luxurious interior, noting the bar, flat-screen TV, and buttery soft black leather.

"Isn't this fun?!" laughed Gilbert, bouncing in his seat like a toddler.

"Oodles," deadpanned Claire. "So, what's the job?"

Gilbert put a warning finger to his lips and jerked his head back to where Dimitri stood loading our luggage into the trunk.

"We can't talk in the car," he said. "Dimitri has big ears and he's very loyal to Max. We can't risk him ratting us out."

"What don't you want Max to know?" I asked.

He smiled impishly. "Let's just say it wasn't easy getting you two in on this. I had to fudge a few things."

"We'll contain our astonishment," said Claire.

"Chateau Marmont!" exclaimed Gilbert once Dimitri had taken the wheel.

"And lay on the speed. My guests need to change for dinner."

It was maddening that the one topic we burned to discuss was off-limits, but the luxury had a certain lulling effect and we contented ourselves to sit back and watch the palm trees glide by while listening to Gilbert rhapsodize about the joys of LA. Knowing that Dimitri was listening, he reserved his highest praise for the man who was subsidizing his stay and who might, if properly buttered, refresh the linens indefinitely.

"You're going to *adore* Max. He's an absolute prince. Charming, generous—and talk about smart!"

This last at least I had no trouble believing. I knew from what little I'd read of Max Mandelbaum that he was, if not quite the town's richest mogul, widely considered its shrewdest. He'd managed to turn a small record company into a media behemoth, comprising TV and radio stations, magazines, theme parks, and, most famously, Hollywood's second-oldest studio, Pinnacle. His zest for acquisition had caused him to be so often caricatured as an octopus that people's first response on meeting him was to marvel at how well his tailor had concealed the extra arms.

When we reached the hotel, Dimitri saw to our luggage while Claire and I followed Gilbert into a small elevator that brought us up to the reception desk. The clerk apologetically informed us that our rooms were not ready, as the previous occupants had been a rock band and untidy even by the standards of their profession. Gilbert ordered champagne, then asked the bellman to have Dimitri wait while he discussed key creative matters with his colleagues. He then led us across the lobby to a cozy corner far from prying ears.

Like most people who only knew the Chateau Marmont as the place where John Belushi's demons yelled, "Checkmate!" I half expected to see a chalk outline on the carpet. What I saw instead was a large, lovely time warp of a room, decorated in the grand Hollywood Spanish style of the twenties. It had a high-beamed ceiling and soaring arched windows giving onto a lovely vaulted portico and garden. So completely did it evoke the silent era's languid glamour that it would not have surprised me to turn and spot a young Gloria Swanson sipping bootleg hooch from Joe Kennedy's hip flask before retiring to walk her ocelot.

We settled onto a plump sofa next to an arched alcove hung with richly brocaded drapes. Gilbert plopped his feet on the coffee table and spread his arms like a genie taking a bow after delivering on a particularly tall order.

"Not too shabby, huh?"

"Not too," I agreed.

"First-class travel, limos, legendary hotels! Stick with me, kids!"

"From what I gather," said Claire, "we're pretty well stuck. You've told people we're writing partners?"

"And so we will be!" he said cheerfully. "I hope you're looking forward to it as much as I am. I've often wondered what the result might be if you two pooled your talents with mine."

I sensed that Claire did not consider "pooled" quite the mot juste and would probably have chosen the more straightforward "diluted," but she just smiled dryly and asked how our happy union had come to pass.

"Well, it all started when—oh, good, just in time!"

A darkly handsome tray bearer was approaching with a bottle of Dom Pérignon. Gilbert beamed at the sight and I wasn't sure if this was just his usual delight in champagne or if he felt that now would be an excellent time to start addling our brains.

"Cheers!" he said, raising his glass. "To the Oscar we'll win for this!"

We offered our dubious toasts, then Gilbert said, "So! This restaurant we're going to tonight's *the* most exclusive in town, but thanks to good old Max—"

"The project?" Claire said firmly.

"Oh, right."

His eyes swept the lobby as though to make sure Dimitri wasn't skulking behind a potted palm. Then, satisfied that our privacy was sufficient, he leaned toward us with a conspiratorial smile and unfolded his improbable tale.

Three

★

T RUTH TO TELL," HE BEGAN, "I'VE been planning this ever
since Mom let drop ever so casually that the old fart she'd
met at a party and who'd sent her roses the next day was none
other than Max Mandelbaum. I mean, talk about your lucky breaks! I
think, Philip, that I may have said something to you at the time about
how perfect it would be if they really clicked."

I said that yes, he'd mentioned the blossoming romance frequently
over the last months and had seldom failed, when requesting a loan, to
cite it as proof of his future solvency.

"Well, I was right, wasn't I? Anyway, I did my best to help things
along, you know, encouraging her to go for it. She liked him well
enough, but she found his weight a bit off-putting. I mean, her last
husband was an absolute hunk, but Max—you could tear him down
and build a stadium. But I kept pointing out what a romantic he was,
which, thank God, he really was. Between the daily flower deliveries
and the packages from Tiffany's, the old blimp finally wore her down.
I mean, Mom's no gold digger but if you keep the bracelets coming,
well, c'mon, she's only *human*.

"Once they got engaged I played things pretty carefully, y'know, not wanting to seem too eager. I waited two whole months to come visit and even then I didn't mention my work to Max or ask him to introduce me to his big-shot friends. No, I went completely through Mom. I encouraged her to throw dinner parties—she *loves* entertaining—and helped her draw up all these 'fun' guest lists. I knew if she threw enough A-list dinners with me there piling on the charm that lightning *had* to strike eventually. And it did!

"It was last week and there were just twelve of us at table. I'd fiddled with the place cards and snagged myself a seat next to Bobby Spellman. You know, the producer?"

"Lucky you," Claire said sardonically, and I snorted in agreement. "I can't stand that asshole."

"You might try to be a little nicer," chided Gilbert. "He paid for your plane fare and hotel."

"Bobby *Spellman?*" said Claire, stunned.

"*That's* who we're working for?"

"He's the man! So you can see we're not talking low budget here!"

Bobby Spellman, I should explain for those rarefied souls whose nights out are confined to opera and stimulating lectures, is Hollywood's leading purveyor of those noisy, extravagantly budgeted action films that the press cannot seem to describe without recourse to the phrase "high-octane." I've seen three of them and found each more unstomachable than the last. I've nothing against the genre, mind you, having passed many a happy hour watching attractive stars outrun fireballs. It's just that Spellman's films are, like the man himself, filled to bursting with snide machismo. His heroes are all cocksure bad boys whom we're invited to admire not for their courage or heroism but for their unfailing flippancy under pressure. Their response to mortal danger is sarcasm and they're never more snarky than when they've just been shot, which is always in the shoulder or thigh, no villain in these films ever possessing the good sense to aim for their hearts or, better still, mouths.

"Bobby *Spellman?*" I repeated, aghast.

"Wants *us* to write a movie?"

"Isn't it great?! Of course, this won't be his usual sort of picture."

"Let's hope so!" said Claire.

"What sort is it?"

"I'm getting to that. So anyway, we're at dinner and he starts talking about this book his aunt sent him. It was written back in the fifties and he put off reading it forever, but he finally did and was blown away by it. It's called *A Song for Greta* and you're going to love it."

Claire asked if it was a comedy.

"In parts. And there's room for lots more. But it's got everything! Great plot, amazing characters, romance, intrigue. It's a lost classic, which is why Bobby's dying to make it—it's his bid for respectability. He wants to show people he can do something besides make money and maim stuntmen.

"So anyway, I asked who was writing it and he said no one yet. And that's when Mom, bless her, piped up about me—how talented I was, what wonderful scripts I wrote. And I knew then and there the job was mine!"

Claire and I exchanged a baffled glance. We couldn't imagine anyone, even Bobby Spellman, putting much stock in the literary judgments of Gilbert's mother. Maddie Cellini is a warm, thoroughly delightful woman, but even her fondest admirers will concede that her brain is 90 percent meringue.

"He took her *seriously?*" marveled Claire, adding hastily, "I mean, she is your mom."

"Hell, no," smirked Gilbert. "But what could he do? He can't blow Mom off without insulting Max, and he's the last guy anyone in this town wants to offend. So he said, 'Great, send me a writing sample and I'll send you the book.' I said, 'Fine,' then I sent him *Imbroglio*. And that's how we got hired!"

"*Imbroglio?*" I asked, confused.

"Oh, right, I haven't mentioned that. I just wrote a new spec script."

Claire and I exchanged a second goggle-eyed glance as I mopped up the champagne spill from the flute I'd just knocked over.

"You wrote a spec script?"

"Yes."

"And *finished* it?" asked Claire, whose astonishment could not have been greater had he claimed to have licked cold fusion.

"Yes. Just last week."

We exchanged a third and still more mystified glance.

"And Bobby *liked* it?"

"Yes!" he said, getting peevish. "Is that so hard to believe?"

"No!" I said, flabbergasted.

You might have assumed from Gilbert's references to his "work" that there exists somewhere a set of actual completed texts of which Gilbert is the author. There does not. There are many things Gilbert likes about being a writer. He enjoys the drinking, the convivial shoptalk with fellow scribes, the sense of superiority to less creative beings. The one thing he does not like about being a writer is writing. Every project he embarks on soon falls prey to his fatal lack of perseverance, and his longest completed work to date is a haiku. For him to claim now that he'd dashed off a spec script brilliant enough to win him a fat Hollywood contract did not merely strain Credulity; it beat the crap out of Credulity and sent Credulity's next of kin scurrying to its bedside.

"When did you write this?" I asked.

"I started it, oh, about a month ago, and I was done by—stop that!"

"Stop what?"

"Every time I say something you two look at each other. It's very annoying."

Claire replied diplomatically that we were merely wondering how we fit into all this. Gilbert assured us he was getting there and ordered more champagne. He then explained that Bobby had sent a messenger to deliver *A Song for Greta* and pick up Gilbert's spec. He paused here and his tone strained for poignancy.

"I saw him, the messenger, standing on the doorstep—this morose, badly dressed fellow. Naturally I thought of you, Philip."

"Thank you."

"I mean it. It broke my heart to think that's what you'd been reduced to—a genius like you, schlepping packages around midtown.

And you, Claire, scraping by as a rehearsal pianist, flogging your songs in grimy little cabarets. The more I thought about it the more unfair it seemed. Why should I be out here getting rich and famous while my two most gifted friends were back east, toiling fruitlessly away in their squalid apartments? So I decided if Bobby wanted me he'd have to hire you guys too."

"And how'd you manage that?" asked Claire a bit coolly, as her apartment was not remotely squalid.

"Easy. I just typed up a new title page and put your names below mine. As far as Bobby knows we wrote it together, which is good news for you because he *loved* it! Called it the best spec he's ever—what did I say about not looking at each other?"

The impulse had been impossible to resist. Credulity-wise we were now at the memorial with Credulity's best friend belting out "Time Heals Everything."

"So," said Claire evenly, "you just decided to cut us in out of the goodness of your heart?"

"Now please! I know what you're going to say—you feel funny about riding my coattails. Well, don't. I can't think of two people who deserve a break more than you guys and it thrills me to be the one who can give it to you."

He raised his glass in a toast.

"To partnership!"

We toasted limply, then Claire said, "So, your script . . . ?"

He wagged a cheerful finger. "*Our* script! Don't forget that—especially when we meet Bobby. That's tomorrow at two by the way."

"As we're supposed to have cowritten it, perhaps you might tell us a bit about it?"

"Happy to!" said Gilbert, refilling my glass. "It's basically a good old-fashioned love story, but funny, with strong suspense elements and—oh look! I think your room's ready!"

I turned and saw the desk clerk crossing the lobby toward us. Gilbert rose then, glancing at his watch, bugged his eyes like the bad high school actor he once was.

"Gosh, I'd better run if I'm going to get home and make myself pretty. Dress up, kids! We're going to the hottest place in town. I'll pick you up at eight!"

"Perhaps," suggested Claire, "you might bring along a copy of 'our' script?"

"Good idea! I can't wait for you to read it!"

And with that he left, walking, we agreed, a touch briskly for a boy with nothing to hide.

TEN MINUTES LATER CLAIRE and I sat nibbling from the complimentary fruit plate in my large, sunny suite while dissecting Gilbert's story, which was, we concurred, fishier than last week's seviche.

"He says he wrote it in three weeks?!" snorted Claire. "As if he could finish a letter in that time!"

Most preposterous of all, we agreed, was his assertion that, having hit the Hollywood jackpot, he'd decided in a fit of altruism to give two-thirds of his winnings to us. This was just goofy talk. It was not often that Gilbert came into money, and when he did philanthropy was not his first impulse. Gilbert, as a rule, used money the way women use pepper spray; he liked having some handy but only produced it when physically threatened. If he was sharing the wealth now there could be only one reason: he needed us. The question was why, or rather why both of us when he could have flown just me out and only parted with half the take? We donned our deerstalkers and sifted the evidence.

A mere ten seconds later Claire smiled and said, "I'll tell you why our names are on that script, ducky."

"Why?"

"Because we *wrote* it."

"Excuse me?"

"You heard his description—romance, intrigue, comedy. Sounds more than a bit like our own *Mrs. McManus,* doesn't it?"

She referred to our first and to date only screenplay. It was a jaunty housewife-gets-mixed-up-with-spies caper that we'd written "for" Julia Roberts, hoping to get it to her through a connection too humiliatingly tenuous to relate here. Claire asked if I'd given Gilbert a copy, and I said I'd not only given him one but, seeking to save on paper, had e-mailed it to him. If he'd brought his laptop, he could easily have printed a copy for Bobby.

"Well, there you are," said Claire. "He needed a spec to win the job so he borrowed ours. Probably considered stealing it outright. But then he realized he could never deliver the goods on his own, so he cut us in, making it sound like some big, munificent gesture."

"The little skunk!"

"Mark my words, dear, when he shows up here tonight there'll be no sign of 'our' script. He'll have forgotten it."

"So what do we do?" I asked. "Break out the thumbscrews and force a confession?"

"Oh, no," said Claire, with a devious smile. "Let's play along for a while. It'll be fun watching him tap-dance."

Perhaps it was the champagne or the golden light shining through the bougainvillea outside the window, but we found it hard to muster much indignation over Gilbert's skulduggery. Yes it was larcenous, shifty, and unethical—in short, thoroughly Gilbertian—but unlike his previous schemes, which had shattered our nerves and shortened our fingernails, this one had landed us in a suite at the Chateau Marmont with a lucrative film deal. And how cheering it was too to find that our poor neglected screenplay had at last been recognized as the corker that it was.

"Just think," marveled Claire, "all this time we thought it was just moldering away in a drawer. But no, the plucky little dear was out there in the world, winning us fame and treasure."

"I always believed in that script."

"Me too. A touch formulaic in spots, but still—"

"Damn funny."

"The scene in the embassy—"

"Priceless."

I gazed thoughtfully out at the pretty houses dotting the hillside.

"Do you suppose Bobby knows Julia?"

OUR PLAGIARISM THEORY WAS briefly shaken when Gilbert arrived on schedule bearing two manila envelopes.

"Oh, good," I said, baffled, "you brought the scripts."

"No, these are copies of the book we're adapting. Oh, damn!" he cried, literally smiting his forehead, "I knew I forgot something! Well anyway, it's much more important that you read the book before we talk to Bobby. If he mentions our script, just smile and accept the compliment."

"Oh," said Claire dryly, "I think we can manage that."

We drove down the Sunset Strip, Gilbert boasting all the way about Bobby's enthusiasm and the "buzz" he'd created around us. You might suppose Claire and I would have quickly tired of being played for such saps, but we actually sort of enjoyed it. Gilbert may be a con man, but he's one of the dreamy Harold Hill variety who tend to get lost in their own fictions. He so enjoyed playing our heroic benefactor that not playing along would have seemed somehow churlish, like refusing to clap for Tinkerbell.

We soon reached our destination, a restaurant called BU after the initials of its celebrated chef, Brian Urban. Its luster has since dimmed but at the time it was fiercely embraced by that sector of the industry who don't much care what they eat but are deeply concerned about where and with whom they are seen eating it. They cherished BU for the drama of its circular dining room and for its ruthless exclusivity.

As we entered the spare gray foyer, I was uncomfortably aware how dated my threadbare Armani was. Maître d's can, of course, smell fear, and this one, who appeared to have been hired chiefly for his unsettling resemblance to a hawk, seemed to peg us instantly as gate-crashers.

"Yes?" he inquired coldly, his perfectly manicured fingers tapping on his lectern as though itching to activate the Nonentity Chute. Gilbert couldn't help smirking, for he knew what was in his holster. He savored the hawk's imperious stare for a moment, then, adopting that gently reproving tone with which diplomats correct the gaucheries of their subordinates, said, "I'm Gilbert Selwyn and these are my guests. We're with Max Mandelbaum's party."

The hawk blinked, then, switching personalities with unembarrassed rapidity, became our best friend.

"Of course!" he said. "So glad you could join us. Right this way."

The main room had an austere, Zenlike feel to it. Practically everything in it—the bar, walls, and tables—was made from thick frosted glass, and my first impression was that I'd wandered into the home of an affluent Buddhist Eskimo. It was undeniably stylish though, especially the way various sections of the floor were lit from beneath, a sensible feature, I supposed, in a town that spent so much on shoes. Our guide steered us through a sea of celebrity to a booth that was smack in the center of the far wall and slightly larger than the rest.

"Don't gawk," scolded Gilbert as a square-jawed waiter materialized to take our drink orders. Our request for martinis was interrupted by a loud jubilant voice that pierced the room's low conversational hum and turned every famous head in the place.

"There they are! Hey, kids! Sorry we're late!"

Gilbert's mother, Maddie, stood atop the curved steps leading into the room, looking, as always, smashing and preposterously young. Next to her, his arm proudly encircling her waist, stood an obese but immaculately dressed man of seventy. His shaved head and lack of any discernible neck made him look like a prosperous retired wrestler. This was Max Mandelbaum.

As they navigated toward us, every table they passed paid some sort of homage, a wave, a smile, a greeting. I hadn't realized how firmly Maddie had established herself among the town's power crowd. It was nice to see that her manner among them was marked by the same breezy good cheer I'd seen her display in far less exalted company.

"Peter, I loved your column today . . . Jack, you scamp, we haven't seen you since the Lakers game. Who's this, your granddaughter?"

When they reached our table we rose and Maddie gave us all big loud kisses.

"Mwah! Philip, honey! And Claire! Don't you both look fantastic? Is this a kick or what, us all being together out here? Max!" she bellowed cheerfully. "Quit schmoozing and come over here!"

Max bade farewell to Jack and waddled over to our table.

"Max, I'd like you to meet Philip and Claire. Kids, this is my wonderful fiancé, Max. Isn't he adorable?"

"Adorable" wasn't the first word that leaped to mind in describing a man whose body seemed designed for the sole purpose of thwarting stranglers, but we smiled and said yes, he certainly cut a dashing figure. Max let out a raspy laugh, being a mogul who liked his cigars. "You're good liars—you'll go far in this town!"

"Oh, drinks!" said Maddie, spotting our approaching waiter.

"What a good idea! Now, remember, hon, the doctor said just one."

"He didn't say how big it could be!"

Maddie giggled and pinched his cheek. "I swear, Max Mandelbaum—to you the whole world is just one big loophole!"

In describing Maddie to you earlier I fear I placed undue emphasis on her somewhat spotty intellect and not enough on her abundant and contagious joie de vivre. You can't spend five minutes with her without feeling you've been thrust into a big Broadway musical. And I don't mean one of those nobly intentioned pop operas where choruses of stern-faced sequinphobes crusade against poverty and injustice and humor—I mean one of those peppy fifties shows where strangers form spontaneous conga lines on the subway. This ebullience, combined with what might more charitably be termed her "refreshing simplicity," has long made her catnip to men whose lives, though amply supplied with power and stress, are sorely lacking in fun. They meet Maddie and are instantly intrigued by her comely face and infectious Gracie Allen giggle. After ten minutes they're thinking, "Jeez, this dame lives in a world of her own." After twenty they're thinking, "How do I get in?"

Her naïveté, which can border at times on coma, is another trait that endears her to the sort of man for whom shrewdness in a wife is no asset. Her previous husband was a noted mafioso; noted, that is, by all except Maddie, who never questioned his claim that he was an importer with many accident-prone friends. Her tendency to view everyone and everything in the kindest possible light had not deserted her even in this most notoriously cutthroat of towns. Her rose-colored lenses were more firmly in place than ever.

"You kids are gonna love it here! The people are so damned *nice!* Everyone I've met—oh, hiya, handsome! I'll have a sidecar and Max wants a Sapphire martini in his usual glass, the one with the diving board—everyone I've met has gone out of their way to make me feel welcome, taking me to lunch, inviting me to their houses. They say Disneyland's the friendliest place on earth. Forget it—it's Beverly Hills."

I smiled at her innocence. It would never occur to Maddie that the welcome she'd enjoyed owed everything to her status as Max's consort and would promptly vanish if he withdrew his affection. Fortunately for Maddie, there seemed little chance of that. The old boy was smitten with her, and small wonder when you compared her to the vixen from whom he'd recently disentangled himself.

"How long have you been together?" asked Claire.

"Five months," said Max. "She's completely changed my life."

"I don't know if you heard," said Maddie, "but Max went through kind of a messy divorce last year. His wife was—well, I hate to speak ill of people—"

"Feel free!" croaked Max.

"She was sort of a stinker. I mean when you have a man like Max at home, you don't go tramping around with polo players."

"And junkies," prompted Max. "Don't forget the junkie!"

"Of course when he married her he didn't know she was a hussy. It's like me and Tony. It never crossed my mind he was a gangster!" She sighed philosophically. "But that's what happens when you're in love. You overlook things."

"So," said Max, switching gears. "Your script!"

"Have you read it?" asked Claire.

"I only wish I had time to read!" said Max. "But Bobby raved about it."

"You must be so proud to have written something that good," said Maddie.

"Oh, we are," said Claire, coyly draping an arm around Gilbert. "We think it's our best work so far."

"Bobby said it had some of the best dialogue he's read in years."

"No kidding?" I grinned. Part of me knew it was no great honor to have one's dialogue praised by a man whose films teemed with lines like "That meteor picked the wrong dude to mess with!" and "Uncle Sam, one. Allah . . . *zip!*" But another part couldn't help conceding that Bobby was, after all, a canny showman and perhaps more astute than I'd given him credit for.

Noting a certain widening of Gilbert's eyes, I turned and saw our waiter heading toward us along with a sidecar, a very large martini, and Sir Anthony Hopkins.

"Forgive my intruding," said Sir Anthony.

"Tony, hon!" said Maddie.

"I just wanted to tell you both how much I enjoyed your extravagantly beautiful party."

Maddie explained to us that Max had turned seventy last month and had marked the occasion with a "shindig" the lavishness of which had dazzled even the town's most jaded partygoers. Max, noting our star-struck gazes, leaped in to make introductions, explaining that we were writing a picture for Bobby Spellman.

Sir Anthony, who, like all of us, has bills to pay, said he'd once done a picture for Bobby and asked us to say hello for him when next we met. I said I would and Tony (for I felt I knew him well enough now to call him that) shook our hands, said how nice it had been to meet us, and withdrew.

Having spent the previous afternoon schlepping envelopes and getting the fish-eye from receptionists, I found this encounter indescribably pleasant. I wondered how I might work it into the letter I planned to write Charlie O'Donnell telling him how nice it had been to bump into him while researching my screenplay about outdoor messengers.

As it turned out the evening would hold no shortage of such glittering encounters with which to enliven my future correspondence. Sir Tony was not the only luminary at BU that night who'd attended Max's fete. Several others present had been there as well, and they all trickled over to say what fun they'd had. Some, like my new pal Tony, did so purely out of politeness, though others voiced their thanks a shade too audibly, clearly keen to let the room know they'd been in-vited. I didn't care what brought them over so long as Max, after ac-cepting their tributes, waved a meaty hand toward us and said, "I'd like you to meet Maddie's son and his fellow geniuses."

"You see?" said Maddie. "What'd I tell you? The people here are just so damned nice."

Though I'd smirked at this assertion at the evening's outset, the martinis and chardonnay had sharpened my insight and I saw now how right she was. Viewed from our cozy table at BU, Hollywood really was a remarkably friendly town, a sunny Prada-clad Mayberry with a heart as big as an IMAX screen.

Claire, ever the staunch realist, tried for a while to maintain per-spective. She enjoyed the parade of ring-kissers but she knew that spending your first night in LA at Max Mandelbaum's table was like first glimpsing Rome from the popemobile. At some point, though— I suspect it was after Alec Baldwin kissed her hand—she stopped fighting and surrendered to the same star-drunk euphoria to which Gilbert and I had succumbed immediately and without struggle.

As the glamorati came and went we kept exchanging furtive glances of delight, our minds racing with the same intoxicating thought. We were in! Arrived! Players! Not for us the hardscrabble life of the wannabe. All the things we'd pined for but feared we'd never possess would now be ours! Careers! Recognition! Respect! Gardeners!

We contained our exhilaration through dinner, comporting our-selves with a cheery nonchalance meant to suggest that we were (don't ask how) accustomed to such evenings. But once we left and were whizzing home in Gilbert's convertible we were free at last to carry on like the drunk, giddy mooncalves we'd become.

"Gawd," crowed Gilbert. "And to think I practically had to *beg* you to come out here!"

"All right, all right!" I laughed. "We'll never doubt you again."

"What a night!" said Claire.

"That back there?" sniffed Gilbert. "That was nothing! Do you have any idea how *big* we're going to be? How much money we're going to make?"

"None, if you don't slow down!" said Claire.

"Millions!" he said. "Tens of millions!"

And with that he launched into an exuberant rewrite of Bernstein's famed "New York, New York."

"LA, LA! A wonderful town! The skies are blue and the people are brown!"

Inspiration failed him and Claire rushed in with "You waltz right in and they hand you a crown!"

We finished together, Claire providing the harmony.

"LA, LAAAAA! It's a wonderful towwwwwn!"

I ESCORTED CLAIRE TO her room and as we entered her phone rang. Claire regarded it warily. She'd left the number on her New York machine but it was now after two there. She answered and immediately grimaced, leaving no doubt who the caller was.

"Marco," she said brightly. "How lovely to hear from you."

I pointed toward the door to ask if I should leave but she shook her head, wanting an audience for this as much as I yearned to listen.

"Glad to hear that," she said warmly. "There's no one I'd rather be missed by."

"Drunk?" I whispered.

"Very."

"Crying?"

"He will be."

Things went back and forth for a bit, Marco offering sloppy promises and Claire asking, in the sweetest possible tone, what species of idiot he imagined her to be. "Lunch tomorrow?" she cooed. "Well, that's a terribly tempting offer, but as you may in a less drunken state have gleaned from the area code and hotel operator, I'm not in town just now."

She went on to explain that she'd accepted a commission to write a screenplay for the producer Bobby Spellman and would not be returning to New York for at least two months, though possibly much longer, as one high-profile job did have a way of leading to another. She wished him luck with his ceramics career and assured him that, despite

his behavior toward her, she would keep him in mind for all her earth-
enware needs.

"Brava!" I cried. I applauded loudly, then, feeling this was insufficient, whistled a bit.

"God, that felt good."

"Whoo-ee," I said in my cowboy voice, "that was some fancy
knife-twistin', ma'am."

Claire sank onto the couch, gazed out the window at the twinkling
lights of the strip, and gave a little laugh of disbelief.

"I never dreamed I'd say this but—thank God for Gilbert!"

"He certainly came through, didn't he?"

"So it appears."

"We always knew he would someday."

"No, we didn't."

She announced her intention to order up some coffee and to read
as much as she could of *A Song for Greta* before morning. I said this
sounded like a sensible plan and retired to my room to do the same.

After calling down for coffee I settled into a chair with the slightly
battered old paperback Gilbert had provided.

I was six pages in when I called room service to cancel my order. It
was already painfully clear to me that there was no point in consuming
coffee while trying to read *A Song for Greta* late in the evening. If
you're reading it for pleasure, no amount of caffeine will stave off
slumber. And if, God help you, you're reading it because you've
agreed to adapt it for the screen, staying awake is not the problem.

It's ever sleeping again.

Four

★

Greta, her kind, gray, sensitive eyes puffy from the sleepless night she had passed listening to the fearsome explosions and heartbreaking cries of sad despair that had pierced the cobblestoned serenity of her lovely, beloved, now war-ravaged city, watched intently as General Snelling, his arrogant belly straining the buttons of his gestapo uniform, thrust his fork viciously into the yielding surface of the rich moist Schwarzwalder kirschtorte she had made from the recipe handed down to her by her mother, a great beauty, now dead.

His cold black eyes glittered with hungry, rapacious greed as he brought the fork to his plump crimson lips and opened his brutish mouth, revealing his cruel teeth. He thrust the cake into his mouth like a stoker who was stoking a furnace, a greedy furnace that could never be too full or even satisfied. Greta watched nervously as he chewed the cake, sensually savoring the dark sweetness of its chocolaty richness.

"It is good, Mein General?" she asked.

"You have done well, Greta," he replied, his insatiable jowls quivering with pleasure.

"Ach," she thought to herself, not for the first time, "you would not like my cake if you knew my secret!"

*   *   *

SO BEGINS *A SONG FOR GRETA*, the 370-page novel that one Prudence Gamache unleashed upon the world in 1955.

As this excerpt illustrates, it is set during World War II and is so badly written that had Hitler survived the war, his punishers would have consigned him to a Spandau cell with a copy of the thing and a jackbooted thug who had ways of making him read. Subtitled *A Tale of Hope and Heroes*, it's one of those ruthlessly sentimental books that make you feel as though your heartstrings are being plucked with a lug wrench. On page after page it strives to achieve uplift and, in the case of my dinner, damn near succeeded.

The plot revolves around the double life of the book's title character, Greta Schumman, a woman so virtuous she makes Maria von Trapp look like a Kit Kat Klub girl. Greta keeps house for the brutal gestapo general Ernst Snelling and his handsome son Heinrich. Heinrich, raised by Greta after his mom died in childbirth, is in the gestapo too but, thanks to Greta's tender influence, is a kinder, gentler Nazi. As Ms. Gamache puts it, "His twinkling eyes sparkled with a gentle light and in his heart there burned a fragile flame of goodness that not even the brackish tide of evil washing over this once green and hopeful land could drown or otherwise extinguish."

Greta, who's secretly Jewish, risks all by smuggling food to her sister, who's hiding in the basement of a bombed-out bakery along with her four children. The children, in ascending order of grisliness, are Lisabetta, a beautiful and spirited eighteen-year-old, Rolf, a manly little fellow of ten, and the twins, Hilda and Heidi, two revolting moppets whose every lisping utterance is crafted to extort tears. When they're not pretend-phoning Daddy in heaven, they're staging puppet shows about brighter tomorrows, and after three chapters of this I was rooting for the snipers.

The general, his suspicions inflamed by a missing roast beef, orders Heinrich to follow Greta. He obeys and discovers her double life. He denounces her treachery to the Reich and vows to turn her in to Dad but finds, in a dinner scene staggeringly devoid of suspense, that he cannot bring himself to do so. Before you can say "Oskar

Schindler," he's smuggling food along with her and falling hard for pretty Lisabetta, who's a feisty one and takes some wooing.

Little Hilda falls gravely ill and Heinrich, who by this point is practically sporting a yarmulke, frees a Jewish doctor from a work camp. Hilda rallies briefly before dying in a deathbed scene so excruciatingly maudlin that only the promise of her eventual demise kept me turning the pages.

"One down, one to go!" I thought, pouring myself an altogether necessary scotch from the minibar. But I soon found that in the world of Prudence Gamache saintly tots do not quit the stage simply because they've expired. No, their dear little ghosts linger on, watching over their families, snuffing out candles when danger looms, and generally pitching in. The nadir of this gambit comes when Hilda's ghost blows a kiss to two Jew-sniffing Dobermans who whimper contritely and lead their masters away. By that point I'd just about had it and only skimmed the rest to get the gist of the story.

I could at least see what had attracted Bobby to the material. Amid the schmaltz there was no shortage of action and preposterous heroics. My question vis-à-vis Bobby was not "Why *Greta?*" It was "Why us?" The answer clearly lay with Gilbert, and I resolved to track him down come morning and, if need be, throttle it out of him.

I PHONED HIM THE next morning and left a message sternly demanding he call the moment he woke. I then tried Claire's room and, getting no answer, dressed and went downstairs, hoping to find her in the dining room. She was there, sitting at a corner table and looking as morose as you'd expect a girl of her taste and discernment to look on finding she's been hired to rewrite *The Diary of Anne Frank* as an action film.

I joined her as our waiter arrived.

"Just coffee for now," I said.

"Black," intoned Claire. The waiter withdrew and she went on, "Black—like the black, pitch-dark heart of General Snelling, a heart never pierced by the radiant light of love or the sunshine of kindness or even a faint tender ray of—"

"All right. You finish it?"

"Yes. I decided to just read the verbs and it flew by. Have you by chance spoken to our collaborator this morning?"

"I left a message."

"When he calls back tell him please to swing by. And ask if he'd be so kind as to bring a garrote."

Our coffee came and we consumed several cups as we probed the mystery of our hiring. Everyone insisted we'd been chosen on the basis of our brilliant spec, a script Claire and I had confidently assumed to be our own *Mrs. McManus*. This now seemed decidedly less likely. Why would Bobby, seeking to adapt this brutally unfunny book, hire a team whose spec was a lighthearted comedy? We wondered if perhaps Gilbert hadn't been lying and the spec really *was* his, a notion we swiftly rejected as too preposterous to entertain.

Claire opined that it might just be flat-out nepotism, Max asking Bobby to hire Maddie's son in exchange for some favor from Max. In that scenario Bobby wouldn't much care what the spec was and might not even have read it. I said I didn't see what good it did Bobby to hire writers he didn't believe in.

"Oh, darling," she drawled with maddening condescension, "you don't think Bobby plans to actually *film* what we write? You know how it works out here. Nothing makes it to the screen until at least a dozen ink-stained wretches have had a whack at it. So if we agree to actually do this—"

" 'If'?" I repeated, startled. "What do you mean 'if'?!"

"I'm sorry, but I'm not sure I want any part of this."

"But you can't quit!" I said, panic and caffeine sending my already cantering heart into a brisk gallop. The task of adapting *Greta* would be hellish enough even with Claire's help and unimaginable with no one's "assistance" save Gilbert's. "I mean, I'll grant you it won't be a picnic—but, God, hon, think of the money!"

"I have. I've thought of it a great deal. I'm just not sure if it's worth spending the next few months writing adorable dead moppets and, what's-his-name, Nazi with the Laughing Eyes."

"I am begging you!" I said, clasping her forearms. "Do not consign me to everlasting Gilbert!"

"I don't want to, dear. I'm just not sure I have the stomach for this."

I whined, wheedled, and cajoled but to no end. Claire insisted she'd make no decision until we'd met with Spellman and ascertained how much of the book he was married to. I could only bow to this and pray that Bobby would not prove so insufferable as to obliterate all hope of keeping her on board.

I tried Gilbert again and once more got his voice mail.

"I wouldn't bother," frowned Claire. "He's obviously gone to ground."

I tended to agree. Gilbert had known when he'd dropped them off just what lurked in those envelopes. He would not, as such, care to face us again till we were seated in Bobby's office and could smell the ink on the paycheck.

THE TAXI DEPOSITED CLAIRE and me at the famed main gate of Pinnacle Pictures promptly at two. A guard gave us directions to Bobby Spellman's office, which we reached an acceptable five minutes late. Gilbert had not yet arrived.

The outer office was quite large, its walls predictably crowded with posters for Bobby's shrill blockbusters. The absurdly beautiful woman behind the desk informed us that her name was—what else?— Svetlana and that Bobby was finishing a call. Would we care for something to drink? We declined and sat to wait for Gilbert, who showed up five minutes later carrying a briefcase.

"Have a seat, dear," said Claire, her tone murderously cordial. Gilbert hung back, smiling nervously, but then, deciding we couldn't dismember him in front of Miss Moscow, sat across from us.

"Can I get you something?" asked Svetlana. "Coffee, water, soda?"

Claire, shrewdly noting the lack of a coffee machine in the room, said she'd changed her mind and would love a coffee; could she warm the milk if there was a microwave on hand? Svetlana happily complied, disappearing into a small adjoining kitchen.

"So, kids!" began Gilbert, jabbering a mile a minute. "There are a few things you should know about Bobby before we go in let me run them down for you real fast for starters—"

"Can the filibuster!" barked Claire.

"You could have warned us what a shitty book it was!"

He regarded us with injured surprise.

"You didn't like it?"

"You *did?*" snorted Claire.

"Loved it! I laughed, I cried. Mostly cried of course. I thought you'd adore it too, but what can I say? *Chacun à son goût.*"

" 'Goo' is right!" snapped Claire.

"Thank you. Anyway, don't bad-mouth it in front of Bobby. I already told him you both loved it 'cause I honestly assumed you'd—"

"Bullshit!" I hissed. "You knew we'd loathe it. That's why you lied to us."

"When did I lie?" he asked, his tone less defensive than puzzled, as though he'd lost track.

"You said it was a comedy!"

"I said it had *room* for comedy. And I stand by that. Why, think what fun Coward got out of an impish ghost in *Blithe Spirit.* And it should be even easier for us, our ghost being a kid and all."

It was lucky for Gilbert that Svetlana chose this moment to return, as Claire and I had started advancing on him with defenestration uppermost in our thoughts. She gave Claire her coffee, said Bobby would see us now, and led us down a short hall.

Bobby's office was a striking, somewhat futuristic chamber with gray suede walls and a curved brushed-steel desk I recognized as a prop from the planet-saving hero's spacecraft in his asteroid thriller, *Kingdom Come.* The room couldn't have screamed "power" more loudly if it had had a platinum throne flanked by twin dynamos with bolts of electricity zapping between them.

Bobby, seated at his command console, rose to greet us. It was immediately clear that he was not one of those cunning Hollywood potentates who like to confound expectations by affecting a schlubby or innocuous appearance. Just as our lady friend on the plane had striven to make it apparent to all that she was a once-famous actress, so Bobby's costume and grooming loudly announced his profession and status within it. His black Dolce & Gabbana suit was *le dernier cri* in Italian tailoring, as was the black open-collared shirt he wore beneath it. His salt-and-pepper hair was combed back above his long wolfish face, which sported a Mephistophelian goatee. His smile was as crooked and smug as those of his bad-boy heroes and his gaze held a calculated hint of menace as though to say, "I like you at the moment but reserve the right to crush you."

"Bobbeee!" sang Gilbert, as though they'd been friends for years. "Love the suit."

"Come in! Sit!" said Bobby, gesturing to a gray boar-skin sofa. "It's not every day I get three geniuses in here. Which one's Philip and which one's Claire? Kidding!"

We laughed, piglets humoring the wolf, and seated ourselves. Bobby said he'd heard this was our first trip to LA and asked how we liked it. We replied, of course, that we liked it very much.

"I took them to BU last night," said Gilbert, not mentioning Max so as to imply he'd gotten us in on his own.

"I *love* that place!" said Bobby with what struck me as unwarranted vehemence. I'd soon learn though that Bobby never made mere statements; he issued pronouncements, and no subject was too trivial to merit this stentorian intensity.

"BU is like my *dining room*. The crab cakes are fucking brilliant. You have the crab cakes?"

"No," I said.

"Do not," he said gravely, "go again without having the crab cakes."

"They're amazing," said Gilbert.

"They're a fucking *rhapsody*."

A strained silence fell. Bobby broke it by saying, *"So!"* with great gusto.

"So!" I repeated, *"A Song for Greta . . ."*

"No," proclaimed Bobby. "Shitty title."

"I was just saying that," remarked Gilbert.

"No, no—our picture will be called . . ."

He paused and swept his hand through the air as though conjuring a marquee. His voice dropped to a reverent hush and he said, *"The Heart . . . in Hiding."*

It was clear that he couldn't have been prouder if he'd picked up a legal pad that morning and torn off *A Streetcar Named Desire*. I supposed the title did capture that majestic vagueness Hollywood aims for when christening films of high purpose suitable for December release. It was clear too that Bobby expected praise if not actual salaams for having thought of it. This we hastened to provide.

"It's beautiful!" I said.

"Very apt," nodded Claire.

"It's like some perfect four-word sonnet," said Gilbert.

"Fucking luminous," agreed Bobby.

Gilbert gushed some more, then explained to Claire that the title referred not only to Greta's hidden family but also to Heinrich, whose own heart is in hiding until Greta gently draws it out. Claire, who looked ready to draw Gilbert's heart out and not gently, replied that she'd gotten that.

"This," said Bobby, punctuating his words with little karate chops, "is going to be a phenomenal picture. Life changing. There's only one thing I want you guys to fix."

"The ghost?" said Claire hopefully.

"Exactly!" he said. "I LOVE it that we went straight to the same place. *Very* good sign. The ghost is all wrong!"

"Well, we're with you on that," I said, encouraged for the first time since reading the damned thing.

"Totally wrong," declared Gilbert.

"It should be a boy," said Bobby.

Gilbert turned excitedly to Claire. "What did I *just say* in the waiting room!"

"Fantastic!" boomed Bobby. "It's like some fucking mind meld! I think you guys are the *perfect* team to write this picture."

Why?!

"And I'm not just blowing smoke up your asses. The minute I finished your script, I knew you guys were it."

"We're glad you liked it," I said.

"I. Fucking. Adored. It."

"You know," said Claire, smiling shyly, "this may sound like a dreadfully conceited question, but I'm curious—what was your favorite scene?"

"Now, Claire!" chided Gilbert. "I think our heads are swelled enough without you begging Bobby to stroke us even more. Let's get back to *Greta*—excuse me, *The Heart in Hiding*—goose bumps!—what say we get Springsteen to write the title song?"

"Love it," said Bobby, "but Claire's question's a fair one. And, hey, who doesn't like to be stroked? Only most people don't earn it the way this lady has."

He plucked a script, presumably ours, from a pile on his desk. He began with general praise for our deft plotting and crackling dialogue, then began citing favorite scenes. The first of these, which dealt with an amusingly corrupt local official, seemed oddly familiar. I wondered with desperate optimism if it was something we'd written years ago and somehow forgotten. But then, in one ghastly instant, I realized at last the full staggering audacity of what Gilbert had done.

"The whole flashback to Paris!" raved Bobby. "And the way she leaves him the note—heartbreaking! But the scene that really blew me away is the one at the café where those asshole Germans start singing 'Watch on the Rhine' only to have Molnar and the whole café stand up and drown them out with 'La Marseillaise.' Loved it!"

It has been advised by Mr. William Goldman, among others, that during initial meetings with producers, screenwriters would do well to let the men with the dollars dominate the discussion. The writers should just listen attentively while maintaining a mien at once receptive and inscrutable. This amiable neutrality can be difficult to affect when the job on offer has little to commend it save its preferability to starvation. And the same look, I now discovered, becomes well-nigh impossible to maintain when you've just realized that your underhanded writing partner has persuaded your film-history-impaired producer that he and you are the proud authors of *Casablanca*.

"Actually," said Gilbert modestly, "I can't take credit for the 'Marseillaise' scene. That was Claire's inspiration."

"Brilliant!" said Bobby. "I would *love* to film that scene someday. And that first Frenchman who stands up to join the freedom fighters in song—I'm thinking Pavarotti."

"Or Sting," offered Gilbert.

"Better still."

Five

★

AT MOMENTS SUCH AS THIS, WHEN I feel that the weatherman, in predicting the day's precipitation, ought really to have mentioned the falling anvils, I can never entirely conceal my distress. My legs take on a life of their own, crossing and uncrossing at will, and I writhe in my chair like a lap dancer in need of a pee break. Gilbert, noting this, kicked me smartly and I willed myself to be still. Claire, in contrast, absorbed the shock with a poise that impressed me deeply. She even managed to smile once or twice at Gilbert, a remarkable feat given her scarcely containable urge to fall upon him and commit such acts on his person as would make Hannibal Lecter cluck his tongue and counsel moderation.

"And that scene at the roulette wheel," enthused Bobby, "where the hero rigs the wheel so the young couple can afford their exit visas—it shows us the guy's really got a heart!"

"A heart *in hiding*," said Gilbert.

"You know," said Bobby, giving "our" script a pat, "when we're done with my movie, I might be interested in making this. What would you say if I wanted to option it?"

"For how much?" asked Gilbert incredibly.

"Gilbert forgets," said Claire, "that it's already optioned."

Bobby frowned.

"Who's doing it?"

"This fellow back in New York," I said. "Rich dilettante."

"Never heard of him."

Bobby steered things back to *The Heart in Hiding*, offering thoughts and suggestions I hoped Gilbert was heeding since my mind was reeling so wildly it was all I could do to feign attention.

At least the mystery of our hiring had been solved. It was not, as Claire had theorized, a mix of nepotism and studio politics. Hell, no— we were good! We were the kind of writers they don't make anymore, skilled craftsmen who could blend romance and intrigue while capturing a bygone era so convincingly you'd almost think we'd lived through it!

"So," concluded Bobby, "we see eye-to-eye on all this?"

"Absolutely!" said Gilbert.

"Fan-fucking-tastic!" said Bobby. He rose, signaling that the meeting was over.

"This picture," he intoned solemnly, "could be a fucking classic. That's what I need you guys to write for me, okay? A *classic*."

"It's what we do best," replied Claire.

Bobby walked out with us, saying he was late for a meeting across town.

"Oops!" said Gilbert when we'd reached the exit. "Forgot my briefcase!"

As he nipped back into the office Claire and I exchanged a look, wondering if he was planning to flee down Bobby's fire escape. He returned promptly, though, jauntily swinging his briefcase. We then exited the office and descended Bobby's private staircase. He was not, like lesser mortals, compelled to park in the studio lot, and his Ferrari was waiting for him at the base of the stairs. We watched him drive off, then rounded on Gilbert, who, far from turning tail and sprinting to his car as we'd expected, burst into giggles and enfolded us in a boisterous hug.

"You two are amazing! You handled that *so* well in there! I mean, you did get a bit twitchy, Philip, but who could blame you? I can imagine how jarring it must have been for you when Bobby started congratulating us for *Casablanca!*"

"Can you?" asked Claire.

"I was kicking myself for not having warned you. I would have but I didn't think he'd go on about it so much and I figured why make you skittish going in? I'm sensing from your expressions that you're worried someone else might read it and blow the whistle on us. Well, don't be!"

He opened his briefcase and, with a magician's flourish, plucked out Bobby's copy of *Imbroglio*.

"That whole briefcase bit was just a ruse so I could go back in and swipe it. So there's no way he can show it to anyone now. Quick thinking, huh?"

"Could I see that please?" asked Claire politely.

Gilbert handed her the script, whereupon Claire swiftly rolled it up and commenced whaling him on the head with it.

"Ow! Cut that out!"

"How DARE you!" she cried. "How fucking dare you!!" she added, resorting to the sort of language she reserves for rare occasions, usually Gilbert-related.

"That hurts! Philip! How long are you going to stand there and let her do this?"

"Till her arm gets tired and I take over."

She gave him one last wallop, then savagely opened the script to the title page.

"Do you see that? That is MY name! In black and white! On fucking *Casablanca!*" She hurled the script back at him. "You moron! You contemptible, brain-dead weasel! How could you do this to me? And Philip! Just sit there and watch us take bows for this thing when you know damn well what'll happen to us when word of this insane scam gets out!"

"Jeez!" said Gilbert, massaging his ear. "This is why I keep stuff from you. You freak out over the least little thing!"

"Have you lost your tiny mind? This isn't a little harmless résumé padding—this is open-and-shut plagiarism!"

"Uh, Claire," I said, gesturing toward three tuxedo-clad extras who were smoking outside the next soundstage and eyeing us with frank fascination. Prudence dictated a change of venue, so we started toward the parking lot.

"I don't see what you're getting so worked up over. It's not as if you two had any ethical problems with it."

"EXCUSE ME?!" inquired Claire.

"Let's not be hypocrites. You had no trouble taking bows for the script when you thought *I* wrote it—"

"WE *NEVER* THOUGHT YOU WROTE IT!"

"Well, whoever you thought wrote it, you knew *you* didn't."

"Actually," I said, embarrassed, "we thought we did." I quickly outlined our initial theory, which he greeted with a patronizing snicker.

"Leave it to you two to assume that if Bobby loved the script it *had* to be yours! Not," he added, fearing another thrashing, "that your script wasn't marvelous. It just wouldn't have gotten us this job. Bobby specifically asked me for a World War II script."

"And why on earth," inquired Claire, "would he assume you of all people would have a World War II script up your sleeve?"

"I might have told him I did. I mean, I *had* to pique his interest. I figured I'd pull one of my other scripts out of the drawer and change the period. Y'know, plop in the Third Reich."

"As if you had anything finished!" I snorted, the time for diplomacy on that issue having passed.

"Well, I had things that were *close*," he said huffily. "But when I tried changing the period on them, it wasn't easy. The cyber-thriller was a complete nonstarter. And forget *Log Cabin Republican*."

He referred to a script he'd started based on his dubious theory as to why young Abe Lincoln first became devoted to the cause of racial justice. Hint: think hot runaway slave and moonlit hayloft.

"You can see the jam I was in. I'd told him I'd get something to him by the weekend, so I had no choice but to borrow something."

"But to rip off a masterpiece—!"

"What was I supposed to use? Something bad? Anyway, I was pretty sure Bobby hadn't seen it."

He explained that during Max's dinner there'd been a general discussion about what classic films had most influenced those present. Bobby had proudly claimed to have no such influences, saying that while his pretentious colleagues were in film school earnestly analyzing Hitchcock and Lubitsch, he was soaking up real life and building a business. He claimed that apart from *Schindler's List* and some old Westerns he'd watched on TV as a child, he'd never even seen a black-and-white movie.

"He was really pretty obnoxious, making it sound like everyone else is busy churning out 'homages' while he's this complete original. So I thought, 'Hell, if he doesn't know his classics, why not slip him one and see if he likes it?' "

"But *Casablanca?!* Even if you haven't seen it, you know it. All those famous lines—"

"Oh, there aren't that many. And of course I changed the really well-known ones. In our script—"

"Stop calling it that!"

"—Rick, or, as I call him, Frank, doesn't ask Sam, or rather Smoky, to play 'As Time Goes By.' He asks for 'I'll Be Seeing You,' which works every bit as well. The farewell scene at the plane was tricky—practically every line is famous! Took a bit of rewriting, but I actually prefer some of my dialogue to—"

"Oh, shut up!" fumed Claire. "I refuse to stand here and listen to you boast about how you improved *Casablanca!*"

We reached Gilbert's car and Claire hurled herself into the backseat. Gilbert, growing testy now himself, slammed the door and took the wheel.

"I'm getting a little tired of your attitude, Claire. I take this incredible gamble to help *all* of us get ahead. It pays off brilliantly and you're not even grateful!"

"*Grateful?!*" she thundered. "I should be *grateful* that I get to go home now—"

"*Go home?!*" I gasped.

"—and spend the rest of my life praying Bobby Spellman never turns on his TV and catches *Casablanca?*"

"What do you mean, 'go home'?!"

"Gawd!" groaned Gilbert, peeling out of the space. "You're worrying over nothing! Once our movie's made it won't *matter* if Bobby finds out. You've seen his ego—you think he'd let people know he was duped?"

"You're *leaving?*" I bleated piteously. Claire's response was a stare of incredulous disdain.

"And you're *not?* Don't tell me you're actually contemplating going through with this?"

"Well," I said weakly, "we did sort of promise we would. It doesn't seem right to renege."

"Thank God *someone* here has a few scruples!" said Gilbert.

"And besides," I argued, as if my lame sophistries could persuade a girl of Claire's unshakable rectitude to remain a party to such chicanery, "if we back out now, how do we explain it to Bobby? Or Maddie and Max? I mean, I don't *approve* of what Gilbert did any more than you do. But that's water under the bridge. And it's not as if we can plagiarize *this* script. No, this one will be our work start to finish, so it's not as if we won't be earning our money and . . ."

I trailed off, thoroughly cowed by her expression. It was a stare of bewildered revulsion such as an abbess might bestow on a young novitiate she's just caught test-driving a dildo.

"Philip," she said slowly, each word an ice cube, "you may lack the common sense to run screaming from a job that promises untold creative misery plus the looming threat of fraud charges and lifelong disgrace, but I do not. And for God's sake, Gilbert, this is not the Daytona 500!"

"If she wants to bail, let her!" brayed Gilbert, running a stop sign. "More money for us!"

"You'll need it for your defense."

As we drove the rest of the way to the hotel, Claire's silence was steely, Gilbert's petulant, and mine wretched as I pondered my future. Would Claire's defection sabotage our deal? And even if it didn't, how could I write the script with just Gilbert? I'd always relied on Claire to handle the heartfelt bits in our comedies, and *Greta* was nothing *but* heartfelt bits. As I gazed at my partners' surly faces I couldn't believe how quickly last night's euphoric unity had given way to such rancorous discord.

You might suppose that the demons assigned to torment me would have agreed at this juncture that they'd put in a solid day's work and could retire to the clubhouse for drinks. But no, they're a gung ho bunch, my demons, and, unlike my guardian angel, never averse to a spot of overtime. Their next assault came an hour later, and as with their previous salvos, they took care to soften me up before going in for the kill.

I was in Claire's room watching her pack, pathetically hoping that my sad puppy stare might alter her decision, when Gilbert, a crazed grin on his face, burst in without knocking.

"Philip, there you are! Claire—what are you doing?"

"What does it look like I'm doing?"

"Well, stop it," he said lightly. "You can't quit on us. Not now. I have the most amazing news!"

Claire said, "Let me guess—Cameron Mackintosh wants us for his next show on the strength of our score for *Porgy and Bess?*"

"No. I just talked to Josh—our agent, swell guy, you'll love him—and he got a call from business affairs at Pinnacle. The studio is offering us—brace yourselves!—half a million bucks to write this baby!"

"My God," I gasped, attempting unsuccessfully to do the math. "That's like . . . more than a hundred fifty grand each!"

"*And,*" said Gilbert, "we share a million-dollar bonus if the movie gets made!"

This was not happy news for a girl whose honor code compelled her to fly back east to a gloating ex-boyfriend and glittering career as a rehearsal pianist.

"Thank you," she deadpanned, "for making this easier for me."

"Oh, honey!" smirked Gilbert. "I haven't even gotten to the good part yet!"

"There's a *better* part than that?" I asked.

"I called Bobby to say thanks and he'd just gotten a call from Mr. Überagent himself, Irv Hackel. It seems he has a certain client that Bobby sent the book to and this client's just *dying* to play the lead."

"Who?"

"You may want to put a pillow on the floor so your jaw doesn't get hurt."

"Just tell us!"

"And . . . that . . . client . . . issssssssssss—"

"*WHO?!!*"

"Stephen! Donato!"

I shrieked like a castrato.

"*Stephen Donato?*"

"His colleagues call him Steve."

"*We're* writing a movie for Stephen *Donato?*"

"Annnnnnnd—!" said Gilbert, slapping out a drumroll on his thigh.

"There's an '*and*'*?!*"

"Guess who wants to play Greta?"

"Who? His mom?"

I said it facetiously, of course, a casting coup of that magnitude being an inconceivable bonanza for a trio of newbie screenwriters. But Gilbert did not roll his eyes at my outlandishness nor did he ask me to guess again. He just smiled puckishly and waggled his eyebrows like Groucho Marx.

"*NO! Diana fucking MALENFANT?!*"

"Mother and son, together again!"

I sank weak-kneed onto the bed, speechless at the thought that this long and breathlessly awaited pairing, this embarrassment of stardom, was to be lavished on our little script. If any acting team on earth could ram this stinker down the public's throat and make them say "Yum," this was the one.

Not even Claire, who'd managed to maintain her look of vinegary disinterest at the mention of Donato, could feign indifference now. She sank onto the bed, her mouth agape as she struggled to make sense of a town in which adored and wildly sought after megastars committed their talents to projects of such dubious merit.

"They *both* want to do it?" she asked. "All the projects they've turned down over the years—and they want to do *this* one?"

"And soon!" said Gilbert. "We'll need to get cracking. Now I realize, Claire, how silly you must be feeling over your little snit, but don't beat yourself up. We artists are entitled to our little displays of temperament. Just unpack and we'll say no more about it."

"You will stay, won't you?" I pleaded. "I mean, you *can't* walk away from something like this!"

She scowled and resumed folding her blouse.

"And just what exactly do you imagine this changes?"

"Are you kidding? They haven't acted together since his first movie when he was, like, ten! Now they're finally doing their reunion picture—and WE get to write it?! This changes everything!"

"No arguments there! *Now* if the whole *Casablanca* stunt gets out— excuse me, *when* it gets out—the stink will be a hundred times bigger!"

"God!" fumed Gilbert. "I'm so sick of your negativity! You only see the downside!"

"Has there ever *once* been an upside with you?" she asked and I winced at the cogency of the question.

"Let her go, Philip! Who needs her?"

"We do, you idiot!"

"No, we don't. Let the turncoat abandon us—we'll still write a beautiful, heartbreaking script and after Stephen and Diana star in it there'll be no end to the offers we'll get! Producers will be lined up, begging for that Selwyn and Cavanaugh magic! I swear to you, Philip, we will *own* this town!"

As if to punctuate this speech Gilbert's cell phone rang. He whipped it out and opened it with a practiced flick of his wrist.

"Selwyn here!" he said debonairly. He listened a moment, then covered the phone. "Our agent. Wondering, no doubt, where to send the Cristal . . . Yes, Josh, old man! If you're calling with the glad tidings, we've already heard."

He listened a moment, and his raffish smile suddenly vanished. His eyebrows shot upward and his jaw plummeted as though suddenly loath to be on the same face.

"You can't be serious!" he said, hitting a high A-sharp on "serious."

"What?" demanded Claire and I, though we both knew.

"We're off the picture!" he blurted, looking like a man about to burst into loud hysterical sobs.

Which, of course, he was.

Six

★

AN HOUR LATER, AFTER FRANTIC CALLS had been placed to
Maddie, Max, and Bobby Spellman, a clearer if only marginally less bleak picture of our situation had emerged. We were
advised to remain calm as we were not yet officially off the project. Our
hopes of staying, though, hung by a thread, one so slender that even
the tiniest spider, offered it for use in constructing a web, would have
declined, citing safety concerns.

Had we been wiser to the ways of filmdom we'd have realized we
were toast the minute we heard the names Donato and Malenfant.
Megastars as a breed pride themselves on their authority to approve all
key players on any project they undertake. Stephen was no exception
to this rule and Diana was notorious for the ruthlessness with which
she exercised the prerogative. It was not difficult as such to imagine
their response on hearing that the screenplay for their reunion picture
had already been assigned to a trio of neophytes. Four flared nostrils
and an icy "Oh, really?" about sums it up.

We were assured that Bobby had heartily endorsed us to Stephen
and Diana but that there was little he could do if they preferred to hire
some more established writer they'd worked with before and with

whom they felt a greater "rapport." This assurance came not from our great pal Bobby, who, so far as we were concerned, was now, like Heinrich's tender heart, in hiding, but from our agent. Josh also warned us that overtures had already been made to several A-list writers and that the odds of our being chosen over these scribes were small indeed. He said that our best, indeed only hope would be to send Stephen and Diana a copy of the spec that had so impressed Bobby and pray they were equally dazzled.

"Great idea!" said Gilbert. He then explained that the script was, alas, trapped on his computer back in New York. He'd only brought one print copy to LA and this he'd given to Bobby. He told Josh to call Bobby and ask him to make copies for the stars. Josh shortly reported back that he'd spoken to Bobby, who claimed to have misplaced the script.

"*Misplaced* it?!" raged Gilbert. "What kind of bullshit is this?!"

Josh found it fishy as well and took it as a sign of Bobby's faltering faith in us. Gilbert implored Josh to arrange a meeting with Stephen and Diana. If "rapport" was such a key criterion for their choice of writers, couldn't we at least be given the chance to establish one?

More calls were exchanged and then Max, bless him, intervened. He phoned Stephen and Diana's agent and said that while he'd certainly understand if they ultimately decided to go with more seasoned scribes, he'd consider it a personal favor if they'd at least meet with the gifted newcomers who'd first been offered the job. An hour later Josh called to inform us that Diana and Stephen would receive us at eleven a.m. two mornings hence.

Gilbert hung up, then, snagging a beer from Claire's minibar, plopped onto the couch, looking drained but pleased at a job well done. "Whew," he sighed. "Was that a close one! For a while I thought we were goners!"

Claire just stared at him, her exasperation tinged for the first time with something like pity.

"Exactly what do you imagine just happened?"

"I saved our jobs, that's what."

"*Excuse* me?"

"Oh, all right," he allowed, "we may not be *officially* in yet. But our foot's in the door and I can handle things from there."

"At least we're still in the running," I said, prompting Claire to favor me with an equally patronizing stare. She formed a little megaphone with her hands and shouted across the room.

"We are NOT in the running! They've offered us a *courtesy* meeting purely to avoid offending Max. Period. There's not a chance in hell they'll actually hire us."

"They might," said Gilbert, miffed. "I'm a damn good salesman."

"You're an unscrupulous, self-deluding jackass. Do you have the remotest idea how out of your league you are? Those two can snap their fingers and get any Oscar winner in town to hold his nose and write this for them. How do you plan to make them choose *you*? Not by waving *Casablanca* at them — even you know better than to try that stunt again. Face it, it's over, and a damn good thing if you ask me."

"Well, then," sneered Gilbert, "since you're so positive I can't *possibly* get us the job, maybe you'll agree to a little wager?"

Claire eyed him warily, then asked what he was proposing.

"Simple. If I get us the job, you'll stay and help us write it."

"And if — excuse me, *when* — you don't?"

Gilbert smiled and shrugged, inviting her to name her price.

I'd expected Claire to dismiss Gilbert's wager as childish posturing not worthy of a serious response. To my surprise she seemed to be considering it, pondering what she might extract from Gilbert in the event, inevitable to her, that we were passed over. She frowned pensively at her half-packed suitcase, then addressed Gilbert in a crisp businesslike tone.

"Get me a job."

"That's what I'm planning to do."

"No, a *real* job. Something at the studio. An assistant job, anything. And one for Philip if he wants one. Have your mom ask Max. He can certainly arrange it."

Gilbert, who'd sooner have asked Max for a quickie than an assistant's job, asked Claire why she'd request so menial a post.

"It's called being realistic, a concept that I know is, like 'honesty,' completely beyond your ken. We can't expect Max to make us execs just because our feelings were hurt. But he can find us something that'll pay the rent."

"You want to stay here?" I asked, amazed.

"What's my alternative? Crawling home in defeat two days after I've boasted to Marco that I'm the toast of Hollywood? I can do without that humiliation, thank you. Better for us to stay here, get day jobs, meet people, and work on a new spec—without this one's invaluable assistance."

I said that sounded like a plan to me and she extended a firm hand to Gilbert.

"Is that a deal? You'll do that for us?"

"Oh, absolutely," smiled Gilbert.

"You won't renege or forget?"

"You have my oath. And you won't renege on us either? If I bring home the bratwurst, you'll stay and pitch in?"

Claire rolled her eyes and placed her hand on an imaginary Bible. Her voice dripping with sarcasm, she spoke the words she would so often and bitterly repent in the days ahead.

"No, Gilbert, my angel, I will *not* renege. If Diana Malenfant (worldwide box office to date, two billion dollars) and her little boy Stephen (six and a half billion) should say, 'Who needs David Koepp or Steve Zaillian for our big reunion picture? Get us Gilbert Selwyn and his plagiarizing chimps!' then yes, yes, yes, my love, I will stay here and write the damned picture with you!"

Gilbert smiled, serene as always in victory.

"You heard her, Philly. She promised."

TWO DAYS LATER GILBERT and I found ourselves sitting in his convertible, timorously eyeing the majestic wrought-iron gate beyond which, at a point not visible from the road, stood the Bel-Air manse of Diana Malenfant.

We were alone. Claire had refused to accompany us, declaring it beneath her dignity to grovel to two self-important stars for a job she didn't want and which they hadn't the slightest intention of giving her.

This had been fine by Gilbert, who'd feared that if she did come she'd find some way to sabotage us.

Gilbert pressed the intercom button and a metallic voice asked our names. He supplied them and after an unnervingly long pause the gate swung open. I did not imagine that any house lying at the end of so long and stately a drive would do much to lessen my anxiety, but I was still unprepared for its sheer intimidating grandeur.

Maison Malenfant was a three-story beaux arts pile that appeared to have been designed with an eye toward formal events like lawn parties and treaty signings. The architect had been instructed to pay tribute to Diana's aristocratic French forebears. His suspicion, entirely correct, that she possessed no such forebears had not prevented him from rolling up his sleeves and doing her bogus ancestors proud.

The resulting edifice boasted a regal entrance with curved stairs flanked by two rather petulant stone lions. Centered above this on the second floor was a large ornate balcony, ideal for waving to peasants while keeping an eye peeled for approaching tumbrels. From each side of this homey entrance there extended the house's two vast wings. In designing these the architect had not stinted on soaring French windows giving onto still more balconies, nor had he neglected to adorn these with cherubs and cornucopias of stone produce. As I stood, awestruck, taking the place in, Gilbert nudged me sharply.

"Close your mouth. It's a *house* for Chrissake! We need to look confident in there, not like a couple of rubes who've never seen a mansion before."

We mounted the grand stairs to the front door and rang the bell. Once more we were made to wait an unsettling length of time, during which we could dimly hear shouts and doors slamming somewhere deep within the house. At length the door opened and a white-jacketed houseman beckoned us into an opulent foyer with a marble floor and a central flower arrangement the size of a hot air balloon. The houseman, a thin bespectacled man, had the besieged, jittery look of a servant whose mistress, cranky on a good day, has just received unflattering news from her talking mirror. It seemed clear from this and from the look of discreet sympathy he gave us that, as if enough factors weren't already working against us, we had come on a Very Bad Day.

"I'm afraid Miss Malenfant's a bit . . . behind schedule this morning. It may be a while before she can see you."

Gilbert checked his watch. "Well, Katzenberg's not till three. We can wait."

The fellow handed us off to a second functionary, a uniformed maid with darting eyes. She led us up a grand curved staircase to the second floor, then down a wide hall hung with tapestries. These appeared at first glance to be frayed and ancient but on closer inspection proved to depict Diana herself in scenes from her most famous movies. Gilbert and I exchanged a look of wonder. We could see a movie star displaying photos of her screen triumphs—but *tapestries?* The maid showed us to a room halfway down the hall, then hastened back downstairs with the carefree gait of a battlefield medic.

The room was a library and a pretty damned nice one. It was two stories high with a forest's worth of oak paneling and rows of leather-bound books no less impressive for having been purchased by the yard. The surfaces were laden with objects chosen to belie the youth of the money that had purchased them—antique globes, clocks, and busts of great thinkers. Diana's two Oscars were on display, but she'd consigned them to a corner shelf as though to demonstrate how lightly she viewed her accolades, a gesture somewhat undermined by the life-size portrait of her that hung over the fireplace. It depicted her in a period gown, raptly reading a book. I wondered if this portrait of Literary Diana was something she'd commissioned specially for the library and if the kitchen had a painting of Culinary Diana with her clad in a toga contemplating a pot roast. Then I realized the picture was a prop from *Tomorrow Be Damned*, an overripe epic in which she'd portrayed the mistress of Alexandre Dumas.

"Catch that one?" I asked.

"The first half."

"*Quelle* stinker."

"Be sure to say that."

We heard another door slam somewhere in the distance, followed

by the unmistakable voice of Diana. She seemed to be reading someone the riot act, though the only phrase we could make out was a shrill,
"I said NO!" This was followed by another thunderous door slam.

"Do you get the impression," asked Gilbert, "that all is not well
today chez Malenfant?"

I concurred and wondered aloud if all this turmoil might leave our
hostess in a less receptive frame of mind than that in which we'd hoped
to find her.

"Now, now," said Gilbert, tenaciously clinging to optimism, "you
heard the butler. He said we'd have to wait awhile. By the time she gets
around to us this may all have blown over."

No sooner had he voiced this hope than we heard another door slam,
followed by the clacking of heels advancing our way down the hall. We
turned just as the library door was flung open by Diana herself.

The great lady wore a tan cashmere lounging outfit, fluffy white
mules, and no makeup whatsoever. The lack of it exposed a sea of
freckles I'd never imagined lurked beneath the invariably creamy com-
plexion she displayed on film and in public. It was startling to see those
large, famously smoldering eyes as devoid of enhancement as those of
a mackerel.

She obviously hadn't expected to find us in her library. She
stopped short, regarding us with consternation as though we were bur-
glars. Good lord, I thought, had we not even been *announced?*

Gilbert, immune to the paralysis that had gripped me, sprang
suavely to his feet.

"Miss Malenfant! How lovely to meet you. I'm Gilbert Selwyn
and this is my partner, Philip Cavanaugh." This produced little
change in her expression, so he gamely continued. "We're the writers
Bobby Spellman hired to adapt *A Song for Greta.* You graciously consented to see us."

This seemed to prompt some vague recollection. Her lips parted
slightly and she gave a little nod. "Thank heaven," I thought, "she remembers us! There's hope!"

"All right," she said, baring her teeth in a grotesque parody of a
smile. "I've *seen* you. Now get the fuck out of my house!"

Aside:
Who's Who in the Cast

★

I T WAS NOT, YOU'LL AGREE, the most auspicious beginning for a
partnership. But a partnership was forged that day, albeit a far
stranger one than we could ever have anticipated.

Now don't get annoyed, please, but before I share with you the
details of the arrangement Gilbert and I entered into that day, I feel a
certain duty to pause and provide a spot of background on Diana,
Stephen, and their storied clan. I know most of you will heave an irri-
tated sigh, the information being as familiar to most readers—
especially, let's face it, mine—as the news that Elizabeth Taylor has
had many husbands and Jodie Foster has not. Why bother, you ask,
to stop and rehash what everyone surely must know? And I see your
point.

But what of the gay Amish teenager?

What of this poor youngster—let us call him Amos—who re-
turns each night to his stark little room, weary and glamour-starved
after a long day of furniture making and barn raising? He waits patiently for his family to fall asleep, then cautiously lights his candle and
removes this volume from beneath his mattress. (Don't ask how he got

it. Gay teenagers, even Amish ones, have a way of laying their hands on things.)

He has read avidly up to this point, but for the last chapter or so a question has gnawed at him. "Who," he keeps asking, "are these Malenfants? How came they to be so grand? Be they like this Streisand woman friend Seth keeps whispering of behind the schoolhouse? Do they play all the day and never eat porridge? And the menfolk—be any of them like me and, I think, Seth?"

It is for the sake of young Amos and his gossip-deprived brethren that I now outline the basic saga of the Malenfants. The thousands of you who've read (and the hundred or so who've written) whole books about them may feel free to skip ahead to the next chapter.

THE MALENFANT SHOWBIZ DYNASTY began in 1938 when an exotic dancer, Mrs. Lotte Kurnitz (stage name Lotte Funn), met Claude Malenfant, a French-Canadian vaudevillian best remembered for his pioneering use of bear traps in a juggling act. Sparks flew, as did Lotte's husband, and soon the pair were married. Lotte promptly produced a baby girl (some say *very* promptly) and a year later a second daughter was born. Though each of the sisters, Diana and Lily, maintains firmly that she is the younger, we do know that both are several years older than Monty, the baby of the family.

The Malenfant girls, though vile little thugs at heart, had indisputably dimpled and adorable surfaces, and, as this was the heyday of the child star, their parents wasted no time in hauling them off to Hollywood. Ironically it was their brother who struck gold first when he was cast as the juvenile lead in *Careful There, Elsie!* Monty, affecting a British accent he has never entirely lost, played the son of a British war widow who marries a Yank fighter pilot and must then adapt hilariously to life in Brooklyn. The film, a surprise hit, inspired two sequels and a brief vogue for the catchphrase "Talk American, wouldja!"

Diana and Lily watched enviously as their baby brother ascended fame's ladder while they settled for extra work in pictures calling for schoolgirls en masse. They were persistent, though, and finally landed speaking roles, playing the ingenue's flighty sisters in the operetta *Krakow Serenade*. A scene in which Lily naughtily smoked Papa's pipe convinced a producer to cast her as Lorna, a farm girl seduced into a life of vice in the gritty film noir *Soiled*.

The film was a solid hit. For the next year or so Lily rode high while Diana, now the sole unsung Malenfant, struggled and seethed. But, as everyone (save, of course, young Amos) knows, it was Diana who got the last laugh.

She won her first lead after starting an affair with a producer who'd bought the rights to a syrupy novel written by—you guessed it!—Prudence Gamache. Its heroine was a young nun whose sister, a gangster's moll, shoots her boyfriend in self-defense and gets sent up the river. The nun, heartsick, forsakes convent life and hauls her beads off to the pen. There she ministers to the inmates, stares down many a knife and knuckle, and helps Sis and pretty much the whole prison find God. The picture, *No Shield but a Wimple*, won Diana her first Oscar. From then on her ascent to fame's zenith was as inexorable as her siblings' decline.

In Monty's case the word "decline" is perhaps unfair. He'd never burned with his sisters' white-hot ambition and was quick to make sport of his limited gifts. He pursued his career haphazardly into his twenties, at which point the studio, alarmed by his indiscreet cavorting with Hollywood's gay demimonde, laid down the law—marry or else. Monty merely curtsied, told them on what they could lunch, and quit. He became a realtor, invested shrewdly in the Valley, and made himself a bundle.

Lily, by contrast, has clung to her dwindling fame with grim tenacity, exploring every avenue open to an actress whose brief stardom has faded. She has tried character roles, TV, and summer stock, with stops along the way in nightclubs, game shows, commercials, and state fairs. She remains active or, at any rate, available to this day.

We come now to the present generation. Both sisters shared their parents' desire to produce illustrious offspring, and in this ambition as well, Diana's triumph over Lily was brutal and complete.

For most of the sixties Lily was married to Buddy Biggs, who'd produced her daffy schoolteacher sitcom *Sorry, Miss Murgatroyd!* The marriage was childless, a great sadness to Lily though she could hardly blame Buddy, given his success in impregnating both her best friend and her housemaid.

Diana by contrast produced a son who proved remarkably precocious at the fame game, managing to win worldwide attention seven months in advance of his actual birth.

His father was the Italian film star Roberto Donato, whose marriage to Diana was one of those tempestuous, plate-throwing liaisons that leave gossip columnists misty-eyed with gratitude. On the very eve of Diana's petition for divorce, a drunken Roberto drove his Lamborghini off a bridge. Diana promptly went into extravagant mourning, fainting daily in some suitably public place. A month later, just as the clamorous coverage of the grief-stricken widow had begun to subside, Diana announced she was carrying Roberto's child. The ensuing frenzy of sympathy didn't let up till Stephen's birth, which was greeted with the sort of fanfare usually reserved for heirs to the British throne and human litters of not less than six.

Little Stephen made his film debut at the age of ten, starring opposite Mom in *Sophie and Sam,* a depression-era comedy about a light-fingered street urchin taken in by a softhearted saloon singer. Stephen's performance earned him his first Oscar nomination. Diana, who was not nominated, put an immediate moratorium on her son's acting career, citing her desire to give him a "normal, wholesome childhood," which, in this case, meant a Swiss boarding school.

Stephen did not resume his career until he was twenty-two, by which time he'd grown into a world-class dreamboat, combining his mother's luxuriant chestnut hair with his father's aquiline nose and bedroom eyes. In his first film as an adult, he played a brilliant schizophrenic violinist in the three-hankie classic *Chamber Music.* This won him his second Oscar nod, and though he lost again, his stardom was now firmly established and has remained undimmed for fifteen years.

Like many a savvy star, he divides his projects between "art" and commerce, alternating high-minded dramas with comedies and thrillers. His most financially successful movies thus far have been the

Caliber films. In these, three to date, he plays Simon Caliber, a private detective whose every case, no matter how mundane at the outset, soon plunges him into some crisis of global proportions. Were Caliber hired to rescue a kitten from a tree, you could be sure the tabby would turn out to be some genetically altered mutation whose fur balls were pure doomsday virus.

His most recent picture was *Lothario,* a drama about a shallow playboy who, faced with a terminal illness, revisits his many conquests in the hopes of experiencing true love before he dies. He finally finds it with Frances McDormand, who plays a plain but compassionate hospice nurse fifteen years his senior. The picture, though derided as shamelessly manipulative by some, grossed a fortune, and Stephen, who'd starved himself whippet thin for the wrenching final scenes, was widely considered a shoo-in for the Oscar that had twice eluded him.

Throughout Stephen's career rumors have persisted that he's secretly gay. The press, displaying its usual deference to megastars, has mostly tiptoed around these rumors but has, on occasion, gently elicited his response to them. His answers have spanned the full panoply of tactics available to the closeted megastar.

He has played coy, refusing to be nailed down while deftly leaving the impression that his evasiveness stems solely from a waggish impulse to twit the reporter. He's been statesmanlike, citing the bond he feels with his gay fans and professing to be flattered that some among them wish, however mistakenly, to claim him for their own. He's waxed indignant, saying he's answered the question so often that to pose it again impugns his integrity. His most frequent and cleverest ploy is to simply bore the press into submission, pontificating on the masculine and feminine dualities within all of us until even the most prurient scoop hound changes the subject to how he enjoyed shooting in Prague.

Five years ago a tabloid published a story about a long-ago roommate of Stephen's who claimed they'd enjoyed a brief but torrid affair. Stephen denied the story but declined to sue, arguing that his accuser, a failed actor, had only made the charge to gain notoriety and that a lengthy, sensational trial was just what the scoundrel wanted.

This argument seemed to satisfy the great unwashed. The washed, however, were still plenty suspicious, so Stephen fired his publicist and hired Sonia Powers, the town's most formidable media tamer. Six months later he married Gina Beach, a spokesmodel turned actress who'd appeared in his second Caliber film as the sexy physicist Caliber finds murdered in his bed. Wags joked that it was her turn to find him dead in the sack, but the marriage has lasted four years and the couple are still, as they confide to the press with numbing regularity, "very much in love."

THERE, THEN. That should set the stage for the Amish contingent as well as any recently rescued castaways. To the vast majority of you who already knew all this and a good deal more about the Malenfants, I apologize. Of what follows, I assure you, you know nothing.

Seven

★

S O THERE WE WERE WHEN LAST GLIMPSED, standing face-to-face with an implacably inhospitable screen legend. Her ferocity robbed me of speech, but Gilbert, who's made of smoother stuff, actually smiled as though the phrase "Get the fuck out of my house" were some Wildean bon mot.

"There, Philip!" he said with what struck me as positively insane good cheer. "What did I tell you?"

He turned his congenial smile to Diana.

"I knew the moment we walked in that we'd come at a bad time. I suggested we slip away and reschedule but Philip, he's *such* a fan of yours—well, we both are!—he *insisted* we at least stay to meet you, however briefly. Now we have, and may we say what an honor it's been. Please forgive us for intruding at a time when something's so obviously troubling you. I don't suppose it's anything we could assist you with in some way?"

I'd never until this moment quite realized how potent a weapon pure charm could be. Diana, hearing so gracious a response to her truculence, just stood there, flummoxed, like a confused repertory actress who's barged onstage as Lady Macbeth only to find the rest of the company playing *Hay Fever*.

"Well," she said, her tone calmer and more refined, "that's terribly nice of you, but it's a family matter. It involves my sister and . . . well, that's all I can say."

"Is she ill?" asked Gilbert, concerned.

"If only."

A brief silence descended. I was uncomfortably aware that Diana's newfound civility toward us was based in part on our promise to leave immediately. Gilbert knew this too but, loath to depart without the prize we'd come for, kept the flattery flowing in the hope of prolonging our tenuous welcome.

"Well, we're off!" he lied. "But first, could you satisfy my curiosity about that stunning painting of you over the fireplace?"

"It's from *Tomorrow Be Damned*, isn't it?" I asked.

"Yes. Can you believe they wanted me to *pay* for it?"

"No!" said Gilbert, deeply affronted.

"But what a movie!" I said. "I won't embarrass you by saying how many times I've seen it."

"I'm glad *someone* enjoyed it. I went through hell making it. The director was a monster."

"Yes," said Gilbert with a knowing nod. "One hears that."

What one in fact heard was that the famously rancorous shoot owed most of its turmoil to Diana, who, convinced that the actor playing Alexandre Dumas was stealing the picture from her, threw such frequent and violent tantrums that the crew nicknamed her the "Cunt of Monte Cristo."

"Well, lovely meeting you," said Diana with warm finality.

"Off we go!" said Gilbert. "And as for rescheduling—?"

"Yes," she said vaguely. "Some other time."

She swept out the door and proceeded down the hall so briskly we had to scamper to keep up with her.

"Knowing how busy you must be, we're happy to work around your schedule," said Gilbert.

"Well, this week is *terrible,*" she replied. "And I doubt the next will be much better. You know, I'm not sure we really *need* to meet again at all."

Gilbert and I exchanged a panicked glance as Diana regally descended the staircase.

"Don't you want to talk about the script?"

"Oh, I don't think we need bother with that. I can see you're both very bright and I'm sure you'd do a wonderful job. There are a few other writers we're talking to. Once we've decided we'll let you know."

She timed this speech to end precisely as we reached the front door, and not even Gilbert, who'd thus far maintained the silkiest poise, could conceal his dismay at being sent packing without a rain check.

"Give my love to Max," smiled Diana, clearly pleased at how efficiently she'd discharged her obligation to him. She then gave us her back and marched briskly toward the stairs.

It was at this precise moment, as the bassinet containing our careers was hurtling toward the falls, that the front door opened and Stephen Donato, like some Adonis *ex machina,* entered the foyer and our lives.

The Star had apparently arrived fresh from a workout or a run. He wore black cotton gym shorts and a gray T-shirt that clung damply to his broad chest, leaving a sweat stain that nestled in the cleft between his pectorals like some Rorschach of desire. His wavy brown hair was tousled and sweat-dampened and his square dimpled jaw was darkened by a two-day growth of beard so sexy as to make death by razor burn seem the happiest of fates. The dreamy hazel eyes regarded Gilbert and me with what may, I suppose, have been mere courtesy, but which seemed, after Diana's Gorgon glare, like the radiant compassion of some benevolent yet fuckable saint.

"Stephen!" cried Diana, wheeling dramatically. "Thank heaven you're here!"

"Hey, Mom," he said. Casually. As though mortal.

"Where have you been, Stephen! I've been calling you for the last hour!"

"We were out taking a run."

He turned to Gilbert and me, who were staring at him like two dogs eyeing a rotisserie. He smiled, extending his hand for us to shake, and though I was a good half foot closer to him, Gilbert darted in first.

"Hi. Stephen Donato."

"Gilbert Selwyn. *So* good to meet you," he trilled. He continued to shake Stephen's hand well past any seemly span of time, compelling me to nudge him discreetly aside. I gave Stephen's hand a firm masculine shake while offering a wry smile meant to convey that I shared his politely concealed amusement over my colleague's absurdly kittenish behavior.

"Phil Cavanaugh," I said crisply even as a voice within me cried, *"I want your T-shirt for a pillowcase and death to the maid who washes it!"*

"Sorry we're late," said Stephen.

"They were just going," said Diana.

"Oh, did we miss the meeting?"

I wondered what he'd meant by "we." Then I noticed that Diana was gazing past us with a look of weary distaste. I turned around and there, framed in the doorway, was Stephen's wife, Gina Beach.

It will give you some idea how swiftly and completely desire had unhinged me when I confess that I viewed her on first sight with that beady critical eye we reserve for our rivals in romance. Her wee nose seemed to me insufferably pert, her hair unpersuasively blond. Her breasts, I granted, were bouncy perfection but so large in relation to her scrawny torso as to render their authenticity dubious in the extreme. She had, it appeared, joined Stephen on his jog. Sweat did not become her.

"Gina," said Diana, her voice swooping a disappointed octave, "I hadn't realized you'd be joining us."

"Stephen asked me to. I read that book *A Song for Greta* last night—cried my eyes out!"

How uncultured her voice was. How lamentably twangy.

"I thought," she continued, "that is, Stephen and I *both* thought, that I could play Lisabetta. Y'know, the one Heinrich falls for?"

"You'd be *perfect!*" fibbed Gilbert.

Gilbert's endorsement won a grateful smile from Gina and we introduced ourselves.

"So, you're the ones who know Max?" she said.

"Know him? He's practically my dad."

She gazed around the foyer as though doing a head count.

"Weren't there three of you?"

We said that our partner Claire sent her regrets but she was nursing a cold and would never have forgiven herself if she'd passed it along to any of them.

"Well, you tell her thank you for me," said Gina emphatically. "I wish more people were considerate that way. I had a photo shoot last week and this guy doing my hair, he's hacking his lungs out and, I'm like, *hello!*"

"Did you hear the way she said that, Philip? Pure Lisabetta."

We were now facing away from Diana, and I wondered nervously how she was taking all this. Not only were we blithely ignoring our banishment, we were bolstering her daughter-in-law's impertinent assumption that she was fit to share a screen with her. I stole a glance at Diana and saw that my anxiety was well-founded. She was standing ramrod stiff by the stairs wearing an expression that called to mind Hedda Gabler as portrayed by Yosemite Sam. Stephen, noting her demeanor, asked gently—such tenderness in his voice!—if something was wrong.

"YES! As I thought I'd made perfectly damn CLEAR I cannot deal with this project today! Something's come up, something very upsetting, and I need to discuss it with you!"

"Right this minute?"

"YES!" she barked and, glowering at Gina, added, *"Alone!"*

She turned, stormed off down a short hallway, and, extending her arm like a battering ram, disappeared through a swinging door.

"Sorry, hon," said Stephen to the woman who could never love him as I could. "You don't want to be around her when she's this way."

"She's always this way," noted Gina. She spun around and, in a pale imitation of Diana's imperious exit, flounced petulantly into the living room. He watched her go, then favored us with a beleaguered smile.

"Sorry, guys," he said. "We're not always this crazy."

"Just one of those days," I said.

He turned and disappeared down the short hall. I was sorry to see him go though delighted to watch him go, the view from behind being a honey and one I could ogle freely without him noticing. After he'd gone we stood a moment in dreamy silence, mired in that trancelike zone where worship and lust collide.

"He's gorgeous!" whispered Gilbert.

"Stunning."

"In shorts yet!"

"We sure won that lottery."

"We have *got* to get this job, Philly!"

"I know!" I concurred from the depths of my soul. "If it weren't for Diana—"

"Yikes, what a bitch!"

"I'll say!"

"And looking pretty rough too."

"Tell me. That face has more fine lines than *The Importance of Being Earnest.*"

We agreed that our one slim hope of victory would be if Diana, having unburdened her woes to Stephen, retired to her fainting couch. Then Stephen, finding us still waiting, would surely consent to hear us out. In the meanwhile we'd suck up to Gina, who might, despite Diana's clear disdain for her, prove a useful ally.

We sidled discreetly into the living room, a vast high-ceilinged chamber that seemed designed to make you kick yourself for having left your powdered wig at home. Gina, looking incongruous in her running togs, sat sulking on a richly brocaded gold sofa. I feared she'd resent the intrusion but she seemed, if anything, to have been waiting for us.

"She loves to do this to me," she declared with a wounded frown.

"Diana?"

"Constantly! She loves to make me feel I'm not part of the family, like I'm some . . . interloper! I've reached out to her *so* many times but nothing I do is ever good enough."

At first we felt surprised, even flattered that a glamorous film star (albeit one whose acting we abhorred and whose husband we longed to purloin) had taken us so swiftly into her confidence. We did not yet realize that her openness owed less to our empathic faces than her impulse to talk about herself during all hours not given over to sleep. When there was no suitable friend or relation on hand to listen, then a screenwriter would suffice, as would a stylist, driver, or elevator occupant. To be Gina's confidant you did not need to be her peer. You just had to be in earshot.

"This so-called crisis," she continued, "I'll bet it's nothing. She's just making it sound important for the fun of shutting me out."

"Actually," I said, "she did seem pretty upset when we got here."

"Yes," said Gilbert. "She told us something really bad had come up."

"See!" she cried in bitter triumph. "She tells *you* about it and she doesn't even *know* you. But I have to hear it from strangers!"

We assured her that Diana had confided no details of the crisis to us except that it involved her sister. Then Gilbert, spotting the houseman trembling in the foyer, suggested that he might know the scoop, having been tantrum-adjacent all morning.

"What a good idea! Phelps knows everything that happens around here!"

She raced off to intercept him, and when she returned it was clear from her malicious smirk that the shakedown had yielded results.

"Well!" she said, plopping herself between us. "No *wonder* she's upset—she's writing her memoirs!"

"Diana?"

"No, Lily. Her sister."

"And that's bad?" asked Gilbert.

Her laugh was as merry as it was vindictive.

"Well, yeah—for Diana. They *hate* each other. Apparently she's just signed with a publisher and Diana's going nuts."

"Why?" asked Gilbert, thrilled to be privy to such inside stuff. "What's Lily going to say about her?"

"That's just it—she doesn't know. And it's making her *crazy*. She got wind of it this morning and called Lily demanding to know what she planned to say about her. Lily just blew her off—said she could read it when everyone else did. Poor Diana!" she hooted, giddy with sympathy.

I said I failed to understand why Diana should be so upset, noting gently that this would not be the first time she'd been denigrated in print.

"This is different. Lily knows *everything*. Gawd, if she tells even half the stories she told me at my wedding—!"

"She trashed your mother-in-law at your *wedding?*"

"She wanted me to know what I was getting into. I thought it was pretty tacky myself. We'd just met and there she was telling me all this really personal stuff. But some people are like that. No boundaries."

Gina, fearing perhaps that her lip smacking over Diana's woes had made her seem less than kind, softened her tone. She assured us she sincerely pitied Diana even if she had brought this upon herself through a lifetime of "negative karma." As she continued in this vein, my mind began to wander.

It wandered, of course, to Stephen. It began by conjuring once more those piercing amber eyes, loitered briefly around his sweaty, still-heaving chest before drifting due south. It then swerved painfully to the depressing likelihood that I'd never see him again after this interview. What could I possibly do to win his favor and the job? My mind went into overdrive, searching desperately for some argument or angle that might sway him.

I was much vexed by Gina's jabbering, as the need to feign attention was hampering my concentration. But then something she'd said earlier echoed in my mind. And that's when it hit me.

It was a cunning little plan, so cunning, in fact, that I couldn't believe it hadn't occurred to Gilbert, in whose brain "guile" is the default setting. I glanced at his face but saw no hint of the smirk that would have been blooming there had he thought of it.

As Gina droned on I pondered my plan further. Its one drawback was that, centering as it did on Lily's memoir, it served Diana's ends more than Stephen's. How much better for me if my beloved shared his mother's anxiety over the book's possible contents. Gina had betrayed no hint of concern as to how she and her rumor-plagued husband might be portrayed. Was this because they were so friendly with Lily they had no need to fear her wrath? Or was Gina just too busy savoring Diana's discomfort to wonder what grenades might be lobbed their way?

"Well," I said when she finally paused for breath, "I'm glad for your sake Lily seems to like *you.*"

"Why?"

"So she won't write nasty things about you. Or Stephen. You two get along with her all right, don't you?"

I've watched many a face fall in my day, but I've never seen one bungee quite so spectacularly as Gina's did now.

"Gawd!" She gasped. "You think she'll go after us too?"

"No!" I said, exulting in her fear. "I mean, you've always been nice to her—haven't you?"

She made no reply, but I surmised from her stricken frown that neither she nor Stephen had ever extended to his aunt those small kindnesses that do so much, come memoir time, to stave off the stink bombs. Gina rose and began to pace fretfully.

"Gosh," I said, "don't tell me she's mad at you guys too?"

"Who knows? She's a very bitter woman! We've *tried* to be nice but that doesn't mean we can rush off to every stupid play she does or give her parts in our movies."

"Has she asked for them?"

"She's *constantly* dropping hints. Which we ignore, of course. She was never a good actress."

"Hmm." I frowned. "I doubt she sees it that way."

"Dammit!" she exclaimed, tears welling in her eyes. "Now you've got me all worried!"

"Sorry. Didn't mean to."

Gilbert, blind to my purpose, kicked my shin to remind me that we were here to charm the stars, not to panic them. He rushed to comfort Gina, offering his handkerchief. She gratefully accepted and it was this fraught tableau that Diana and Stephen beheld on reentering.

Diana, finding us still infesting the place, froze. It was clear from her outraged stare that she felt our presence had ceased to constitute a creative meeting and was now more of a home invasion. Stephen wore a harried frown—proof, I hoped, that news of the memoir had perturbed him as well. His frown deepened when Gina turned to him, revealing her tear-streaked face.

"Jeez! What'd you guys do to her?"

"It's not our fault!" mewled Gilbert. "She heard about the book— your aunt's memoir."

"Who told you about that?" demanded Diana.

"Phelps," sniffled Gina. "It's nice that *someone* around here lets me know what's going on." She raced melodramatically to her husband's side. "Gawd, this is awful! What do you think she'll say about us?"

Stephen's response was an incredulous stare, which I interpreted as meaning, "You expect me to *answer* that?! With *people* here?! Why did I ever marry you, you penis-lacking albatross?"

"We'll talk about it later, okay?"

"I'm sorry," she replied sulkily. "I'm upset. You know how crazy she is, how desperate for attention! Who knows what kind of horrible lies she might make up about us just to sell books?"

"Nobody knows," snapped Diana. "That's the maddening part! She can write whatever she wants and until the damn thing comes out we have no way of knowing what she's saying."

"But you could know," I said, rising suavely to my feet. "You could know everything."

It was an elegant gambit, worthy of the best courtroom drama, and succeeded in drawing the eager gaze of all present.

"How?" asked Stephen.

"Yes, how?" echoed Diana. Her tone was withering and skeptical but her eyes betrayed a glimmer of hope.

"Well," I began, "I'm assuming Lily won't write the book by herself. These things are always ghostwritten. So what I propose to you is this . . ."

I paused for effect, then took a step toward them.

"*I* go to Lily, butter her up royally, and win the ghostwriting job. Then you can read every page the very day it's written because *I'll* be the one writing it and I'll give them to you. What you do with it all, well, that's between you and your lawyers. But the point is, you'll *know*. And you'll know early when you can still maybe take some action—not when it's in print and every gossip in the country's talking about it. So, what do you say? Interested?"

I have seldom beheld anything so gratifying as the look that now shone on the faces of all three stars. It was a look of sudden, glowing reassessment, and basking in it, I felt like some lovely stenographer who'd finally removed her glasses. Equally satisfying was the look of upstaged consternation adorning Gilbert's puss. I couldn't blame him. Not only had I managed in one bold stroke to cast myself as the brains of the team and him as my slack-jawed sidekick—I'd done so employing techniques he regarded as proprietary.

The stars' stunned and admiring silence was at last broken by Diana.

"Well," she drawled prettily, "aren't you a clever boy?"

"I'll say!" marveled Stephen. "You would actually *do* that?"

"Happily."

"Just imagine," purred Diana. "Our own private pipeline into Lily's diseased imagination."

"That's one smart friend you've got there!" remarked Gina to Gilbert, who responded with a small, curdled smile such as Iago might have mustered for Othello Appreciation Day.

Stephen asked how I could be certain I'd win the ghostwriting job. I'd already considered this obstacle but pretended not to have, the better to dazzle him with my improvisatory brilliance.

"Hmm," I murmured, frowning thoughtfully. "Well, perhaps—"

"Don't bother," pounced Gilbert. "I'll take it from here. What we need, Stephen—"

"I can manage, thanks!"

"—is someone close to Lily who's greedy and who'd go for a bribe."

"*Exactly* where I was heading. A friend, perhaps, or an agent—"

"Her manager." This from Diana. "Lou Perlmutter."

"Weaselly?" asked Gilbert.

"He'd steal the freckles off a child star."

"Perfect!"

"*So!*" I said loudly, determined to regain control of my presentation, "I contact Lou—"

"He doesn't say a word about *you* people, of course."

"I should think that was obvious. I say I'm an aspiring writer—"

"—who *adores* Lily—"

"Her biggest fan and I'd be grateful if he'd recommend me for the job. I offer a bribe—"

"—which Lou, being Lou, takes."

"Then I meet Lily, lay it on with a trowel—"

"And voilà! We're in!" concluded Gilbert, bowing like a proud magician—as if the rabbit had so much as glimpsed the interior of his own hat!

"I love it!" Diana said gleefully. "Using her own vanity against her. Just what the vengeful cow deserves."

"So you think she'll hire me if I flatter her enough?"

"Please! Tell her you like her movies and she'll *adopt* you."

"Gawd, we are so lucky you two showed up here today!" twanged Gina, and Stephen, to my delight, hastened to concur.

"I'll say. You're like the goddamn cavalry!" As he said this he reached over and squeezed my shoulder, triggering an erection so swift it was nearly audible.

"Selwyn and Cavanaugh, at your service," chirped Gilbert, saluting buffoonishly.

"I'm just happy I can help," I said, striking a more modest tone. "I mean, I admire you all so much. And when I see someone trying to exploit you—your own family yet—well, it's an honor to help defend you."

My words, I could see, had touched the stars.

"How veddy kind of you," said Diana in that warm, quasi-British voice she reserves for period dramas and acceptance speeches.

"We really appreciate it," said Stephen, his gorgeous eyes boring like some divine augur into mine.

"And we want you to know," vowed Gilbert, "that Philip's ghostwriting won't interfere one bit with our work on the screenplay. There are three of us, after all, and Claire and I will be writing away during the hours Philip has to give to Lily."

It is impossible to know Gilbert without periodically wishing to disembowel him with a grapefruit spoon, and I've never felt the impulse as keenly as I did in the moment following this demand. For it *was* a demand, however artfully disguised as a promise, and while this sailed over Gina's head with ample clearance, it was not lost on Stephen or Diana. Their eyebrows arched ever so slightly and their smiles turned cool and inscrutable. What had mere seconds ago been the tenderest lovefest now felt more like a poker game and a none too friendly one at that.

Had he lost his mind? Couldn't he grasp as I did that Stephen and Diana knew we wanted the job badly and were on the verge of offering it in gratitude for my heroism? By twisting their arms he'd accomplished nothing but to annoy them and make my offer seem less generous than calculating.

"By the way," he added lightly, "we want to be careful who we mention this ghostwriting business to. If the wrong person got wind of it—a disgruntled ex-employee, say—they might tip off Lily and spoil everything."

"*Holy fuck!*" I thought, utterly beside myself. "*Now he's THREATENING them?!*" For clearly the remark was meant to warn them that if they passed over us then stole our idea we'd rat them out to Lily. The stars did not fail to grasp this (excepting, of course, Gina, who nodded gravely and said, "Good point").

"Oh, yes," said Diana with lethal coyness. "We wouldn't want that, would we?"

"You're right, Gilbert," said Stephen, sounding for the first time like his debonairly dangerous Caliber character. "We should all be careful what we say."

Stephen and Diana exchanged a freighted glance as though conducting a telepathic debate. Should they banish us for our effrontery? Or should they accept as reasonable the terms Gilbert had laid so discreetly on the table? It was an excruciating moment and seemed to last longer than *The Iceman Cometh*. At last Diana shrugged and stared languidly out the window, leaving the decision to Stephen. He turned to us, his face maddeningly unreadable.

"So . . . you guys know Bobby?"

"Oh, yes," I croaked, my throat having gone very dry.

"Wonderful guy!" said Gilbert.

"We love Bobby," said Gina.

"And he, uh, offered you this job? Before we got involved?"

"Yes, he did," I said. "We had a really great meeting."

"He *flipped* for our spec. By the way, what'd you think of it?"

"We haven't seen it."

"Really?" frowned Gilbert. "Make a note to send them one, Philip."

Gina changed the topic to *Greta*, asking how we'd liked it. I perjured myself with gusto. She echoed my sentiments, then pointed to Stephen.

"This one, he just went *nuts* for it. Didn't you, hon?"

He leaned forward in his chair. The move caused his gym shorts to ride up, exposing another inch of his thighs, which were tan, powerful, and, as thighs go, oddly expressive. He spoke in a quiet, heartfelt voice with none of the coolness he'd displayed following Gilbert's gauche finagling.

"I think it's an astonishing book. By the time I got to the end, I was weeping."

"Me too," I said, truthfully enough.

"The themes are so . . . universal."

"Yes. Resonant."

"Morality. Conscience. Courage. Growth. Transformation."

"They're all in there."

"That struggle to find the humanity inside you and . . ."

"Push it along."

He continued describing the book's powerful effect on him, and the more I listened to his deep, masculine yet strangely musical voice, the more ashamed I felt at my own more cynical response to it. How shallow I'd been! How snide and flippant not to have grasped the story's richness and beauty simply because its author, a woman of the loftiest aspirations, had an adjective problem. Stephen hadn't missed it, and this glimpse into his deeper, more soulful side left me more besotted than ever. Here was no brainless Hollywood hunk. Here was a man of vision, a passionate and sensitive idealist, and I prayed with all my heart that he might someday instill these noble qualities in me, preferably via fellatio.

"You're right. It's a magnificent book," I declared, my admiration now unfeigned, "and we would consider it an incredible honor to help you bring it to the screen."

I could see from their faces that this sincere, appropriately humble petition had gone over much better than Gilbert's vulgar machinations. Stephen in particular looked relieved to see that at least one of us was a like-minded artist and not just another Tinseltown careerist. He pursed his lips thoughtfully and gazed out the window. After a moment he said, "Well, if Bobby thought you were right for it, who are we to second-guess him? Let's do it."

"We're hired?" I asked in joyous incredulity.

"Yes." He smiled. "Congratulations."

Gilbert, never restrained in victory, leaped to his feet with an exuberance Roberto Benigni might have found unseemly.

"*Thank you!*" he cried. "This is great! This is fantastic!"

"We really do appreciate this," I said, my warm professionalism a welcome contrast to Gilbert's jejune display.

"I am so glad this worked out!" said Gina, clapping her hands like a little girl. "I have to say, Stephen didn't think it would."

"Well," he amended gallantly, "we hadn't met you guys yet."

"And we were only doing *that* as a favor to Max."

Stephen let this pass with the wan smile of a man long inured to his consort's leaden faux pas. He extended his hand to me and I clasped it, exerting as much pressure as I dared.

"I'm really looking forward to this," I said, flashing my most winning grin.

"Me too, Philip," he said, smiling back.

As I gazed into those exquisite eyes, no effort at restraint could conceal the adoration shining in my own. Stephen, as though in response, gave my hand an extra little squeeze, and as he did an astonishing thing happened. His smile changed subtly; it became slyer, more playful, a discreetly salacious look such as a Rat Pack member might have bestowed on a showgirl whose husband was inconveniently present. The look came and went in the merest instant, yet I was sure I hadn't imagined it.

I felt as though my stomach had just been invaded by several dozen hummingbirds, all waving sparklers. What had *that* meant? Was it a come-on? A tease? A joke? Should I acknowledge it? *How?!* A wink was too obvious, but a little squeeze or a well-chosen double entendre might—

"Stephen!" cried Gilbert, hip checking me aside, "I can't wait to get started!"

Stephen released my hand (Reluctantly? Surely reluctantly?) and shook Gilbert's. I moved on, first to Gina, who pecked me on both cheeks (*her* I got a kiss from!), and then to Diana.

"I'm *so* pleased," she said, adopting once more her plummy thanks-for-the-statuette voice. "I'm sure you'll do a marvelous job."

"I can't tell you how excited we are to be working with you."

"Please. It is we who are excited. Such a thrill to discover fresh talent."

Then, as if it were the most inconsequential afterthought, she added, "Oh, and that other business? With my sister . . . ?"

"I'll get right on it."

"Do that."

Eight

★

AS WE DROVE BACK TO THE Chateau Marmont in the glorious midday sunshine, our mood was so jubilant that I chose at first not to dampen it by chiding Gilbert for his ill-judged and nearly ruinous bargaining tactics. But his long-winded odes to his own deftness, combined with his somewhat perfunctory acknowledgment of my vastly more pivotal contribution, compelled me finally to speak.

"Just do me a favor, genius, and don't play hardball with them again."

"What do you mean?"

"Putting the screws on them. They didn't like it."

"What do you think got us the job?"

I voiced my opinion that they'd been only moments away from offering us the job in gratitude for my daring and brilliance and that his cheeky maneuver had come perilously close to derailing the whole thing. His reply was a cascade of merrily derisive laughter.

"Poor naive Philip! Do you really suppose they would have just *given* us the job? Out of the goodness of their hearts? If that was your plan it's a damn good thing I was there!"

The problem with my scenario, he explained condescendingly, was its failure to take into account the stars' notorious egomania and stinginess. Diana in particular was renowned for possessing a sense of entitlement that made Faye Dunaway look like a Carmelite. Many were the stylists, decorators, and couturiers who'd been confounded by her apparent conviction that to garb, feed, or in any way assist her was so heady an honor as to require no additional compensation.

"You heard her bitching about that dumb painting—how pissed she was that they asked her to pay for it! She's like the fucking queen. She doesn't expect to pay for anything. Including us spying for her."

"*Us?*"

"Trust me, as far as she was concerned, it was thrill enough for us to be doing a Great Star's dirty work. It was up to me to make it clear, in my usual diplomatic fashion, that we either got what we came for or it was no dice. And say what you like, sweetie, it worked."

"All right," I countered, "maybe Diana's a self-important old skinflint, but I still think Stephen would've come through for us."

"Oh, puhleeeze! Just because you're in *love* with him—"

"I'm not in love with him."

"Of course you are. I am, you are, everyone is. And if I thought there was the tiniest chance I might get me some Stephen, trust me, I'd be all over it. But I don't because a.) that's not a closet he's in, it's a goddamn bunker and b.) I don't think he likes me. If you want to dream the impossible dream, be my guest, but jeez, try to be a little more subtle. If you'd drooled any more they'd have billed us for the carpet."

I had no intention of discussing my feelings for Stephen with a lad who lacked the purity of heart to comprehend them. I changed the subject, allowing that Gilbert's coercion may have been a necessary evil and that it was perhaps the combination of gentler and tougher approaches that had won the day.

"Exactly. It was the classic maneuver," said Gilbert. "The old good writer, bad writer."

With this I declined to argue.

* * *

CLAIRE TOOK THE NEWS like a Frisbee to the head, gaping at us in pained astonishment.

"*Please* tell me you're joking."

"Nope!" said Gilbert, lolling smugly on her couch. "We're in, toots."

"But, I don't—! I mean, it's . . . *how?*" she sputtered.

"We just hit it off," I said. "We liked them, they liked us, they liked our take on the book—which by the way isn't half so bad as we've been making it out to be."

"I am not hearing this."

"I mean it. The writing may be clunky, but hearing Stephen talk about it I was actually sort of moved."

"He's in love with him!" stage-whispered Gilbert, fluttering his eyelashes.

"Obviously," sighed Claire. She sank miserably into a chair and glared at us, for she knew what was coming next.

"May I remind you—?" began Gilbert.

"No you may not! I know perfectly well what I said."

"Vowed," he corrected.

She turned a flinty eye toward me. "They actually hired us? I mean they said those words, 'You're hired'?"

"Oh, absolutely."

Her stare became flintier.

"And there's *nothing* you're not telling me?" she inquired with unnerving shrewdness. "Nothing you're deliberately leaving out?"

"Of course not," I said, struggling not to avert my eyes from her javelin gaze.

Gilbert and I had agreed it would be imprudent to inform her about my dual chores as scriptwriter and undercover biographer. Though we felt sure that Claire, given her (for once conveniently) rigid scruples, would honor her promise, we knew she'd be doing so with the utmost reluctance. If we confessed we'd only won the job by consenting to perform nefarious extracurricular chores, she'd seize on this loophole, declare that her promise applied only if the job were won solely on merit, and wriggle away.

"You're sure about that?"

"Absolutely!"

"Oh for God's sake, honey," huffed Gilbert. "A week ago you were starving in a crummy little apartment, crying your eyes out over Hairy Potter. Now you're in the lap of luxury, making a fortune to write for the biggest names in Hollywood! This town's crawling with people who'd fricassee their firstborn to be where you are, so jeez, lighten up!"

Claire replied hotly that she doubted she'd inspire much envy once our *Casablanca* ruse became public, forcing her to abandon her career as a writer/composer to pursue one as a defendant/punchline. Gilbert assured her there was not the slightest danger of anyone else reading *Imbroglio*, as the sole copy was safely in his possession. Claire countered that even if no one else read it, Bobby knew the plot and might describe it to the wrong person, which, in this instance, meant just about anyone.

"You worry too much!" reasoned Gilbert. "There's only one script of ours anyone's going to be talking about and that's the four-hankie Oscar winner we're going to write next, baby!" And yes, he actually said "baby."

Claire was unconvinced. She raged. She cajoled. She prophesied doom. She jeered openly at Gilbert's writing ability, hoping to goad him into "Fine! Who needs ya!" territory, but all to no avail. She knew as well as we that in the end, one thing alone mattered. She had given her word, and where Claire was concerned, that, poor darling, was that.

IT WASN'T LONG BEFORE we received our first lesson in the politics of writing for megastars. As Gilbert and I were trying to cheer Claire up with another chorus of "For She's a Jolly Good Hostage," my cell rang. A British accented woman informed me she was calling on behalf of Sonia Powers, who wished to meet with us at our earliest possible convenience.

This was not welcome news. Sonia, you may recall, ran the PR firm that handled Stephen and Diana. She was widely famed as a dictatorial, paranoid gatekeeper who demanded and got full approval on all client interviews and photos and who, when crossed in even the mildest way, hunted down and destroyed the offender with an implacable resolve once thought confined to homicidal cyborgs. I did not look forward to meeting her.

"Are you available today?" asked her henchlady.

"*Today?*"

"Yes. I know your partner Ms. Simmons is ill but if you and Mr. Selwyn could come, say, around three? It's very important that she see you." It seemed best to get it over with, so I said we could manage and scribbled down an address on Wilshire Boulevard.

Given Ms. Powers's well-known mania for power and secrecy, I'd expected her stronghold to be a cold, fortresslike place patrolled by grim, tunic-clad minions, all eerily silent thanks to the mandatory tongue-ectomies. I was surprised to enter a reception room done in a country farmhouse style so homey you could practically smell the pie baking. We were duly watered, then led to an equally cozy office with overstuffed furniture upholstered in floral silks and a bowl of sunflowers on the coffee table. The sole uncheerful object in the room was its occupant, who sat behind a rustic oak desk eyeing us with the disgruntled pugnacity of a woman wondering who threw the snowball.

As a dutiful show queen I had long been aware that the great Ethel Merman was once married quite briefly to *Marty* Oscar-winner Ernest Borgnine. Never before meeting Ms. Powers had I paused to wonder if the union had produced issue. A burly woman somewhere north of forty, Sonia had Mom's big hair and brassy, cocksure manner, but her face owed more to Dad than was entirely fortunate. When I voiced this later to Gilbert, he said he saw my point but that his own thoughts had run more toward Shrek in whiteface.

"Have a seat," she said, indicating two chairs in front of her desk. The voice was low and gruff, with a raspy adenoidal quality as though she'd spent years smoking through her nose.

Gilbert, attempting the same burbling courtier routine that had so disarmed Diana, said, "Hello, Ms. Powers! I'm Gilbert Selwyn and this is my partner, Phil Cavanaugh. What a tremendous pleasure it is for us to meet you."

The look she shot him amply conveyed her contempt at his belief that such tactics would cut any ice with her.

"Like hell it's a pleasure. *No one* enjoys meeting me. And that's just how I like it. It's how I know I'm doing my job. Heard a lot about you boys."

"All positive, I hope?" simpered Gilbert.

"I hear you're smart. Also pushy. But who isn't out here?" She leaned forward, her eyes narrowing to a dangerous squint. "But now you're working for Diana Malenfant and Stephen Donato. And that's different from working for anyone else. You know why?"

"Because they have you?" I ventured.

"Bingo. You are smart. So I'll only need to say this once . . . Do not ever—*ever!*—try to fuck with my clients. You understand me?"

"We wouldn't dream of it!" I said.

"We admire them!"

She snickered unpleasantly and waved a dismissive paw.

"Save it. You're ambitious kids, right?"

"Well . . ." I demurred.

"You'd better be. It's the only reason I'm trusting you."

"Oh, yes!"

"Wildly ambitious!"

"Sammy Glick, *c'est nous!*"

"You want this job to lead to more jobs? You want to be in this business a long time, make lots of money?"

"Who doesn't?"

"Good. That's why I'm willing to believe you'll be nice, smart boys and not do anything stupid."

She leaned back in her chair and eyed us warily.

"Which one of you's ghosting the book?"

I raised a timid hand.

"The woman you'll be writing for . . . *Lily.*" She spat the name out like it was an escargot that had somehow survived the sauté pan. "You're gonna hear a lot of stuff from her. All bullshit. Pure malicious invention. She's a vindictive lunatic and I've spent my life dreading the day she'd decide to commit her alcohol-induced fantasies to paper. And the fucking brother's even worse."

"Brother?"

"Monty," she said, pronouncing the name with contemptuous feyness. It was the sole display of femininity we would ever see from her.

"He's a total fucking degenerate. Lily lives with him, or rather *off* him. You are not to believe one damn thing you hear from either of them. And if you repeat a word of it—" She jabbed a plump unlovely finger at me. "*One! Single! Word!* to anyone except me, Diana, or Stephen, you will pay the most horrible price you can imagine. No, the most horrible price *I* can imagine, which, trust me, is worse. We clear on that, precious?"

"Absolutely."

"We won't breathe a word," vowed Gilbert.

"I know you won't. 'Cause you're signing these."

She tossed some documents across the desk at us.

"Confidentiality agreements. There's one for your partner too."

We examined the documents, which ran to eight single-spaced pages. In brief we were forbidden to divulge to anyone whomsoever any "confidential information" regarding the stars, their families, or their associates. The more I read the clearer it became that the phrase "confidential information" was redundant, as the contract did not concede there to exist any information concerning the stars that was not confidential.

The agreement, whose author was inordinately fond of the phrase "including but not limited to," stated repeatedly that any disclosure we might make regarding the stars' statements, appearance, or activities of any nature would cause them "irreparable damage." While it allowed that such damage was difficult to quantify monetarily, it did not shrink from attempting to. It placed a modest $50,000 tariff on secrets divulged to individuals but upped the toll well into the millions if a disclosure hit the media. This seemed a bit steep, given the agreement's rather expansive definition of "confidential information."

Never mind sexual kinks or drug use—we could be bled dry for saying they drank milk out of the carton.

"Goodness," said Gilbert, slogging through page three, "they do like their privacy, don't they?"

"Take your time reading. I want 'em signed before you leave."

Gilbert, never one to look before leaping, shrugged and signed two copies. I exhaled and followed suit, reasoning that even were I to find a clause to which I objected, the odds of Sonia agreeing to strike it were nil.

She collected her copies, then, reaching behind the desk, produced a shopping bag filled with videocassettes. The tapes, she informed me, were from Diana's private collection and represented a comprehensive survey of Lily's film and TV work. I'd need to study them if I was to pass myself off as an ardent fan. She then handed me an envelope containing $5,000 in cash, my bribe for Lily's manager. I took the cash and the tapes, vowing to spend the days ahead transforming myself into the nation's leading Lily Malenfant scholar.

"Just out of curiosity," I said, rising, "what happens if it turns out Lily already has a ghostwriter?"

She just stared at me with a "Who farted?" sort of look, clearly nonplussed by my idiocy.

"You have to *ask?*"

I PHONED LOU PERLMUTTER from the car. Since Philip Cavanaugh the rising young screenwriter would shortly become a well-known associate of Stephen Donato's, I used a false name, identifying myself as Mr. Glen DeWitt. I begged for an audience, saying I wished to be of service to one of his clients. Was he free for a drink at six? He said what about five and we agreed to meet at the Coronet Pub on La Cienega.

Having subjected you to the charms of Sonia Powers I'll spare you the equally repellent Mr. Perlmutter. Suffice it to say that the hour I spent pondering the most tactful way to offer a bribe proved wasted as he demanded one within seconds of grasping that I wanted something from him. He'd have fared better had he waited for my bid, as his own price was a mere tenth of what I'd been authorized to offer. On receiving the cash he phoned Lily and said he'd found her an ideal ghost-writer, claiming with an agent's casual mendacity to have been searching tirelessly for one all week. ("You know me—always looking out for my best girl!") The writer, he said, was a brilliant young author and as worshipful an admirer as she could hope to meet. ("Thinks you're the goddamn Queen of Sheba!") Even I, seated across the table, could hear the enthralled *"Really?!"* that greeted this. When Lou hung up he informed me that Lily was eager to meet me—rather too eager in fact. She was expecting me at her home at eleven the next morning.

Lacking even the slightest acquaintance with her films, I'd hoped to have more time before trying to pass myself off as her Boswell. I was about to ask Lou to call back and reschedule when it occurred to me how dazzled Stephen would be by the speed with which I'd delivered on my promise. "Who," he'd ask in wonder, "is this dauntless young man who has so swiftly scaled the gates of mine enemy?" I resolved to keep the appointment even if it meant subjecting myself to an all-night Lilython.

I returned to the Chateau, stopping en route at Book Soup, where I found several books to assist me in my research. I then retired to my room, ordered up a burger, and emptied the bag of cassettes onto the bed.

I've no wish to tax the reader with a detailed survey of the cinema of Lily Malenfant. Most of you will have gathered from the films I've already mentioned the general tone and quality of her oeuvre. Those seeking a more in-depth account should study the two excellent books I purchased: Naomi Lawrence's *The Siren in the Alley: Transgressive Female Sexuality in American Film 1940–1960* and Chip Winkle's *Even THEY Forget Their Names! Those Fabulous B-Stars!* Permit me, though, to briefly describe a few of the films that unspooled before my glazed and disbelieving eyes, if only to make clear the challenge I faced in having to feign admiration for them.

I began with her first hit, the aforementioned *Soiled.* In it Lily portrays Lorna Appleby, a sweet-natured farm lass whose preeminence in the church choir inspires her to seek work as a band singer in Chicago. The city has its vile way with her and by the film's end she's a hard-bitten dope fiend who expires for her sins on the steps of a church, smiling in tender nostalgia at the hymn wafting from inside. Produced on the cheap, it raked in a tidy bundle, prompting the studio to star her in a more lavishly produced version of the same basic story. The second picture, *Brazen*, made twice as much as *Soiled*, and it seemed, to her sister's boundless chagrin, that a Star had been born.

These first films, while hardly classics of the genre, remain solid popcorn fare. Lily was one juicy morsel, and if her acting suffered from a certain excess of conviction, it was hardly out of keeping with the films' overheated storylines.

Her next picture, *Shame Is for Rich Girls,* was less successful both artistically and at the box office. Lily plays Glenda, an impoverished coed who, forced to do her sorority sisters' washing, boils with secret rage. Determined to wed the rich but engaged Oliver Bredwell (Farley Granger), she befriends his fiancée, Hope, poisons her, and by bonding with the grief-stricken Oliver over "their" loss, wins his hand. Her fortune made, she heartlessly neglects her husband and child while romancing a still richer candidate for hubby number two. Through a plot twist so contrived I rewound twice to make sure I'd seen it, evidence arrives that proves her guilty of Hope's murder. She's arrested during her swanky engagement party and dragged off to death row, where she undulates her way to the chair, unrepentantly snarling the film's title line to the sad-eyed chaplain.

Lily began filming *Shame* just after the release of Diana's first smash and it is perhaps the resulting competitiveness that accounts for the sheer manic awfulness of her performance. Watching it, you picture dental hygienists poised just off camera, rushing in between takes to extract the scenery from her teeth.

Diana's triumph as a nun caused Lily to broaden her range beyond bad-girl roles. It did little, though, to curb the insane gusto of her acting, which worsened with each picture. I will provide no summaries of her many subsequent flops, as their contents are admirably conveyed by their titles, among them *I Sold My Baby!*, *The Monster from Creature Lake,* and *Third Floor, Lingerie!* One sensed that Lily's response to increasingly feeble scripts had been to say, "Hmm, not very good, this—I shall have to act all that much harder!"

By three a.m. I was watching episodes of her daffy high school teacher sitcom, *Sorry, Miss Murgatroyd!*—a title that frankly could have done without the comma. I finished up at four, blearily surfing through her more recent work, mostly teen slasher films in which she portrays various old bats who pay a mortal price for their sins (their chief sin, of course, being oldness). After the evening I'd put in, the sight of her head tumbling neatly into a knitting basket was one I found indescribably soothing.

Nine

★

I OVERSLEPT THE NEXT MORNING AND, after downing enough coffee to simulate the early stages of Parkinson's, drove to the address
Lou had given me. It was a large Spanish-style house on a somewhat parched hilltop in Los Feliz. I passed through a wooden gate in a
moldering stucco wall and found myself in what must once have been
a gracious courtyard but which now looked pretty sad and seedy.
There were weeds sprouting from the central fountain and the vegeta-
tion ran toward frayed palms and tatty birds-of-paradise. I approached the front door and rang the bell, which was answered by a
middle-aged ample-bosomed black lady dressed in a gray-and-white
maid's uniform. Seeing me, she crossed her arms and regarded me with
frank distaste, as though I were a purveyor of tainted meats unwisely
attempting a second sale.

"Hello," I smiled, attempting a Gilbertian charm offensive, "my
name's Glen DeWitt and—"

"Mr. Malenfant's busy. With another *student*," she added, her
snide emphasis on the word suggesting a clear if somewhat baffling
disdain for higher learning. I explained that I was neither a student nor
there to see Mr. Malenfant. My appointment was with Lily and had

been arranged through Mr. Perlmutter. It was clear from the look that greeted Lou's name that she couldn't have liked him less had he been a Rhodes scholar, but she let me in.

Seen from inside, the place resembled a scaled-down Chateau Marmont three weeks into a housekeeping strike. I'd heard of maids refusing to do windows, but this one appeared to draw the line at floors. I followed her through the terra-cotta-tiled foyer into a large, dark living room with a lovely coffered ceiling. The furniture, in sad contrast, looked to have been purchased in 1970 by a designer inexplicably enamored of the color orange. We took a left into a much sunnier dining room, the table barely visible under piles of books, old magazines, and photo albums. Sliding doors led out to a covered terrace with rows of ornate stone planters and a lot of badly cracked white wicker furniture. The garish pink-and-green cushions distracted one's eye from the flowers, a good thing since the place was basically a geranium hospice.

Beyond the patio was a pool. To the left of this was a pool house, and to the right a lawn and garden maintained, it appeared, by the Miss Haversham Landscaping Service. A petite figure in clam diggers and a man's shirt several sizes too large was harvesting the few presentable roses in a straw basket. I presumed this was Lily, though I couldn't be certain as her face was concealed by a huge sunbonnet with an attached veil that tied under the chin.

"Miss Malenfant!" yodeled the maid. The little figure turned and waved gaily in greeting. She undid the veil and lifted it over the brim, revealing the face of the thwarted seat bandit from the plane. She flashed a radiant smile, then proceeded jubilantly toward me, her arms flung wide like an Oscar winner parading in triumph toward the stage. "Dear God," I thought, "please don't let her recognize me as the young cad who'd refused to surrender his seat to her."

"Mr. DeWitt!" she throbbed, taking my outstretched hand in both of hers. "How terribly kind of you to drive out to my far-flung abode!"

"Wow, it's really you!" I said, my gaze wide-eyed and worshipful. "This is such an honor!"

"Please! 'Tis I who am honored to have such a fine-looking young man take an interest in my little films. Louise," she said to the house-keeper, handing her the basket without a glance, "do be an angel and put these in water." Louise snickered openly at Lily's lady-of-the-manor routine and Lily shot her a peevish look.

"*Now*, please, Louise. And perhaps a pitcher of my special lemon-ade for my guest."

Louise curtsied satirically, then withdrew as Lily removed her bonnet.

"Forgive the hat, Mr. DeWitt," she said, tossing it over an expired geranium. "My skin, you know. So delicate. I won't let mean Mr. Sun do to me what he's done to my sister."

"Oh?"

"She hides the ravages as best she can, but the makeup it takes! So heavy! Like Spackle."

We sat at a rickety table on equally precarious chairs. She crossed her legs as though posing for a cheesecake shot, then peered at me curiously.

"You seem familiar. Have we met?"

"Oh, I think I'd remember *that!* You probably recognize my face from your plays. I've seen them all and I always ask for the first row."

"How dear of you! So you saw my *Nunsense?*"

"Three times!"

"And *Hallelujah Hollywood!?*"

"Pure magic!"

"And *Hats Off to Shakespeare!?*"

"Transcendent!"

"How lucky I am to have such a supporter! If there were more like you we'd have played out the full week."

Louise reappeared, bearing a tray with glasses and a pitcher of lemonade. "Allow me!" I said chivalrously and poured.

"I must say, Mr. DeWitt, I already like you much better than that other writer my publisher sent to help me. Cheers!"

"Cheers!"

"Not that I'll need much assistance—I've written all my life, you know. Stories. Poems. Little plays. I'm a hard worker and fiercely disciplined!"

"Is there gin in this?"

"Just for flavor. This other writer, he seemed to barely know my movies at all. All he wanted to talk about was my sister and nephew. As if the book were about them, not me!"

"When your eyes flash like that, you look just like you did in *Switchblade Sadie* right before you threw the acid in William Bendix's face."

"What a memory you have!" She laughed delightedly and downed half her drink in one ladylike gulp. "Of course, that's not to say I plan to keep them out of the book entirely. Far from it. They're both incorrigible liars and it's up to me to set the record straight. But that's hardly the whole *point* of the book. *I'm* the one people want to hear about. The public's sick to death of Diana."

"God knows I am! I have to say, Miss Malenfant—"

"Please—Lily!"

"I have *never* understood," I said with the gravest umbrage, "why your sister gets so damned much attention when you are *such* a better actress!"

When I was thirteen I was marooned for the summer with my mother in a New Hampshire cottage owned by my great-aunt. Having recently discovered Theater, Sophistication, and Boys, I found the town provincial and the lack of Art and Culture stifling. Ordered to enjoy the outdoors, I trudged every day to the local library, which offered air-conditioning, privacy, and a small performing arts section. Three weeks into my sentence I made my way to the arts alcove and there, rocking on his haunches, was a slim, pretty lad about my age. I saw that he was engrossed in *A History of the Tony Awards* while he noted that I was holding *The Making of* No, No, Nanette. I'll never forget the expressions that greeted this mutual discovery. "Can it be?" our faces asked, tremulous with hope. "Is there another of my tribe in this philistine backwater? Have I at last found a true soul mate, one who shares my most secret desires and convictions?" This pretty much sums up the look Lily gave me when I pronounced her a better actress than Diana.

"You are *very* kind, Mr. DeWitt," she said, her voice thick with emotion.

"You mean 'very perceptive.'"

"Perhaps I do!" She giggled and coquettishly freshened my lemonade.

I sensed at this point that the job was pretty well mine, but just to be safe I began gushing about her films, starting with a panegyric to her famed flop *Shame Is for Rich Girls*. Actresses, even minor ones, are used to receiving compliments on their hits; praise their stinkers and you establish yourself immediately as a discerning connoisseur.

"I had such hopes for that picture!" she sighed. "Its failure was due entirely to my sister."

"No!"

"She had her own film coming out at the same time. She'd gained a lot of influence with the studio head through means too disgusting to go into (except in the book, of course) and she convinced him to give tons of promotion to her picture and none at all to mine. And, of course, the little whore got her way."

"It's time the world knew that."

I kept the unction flowing, citing "favorite" scenes from other films and pausing occasionally to just gape at her and say, "I can't believe I'm actually sitting here talking to you!" ("Calm yourself, Glen!" she'd titter. "I'm not a goddess!") Though her appetite for praise was limitless, my hastily acquired knowledge of her work was not, so I changed the subject, asking what was on the horizon for her.

"Oh, big things," she said, her tone suddenly hushed and cryptic. "Very big things."

"Really?"

"My biggest picture yet. I can't say any more just now—you talk about these ideas too much and the next thing you know someone's stealing them."

"So," I asked, "is this like a big comeback vehicle?"

She bristled slightly. "I wouldn't say 'comeback.' It's not as if I ever left—not that you'd know that, to hear Diana talk. She likes to make out that my career's in some sort of decline, which is nonsense.

She's jealous because I'm still working while she hasn't made a picture in three years. Being 'choosy,' she calls it. Rubbish! There's simply no demand. I made three movies this year. One's doing quite well in Portugal and another comes out in February. Major release."

"Really?" I said.

"It's a wonderful thriller called *Guess What, I'm Not Dead.* It's about this horrible young man—or woman, we're never quite sure—who goes about killing people in very interesting ways. You know, gruesome but clever. I play the mysterious landlady of a boarding-house where the hero's sister, that Barrymore girl, is hiding be-cause—"

Her synopsis was interrupted by the abrupt slam of a screen door. The sound had come from the pool house. Peering over, I saw that a slim, dapper gentleman in his sixties had emerged from its shuttered darkness out onto the deck. He wore tan linen trousers, a white V-neck sweater, a trim gray mustache, and a mysterious little smile. The smile was soon rendered less mysterious by the emergence from the pool house of a well-built young man of perhaps twenty-five clad only in minuscule hiking shorts, boots, and a white tank top.

"Ah," said Lily brightly, "I see Monty has finished with his new student."

Monty ambled up the short steps to the patio, his campily inquis-itive gaze clearly posing the question "Whose little boy are *you?*" His "student" (for I already had grave doubts about that) prowled lan-guidly behind as though on his own private catwalk.

"Monty, dear," said Lily, rising a bit unsteadily, "I'd like you to meet Glen DeWitt. He's going to help me with my book."

I was in! Exulting inwardly, I extended a cheerful hand to Monty.

"Well," he said, shaking it heartily, "aren't you a brave boy? You're actually prepared to sit for months on end transcribing my sis-ter's lurid reminiscences? My advice to you is cocktails and plenty of them. Fortunately, as you can see, we provide them at all hours."

"He's a very impressive young man. He remembers films of mine I'd quite forgotten."

"There's no skill in that, darling. I've seen films of yours I couldn't forget if I tried and, believe me, I have."

"Monty's a horrible tease. Pay no attention to him."

Monty smiled. "Oh, I do hope he'll pay *some* attention." Though frank come-ons from gentlemen over sixty usually send an anxious shiver up the Cavanaugh vertebrae, Monty's manner was so friendly, so cheerfully straightforward that my first impulse was to flirt back, as though decorum demanded it. It was my first glimpse of his singular knack for making lechery seem charming.

"Ah, there you are!" he said to the fantasy hiker who'd finally joined our little circle. Seeing him up close I couldn't help noting his drowsy eyes—was he stoned?—the inch of bare midriff between his shirt and shorts, and the two beepers adorning his belt.

"Allow me," said Monty with wry formality, "to present the latest enrollee in the Monty Malenfant Academy of Dramatic Arts—Glen DeWitt, Mr. Cody Masters."

"Hey," said Cody, flashing his palm in lieu of an actual handshake, for which, I sensed, I'd have been charged.

"My brother's one of Hollywood's most sought-after acting coaches," explained Lily.

"I see."

"He takes very few students," she added proudly, "and only one at a time. Though I recall once there were two."

"Ah."

"He was an actor himself, you know. As a child. He was a big star before any of us were."

"No shit?" inquired his dilated pupil.

"Guilty as charged. Have you by chance," he asked me, "seen any of my pictures?"

"I'm not sure," I said diplomatically. "Possibly."

"Oh, you'd remember if you had. My pictures, like Lily's, haunt the memory long after the initial trauma has passed. Counseling is often required."

"Did you have a good class, Mr. Masters?" asked Lily.

"Yeah, great," smirked Cody, gamely throwing himself into the charade. "We did something by, uh, Shakespeare and also, um . . ." His knowledge of playwrights depleted, he let out a stoned giggle and his beeper went off.

"Can I use your phone on my way out?"

"Of course. And splendid work today. Your Malvolio was wonderfully nuanced, but next time you might imbue your Trigorin with a touch more world-weary insouciance."

Cody emitted a baffled snigger and shook his head.

"Man, you are too much."

"I am tempted to return the compliment. Good day, Cody."

He prowled out through the dining room, passing the baleful Louise, who pointedly positioned herself between him and a table covered in easily pocketable tchotchkes. At least I now understood the fish eye I'd gotten when she'd taken me for a fresh applicant to Monty's academy. I caught Monty's eye and cocked an eyebrow as though to inquire just how recently he felt the turnip truck and I had parted company. His response was a droll parody of innocence, the eyes cast casually skyward, the lips whistling a little tune, and I found myself giggling as helplessly as Cody had.

"I share your mirth, Mr. DeWitt," said Lily. "Really, Monty! I know you sometimes accept a student just because he's good-looking but I don't think you'll *ever* make an actor of that one."

"You see no potential?"

"His diction! Quite hopeless."

"I have an exercise to correct that. It's loosely inspired by Demosthenes. *Very* loosely."

"My brother's problem," said Lily, "is that he's too nice to tell people when they have no talent. He means well but if I were him I'd be ashamed to take their money."

"On that score, I assure you, I feel no guilt whatsoever. Can you join us for lunch, Mr. DeWitt?"

I feared that further conversation might expose my limited acquaintance with Lily's oeuvre, besides which I was bursting to report my victory to Stephen. I told them that while nothing would give me greater pleasure, I had a pressing appointment for which I had to leave shortly.

The question of my fee arose. I knew things could get sticky if her publisher tried to pay me, necessitating tax forms and such for the nonexistent Glen, so I suggested we keep our arrangement informal for now. After all, I could hardly expect a woman of Lily's stature to enter into a contract with me until I'd proven my mettle. Once we were, say, a few chapters in, we could take the matter up again and decide on a reasonable fee. Lily agreed and I rose and thanked her again for entrusting me with her story.

"Please! It's I who am grateful to you. But I must warn you," she added darkly, "that it will take more than talent to write this book. It will take courage!"

"Oh?"

"You don't know what powerful forces are working against us."

"Who?"

"My sister for one. She's absolutely panicked about this—as well she should be. There are quite a few things she doesn't want the world to know about her—shameful things. It will pain me to tell them, but what can I do? Sugarcoat the truth? I think not!"

"And of course," added Monty, "there's Stephen and his lovely goatee, Gina—"

"I'd hardly call her a goat, Monty. She's quite pretty in her way."

"I said 'goatee.' "

"Sorry?"

"As in 'beard.' "

"She hasn't got a beard."

"How many of those have you had, love?"

"You mean Stephen's gay?" I exclaimed, sounding more overjoyed than I'd meant to.

"Heel, boy. Yes, he is. Or, at any rate, was. He lived with us through much of his teens while Mother was off on location and at that time—"

"Oh—*beard!*"

"—he was, I assure you, gayer than a Mardi Gras float. When

magazines from my private collection went missing, they could invariably be found under the guest room mattress."

"And that day in the pool house—!"

"With the tennis coach!"

"*So* embarrassing!"

"And you're putting all this in the book?" I asked, shocked.

"Well, it's hardly a secret," said Lily, freshening her drink. "All *my* friends have known he's gay for years."

"That's because you tell them, dear."

"Besides," added Lily, "how can I possibly convey Diana's failings as a mother without describing her monstrous insensitivity to Stephen when she found out? Couldn't deal with it at all. She was horribly mean to him whereas we accepted him just as he was. She had her way in the end of course. It's because of her that he's living a lie today."

"Well, that," allowed Monty, "and the thirty million a picture. So I doubt he and Gina are turning cartwheels over this book, to say nothing of that human pit bull they've put on retainer."

"Sonia Powers!" scowled Lily, washing the name off her tongue with a hefty swig. "The rude cow! Calls me every day!"

"Their publicist," explained Monty. "She guards like a mother tigress the padlock on Stephen's closet—a curious vocation for a woman well known to be the town's leading vaginavore."

"Let her try to stop us!" said Lily defiantly. "Our voices will not be stilled!"

"So," said Monty, clapping my shoulder, "are you with us, Glen? You'll stand side by side with us against the enemies of truth?"

"Oh, absolutely."

"You'll scoff at their threats and sneer at their bribes?"

"I'm working for you, not them," I replied less than accurately.

"That's the spirit!" cried Lily. And with that, she rose and showed me to the door, warning me as she did to be discreet about my assignment, discussing it only with those whose trustworthiness was beyond question.

"You know. Like my manager, Lou."

*   *   *

MY FEELINGS AS I drove back to the Chateau were mixed. On the one hand I was thrilled I'd gotten the job and elated to have found that Stephen was not the rumor-plagued straight boy his handlers so vehemently proclaimed him but the genuine man-loving article. At the same time I was unsettled to find that Lily and Monty did not seem at all like the base fiends their family and Sonia had made them out to be.

Readers of my earlier histories will recall that on my one previous foray into home infiltration my victims had possessed the good grace to be so odious that any backstabbing mole in their employ could consider it a privilege to betray them. But Lily, while undeniably gaga, seemed rather sweet—sweeter certainly than her imperious sister— and Monty was downright delightful. The thought that I'd signed on to be the viper in their midst pained me. To avoid dwelling on it, I turned my thoughts to Stephen.

There is, of course, no more effective qualm suppressant than lust. By the time I'd passed an agreeable five minutes imagining how pleased Stephen would be with me and another five viewing a mental slide show of his astonishing face, shoulders, and thighs, my misgivings had seeped away like bathwater from the heart-shaped tub we shared in my reverie. Hadn't Sonia warned me not to believe anything Lily or Monty said? So they'd seemed nice—what of it! Was this not a world in which the low and cunning could, as the bard put it, smile and smile and be a villain? The fading voice of my conscience muttered, "Well, you're certainly proving *that*, dear."

"Fuck you!" I replied, "Stephen's nipples!" and it shut up.

WHEN I RETURNED TO the Chateau I was so eager to report my triumph to Stephen that I bypassed the sluggish elevator and sprinted up the four flights to my room, a pointless exertion, as it struck me on entering that I hadn't a clue what Stephen's phone number was. I mulled my options and realized I had no choice but to call the abominable Sonia and beg her assistance.

"You think I give that number out?" she asked, sneering audibly.

"Then he can call me. I'm at the Chateau Marmont."

"Look, precious, Stephen's a busy man. Just tell me what's up and I'll pass it along to him."

I literally recoiled at this suggestion, yanking the phone from my ear and glaring at the receiver. When wooing a fair prince one prefers of course to present all love offerings in person, not hand them off to the troll at the drawbridge. Fortunately this was one of those days when the Cavanaugh brain was firing on all cylinders and I grasped immediately that Sonia herself had provided me the grounds on which to resist this demand.

"It seems to me I just signed a document forbidding me to divulge confidential information to anyone outside Stephen's immediate family."

"I'm *employed* by Stephen."

"So's his gardener and I'm not telling him."

Sonia did not like this line of reasoning one bit. She thundered, threatened, and pelted me with epithets of which "snotty little fag" was by far the gentlest. Love had made me bold though, and I held my ground. Repeating that I would report to Stephen and only Stephen, I hung up on her. Forty minutes later my phone rang and I pounced on it like a coyote on a kitten.

"Philip?"

"Stephen!"

"Boy," he said with a musical laugh, "you sure pissed Sonia off!"

"There are harder things to do in this world."

"I know she can be a little hard to take."

Be wry, I admonished myself. Be bland. Think David Niven.

"Nonsense. I find her delightful in a snarling, feral sort of way. Oh, before I forget, you're now talking to Lily Malenfant's official biographer."

Awed silence.

"You're *in?*"

"Yuh-huh."

"*Already?*"

"Yes. Or rather, Glen is."

"Glen?"

"I felt it wise to use a pseudonym. Can't have the old dear getting wind that I'm also writing a movie for you guys, can we?"

Stephen's response was another gratifying burst of laughter.

"Man, I've played a spy on screen but you, you're the real thing."

Having never before heard a sexy megastar compare me favorably to his dashing signature role, I lost all grip on my suavity and giggled like a chorus boy being tickled by Bernadette Peters. Stephen, tactfully ignoring this, asked, a bit too casually, if Lily had offered any preview of what she planned to say about her nearest and dearest.

"Well—!" I began, prepared to reveal all, then realized at once what a serious tactical blunder this would be. If you're smitten with a secretly gay film star and eager to establish a more intimate rapport, is this how you tell him his aunt's planning to out him? Over the phone? When you can't even see his face? Of course not. When the news is this juicy you want to save it until you're alone with him in some appropriately snug setting. Only then do you release the cat from the bag, minutely scrutinizing his face while composing your own into a compassionate and receptive mien that says, "Tell Philip. He can be trusted."

"Well, what?" he asked.

"Well, she *hinted* like crazy. 'Bombshells' is the word she kept using. But nothing specific. And I didn't want to press her. She'd just got through bitching about how the first ghostwriter she'd interviewed was more interested in you people than her. I thought if I dwelled on you too much I'd piss her off and lose the job."

"You did the right thing," he said, sounding nonetheless disappointed. It occurred to me that I did have at least a few tidbits I could serve up to keep the conversation lively.

"Boy, Lily sure likes her cocktails."

"Tell me."

"Almost as much as Monty likes his hustlers."

"Excuse me?"

"When I got there he was entertaining one in the pool house."

"No!"

Surprise had lowered his guard and he said this in a voice that was thrilled, gossipy, and—dear diary!—very gay.

"Scout's honor. And this before lunch, mind you."

"You're sure it was a hustler?"

"Teeny little cutoffs and two beepers on his belt. I didn't see his ass but I'm guessing it had a bar code on it."

"Did *Lily* see this?"

"Sees it all the time apparently. He tells her they're his *students*. Says he's giving them acting lessons."

"Acting lessons?" said Stephen, roaring with laughter. "That old goat! He's fucking shameless!"

"My God," I thought, "*I'm dishing with Stephen Donato!!*"

"Anyway, I'll be seeing Lily every day starting tomorrow, so I should have lots to report soon. Perhaps," I said, screwing up my courage, "we could talk over coffee or a drink?"

He said he was leaving tomorrow for a week of "fucking reshoots" on his most recent film, a fourth Caliber picture, but would be happy to meet when he returned, presuming I had anything of substance to report.

"Oh, I'm sure I will!"

"How about, uh, a week from Wednesday? Say around seven?"

"Works for me!" I replied, my heart beating so briskly I was afraid he'd hear it over the phone.

"It's a date," he said and hung up.

A date!

He called it a date!

Not me—*him!*

"I have a date with Stephen Donato!" I cried as though cueing the orchestra to strike up the title song in the giddy musical my life had suddenly become. I bounded ebulliently from my suite, danced down the stairs, and practically floated across the street to Sunset Plaza, my feet only touching the ground when I reached Crunch Gym, where I took out a one-year membership and inquired about personal trainers.

Ten

★

O
H, ALL RIGHT, ALL RIGHT.
          Just what, I hear you asking, did I imagine in my most girl-
ish flights of fancy was going to happen romantically between
me and a film star twice voted *People* magazine's Sexiest Man Alive? It's
a fair question and one I asked myself with some regularity. My answers
varied widely according to my mood and recent intake of wine.

There were moments, nocturnal and chardonnay-abetted, when I
actually believed we might fall into an affair, or at any rate a fling, or at
least One Very Special Night to Be Remembered Always. The scenarios I spun ran something like this:

> *Stephen, deeply impressed by my spy craft, writing skills, and re-*
> *cent progress at the gym, invites me to his secret pied-à-terre in*
> *West Hollywood. His ostensible purpose is to discuss the screen-*
> *play but he mainly wants to offer his side of the gay stories I've*
> *heard from Lily and Monty. He admires me so that it pains him*
> *to think I may secretly regard him as a hypocrite. His voice*
> *choked with emotion, he describes to me the demands and pres-*
> *sures, incomprehensible to the nonmegastar, that have kept him*

from publicly acknowledging his sexuality. He speaks of his lone-liness and lifelong dream of meeting a caring, nonjudgmental soul mate who'll understand his dilemma and embrace him as he is. I embrace him as he is.

On other nights, too tired to mint such elaborately romantic sce-narios, I devised more streamlined versions.

I bring new script pages to his trailer on location. He has just stepped out of the shower. "Don't just stare," he drawls saucily, "make friends with it."

These reveries were balanced by moments of rueful realism in which I sadly acknowledged that my odds of bedding Stephen were roughly the same a cocker spaniel might enjoy in pursuit of a pilot's li-cense. Most of the time I hovered between hope and despair. How, I reasoned, could I begin to assess my chances with Stephen until I knew him better? And if the possibility of a dalliance seemed indisputably remote, was it really *impossible?*

Certainly anything seemed possible in those first heady weeks after I'd won Lily's trust and cemented our place in the glittering orbit of the Malenfants. In that brief, idyllic period the news was so consis-tently good I began to feel as though somewhere on high the Showbiz Gods were commencing each morning's meeting with a brisk bang of the gavel and a hearty, "What shall we do for Cavanaugh today?"

For starters there was my lovely mention in *Variety*. I was told to look for it by Bobby Spellman (who, after three days of avoiding our calls, was once more our dearest friend). The morning it appeared I raced down to the lobby at eight to be sure to get one of the Chateau's small allotment of copies. The agreeably large headline read "Spellman Coaxes Donato, Malenfant into 'Hiding.' " I was so excited I began reading it right there at the front desk.

Stephen Donato and proud mom, Diana Malenfant, who've been in hiding as acting partners since playing the

beloved floozy-and-waif duo in *Sophie and Sam,* will pair
up again for *The Heart in Hiding,* a WWII romance/
adventure from producer Bobby Spellman. Making the pic
even more a family affair will be Donato's wife, Gina Beach,
who'll play his love interest. The plot, says Spellman, "has
moving echoes of the Anne Frank story" but with "strong
action elements" and "this time," he promises, "the good
guys win."

I skipped ahead, scanning eagerly for our names, and finally spotted them one paragraph from the end.

In a move that raised insider eyebrows, the writing chores
for the high-profile project will go to three tyro scribes,
Gilbert Selwyn, Philip Cavanaugh, and Claire Simmons.
The trio, with no screen credit to date, won the assignment
on the strength of their spec script. "They are kickass talents," said Spellman, "who share my dynamic vision for
this unforgettable story of courage and triumph." Trio is
repped by Josh Soboloff of CAA.

I was unable to resist sharing this milestone with Sandra, the amiable day manager. Her eyes bulged gratifyingly when she saw the
names Malenfant and Donato. She congratulated me warmly, mentioning in passing that she was an actress.

Some benevolent Showbiz God, observing this scene, gave a worried cluck and said, "How is Philip to get on with his work with all
these new admirers pestering him? I say we move him out of that hip
Hollywood hotel and into an even hipper movie-star home in the hills.
All in favor?"

There was, in fact, an authentic Showbiz God behind this move,
namely Max Mandelbaum. The mogul, though delighted for Maddie's
sake that her son's career was off to such a roaring start, could not help
noting that the job would keep Gilbert in LA and more specifically his
guesthouse for the foreseeable future. Was it fair, he asked Maddie, to

expect so dynamic a young man to molder in sleepy Bel-Air tethered to Mother's apron strings? Wouldn't he be happier on his own enjoying the gay social whirl of West Hollywood and the Sunset Strip? Thanks to his new income Gilbert could easily afford to lease a nice little house, especially if his partners joined him and shared the expense.

As luck would have it an associate of Max's knew of just such a house, a stylish three bedroom high atop the strip. It was now under lease to the Scottish heartthrob Angus Brodie, who'd made waves this past summer as Gwyneth Paltrow's psycho boyfriend in *Forever, Baby*. He was leaving soon for a lengthy shoot and hoped to sublet it. Max endorsed us to Angus's manager and by week's end the keys were in Gilbert's hands.

Gilbert, whose tightness with a dollar has been noted, had not seen his windfall as presenting any reason to cease mooching off Max. He accepted his eviction philosophically though, reasoning that he'd managed an impressive run and that when the Houseguests Guild held their annual awards banquet, he'd be a shoo-in for the Golden Sponge. Besides, for Gilbert, to whom Hipness was all, the cachet of inhabiting a genuine movie-star bachelor pad provided at least some compensation for the regrettable expense.

I was pretty puffed up about the move myself, even though I'd never seen Mr. Brodie's films and wasn't crazy about the house itself. It was one of those spare, starkly modern LA homes that make you feel you've awoken in some future society where fashion favors shaved heads and jumpsuits, and possession of chintz is a felony. I kept this opinion to myself, though Claire, who came with us to inspect the place, voiced it freely.

"You don't find it a tad sterile?"

"No," I fibbed. "I think it's nice and . . . airy. Those huge glass walls."

"It looks like a great party house!" said Gilbert.

"It looks," said Claire, "like a very small airport."

My other reservation was the rent, my share of which came to two thousand a month. I tried to persuade Claire that if she joined us and shared the expense we could find ways to make it homier. She declined, saying that it would be aggravating enough writing with Gilbert; if she had to live with him on top of it, the most she could hope for would be a sympathetic jury. She opted instead for a frugal but charming one-bedroom flat on King's Road.

WITH THE HOUSING SITUATION sorted out, it was time to grapple with my main conundrum, i.e., how to collaborate on two theoretically full-time projects without either Claire or Lily finding out she was sharing me. Here too the Showbiz Gods had provided a blessing in disguise by encumbering Claire and me with a doggedly hedonistic partner whose mornings were given over to restorative sleep and awkward breakfasts with young men whose names eluded recall.

"I've been thinking," I said as I strolled with her through Williams-Sonoma, helping her stock her new cupboard, "we should probably try to get in a good five hours a day. What say we start at one and go till six?"

"*One?*" snorted Claire, who, had she been a pioneer gal, would have built several homesteads by that hour.

"If we start any earlier Gilbert won't be there."

She eyed me quizzically.

"And this hinders us how?"

I argued that it was a matter of principle. Gilbert was getting a third of the money and even if he were no help at all he should at least be compelled to be present. Claire disagreed, seeing Gilbert's absence as less a drawback than a sound efficiency measure. I held firm though and eventually she relented, deciding that it might be nice having mornings free for her music.

AT FIRST LILY WAS more put out at losing my afternoons than Claire had been over my mornings, an odd stance, I felt, given the effect her lunchtime lemonades had on her subsequent lucidity.

"Really, Glen," she frowned, "I don't see how we'll ever finish if you can't stay later than one!"

"I'm really sorry. It's just that you're not paying me till we see how things work out, so I need to keep my other job."

"Other job? What other job?"

Not having anticipated the question, I glanced nervously at my feet, next to which lay my gym bag.

"I'm a personal trainer."

"Well, I wish you'd said something sooner!"

"It's just part-time. Of course," I said, risking a bluff, "I could always quit that job if you started paying me now. But to make up the loss I'd need . . . oh, about eight hundred a week."

Nothing I'd seen in Lily's film work so poignantly exposed her limitations as an actress as the effort she now made to look as though she was actually considering paying me. She cocked her head, pursed her lips, and even, God bless her, brought a finger to them.

"Perhaps I have been a bit unreasonable, Glen. I don't *own* you. We must all do what we must to make a living. Why even I have once or twice done a picture I considered less than first-rate just for the money."

"I can't think which ones you could mean."

"Aren't you a dear!"

Our schedule settled, she seated herself at the dining table, her scrapbooks and albums arrayed before her. I took the seat to her left so as to favor her good ear and began taking notes on a legal pad with a tape recorder for backup. A stickler for chronology, she began with her earliest memory, which was of Diana, "a stout child with cruel, piggy eyes," dropping spiders into her crib.

And so the great work commenced.

WORK ALSO COMMENCED ON our adaptation of *A Song for Greta,* a chore that, alas, entailed rereading it. I tried without success to find any of the virtues my Stephen professed to see in it. Though I could agree with him that Miss Gamache had a good heart, I couldn't read her book without wanting to plunge an ice pick into it while screaming, "That's for chapter four!"

Bobby had instructed us not to begin the script until we'd submitted a "treatment" outlining our vision for it. He encouraged us to take liberties, especially if those liberties bolstered Diana's part or spiced up the romance between Heinrich and Lisabetta, who, as rendered by Prudence, were as steamy as a pair of Hummels.

By the end of day two we'd decided, in broad strokes, what we would do. Our version did not completely expunge the book's grotesque sentimentality—something we dared not do, given the Malenfants' apparent weakness for schmaltz—but we felt it subdued it somewhat and that now only half the audience would race up the aisles retching into their popcorn.

And what, you may ask, was it like writing with Gilbert? I can only reply that should I ever have the pleasure, I'll tell you all about it. Gilbert, it soon became clear, did not care a whit if he actually contributed to the script so long as he could contrive to *feel* that he had.

Toward this end he insisted on manning the keyboard. Claire and I balked at this until we saw what wonders plagiarism had done for his typing speed. When not tapping away he confined himself to making observations that were either uselessly vague ("This middle section— it needs something") or screamingly obvious ("This strudel recipe doesn't advance the plot much, does it?"). He also developed a maddening habit of instantly paraphrasing everything Claire or I said as if to imply we'd merely been intuiting what he'd been *about* to say. This incensed Claire, who swiftly developed counterploys. A typical exchange went something like this:

Claire: "What if we just cut—? Oh, but I see you're ahead of me, Gilbert. Go on, dear."

Gilbert: "No, you go ahead."

Claire: "We could cut Snelling from the scene entirely and have Heinrich give that information to Helga in the base—"

Gilbert: "Basement scene! You totally read my mind!"

JUGGLING THE TWO JOBS was no cakewalk, but I soon fell into a manageable if grueling routine. I rose daily at seven, hit the gym, then made it to Lily and Monty's by nine. We'd work for about four hours, then I'd dash home to meet Claire and the invariably tardy Gilbert. We'd finish at six and only then would I remove the morning's notes from my gym bag and, to the galling accompaniment of Gilbert's cocktail shaker, start coaxing Lily's rambling recollections into something approaching coherence.

I initially assumed that it was my duty as ghostwriter to capture Lily's actual voice. I thought I did a fair job, but after my first efforts met with complaints of inauthenticity (or, per Lily, "Un-me-ness"), I realized my error. Lily didn't want the voice in the book to sound the way she really did. She wanted it to sound the way she *thought* she did. She wanted the voice to be cultured and articulate, ladylike yet capable of slashing wit. She wanted, in short, to sound like a long-lost Mitford sister. I began doing my best to write her this way.

A tape-recorded snatch of memory such as this:

Look at this picture—see how much thinner I am? What a little butterball she was! This was right after she gained all that weight at Christmas— and this, mind you, while playing Wendy in Peter Pan! *The part should have gone to a thinner, prettier girl like me. I'd watch her in that damn chestnut and think, "Serve her right when that cable finally gives out. Splat!" You couldn't have paid me to sit in the front row.*

was rendered as follows:

I was a slim, delicate child, my natural energy and love of jump-rope games keeping me, as Mother used to say, "no bigger than a minute." I always pitied my elder sister, whose lifelong battle with avoirdupois began in girlhood. One Christmas season she was cast as Wendy in Mr. Barrie's evergreen Peter Pan. *Diana gorged herself daily on Mother's fresh-baked holiday treats with comical results. By the end of the run latecomers to her flying scene could have been forgiven for wondering why the director had placed a nightgown on a wrecking ball.*

This more genteel tone won gushing plaudits from Lily.

"It's too perfect, Glen! It's me to a tee! 'Nightie on a wrecking ball'—I can't believe I said that!"

"Because you didn't, love," offered Monty, buttering a brioche.

"Oh, hush. Glen's doing a marvelous job."

"I just put it on paper," I demurred. "The raw material comes from you."

"If it's raw material you want, wait till she turns twelve."

Between Lily's praise and Monty's rascally charm, I was finding it harder by the day to view them with the pitiless eye my assignment demanded. I could see why Diana and Stephen disliked them, given their cheerful determination to leave no bean unspilled. But sitting with them each morning and hearing their side of things one couldn't help feeling that Diana at least had it coming.

Diana had seldom missed a chance to belittle her sister in print. Though she'd never written a memoir, she'd recounted her family's history in scores of interviews, and in her version Lily and Monty appeared, when at all, in the most dim and patronizing of lights. Did she really imagine that Lily, after decades of such queenly condescension, would not finally cry, "Enough!", empty her bile duct into a fountain pen, and scrawl "Chapter One"?

Even my beloved Stephen's treatment of them had been a bit shoddy, though I ascribed this entirely to Diana's malign influence. Still, having been all but raised by them while Mother gallivanted about, would it have killed him to call them once in a while or to offer Lily a small role in one of his blockbusters? Even Lily's harshest detractors would concede that she could have played the hysterical hostage in *Caliber Unleashed* as capably as Lainie Kazan had.

But just as I was starting to wonder if my betrayal of Lily and Monty was not, on balance, just a teensy bit indefensible, I received a call from Stephen that stiffened, among other things, my resolve to continue.

THE CALL CAME PAST midnight on the day we finally dispatched our finished treatment to Bobby. Our celebratory dinner at Orso had been accompanied by two bottles of amarone, so it took several rings to wake me, and I knocked over my water glass reaching for the phone.

"Shit!" came my charming salutation.

"Phil?"

"Whozis?"

"It's Stephen."

"Stephen!"

I quickly turned on the bedside lamp, then thought better and turned it off. Why talk to Stephen Donato in a lit bedroom when you could talk to him in a dark one?

"Sorry to call so late." He sounded as if he'd had some wine himself.

"No, it's okay! What's up?"

"I just wanted to let you know I won't be able to see you next Wednesday."

"Oh?" I replied, crestfallen.

"I'm stuck here an extra day. But are you free Thursday?"

"Yes! Yes I am! Totally free!"

"Good. Because Sonia and my mom want you to have dinner with us at her restaurant. You know, Vici?" He referred to the trendy Beverly Hills eatery Diana had opened some years back when restaurants were the celebrity accessory du jour.

"Yeah, I've been there," I lied. "So, your mom and Sonia are coming?"

"They just want to hear more about what's up with Lily. The pages you've been e-mailing are great, but it's still all just childhood stuff. They're more interested in what's coming down the line. I'll be back in time for that. Gina too."

I could hardly confess at this early, delicate stage of our courtship that I'd hoped our first date would be long on whispered confidences and smoldering stares and that the presence of his wife, mother, and publicist would do much to curtail these. So I just smothered a sigh and said, "Oh, great."

"But I do wanna see you," he said.

"Likewise."

"I mean alone."

"Oh?" I said, my fallen crest reascending.

"To talk about all this . . . stuff."

"Any time!"

There was a pause and I heard the tinkling of ice cubes.

"Listen, Phil . . . I really like you."

Did he just say that? Did he actually just say that?

"I like you too, Stephen."

"I mean it. You're a nice guy. And I want to think I can trust you. Can I?"

"Absolutely!"

He was whispering now, his tone endearingly tentative. "Good. Because what I would like is for us to have a little . . . arrangement."

My God!

My Gawwwwd!

Stephen Donato's coming on to me! Please, PLEASE don't let this be a dream! And if it is don't let me wake up before I finish like last Tuesday!

For a moment all I heard was Stephen's breathing, and his shy silence emboldened me.

"What sort of arrangement?" I aimed for a sexy throatiness but overshot, practically gargling the question.

"Lily and Monty," he said, his voice quieter still. "The things they say about me—especially Monty—I want you to tell all that stuff to me. *Just* me. Not my mom or Gina or Sonia. I'll tell them anything I think they need to know. But for now let's keep it between us, okay?"

"Of course, Stephen. Anything you say."

"Nobody else."

"Your ears only!"

"Even if Sonia grills you."

"She can break out the bamboo. Cavanaugh won't crack."

Though I blushed to think my failed Kathleen Turner impression might have betrayed my initial (and, let's face it, preposterous) assumption that he was about to propose a dalliance, I was delighted nonetheless by what he was proposing. The thought of Stephen and I sharing his sexual secrets was an immensely agreeable one. It brought our relationship to a new and thrilling level of closeness from whose fertile soil who knew what further intimacies might bloom?

"It's not," Stephen said, "that I'm *hiding* anything."

"'Course not!"

"It's just that some things are . . . y'know—"

"Private."

"Exactly. And I'm thinking of my family too. Why get 'em all worked up over stuff they don't need to hear? Stuff that might not even wind up in the book?"

"Leave it to you to put family first."

"So . . ." he said with absurd nonchalance, "what've they said about me?"

I paused for a brief debate with my penis. It argued cogently that though there were undeniable advantages to waiting as planned to give Stephen the lowdown in person, the chance to masturbate while doing so was not among them. But my more romantic side won out. I remained resolved to speak not of big-dicked tennis pros until I was gazing directly into his dreamy brown eyes.

"Sorry," I murmured, "but you're not even born yet at this point. They've certainly *hinted* there'll be lots about you later on. Big things."

"Fantastic," he muttered.

"Look," I said, inspiration having struck, "why don't I just ask Lily what she plans to say about you? She trusts me now, I'm sure she'll tell me. Then when we all have dinner next Thursday, you and I can meet an hour early and I'll report in."

Stephen deemed this a superb plan and said he'd meet me at Vici at seven. If the bar was too crowded to afford adequate privacy, we'd go for a drive.

"Thank you for this, Phil."

"It's my pleasure, Stephen."

"I can count on you, big guy?"

"Day or night," I replied with passionate sincerity. "I'm entirely at your service."

To this he replied—wryly? coyly? pornographically?—"I'll remember you said that," then hung up.

Fans of the musical *My Fair Lady* will recall the scene where Eliza, fresh from her tango with Higgins, romps exuberantly about her bedroom, informing the housemaids that she doesn't want to go to bed as she couldn't possibly sleep, her heart having taken flight. Subtract the maids, throw in some boisterous self-abuse, and you have the scene in my boudoir after Stephen's call. Half an hour later I lay contentedly asleep. The same could not be said for the Showbiz Gods, who were pulling an all-nighter to debate what laurels to crown me with next.

Having just handed in our treatment, we didn't expect a verdict for at least a few days. But the very next morning Svetlana phoned to ask if we'd be available for a noon conference call with Bobby, Diana, Gina, and Stephen. We alerted Claire that the jury was in and she hastened over. We passed a fretful hour wondering if they'd find our take on the material insufficiently mawkish, especially our decision to drastically prune the postmortem antics of wee Hans (formerly Hilda). But when the call came our fears were immediately dispelled.

"Hey, everyone there?" asked Bobby.

"All here!" we chimed into the speakerphone.

"Are those my three geniuses?" said Diana, provoking broad smiles and pantomimed glee.

"Great job, you guys!" said Stephen. "And Claire too. We haven't met yet. I'm Stephen."

"Nice to meet you, Stephen," said Claire, sounding crisply professional yet unable to subdue a goofy "I'm chatting up a movie star!" grin. "So you liked it?"

"Liked it?" said Bobby. "We. Fucking. Loved. It."

"It was great," said Gina. "I liked the structure," she added in a poignant effort to simulate intelligence.

Stephen, referring to one of Claire's inspirations, said, "The scene where I have to kill my dad—I love the way it's foreshadowed now by that flashback to where he makes me shoot the fawn in the woods."

"Yes," said Gilbert, "I thought that might give it a bit more oomph."

"I don't know how you writers do it!" gushed Diana. "It's perfectly paced, suspenseful, moving. We couldn't be happier."

"Well, thank you," said Claire, shooting me a wary look. I knew what she was thinking. Though newcomers to screenwriting, we'd met with enough theater producers to know that profuse compliments were a frequent opening gambit designed to lull us into a praise-addled stupor in which we'd consent to make changes invariably and laughably characterized as "minor." You can imagine our delight when Claire's request for notes met with a brusque laugh from Bobby.

"Notes? Here's my note—write the damn script!"

We thanked them all again, vowing that we'd get to work the instant we hung up. We did nothing of the sort, of course, even Claire concurring that it would be a shame to ruin our buzz by reentering the treacly world of Prudence Gamache. Our discussion of how best to celebrate was interrupted by a call from Gilbert's mom. Gilbert crowed at length about how the Malenfants had loved our treatment, and Maddie, once made to understand that "treatment" in this case had no medical significance, offered to throw an impromptu dinner in our honor that night.

THE WEATHER WAS UNSEASONABLY BALMY, so we dined alfresco on the elegantly balustraded terrace of Max's Bel-Air manse. Maddie had assembled a small but glittering group, all of whom heartily congratulated us and expressed their certainty that the picture would be a triumph, the first of many in the long, success-drenched careers that awaited us. The conversation was sparkling, the food superb, and the wines all of voting age at least.

After dinner, as the guests trickled into the salon, I lingered a moment on the terrace to admire the shimmering view. Maddie, swaying just a bit, sidled up to me.

"I can't tell you how tickled I am that you kids are doing so great out here."

"We're pretty tickled ourselves."

"I always knew you'd make good, honey. It's like Mama used to say—the cream always rises to the top."

I smiled in tacit assent, my superior butterfat content having been established beyond argument. I was standing on a mogul's terrace. I had just dined with stars (how charming Warren and Annette were), I was writing for stars, I was living in a star's house, and the most desired star of all had chosen me as his sexual confidante.

I chuckled inwardly to think that only weeks ago I'd been gripped by the outlandish fear that I was fated for a life of obscurity and men's neckwear. How absurd of me to have imagined so paltry an existence would ever be mine! Never again would I doubt my destiny, my genius, my inherent God-given creaminess.

It was at this juncture I suppose that some Showbiz God, observing the scene below, turned and addressed a fellow Deity.

"That Cavanaugh."

"What about him?"

"Getting a bit uppish."

"Oh?" said his companion, gazing up distractedly from next year's Oscar winner list. "You think so?"

"Yes. Definite signs of hubris."

"Should we have someone in Retribution attend to him?"

The Showbiz God frowned pensively, then gazed down at the salon where Maddie, thanks to the hints I'd dropped, was "persuading" Claire and me to regale her guests with one of our witty show tunes. The God winced, then nodded decisively.

"Find out who handled Mike Ovitz. Put him on it."

Eleven

★

IN RETROSPECT IT'S EASY TO SEE that it was not very shrewd of me to mock the LA district attorney. DAs, I knew, are notoriously proud, prickly sorts who do not appreciate snide comments directed at them in public cocktail lounges by saucy homosexuals. It's just that Stephen, who'd never liked the man, was already twitting him and we'd been getting on so fabulously (me and Stephen that is, not me and the DA) that the tactful silence I'd maintained at the outset of their skirmish began to strike me as unsupportive. Wussy even. What, I asked myself, would D'Artagnan do if Aramis encountered some surly adversary in a tavern and swordplay ensued? Would he let out a manly *"En garde!"* and leap into the fray, or would he just sit on the sidelines gazing sheepishly into his Cosmopolitan? The former surely.

The problem, as I'd learn to my regret, is that DAs remember these things. They hold grudges. And this one, a Mr. Rusty Grimes, was renowned even among the fiercest of his brethren for the ruthlessness with which he pursued his vendettas.

Given the vast energy Rusty would subsequently devote to our downfall and destruction, it would be nice to at least be able to report that he was the most formidable foe to emerge in the course of my saga.

This was not, alas, the case. He was not even the most formidable foe to emerge in the course of that evening. For no sooner had Rusty slithered offstage than there sprang from the wings an altogether higher form of fiend, one whose cold-blooded cunning, treachery, and ruthlessness would make Rusty seem by comparison like some gruff yet lovable curmudgeon, such as William Demarest endearingly portrayed in the films of Preston Sturges.

But I'm getting ahead of myself. "Foreshadowing," we screenwriters call it—cutting away to the bloodshot eye peering up through the sewer grate so as to assure the more bloodthirsty in the house that gruesome doings await. Having done so, permit me please to digress briefly about the events preceding the dark moment when Fate popped its head into our Nemeses' dressing rooms and yelled, "Places!" To be honest, I'm in no great hurry to usher them onstage.

Once there, you see, they never leave.

I HAVE OFTEN AND masochistically dwelled on the fact that the whole debacle might have been averted if, on the day before my date with Stephen, Gilbert had gotten home ten seconds later than he did. An extra traffic light might have saved us, or a longer line at the grocery. But no, he sauntered in precisely in time to hear the incoming message.

"Philip, this is Ashley in Sonia Powers's office. Just confirming your dinner tomorrow with Sonia, Stephen, and Diana. Eight o'clock at Vici."

"What was that?" he demanded suspiciously.

"Search me. She must have meant to call someone else."

"Then why'd she say 'Philip'?"

I replied that mine was not an uncommon name and that they might well be dining with the actor Philip Seymour Hoffman, Philip Roth, or the composer Philip Glass. Gilbert found this improbable.

"You fucking little weasel! You're having dinner with Stephen and Diana and you weren't even going to *tell* me?"

"Calm down! It's about the book, okay? They just want an update."

"Well, I'm coming!"

"Why? You've never even met Lily."

"Who cares? The whole ghostwriter thing was my idea."

"No it wasn't!"

"I can't believe you tried to squeeze me out of this! After all I went through to get us this job!"

"You retyped *Casablanca!*"

"Do you know how *long* that took?!"

I protested a bit more but I knew it was useless. Nothing would persuade Gilbert to pass up a chance to be seen on the town with the Malenfants, and, as he knew when and where we were dining, he would be killed or be there. It was at least some consolation that he assumed, like the others, that we weren't meeting till eight. He knew nothing of my earlier rendezvous with Stephen, nor would he.

I HADN'T FORGOTTEN MY promise to Stephen to ascertain how much *plastique* Lily and Monty were planning to affix to his closet door. On the morning of our dinner I arrived in Los Feliz bright and early, determined to Learn All.

Louise let me in, and I knew at once from her pious scowl that Monty had a "student" on the premises. I entered the dining room and found him breakfasting with a luscious young man in a white T and faded jeans that fit him like a pale blue rash. In contrast to Monty's more louche consorts, this one had a sweet farm-boy look, with apple cheeks and tousled blond hair. He held an *LA Times* and was studying the comics page with the furrow-browed intensity of a Talmudic scholar.

"Lily might take a while to rouse herself this morning. Her old chum Connie's visiting and they dined quite late, mostly on olives. This is Buster, Glen. He's new in town. I'm showing him the ropes and he's returning the favor."

Not being accustomed to sadomasochistic ribaldry at the breakfast hour, I just stole a glance at Buster's cantaloupe biceps and murmured hello.

"Hey," said Buster. "S'up?"

"Refurl your tongue, Glen, and help yourself to a scone."

"Should I, uh, clear out?" asked Buster.

"No need. Glen's here to see Lily."

"You a masseur?"

"Coauthor," I replied evenly.

"My sister's writing her memoirs and Glen has graciously consented to translate them into English."

"Your sister doesn't speak English?"

"No, she speaks it quite well and, may I add, constantly. It's transferring it to paper that defeats her. If the Mafia wished to take out a hit on English prose, they could find no more capable an assassin."

Monty launched into an extended riff on Lily's failings as a prose stylist, failing to see that literary technique was not a topic likely to enthrall a boy who found *Marmaduke* a bit of a slog. Buster yawned and, grabbing a scone for the road, made his excuses and left.

"Been to the gym, have we?" said Monty, noting my bag.

"Every morning."

"Lily tells me you're a personal trainer."

"Yes."

"How personal?" he drawled and I laughed. His lewdness had come to strike me as both comical and quaint like the tiger growls Bob Hope dispensed indiscriminately to our gals in uniform.

"Not as personal as Buster, if that's what you're asking."

"I won't hear a word against Buster. He doesn't steal and he looks like his ad. One can ask for no more."

It occurred to me that Lily's absence might present an opportunity to pose some questions to him about Stephen that he might not answer as frankly in her presence.

"Can I ask you something, Monty?" I said, my tone intimate and perhaps a tad flirtatious.

"Anything you like," he replied with an intrigued smile.

"Your nephew, Stephen—"

"Ah," sighed Monty. His roguish smile vanished and he rolled his eyes. "You mean is he really gay?"

"How'd you know I was going to ask that?"

"My dear, it is all *anyone* ever asks me about Stephen. Especially the boys. The scoop on my nephew is the holy grail of gay gossip. I usually say 'Ask *him*,' smiling all the while to make it clear that I know more than I'm telling, which never fails to make them buy me another drink. I don't see why *you're* asking though. I've already told you about the tennis pro and his borrowings from my embarrassingly extensive smut trove."

I pointed out that this had been many years ago. What had Monty heard lately? Was he still playing for the home team or had he retired his jersey? Monty glanced enigmatically at his plate for a moment, then said, "Well, this is usually where I go all coy and suck noisily on the dregs of my Mojito. But, seeing as you're practically family now—yes, he's still gay."

"He's *told* you?"

"God, no. We've barely spoken in years."

How did he know then, I asked, and Monty, smiling like the elegant woman of the world he was, replied, "Let's just say we have mutual friends."

An actual gasp is, of course, the highest tribute one can pay to a piece of gossip, and the one I let out with now topped even those Lily had regularly emitted in *Zombie Luau.*

"Friends like *Buster?!*"

"Like uncle, like nephew. Of course," he added, freshening my coffee, "our reasons for choosing the 'buy-sexual' route—you hear the pun—?"

"Yes, of course."

"—couldn't be more different. I'm simply bowing to the realities of the sexual marketplace. I like beautifully sculpted young men and they do not, alas, bestow their favors on dapper gentlemen over sixty unless compensated. For Stephen though, I think it's all about fear."

"Fear of what?"

"Well, he had that one boyfriend who ran to the tabloids. After that he got very worried about discretion and hoped he could buy it. The other advantage of hustlers, of course, is that they're not, as a class, widely esteemed. If one seeks to expose you, he must first con-

fess his profession, which hardly enhances his credibility. Stephen figures who's the public going to believe—him or some youth whose résumé is rather long on fellatio?"

"So you've heard stories about Stephen from your . . . friends?"

"Scads. There's Kyle and Justin and what's his name with the unfortunate piercing . . . ?"

"Recently?" I asked, agog.

"Not for a year or so. I'm told he had a close call with Kyle and a
paparazzo. Threw a scare into him so he's been a good boy lately."

"My poor Stephen!" I thought. How dreadful to think that fear
and a paramour's betrayal had driven him into the loveless arms of
male harlots! On the bright side though he hadn't had dick in a year,
which could only improve my chances.

"Dear God," I said, my head spinning. "So Lily's actually putting
all this in the book?"

"Good heavens, no! Lily knows nothing about it. You don't suppose I'd tell her?"

"I don't know. You seem so close."

"We are. We get on beautifully. And why? Because I tell her nothing she doesn't want to know and because, as you've surely noticed,
her capacity to ignore the obvious is nothing short of breathtaking. It
is the whole secret of her happiness—and I thank you, Glen, for your
chivalrous refusal to tamper with it."

He laid a gentle hand on my shoulder.

"It's endeared you to me, Glen. It has. You sit here day after day
listening to her spout the most appalling drivel about her so-called
glory days and respond with the most angelic tact. I've watched her sit
here among her picture albums and make claims so outrageous the
very photographs do spit takes. But you don't even roll your eyes. It's
positively saintly of you, Glen, and that's why I've told you what I just
have. I lay my family's dirty linen at your feet as my meager thank-you
for your great kindness."

As I noted earlier, if you're going to infiltrate people's homes and
win their trust for the sole purpose of betraying it, it helps a great deal
to dislike them. This is no simple task when they're two old sweeties

who shower you with praise and beatify you over breakfast. Monty's tender tribute, coming on the very day I was to sup in the tents of the enemy, made all the guilt I'd quelled come flooding back, redoubled in strength. So it was no wonder that when Lily finally confided to me the details of her comeback project, I was powerless to refuse her request for assistance.

We were an hour into the day's work when her friend Connie, a plump, salty old dame who'd played the gym teacher in *Sorry, Miss Murgatroyd!*, entered the dining room, clutching a well-thumbed manuscript.

"Oh, good," smiled Lily, "you've started it."

"I'm done, honey. Couldn't put it down. And may I say you are a goddamned genius!"

"Did you really think so?"

I asked if it was the early chapters of the memoir. Connie said, "No, it's her screenplay!"

"Screenplay?"

"It's what I've been hinting to you about. I suppose I can tell you now. You've certainly proved you can be trusted! It's a script I wrote especially for myself."

"A historical epic," gushed Connie, "with one helluva great part!"

"Really?" I asked Lily. "Who do you play?"

"Amelia Earhart!"

As Monty had pointed out, I'd grown skilled at politely absorbing statements that would induce involuntary backflips in others, but I could not restrain a certain widening of the eyes.

"I know what you're thinking—that I'm too old for it. But I'm not. You see, my story takes place seven whole years *after* her plane disappeared."

"She survived!" explained Connie. "On a tropical island."

"But then she's rescued by Portuguese fishermen. She makes her way to France, only it's occupied now."

"By Germans," Connie added helpfully.

"She meets a dashing young freedom fighter and begins flying se-cret missions for the resistance while all France wonders who this daring mystery woman could be! I'm so glad you liked it, Connie! You didn't find it a bit rough in spots?"

"Well, I wasn't sure about a few historical things. But I'm sure you can get some help with that."

On hearing the word "help" I gazed apprehensively at the light-bulb that had just materialized over Lily's head. Why goodness, she exclaimed, the perfect critic was sitting right here. Would I be so gallant as to read her little effort and offer my thoughts?

Though unable to imagine a more gruesome task, I knew that the favor would assuage at least some of my festering guilt. I said I'd be honored and tucked it in my gym bag, suppressing a shudder as I glanced at the title, *Amelia Flies Again!*

DIANA NAMED HER RESTAURANT Vici in honor of her late husband, Stephen's father, the man who'd "conquered" her heart. The place is a posh trattoria decorated with black-and-white photos of the late Roberto, and it serves hearty "peasant fare" at prices that make you wonder if it wouldn't be cheaper to just buy your own peasant and throw an apron on him. It's popular with both Diana's aging contemporaries and that segment of young Hollywood that finds it amusingly ironic to hang out with the Steve and Eydie set. Diana herself, though normally loath to dine in public, knows that the chance of sighting her is one of the few reasons people tolerate its lackluster food and larcenous prices, so she keeps its heat simmering with periodic appearances. Once a year she dons an apron and plays waitress, a shrewd stunt that never fails to keep the small $30 pizzas moving briskly.

I arrived early, found a corner booth in the dimly lit bar, and settled in. I expected a longish wait, but Stephen strolled in five minutes later in tandem with the thickset unsmiling bodyguard who accompanied him on all forays into public arenas.

It was only the second time I'd seen him in the flesh, and faced once more with his astonishing perfection, I could only stare open-mouthed, little lust bombs exploding in my chest. I hastily composed my features into a more decorous expression and waved to him. He saw me and flashed a smile that hit me like a heart-seeking missile.

There were a dozen or so industry types arrayed about the bar and though they seemed as blasé a crowd as ever yawned its way through a Golden Globes, not one could help staring as he passed by. The bartender, poor lad, gawked so helplessly that he poured a martini right onto Christina Ricci's cigarette.

I rose to greet him and was pleasantly astonished to find myself on the receiving end of a full-fledged hug with cheek brush.

He murmured into my ear.

"So how you doing, James Bond?"

"Not bad, Mishtah Caliber. And yourshelf?" I replied, wishing I did a better Sean Connery. He laughed though and we sat, ordering drinks from the saucer-eyed bartender who'd practically teleported himself to our booth. When he'd gone I looked around at the other patrons, several of whom were glancing our way.

"Do you think it's safe to talk here?"

"I think we're okay if we keep our voices down." He jerked his head toward the bodyguard, who'd stationed himself at the bar. "Anyone gets too close, Ravi's here."

Our drinks came and we toasted.

"How's the script coming?"

I said it was going well and he said he couldn't wait to read it. He asked about my background, where I'd grown up, how long I'd been writing. His interest seemed genuine; every answer met with followups and the attention was going to my head faster than the Cosmo I'd ordered as a subliminal hint that he could consider me his bitch.

"Gosh," I said finally, "you must think I'm an egomaniac, prattling on about myself this way."

"I'm curious. When you do what I do the people you meet know a lot about you and you know nothing about them. And I want to know about you, Phil."

"That's really nice of you. It's just . . . y'know," I said, glancing meaningfully at my watch.

"Right," he nodded, then leaned toward me and lowered his voice. "So, let's hear it. Lily and Monty. What are they saying about me?"

"Well," I said, suddenly flushed. "Basically, they say that you're, uh, well . . . gay."

He stared at me, his expression unchanged.

"And?"

It was suddenly clear to me how foolish I'd been to think Stephen would respond to this "bombshell" with gasps and calls for smelling salts. It was hardly news to him that he was gay, nor was it any surprise that his aunt and uncle knew, having once caught him with a mouthful of tennis pro. What he wanted to know was what they planned to actually publish. I repeated their stories about him filching Monty's porn and the tennis instructor, plus Lily's claim that they'd dined with him and Andrew, his now disclaimed, then quite open, boyfriend. He took it all in, his face calm and inscrutable. When I'd finished he sat a moment digesting it, then said, "Anything else?"

I hadn't planned on telling him about the hustlers since Lily didn't even know and I feared embarrassing him. But I sensed he could tell I was holding something back, so rather than sow mistrust, I lowered my voice to a murmur and said, "I didn't bring it up 'cause it won't be in the book, but Monty says he's heard stories about you more recently. He said he's heard them from . . . well, his hustlers. He mentioned a Kyle."

His impassive demeanor cracked a bit. He exhaled sharply and, raising his eyes to heaven, downed the rest of his scotch. The bartender, noting this, practically pole-vaulted over the bar to ask if we'd like another round.

"Please," said Stephen.

When he'd gone Stephen favored me with a weary smile.

"Thank you for this."

"You're welcome."

"Now, I'd like you to do something for me. Two things actually."

"Name it, Stephen."

"Steve. First I want you to keep this to yourself. You haven't told anyone, have you?"

"Of course not!"

"Well, don't. Not my family or Sonia or your partners."

The bartender returned with our drinks, then hovered a moment as though hoping we'd ask him to join us. Stephen shot him a perplexed look and he withdrew, a maidenly blush on his cheek. Once he was out of earshot I asked Stephen what the second thing was. He took a sip of his drink, then leaned in so closely I thought for a breathless moment he might kiss me.

"Talk her out of it."

"Excuse me?"

"Lily. Convince her to leave this stuff about me out of the book."

I sat there a moment, slightly dizzy from both the tallness of the order and the intoxicating proximity of his face.

"Uh, okay," I said finally. "I mean, I'll try."

"It's not enough to try, Phil. You've got to *do* it."

"Oh. Okay, then, I will."

He sat back but his eyes never left mine. He frowned sexily, distending his lower lip in a come-hither pout.

"You think I'm a hypocrite, don't you?"

"No!"

"A self-loathing closet case?"

"Not a bit!"

"I'm glad, Phil. Because I'm not. I just think what Lily's doing is wrong. If she wants to tell her story, that's fine. But this is *my* story. The only one who has the right to tell it is me. And I will."

"You *will?*"

He glanced quickly around the bar, then returned his riveting gaze to me. His eyes blazed with sincerity and there was even a hint of moisture in the corners.

"Yes, I will. Trust me, the day will come when I write my story, and when I do, I'm telling everything. And if my family or the studio or my agents don't like it, well, fuck 'em. My life is *mine* and I'm not ashamed of any of it."

His words had a profound effect on me. I gaped worshipfully at him like some transported pilgrim beholding a saint's tibia. To know that he planned to commit so courageous an act, albeit at some distant and unspecified date, further solidified my belief that he was as noble as he was scrumptious. I struggled to frame some suitably eloquent response, but the best I could manage was, "Wow! That's great."

"It's what I've planned all along. It's just a question of when."

"When were you thinking?"

"When it's time. When it feels right. It has to feel right."

"Well, of course."

"But when that time comes I don't want my aunt to have beaten me to the punch. You can understand that, can't you?"

"Oh, absolutely. It's just . . ."

"What?"

"I'm not sure how to convince her. She seems pretty determined."

He shrugged and blinded me with a grin.

"You're a pretty persuasive guy, Phil. You convinced *me* to hire you even though you'd never had a picture made. If you could pull that off, talking an old lady into leaving some gossip out of a book should be nothing."

He gave me an encouraging clap on my shoulder. His hand lingered, lightly rubbing my upper arm. "Say, you've been working out, haven't you?"

Good God, was he flirting with me?

"A little," I said bashfully.

"It shows," he said. He gave my biceps a firm squeeze, a gesture that carbonated my bloodstream. If two Cosmos can make the nice-looking fellow who's flirting with you seem like a movie star, imagine what it's like when the flirter actually *is* a movie star. A pleasant wooziness stole over me and I feared that any moment my head would loll back and my tongue damply unspool the way Homer Simpson's does when he dreams of doughnuts.

He withdrew his hand from my arm, then leaned in toward me again, his tone thrillingly intimate.

"Can I count on you, buddy?"

"Absolutely!"

"You'll do this for me?"

"Come hell or high water!"

"Thank you. And thanks for being my friend. I don't meet a lot of guys I feel I can . . . *trust*. But I feel that about you. And if you come through for me, I'll be grateful." His eyes traveled shyly south, then rebounded back up to meet mine. "*Very* grateful," he repeated, fixing me with a gaze so smoldering, so freighted with sex it would not have surprised me to glance down and find that my shirt was unbuttoning itself.

I boldly returned his gaze, throwing in a few sex rays of my own, and said, "I won't let you down, Steve. I promise you that—"

"Hey, Stevie! Who's your boyfriend?"

The voice, brash and grating, had come from the bar. I looked up and saw a beefy, fiftyish man wearing a conservative gray suit. He had mottled, leathery skin, short carrot-colored hair, and a bulbous mis-shapen nose that bespoke a lifelong devotion to gin and fisticuffs. His bearing suggested a military background. He had that swaggering, contemptuous air certain old soldiers display when confronting effete men whose bodies, they feel certain, contain an unmanly shortage of shrapnel.

I despised him on sight, partly because of his annoying machismo but mostly because he'd intruded at the very moment when my—my? *Everyone's!*—dream was finally coming true.

The instant Stephen heard the man, his sex face vanished, re-placed first by an annoyed grimace and then, as he turned to face his heckler, a cool insolent smile. The interloper started toward us and Stephen's bodyguard shot over to intercept him. Stephen waved the guard away, informing him the fellow was an "old friend."

"Hey, Rusty. Been a long time. Not long enough, but long."

"Who's your boyfriend?" repeated Mr. Surly.

"Why? Jealous?" He turned to me. "Meet Rusty Grimes. He's what passes for a DA these days."

I realized at once the source of their enmity.

Five years ago Grimes had charged a man named Roger Banks with the murder of Banks's ex-boyfriend. The evidence was flimsy and many felt that in prosecuting the case the state's lurid emphasis on Mr. Banks's fondness for light S and M was both pointless and homophobic. Since Banks, when not applying tit clamps to recent acquaintances, was a model citizen and prominent in many gay charities, his case became a literal cause célèbre with numerous stars, Stephen among them, rallying to his defense. Banks was acquitted and two years later HBO produced an all-star film version of the case. Stephen played Rusty, complete with prosthetic nose, and his brilliantly caustic portrayal had struck Rusty as a more than adequate casus belli.

"Nice to meetcha," said Grimes, not deigning to look at me.

"Philip's writing my next picture," explained Stephen. "So what are you doing in a hip place like this? Besides making it less hip?"

"Saying hi to my kid. He tends bar here. I hope this picture's better than your last one. Whew!" he said, wittily miming a frat boy's response to a fart. "I saw it on a plane and people still walked out."

"If only you'd joined them."

"Maybe this one'll win you an Oscar to put next to your other two. Oh, wait, I forgot—you lost, right? Both times?"

This was a low blow. It was well known that Stephen, the son of an Oscar winner, yearned for one of his own and that his losses had rankled him sorely. It was then that I decided I was letting down Team Donato and risked forfeiting Stephen's regard if I did not rally to his side.

"Are we keeping you, Rusty?" I asked pertly. "Don't you have places to go, faggots to frame?"

Stephen smiled and Grimes, who'd not expected me to stick my oar in, gave me that squinty appraising look long favored by schoolyard ruffians.

"Aren't you a cutie-pie? Wudja say your name was?"

"Philip Cavanaugh."

He took a pad and pen from his pocket and made a note.

"Ooh!" I cried, mock cringing. "He's writing my name down! How theoretically intimidating!"

"Nice seeing you, Rusty," said Stephen.

"I get the picture. The lovebirds wanna be alone. Nice running into you, Stevie."

He started off, then turned back to us.

"Stevie, do me a favor?"

"What's that?"

His lips twisted in a sour little smile. "Make a mistake. Just one, okay?" And with that he turned and left, waving goodbye to his son, who'd watched the whole scene with undisguised dismay.

Stephen said, "Thanks for jumping in. You didn't have to do that."

"Hey, any enemy of yours is an enemy of mine."

"I appreciate that, but watch your step with Rusty. He's a powerful guy."

"What can he do to me?" I asked unprophetically.

There seemed little hope of rekindling the deliciously steamy atmosphere Rusty had so rudely shattered. It wouldn't have mattered if there had been, since within moments of his departure the voice I'd been dreading called out shrilly from beyond the bar.

"Hey, guys!"

"What's Gilbert doing here?" muttered Stephen.

"He got wind of this from our answering machine and invited himself along. He's such a *starfucker*."

Gilbert arrived at our booth and plopped himself brazenly next to Stephen.

"I'm not late, am I? I thought we said eight."

Stephen said that by chance we'd both arrived early and decided to have a drink. I could tell Gilbert thought he was lying but knew he'd never dare say so to Stephen. I, by contrast, could confidently expect brass knuckles the instant we reached home.

Diana showed next, and her arrival caused the furtive oglers in the bar to abandon any effort at discretion. Gilbert, aware of this, leaped to his feet and flung his arms wide in greeting.

"Darling!" he cried, his air kisses swarming around her like gnats. Diana, who'd only met him once and hadn't expected him tonight, endured this with baffled courtesy and seemed on the verge of asking his name. Stephen, observing this, rose and, with undue gallantry, said, "Gilbert was available to join us."

"Oh, good," said Diana vaguely.

Gina arrived next, followed by Sonia, who was much affronted to see her two biggest clients chatting in a public bar without so much as velvet rope to protect them. She gruffly summoned the maître d', who greeted his sovereign with a terrified smile and escorted us from the bar. He led us through the main dining room, Diana bestowing grand "Yes, it's really me" nods on her fortunate patrons, to a private table concealed from public view behind sliding smoked-glass doors.

We perused our menus, exchanging small talk and hearing some spicy gossip from Sonia, who had no compunction about airing the lurid misfortunes of nonclients. It was not until the waitstaff had taken our orders, served our appetizers, and withdrawn that Diana finally broached the topic of Lily's memoir.

"I want to thank you, Philip," she said, "for everything you've done for us. I can only imagine how tiresome it's been for you, listening to Lily chatter on about herself day after day—I'd go mad in an hour! But you've done a wonderful job. In fact, a little too wonderful."

"Oh?"

"I know my sister. She's not a bright woman. But you make her sound quite intelligent, clever even. Is that quite necessary?"

"Mother," sighed Stephen, "we can't hire Philip for a job, then find fault when he does it well. Besides, what better way to get Lily to trust him than to flatter her?"

Diana dourly allowed that Stephen perhaps had a point but was clearly piqued by anything that showed her sister in a positive light.

Sonia said, "Anyway, the pages you've given us so far, it's just childhood crap, which is not what we're concerned about. We realize that if she's telling her life story she's gonna start at the beginning, but we don't want to wait months to find out what we're up against. What I'm talking about are allegations. Lies. Big, fat actionable lies. We know she's told these lies in private. What we want to know is, is she planning to print them? Has she said anything negative about my clients? To either of you?" she said, including Gilbert.

"Actually," said Gilbert, "I've never met her."

"Then what the fuck are you doing here?"

"Well, sure," I said cautiously. "Lily's said a lot of things. It's just a little embarrassing to talk about."

"It's embarrassing for us too," said Stephen gently, "but it's better for us to know than not."

"I suppose so," I said and, composing my features into the contrite expression the polite dinner guest wears when preparing to defame his hostess at length, pulled out a crib sheet I'd made detailing Lily's charges. I was glad I'd brought it. Apart from serving as a memory aid, it gave me something to look at besides Diana's increasingly volcanic countenance.

In brief, I said, Lily was planning to write that Diana was an over-rated actress who'd stolen her signature mannerisms and effects from more gifted and original performers; that she had, starting in adolescence, begun a lifelong habit of trading sexual favors for both material goods and career advancement and that by the time she was twenty a wag had christened her boudoir "the chamber of commerce"; that in her late teens she'd augmented her meager acting income by selling marijuana to jazz musicians and that even as a dope peddler she'd lacked integrity, cutting her wares with herbs and lawn clippings; that her sexual appetite bordered on nymphomania and that once, on a USO tour in Korea, she'd gotten drunk and pleasured no fewer than seven marines; that by the time she was twenty-four she'd had three abortions, the last of these while playing a nun; that she'd been a neglectful mother to Stephen, callously entrusting his upbringing to servants and relations; that she'd cheated on all three of her husbands; that she'd had affairs with numerous married men, several of whom she'd snagged not from passion but resentment over their wives having won roles she'd coveted; that so far as her character was concerned, she was dishonest, petty, vain, envious, cruel to underlings, alcoholic, and a world-class cheapskate.

When I'd finished there was a fraught silence at the table. It was finally broken by Gina, who said, "You've been to Korea?"

"Oh," I added, glancing at my crib sheet, "she also said something about a junkie musician you were seeing in the late seventies? That he overdosed at your house and you had your gardeners bring his body back to his place to avoid the publicity."

"How could she possibly—?!" sputtered Diana, then she cut herself off before uttering the damning words "know about that?"

"Give me those notes!" barked Sonia, snatching them from my hand. "Have you shown these to anybody?" she demanded.

"Of course not!"

"Let's not shoot the messenger here!" scolded Gilbert, winning himself a tender gaze from Sonia. As for Diana, the actress in her had suddenly grasped that her enraged expression was making her look less like an Innocent Maligned than a Villainess Exposed. She promptly replaced it with a poignant look of wounded astonishment.

"How can she hate me so much that she'd make up such dreadful lies?"

Stephen, who, I suspected, knew that the charges were all dead-on, patted her arm and said that jealousy prompted people to do all sorts of strange things.

"What about this one?" asked Sonia, jutting her chins toward Stephen. "What's she planning to say about him?"

"Mainly," I replied without a moment's hesitation, "that he's conceited and ungrateful."

"Oh, please!" harrumphed Gina. "He's the most grateful person you'll ever meet. I could show you ten interviews where he says he's the luckiest guy on earth!"

"I think," said Stephen, "that she means ungrateful to her."

"Yes. She says she did so much for you when you were growing up, more than your own mother—"

"Lies!" cried Diana, wiping away a nonexistent tear.

"—and now that you're famous you consider yourself too important to see her or Monty anymore."

Stephen ruefully conceded that he had, perhaps, been a shade neglectful.

"That's so like you," said Gina. "She attacks us and you blame yourself."

"And that's all?" asked Sonia, her eyes narrowing.

"That's all she's told me," I said, content that, in the acting department, I was more than holding my own with Diana.

The waiters arrived with our entrees and Stephen took advantage of the distraction to give my thigh a little thank-you squeeze. He, of course, performed this gesture with the utmost discretion and suavity. I, however, unaccustomed to having my thighs fondled by sexy megastars in the presence of their wives and mothers, could not constrain a delighted smirk from erupting briefly on my face. Gilbert alone observed this and shot me a questioning look that I pretended not to see.

When the waiters were gone Sonia fixed me with a glacial stare and said, "What do you think of Lily?"

Given the circumstances I could hardly say that I found her a daft yet sweet old darling and that we were working on a screenplay together. I said that I considered her a vain, bitter woman who lived in a world of her own and relied heavily on drink to sustain her illusions.

"Would you testify to that?" demanded Sonia.

"Excuse me?"

"That she's a delusional alcoholic? Possibly a danger to herself and others?"

"Sonia," chided Stephen, "we cannot actually *commit* Lily just because we're pissed at her."

"I'm trying to be creative here!" snapped Sonia.

Gina, who'd lost interest in Lily's book once it ceased to threaten Stephen, asked if we could talk about something more pleasant. Diana, keen to avoid a more detailed discussion of Lily's charges, seconded the motion and began chattering inanely about her polenta.

I did not suppose, given the joy I'd spread during the appetizers, that the rest of the meal would be a very jolly affair. I had, however, underestimated the effects of excellent wine and Gilbert's indefatigable charm. Eager as always to ingratiate himself with the famous, he employed every device he could muster to chase the Malenfants' blues away. He told jokes, many of these lengthy and well-practiced set pieces, he did impressions (his Maggie Smith, as always, spot-on), and he flattered them shamelessly. The specter of Lily's memoir did not completely recede but began to seem more and more like a battle that could be waged and won another day and which needn't further dampen our spirits tonight. The drinks flowed, our laughter grew louder, and by the time the last impossibly dainty cookie had been consumed, an air of tipsy conviviality prevailed. As we rose to leave, I could see from Gilbert's rapturous smile that he considered the evening an unalloyed triumph.

Two waiters pushed apart the sliding doors, revealing a tableau that was deeply gratifying to both Gilbert and myself. We stood at the center of our little group, flanked by Stephen on one side and Diana and Gina on the other. We watched as diners discreetly nudged companions who hadn't seen us, then began our stately procession toward the exit, regally ignoring the necks craning and swiveling all around us.

Gilbert suddenly stopped dead in his tracks, clogging our party's route. I gave him a puzzled glance, and as I did there spread across his face a grin so ecstatic as to make his earlier expression look like that of a small boy watching the final reel of *Old Yeller*.

"Gilbert?" came an incredulous voice just behind us. I turned toward it.

"Oh, dear God!" I gasped.

For there, just four feet away, dressed in black Prada and seated at a small table too close to the kitchen, was Gilbert's ex-wife, Moira Finch.

"Stephen," purred Gilbert, "there's someone you simply *must* meet."

Twelve

★

OR THOSE OF YOU WHO HAVE faithfully followed earlier in-
stallments of the Cavanaugh Chronicles, the fiend Moira
Finch requires no introduction; I don't doubt that any of you
currently residing in Los Angeles, on learning that she walks among
you, have already laid down this volume, bolted your door, and called
small children in from play. I ask those of you whose flesh has already
horripilated to Moira's dark doings to grant me a moment's indulgence
while I throw open the crypt for the newcomers.

A few years back Gilbert, in a move that will surprise no one
who's read this far, decided to get married, his sole motive being to
extort lavish wedding gifts from his wealthy stepfamily. He chose
Moira as his bride. He was not, even then, particularly fond of her,
but her equally prosperous family, combined with her can-do approach to swindling, made her seem a suitable partner for the venture.

Once engaged, Moira revealed herself to be a full-blown so-
ciopath, one whose brazen deceptions and lighthearted treacheries
would have made the Borgia girls hang their heads in shame and resolve to try harder. Gilbert and I, his luckless best man, did everything

in our power to halt the wedding, but Moira thwarted us at each turn and by the end had maneuvered us into a position of literally mortal peril. Thanks to Claire's heroic assistance we escaped with our lives (others were less fortunate), and after a decent interval, Gilbert divorced her, vowing to shun her for the rest of his days.

Given their history, Gilbert's glee at seeing her again might seem puzzling. I knew though that it sprang from the happy fact that she was sitting at a bad table with a stringy-haired female nonentity while he had just emerged from a private dining room, armed to the teeth with movie stars. There are few things as pleasant as rubbing one's latest triumph into an old enemy's face, and Gilbert wasted no time in spackling Moira's with his.

"Moira, my angel! How well you look! It's been ages! Stephen, Diana, Gina, I'd like you to meet a very dear old friend of mine, Moira Finch."

Greetings were exchanged. Moira, whose blood has the approximate temperature of a Slurpee, managed not to look nonplussed, but her companion gaped like a goldfish. Moira, noting this, smiled in mortification and introduced her as Deborah, "a colleague."

"Oh, gosh, hello!" burbled Deb. "You people—I just think you're so . . . *awesome!* Gawd, wait'll I tell Ma."

"So, Gilly," said Moira, preposterously reverting to the endearment she'd employed when feigning affection during their engagement, "what brings you to LA?"

"I'm writing a script for these guys," he replied with brutal nonchalance.

Not even the frosty corpuscled Moira could conceal her amazement at this. She'd lived with Gilbert for months and knew better than anyone that his words-per-day output seldom exceeded that of a one-armed headstone carver.

"*Really?*"

"Philip too," added Gilbert, remembering I was present. "Bobby Spellman read our spec script and recommended us. So what are you up to?"

"This and that," came her evasive reply.

"Moira's a movie producer too," offered Deborah, prompting a subtle but unmistakable wince from Moira.

"Anything we might have seen?" asked Gilbert ruthlessly.

"Not yet. I have a few things in development. You know how it is. Everything takes ages!"

"And sometimes," beamed Gilbert, "it all just comes together overnight. *So* good seeing you again!" he said and, like a cat who knows there's no more life to be shaken from the mouse, released his limp prey and swept jauntily to the exit. The rest of us bade farewell to the deceased and followed behind. When we reached the sidewalk, we found awaiting us there the sole thing that could have made Gilbert's stratospheric spirits soar even higher.

"God!" moaned Gina as flashbulbs exploded in our faces. "They always find us."

Stephen and Diana, long accustomed to such ambushes, took as little notice of the cameras as gazelles in a game preserve. Gilbert, taking his cue from them, affected a bland insouciance as he wished loud good nights to his dear new friends. As I edged forward to take my place in tabloid history, a firm hand gripped my shoulder and yanked me out of camera range.

"Real smart," hissed Sonia. "You want Lily seeing you in the paper with Diana?"

I sulkily conceded the point and sought shelter behind her suddenly convenient bulk. Diana's driver pulled up and whisked her into the car just as the valet delivered Stephen's Porsche. Just before he got in, he turned to where I stood lurking behind Sonia and winked at me.

"Good work!" he called.

"Thank you!" shrieked Gilbert.

My car came next and as I pulled away I noticed Gilbert chatting up a photographer whom he was no doubt advising on the correct spelling of his name.

"WELL, HOW MUCH FUN was that?!" brayed Gilbert as he danced into the house a few minutes behind me. I replied that a good time had indeed been had by all.

"Not by Moira!" he said, collapsing in giggles on the couch. "I ask you, Philip, have you ever in your life seen anyone so *thwarted*? So thoroughly and magnificently *skunked*?"

"She was hurting all right."

"Wait till we tell Claire!"

"Are you crazy? We can't tell Claire!"

"Why not?" he asked.

"How do we explain why we were out to dinner with Stephen and Diana?"

"Oh, right. We could always say it was a meeting about the script."

"That she wasn't invited to?"

Gilbert frowned thoughtfully, then agreed that, as pleasant as it would be to tell Claire how we'd vanquished our ancient foe, it might on balance be wiser to keep mum.

"Oh, and by the way," he said, his eyes suddenly narrowing to a flinty stare, "what was that business with you and Stephen?"

"What business?" I replied with a yawn, as bed seemed suddenly advisable.

"Oh, please—I show up two minutes early and there you are canoodling in a booth!"

"Oh, that," I said with a dismissive wave. "We *told* you. We both got there early and decided to have a drink."

"It was *arranged*," snapped Gilbert. "It's why you wanted to go in separate cars . . . 'Oh, *Gilll*-bert,' " he mewled in the offensively precious voice he employs when imitating me, " 'I have some errands to run before dinner—let's just meet there, okaaay?' You were meeting Stephen!"

I was not, of course, about to betray the trust Stephen had placed in me. I held firm, resolutely maintaining that my encounter with Stephen had been pure chance.

"Puh-leeez!" scoffed Gilbert. "I saw you at dinner—that goofy Kansas-in-August grin. Not to mention the way you ladled out tons of dirt about Diana and nothing at all about Saint Stephen. We're really supposed to believe Lily and Monty haven't said a word to you about him liking boys?"

"They haven't."

"Oh, give it up! I know *exactly* what happened. Stephen doesn't want his wife and mom to know what Lily's got on him. He told you to meet him early so he could warn you to keep your mouth shut— which you did because you're gaga for him and you have this delusion that if you do what he wants he'll throw you a fuck."

It did not surprise me that a boy as blithely devious as Gilbert would so swiftly intuit my arrangement with Stephen, nor that one so lacking in nobler sentiments would characterize it so coarsely. Still, his having guessed the truth placed me under no obligation to concede it. I tossed my head and poured myself a scotch, remarking on the vividness of his imagination.

"Oh, c'mon! I'm right and you know it! I'm not mad, hon—just *tell* me, okay? What's Lily said about Stevie that's got him so nervous?"

"She hasn't said a word."

"Well, I like this! Here I am, your oldest friend in the world, and you won't share the hottest gossip you ever heard! It's not like I'm going to tell anyone!"

"Oh, right!"

"Then you admit there's something to tell!"

"I admit nothing!"

"Gawd!" he wailed, hurling a throw pillow at me. "After all we've been through how can you possibly be more loyal to him than me! Can't you see he's just using you? Honestly, Philip, there are times I think you haven't the tiniest *shred* of common sense!"

The doorbell rang and he sprang eagerly to his feet.

"That'll be Moira!"

"*What!*" I blurted, passing scotch through my nose.

"I asked her by for a nightcap."

"*Moira?!*"

"Yes."

"You *invited* her?"

"She came out while I was waiting for my car. She said she had a favor to ask and when could she see us? I said how about now."

"A *FAVOR?* Have you lost your mind?! We are *not* doing any favors for Moira Finch!"

"Of course we're not," smirked Gilbert. "We'll see what she wants, then turn her down flat."

"If we're just going to say no, why ask her over in the first place?"

Gilbert knotted his brow, clearly marveling at my inability to grasp the obvious.

"So she can see the *house.*"

The Moira whom Gilbert now admitted bore little resemblance to the dazed and defeated wraith we'd left behind at Vici. She'd regrouped and now seemed serene and delighted to see us. Nothing in her demeanor suggested we were anything but the very dearest old friends who'd been apart far too long and were now joyfully reunited. This pose, I knew, stemmed from her native duplicity and need of a favor, but it still made me nervous. Moira is never more dangerous than when she's being nice.

"What a *fantastic* house! The views are just spectacular! I love what you've done with the inside too. So clean."

"Actually," confessed Gilbert, "it's not ours. Our friend Angus is letting us stay here awhile. Angus Brodie? The actor?"

"You *know* him? I'm so jealous I could die! This kitchen's a dream! Is that a Gaggenau?"

Gilbert sweetly offered to give her the tour.

"I would *love* that!" she declared ecstatically. "God, it's so good to *see* you guys!"

When Moira wants something she does not shy from laying it on thick. As she flitted from room to room, she gushed and marveled over every sconce and skylight, carrying on like a Karachi goatherd who'd been snatched from her mud hut and deposited in the Hearst Castle. By the time she'd inquired of a Pottery Barn vase if it was Baccarat or Steuben, I knew that when favor time came she wouldn't be asking us to feed the cats while she visited Nana. The tour concluded in our office, which jutted out from the second floor and, having glass walls on two sides, afforded the most impressive views.

"So," she said, running a reverent hand across the cluttered desk, "this is where it all happens!"

"Yes," replied Gilbert, and I willed him, unsuccessfully, not to add "the nerve center."

He sat behind the desk, the better to create a tableau in which he was the entrenched Hollywood muck-a-muck and Moira the lowly supplicant. She gazed out at the view for a moment, and when she turned back to us her eyes were suddenly dewy with emotion.

"I am *so proud* of you two! I mean, I always knew you'd succeed. How could you not with all that talent? But Stephen Donato and Diana Malenfant? How great is that?"

"And such nice people too," said Gilbert.

"Oh, I could tell. So how long have you been writing together?"

"Not too long. Just our spec script and now this."

"We're writing it with Claire." I said this not out of fairness to Claire but as a veiled warning, since Claire's strategic brilliance had been our most potent weapon against Moira's vile stratagems when last we'd tangled.

"Claaiirre!" sang Moira fondly, as though they'd not daily wished each other a slow agonizing death. "How *is* she? Do say hi for me!"

"So," said Gilbert, "what have you been up to?"

"Where to start?" she said with a jovial laugh. "Well . . . a little after we last saw each other I decided it was time to shake things up. New places, fresh challenges. So I came out here. I was only going to scope things out, stay maybe a few months, but then I met Albert. Gosh, I *so* wish you guys could have met him. He produced a ton of great movies from the fifties right up through a few years ago. He was a wonderful guy, kind and smart—a real gentleman. He totally swept me off my feet and the next thing I knew I was Mrs. Albert Schimmel!"

"You're married?" I said.

"Widowed," she said, glancing downward to convey that this saddened her. "I knew going in we'd only have so much time. He was a good bit older than me. His lungs were terribly weak and he would keep smoking those darn French cigarettes. Still I knew I'd be grateful for however long we had. Such a mensch."

"Rich?" asked Gilbert.

"Comfortable."

"Kids?"

"No. It was his greatest sadness."

"Not yours I'll bet."

"Oh, *you*," she said, playfully swatting his knee. "So anyway, I was a *wreck* after he died. A complete basket case! But after a while I thought, well I can't just sit around this big old mansion crying all day. It's the last thing Albert would have wanted. So I decided to become an independent producer. I rented an office, hired an assistant. I took meetings, optioned some books, made a gazillion phone calls. I'll be honest, guys, I hustled my ass off and after a whole year—nothing! I had no idea how hard it was to get a little movie made! I mean, maybe I'm naive but I'm amazed how cold people in this town can be. You write them the nicest letters and they don't even respond! If you're already a big name they're sweet as pie, but if you're just trying to get started, forget it!"

It was laughable that a girl as canny as Moira should affect surprise at the town's notorious clubbiness and odd too that she had not, in her infinite cunning, found some way around it.

"So after a while I decided why bother? I mean, why does anyone want to make movies in the first place? To make people happy, right?"

We could, of course, have argued with that sugary premise, but we just nodded, curious to see where she was going.

"And there are other ways to do that. To make your own special gift to the world. I just had to find one that, you know, *spoke* to me and would help me nourish my healing, spiritual side."

Lacking toupees that could leap from our heads and spin around three times before landing askew, we let this comment pass as well.

"So one day I was showing my house to some new friends and it suddenly hit me—*this* could be my gift to the world. My home! It's so damn big, so sprawling and beautiful with all this drop-dead landscaping. Why not turn it into a spa and share it with the world? So that's what I did!"

She detailed for us how she'd hired a brilliant architect who'd gutted and redesigned the vast house, converting the ballroom into a treatment center while peppering the grounds with charming guest bungalows. Moira had meanwhile toured the poshest spas of California and Europe, taking notes and luring away top talent. By the time construction had finished she'd assembled a staff unrivaled in its expertise, plus an Italian dermatologist able to dole out the Botox and a few other surreptitiously offered goodies that had not yet won FDA approval.

"So that's the story, kids! I named the place Les Étoiles and we opened last month. Needless to say, it wasn't cheap. It cost me every penny Albert left, not to mention a hefty bank loan, so you can imagine how much it means to me that it succeed. And of course the whole key to that is image. Buzz. And that's where that little favor I mentioned comes in.

"When I saw you guys tonight with Stephen Donato, I thought to myself, 'My God, that's *exactly* the sort of person who should be coming to Les Étoiles. Someone accomplished and admired who has to cope every day with these incredible pressures and who could really benefit from this blissfully tranquil environment I've created.' And I'm not saying it wouldn't be pretty nice for me too! Once word got around that Stephen Donato enjoyed little getaways there, the whole town would be clamoring to get in.

"I'd be *so* grateful if you guys would bring him in sometime. And of course," she added hastily, "you'd both be welcome too. My treat, everything included—meals, drinks, treatments. Stay as long as you like."

I glanced over at Gilbert, who, to my unbounded horror, seemed actually to be considering it. He had the torn, troubled look of a child who knows he's not supposed to enter strange cars, yet can't help noting that the cookie has icing.

"So we could stay like a week?" he asked.

"Two weeks!"

"Gilbert!" I barked, leaping to my feet. There are moments that call for tactful diplomacy and others that demand swift and decisive action, however impolite. This was unquestionably one of the latter.

"S'cuse us!" I said to Moira, seizing Gilbert by the elbow. "We'll just be a minute!" I yanked him out of the office and dragged him down the hall to his bedroom.

"Have you gone insane?" I hissed, shoving him onto the bed.

"Ow! What's your problem? It's not like I said yes."

"But you were thinking of it!"

"What if I was? The place sounds fantastic. And it hardly seems all that big a favor."

"Gilbert!" I wailed. "You dolt! You simpleton! You self-destructive half-wit! What Moira asks for and what she wants are never the same thing and you of all people should know that! Just think, would you, about everything that despicable bitch has put us through! Then think about where we are now, what we're on the verge of! Success! Happiness! Is this really the moment you want to invite Moira fucking Finch back into our lives? And not just ours but Stephen's? *Do you really want to do that?"*

Gilbert clearly saw the folly of his impulse. He stared, chastened, at the carpet and concurred that further association with Moira was unlikely to redound to our benefit.

"Sorry," he murmured.

"Don't blame yourself."

"I don't. It's *her.* She's like some fucking hypnotist!"

"Tell me."

"The gall!" he said, growing indignant now. "What kind of saps does she think we are that we'd actually do her a favor? Or fall for that syrupy new age crap!"

"Okay, then," I said, relieved that his moment of weakness had passed. "Let's tell her we'll think about it, then let the whole thing drop."

"Fuck that! I'm going to tell her just what I think of her, then give the scheming harpy the boot."

Though I questioned the wisdom of angering Moira, I knew from the fire in his eyes that there'd be no dissuading him. A part of me relished the thought of seeing the evening's absurd charade of good-fellowship blown to bits by a refreshing gust of truth. I followed Gilbert as he strode resolutely down the hall and barged through the office door.

"Moira—!" he bellowed, then stopped, seeing that he was about to excoriate an empty couch. Gazing to his left, he saw that Moira was now sitting in an unsettlingly proprietary way at our desk, reading something that lay flat upon it. On hearing Gilbert, she glanced up, and though she could hardly have failed to register his bellicose scowl, all she offered in return was a cool, almost pitying smile. The cause for this smile became devastatingly clear when she tilted her reading matter up so its title was visible to us. It read:

IMBROGLIO
a screenplay by
Gilbert Selwyn
Philip Cavanaugh
&
Claire Simmons

"Sorry," said Moira in her penitent little girl voice. "I peeked at your spec script."

Then she leaned back in my chair, making herself comfortable.

"Tell me, boys—is it just me, or are some of these lines *awfully* familiar?"

Thirteen

★

I N THE BITTER DAYS THAT FOLLOWED THIS FIASCO, Gilbert and I held frequent and rancorous debates over which of us was more responsible for our sudden and regrettable enslavement. I blamed Gilbert, as he'd invited the little virus home in the first place, while he contended with equal vehemence that it was my fault for dragging him out of our office, giving her the chance to pilfer our desk. But if we could not agree who was to blame, one fact remained unhappily beyond dispute: our once independent little firm was now a wholly owned subsidiary of MoiraCorp, and orders from upstairs could not be ignored without peril.

Moira did not gloat over her victory. She did not even acknowledge it, maintaining instead the same false bonhomie she'd affected before her coup. Her manner was like that of some South American despot politely requesting a favor of two subordinates who need no reminding that plan B involves cattle prods.

"God," she exclaimed mirthfully, "you guys are too much! Don't get me wrong—I think it was clever. A little risky, sure, but talk about ballsy! Believe me, no one knows better than I do how *creative* you have to be to get a career going in this town. But, still . . . *Casablanca?* You're telling me *none* of those guys has ever seen it?"

Gilbert, speaking in the sepulchral tone of the vanquished, explained that only Bobby had actually read our "spec" and that the Malenfants had hired us on his recommendation. Moira, glancing at the title page, asked how we'd managed to persuade a Girl Scout like Claire to sign on for so dodgy a scheme. I leaped to Claire's defense, detailing the twisty chain of events that had brought her reluctantly on board.

"Well, I'm just glad it worked out for you! I mean, what's the difference *how* you get a job so long as you do it well? And stop looking so *nervous.* What do you think I'm going to do? Squeal on you? Send Bobby a poison pen letter and a DVD of *Casablanca?* We're *friends,* for Pete's sake! Sure we've had our bumpy patches but we're still *there* for each other . . . Right?"

We nodded listlessly, hoisting the flag of surrender.

Moira yawned daintily, checked her Cartier watch, and rose.

"*So* glad I bumped into you boys! Here," she said, handing Gilbert a card. "Call me and let me know when you'd like to bring Stephen in. And thanks for showing me your house. I love it. So *manageable.*"

WE DID NOT, of course, breathe a word of this to Claire, whose feelings for Moira were slightly less cordial than those Van Helsing held for Dracula. Were she to learn we were utterly at the old she-thing's mercy, our most piteous pleas would not dissuade her from quitting and decamping instantly to New York.

As for Gilbert's and my view of life under our dark lord, our initial anguish gradually gave way to a more manageable level of dread. This was thanks largely to denial and frequent martinis but also to the comparatively innocuous nature of Moira's demands. We doubted if more typical blackmail victims, bankrupt wretches bled dry by their tormentors, would extend much sympathy to two lads ruthlessly compelled to endure a free day of beauty with a movie star. True, the thought of future, more onerous demands was an unsettling one, but wasn't it possible that all Moira wanted or would want from us was our help in promoting her business?

The more troubling question was, Could we deliver?

Fortunately for us, Stephen had inherited not only his mother's full lips and dramatic virtuosity but a soupçon of her avarice as well. It was lucky too that he'd once made a picture with the late Albert and had dined twice at his Bel-Air manse. His curiosity to see what his widow had made of the place, combined with his inborn fondness for high-end freebies, were enough to incline him to accept Moira's offer.

"You say she's a good friend of yours?"

"Oh, yes," I fibbed. "Total sweetie! And talk about taste. She's outdone herself with this place."

"Okay, you've intrigued me. I'll give it a try."

We arranged a date and time and I gave him the address, promising that Gilbert and I would be on hand to offer a more formal introduction to our dear pal Moira.

"Well done!" applauded Gilbert after I'd hung up. "Why the long face?"

I replied that I didn't like lying to Stephen and felt it especially heinous to have portrayed Moira as a sweet harmless hotelier.

"What were you supposed to say? 'Great spa, but watch your back, she's a blackmailing bitch'?"

"I just feel bad, okay? It's like we've lured him into her lair."

"It's not a lair, it's a spa—and a damned nice one. She'll give him a seaweed wrap, drop his name a gazillion times, and bingo, we're off the hook."

"What if we're not? What if she wants something else from us?"

"You worry too much! Olive or twist?"

I WORRIED, IN FACT, a damned sight less than I should have, as my schedule left me little time for fretting. Not only were my hands full with the screenplay and memoir but I'd also committed myself to the ghastly chore of punching up *Amelia Flies Again!*

I put off reading it as long as I could, but Lily's persistent queries finally extracted a promise to read it over the weekend. Come Saturday

I rose late to find Gilbert perusing it on the sofa. I knew the script was a drama, so his nonstop giggles were not an encouraging sign. I poured myself coffee, commandeered the script, and padded out to the patio. Ninety minutes later I closed it and sat staring into the hills with a dull headache and a newfound respect for the subtle artistry of Prudence Gamache.

Though I was forewarned that the story centered on the wartime heroics of an improbably resurrected Amelia Earhart, nothing prepared me for the insane plotting, the unspeakably florid dialogue, or the staggering liberties taken with recorded history. Perhaps you'll get the general flavor if I tell you that the final scene has Amelia, heretofore amnesiac, suddenly remembering who she is as she lies fatally wounded in the arms of her adoring copilot. The scene takes place in Berchtesgaden and the bullet has come from a Luger wielded by Eva Braun. She is seeking revenge, you see, because Amelia has just assassinated Adolf Hitler (who, as rendered by Lily, displays a baffling mastery of American slang).

Despite the guilt that had prompted me to sign on, I saw no reason to labor unduly on improving it. There was not even the slightest chance that a studio would again star Lily in a picture, least of all this one. And even if I'd wanted to give it the massive rewrite it would need to be a remotely viable project, where would I have found the time? No, a quick and dirty job would have to suffice. I left the absurd plot intact, weeded out the more glaring anachronisms, and fixed the dialogue, every purple line of which howled for revision. (When, I wondered, had she grown so fond of the word "alack"?)

That weekend I rewrote the first thirty pages. Lily was ecstatic with the changes.

"It just crackles, Glen! I love how the dialogue sounds more like the way people actually talk. I see now what a mistake it was trying to make it too poetical. I mean, when you think about it, how poetic would a Portuguese fisherman be?"

So grateful was Lily for my slapdash effort that she insisted on cooking me her famous garlic roast chicken for dinner. Too guilty to refuse, I returned that evening and found to my surprise that Lily and Monty weren't alone.

Seated between them on the sofa was a short plump man in his six-ties. He had a blond pageboy hairdo with long bangs over a wide chubby-cheeked face liberally speckled with gin blossoms, the com-bined effect suggesting a dissipated cherub. His white puffy-sleeved shirt, purchased in slenderer days, clung unbecomingly to his sub-stantial belly and man boobs, and his pants were bright orange clam diggers. Beholding him, I found it difficult not to conclude that Oscar Hammerstein had been wrong—there *was* something like a dame.

"Ah, Glen!" said Monty, rising ebulliently. "So glad you could join us. I'd like you to meet my very dear old friend Rex Bajour."

Rex, whose feet did not touch the floor, hopped off the couch and waddled toward me.

"Pleased to meet you, Glen," he said, giving my hand a languid shake. He had a slight southern accent, and his manner, I noted with dismay, was not merely flirtatious but confidently so.

"Uh, nice to meet you too, Rex."

"How flustered you look," observed Lily. "Make him a cocktail, Monty. We're having sidecars!"

"Oh, he's fine," drawled Rex. "He's just looking at me that way 'cause he recognizes me from my show."

"Show?"

"Rex," said Lily proudly, "is a very big TV star. His program's been on for years and years."

"Really?" I said, trying not to sound as baffled as I was. "What show is that?"

"Well!" he riposted, cocking a hand sassily on his hip. "It's not *Guiding Light!*" He then threw back his head and guffawed as though this had been an actual witticism. This was my first but by no means last glimpse of Rex's uncanny ability to convulse himself with "quips" that would not draw a polite smile from a drunken hyena.

I shot Monty a helpless look and he explained that Rex was the producer and star of *Rex Bajour's Hollywood Lowdown,* a talk show that had been airing on public access cable in LA for more than thirty years. I apologized for not having seen it, saying I hadn't been in town long.

"Oh, you *must* watch it, Glen," said Lily. "Rex is a Hollywood legend."

"I've interviewed *everyone*, sweetie."

"All the biggest stars!" she said, adding without irony that she herself had appeared many times.

Even now, mere minutes into my acquaintance with Rex, I suspected strongly that his show would not prove to be superior television, a suspicion borne out by my subsequent viewings.

For the fortunate majority of you who've never seen it, *Rex Bajour's Hollywood Lowdown* is a daily interview show, the production values of which are shockingly threadbare even by the standards of public access television. His guests are "celebrities" whose fame is either long vanished or not yet achieved, though few in the latter group show much promise of joining the former. His interview style seesaws between fey gushing and personal anecdotes so turgid and meandering that his guests don't get a word in. Though nowhere near the "cult phenomenon" Rex claims it to be, the show does have a certain following among connoisseurs of kitsch and indiscriminately nostalgic film buffs who enjoy phoning their friends each weeknight at twelve-thirty to scream, "Guess who's still alive!"

"So," I asked Monty as we sat down to our salads, "how do you and Rex know each other? Did you meet doing his show?"

"God forbid," said Monty. "I may be widely viewed as a queeny old has-been, but I refuse to render it official by appearing on *Rex*."

"Bitch."

"We go back much further than that. We were child stars together."

"So you were an actor?" I asked Rex, who seemed wounded by the question.

"Do you know *nothing* about me?"

"Hard to say which of us was worse," mused Monty. "In terms of sheer volume I, being, let's face it, the prettier one, racked up twice as

many stinkers. On the other hand Rex, when given a chance, could deliver a performance so bad the projectionists would threaten to strike."

I asked Rex why he'd switched from acting to interviewing. On
hearing this query, Monty winced and topped off his wine, for he knew
I'd provided Rex a perfect segue into his favorite topic—the rampant
homophobia of the film industry and how it had robbed him of the
stardom he'd indisputably deserved.

"I see all these actors today who are your age who say, 'What's the
big deal? I'm gay, I'm out, and I work all the time.' I want to *scream* at
them because they have no idea what it was like in my day."

"Well, I think most people my age have *some* idea how—"

"*No* idea!" he snapped. "They weren't *there*. Back then if you were
gay you hid it. And if you were, like me, someone too honest, with too
much *integrity* to pretend to be who you weren't, well, forget it, baby.
It was *over*. And of course the casting directors never had the guts to
say, 'Oh, Rex, I'm still in the closet and your courage frightens me.'
And they'd never say I was 'too gay' either. No, they had their little
code words. I was the 'wrong type' or 'too fat' or 'off pitch.' Though
one director actually said to me, 'God, Rex, you're such a pansy! Can't
you hide it?' "

"Well," I asked unwisely, "could you?"

"Could I what? *Hide* it?"

"Just when you were acting? If the part demanded it?"

"Why should I *hide* it? It's who I *am!* Would you tell Glenn Close
to stop being such a woman?"

"Well, if she were playing a man—"

"*I refuse to pass!*"

There seemed no point in arguing with a man too dementedly self-
righteous to concede that acting was pretty much about "passing" and
that a gay man cast as Stanley Kowalski should keep the flouncing to a
minimum. I tried to change the subject but Rex refused, decrying
"self-loathing" young queers like me who'd sooner side with their
straight oppressors than defend their wronged brethren. Lily and
Monty, dismayed by the turn things had taken, began discussing our
progress on her memoir. This only prompted Rex to pillory "that

closet case Miss Stephen" and urge Lily to expose him as a hypocrite who'd taken the coward's route to success.

On hearing my beloved so maligned, I could no longer contain myself. I asserted sharply that I had no need to loathe myself, as Rex was handling that chore quite ably. And had it, by the way, occurred to him that "wrong type," while possibly a discreet euphemism for "too gay," might just as politely stand in for "can't act to save his fucking life"?

"Well said!" boomed Monty, slapping the table. "And shame on you, Rex, for haranguing poor Glen that way. He's been an angel to us and I won't have him abused at our table. Now change the damn subject or as God is my witness I won't open the second bottle."

This was not a threat Rex took lightly. He calmed himself and spent the rest of the night spouting well-rehearsed anecdotes and cracking himself up. Whenever one of his zingers struck him as especially hilarious, he'd extract a small voice recorder from his pocket and repeat it to make sure it was not lost to posterity.

"For tomorrow's show: 'Nicolette Sheridan's a real girl-next-door type—if you live next door to a *whorehouse!*'"

After dessert I beat an understandably hasty retreat. Monty walked me to my car, offering another apology plus an assessment of his old friend that would prove fatally inaccurate.

"Don't mind old Rex. A bit of a crank, I know. But quite harmless."

THE NEXT MORNING I canceled the day's writing session with Claire, pleading a dental emergency. That afternoon Gilbert and I drove in jittery silence to Les Étoiles. Never having seen the place when I'd extolled its wonders to Stephen, I feared I might find I'd oversold it. But the minute we passed through its stately gates, I saw that my fears were groundless and that Les Étoiles was emphatically not, having grounds as far as the eye could see. Our tires crunched over white gravel as we followed a long gracefully curving drive that ended in a circle around a grand fountain with smiling cherubs peeing in perpetuity.

The house seemed to have been built by some prosperous southerner who'd felt that, while Tara had been a nice little starter home, it was time to open the wallet and get serious. On pulling up we saw that Stephen and Gina had arrived just ahead of us. As our car crunched to a stop, Moira, chastely clad in a peach silk suit, her cloven hooves concealed in matching Manolos, emerged from the house, followed by a waiter bearing champagne.

"Welcome to Les Étoiles!"

I could tell from her patrician air and suddenly mid-Atlantic diction that Stephen and Gina were in for quite a performance. She embraced Gilbert and me affectionately, then bestowed courtly handshakes on the stars.

"I can't thank you enough for visiting my little labor of love! Champagne anyone? I know it's early, but don't forget, you're here to be pampered!"

We accepted the proffered Cristal and Moira led us inside, Stephen regaling her with fond recollections of Albert, who'd produced *Chamber Music* fifteen years ago and who even then had been valiantly battling emphysema.

We entered the spa's foyer, which was palatial yet warm, with two majestic staircases that curved gracefully up to join at a second-floor landing. To the left was a reception desk and a hall leading to guest rooms, to the right a richly paneled lounge with an inviting mahogany bar. Straight ahead through a wide archway was a large sumptuously furnished salon that for sheer acreage dwarfed even Diana's digs. Soaring French windows at the far end gave onto a broad elegant terrace with tables overlooking the arcadian grounds.

It was, as one of Lily's film-noir dames would have remarked, one sweet little setup. As Moira led us into the salon, she tenderly recalled how dear Albert had invited her to lunch here for their very first date. I had no doubt that the minute she'd left she'd choppered straight to the bridal shop, phoning the tobacconist en route to order the groom some nice unfiltered Gitanes.

As it was quite warmish for December, Moira led us out to the terrace, seating us two tables away from where a producer famed for his tantrums sat serenely taking tea with his mistress. We sipped our champagne and admired the charming, ivy-covered guest cottages while Moira, sounding more and more like Dame Diana Rigg, expounded on her spiritual commitment to high-end hospitality.

"When I designed Les Étoiles I thought mainly about my many friends who are, like you, brilliant and accomplished, but forced to live every day with the stress and scrutiny such careers bring. I asked myself, 'What can I provide these people that other spas can't?' And the answer was simple—*sanctuary*. A place of beauty where they can escape every outside pressure. A place that pampers their bodies straight to nirvana, even as it nourishes their souls. A place of complete privacy where no cameras are permitted—even the guests are forbidden to bring them. A place where those two ravenous beasts, the Public and the Media, aren't allowed to set foot."

She continued in this vein, wrapping ruthless exclusivity in pretty new age ribbons, and Gina was eating it up, oh-yessing and how-true-ing her head off. Moira then gave us brochures detailing the broad array of treatments available. Stephen and Gina opted for simple shiatsu followed by facials and I said that sounded fine by me. Gilbert rather showily chose two of the more esoteric options and I was pleased when Moira corrected his pronunciation. Then she led us back into the salon, where frosted glass doors on one end led to the treatment center.

Since my income pre-Hollywood was such that my concept of "luxury" did not much extend beyond dental care and wines requiring recourse to a corkscrew, I'd never before experienced either of my treatments. I found them both so agreeably soothing that even my anxieties about Moira began to subside as I surrendered to pure sybaritic serenity. After my sessions I toddled off to the bar. Gina and Gilbert were already there, looking thoroughly blissed-out, and soon Moira and Stephen joined us. Stephen said he couldn't recall a more relaxing day, and if Moira's purpose in extending such largesse had been to win a new customer, she could consider her goal achieved. Moira took her bows modestly, telling us to come back whenever we liked as we were now part of the Les Étoiles family.

Driving home I allowed myself not only to hope but to believe that the danger had passed, that Moira, having gotten what she wanted, would plague us no further. If this view seems, in hindsight, lethally naive, the weeks that followed offered little to contradict it. Stephen and Gina became regular visitors to the spa, and as each day passed with no additional demands from Moira, my outlook steadily brightened.

Claire's spirits rose too as we grew closer to completing the script, and they positively soared when our agent informed us that a producer wished to option *Mrs. McManus*. This heartening glimpse of a post-Greta future helped us both to unclench a bit. We started getting out more, accepting Gilbert's invitations to join him at the parties thrown by his many new friends, and we soon found ourselves immersed in the frenetic social whirl of the industry's younger set.

Though I did not "go Hollywood" half so shamelessly as Gilbert, I'll admit that I began to display a tendency toward, not arrogance quite, but that breezy self-satisfaction one glimpses in many a young Hollywood turk who finds his star on the rise and cannot at present conceive of its descent.

How pleasant it was to meet new people and ask them what they did. How simple to feign interest while waiting for them to pose the same question to me. How lovely to tell them. I took particularly nasty pleasure in meeting other writers who were even more puffed up than me but on far flimsier grounds. I'd draw them out, letting them prattle about their meager toeholds on fame before casually letting drop that I was a writer as well.

"Right now? Oh, I'm writing a picture for Stephen Donato. His mom's in it too. So this Lifetime Original of yours—do you really think you can get Delta Burke?"

Not even my gym acquaintances were spared the details of my glory. True, it was harder to coax boys bench-pressing two hundred pounds into career chat, but I was nothing if not persistent and it was not long before the whole gym knew what air I breathed.

One day as I was there, attempting to coax one more rep from my biceps—which, had they been masochists, would have been screaming the safety word—a voice behind me exclaimed, "Oh my God, it's you!" Turning, I saw a tall, vaguely familiar fellow in shorts and a tank top. He had a lithe gymnast's physique and carrot-colored hair. His face was densely freckled and, if not quite handsome, open and instantly likable.

"Sorry, have we met?"

"I served you drinks! At Vici! You were with Stephen Donato! Your heads were really close together!"

"Oh, right," I said, remembering now the little hearts that had danced around the bartender's eyes each time he'd looked our way.

He said his name was Billy Grimes and asked if he could buy me a coffee next door. I agreed and for the next twenty minutes he pelted me with questions about Stephen, no detail of whose life, however mundane, failed to inspire his rapt fascination. He begged, of course, to know if Stephen was gay. I replied, of course, that I didn't know but could not resist doing so in a tone so coy as to practically scream that I did know and from personal experience. My evasive replies to his cajoling follow-ups only heightened this impression, and a half-dozen "Oh, c'mons!" later I finally changed the subject.

"So that was your dad who came over to hassle us?"

"Don't bring it up!" groaned Billy. "I was so embarrassed!"

"He must love it that you're such a fan."

"You think I'd *tell* him? I don't even *mention* Stephen around my dad."

I asked if he was out to his parents. He blushed and said he was not. He'd been on the verge some months ago but then Dad had decided to run for governor and this had sapped him of his nerve. I offered my sympathy, ceding that there were easier things to be than the gay offspring of an archconservative politico. We parted with a friendly hug and he beseeched me to come back to Vici, promising to comp me as many drinks as he dared. I said I would and soon Gilbert, Claire, and I took to going there Fridays after work to rinse off the sauerkraut with nice cold martinis.

I grew fond of the place. I liked the odd clientele and the memories it stirred of Stephen and the promise that had smoldered in his eyes in our little love booth. I also liked Billy's charming habit of introducing me to his regulars, never once, bless him, failing to mention what I was up to just lately.

"Sweet boy, Billy," remarked Claire. "Saves you *so* much trouble."

THE PROMISE THAT HAD simmered in Stephen's gaze had, of course, been firmly predicated on my persuading Lily not to tell the world of his teenage discovery that strong, hairy thighs make swell earmuffs. At first I couldn't think of any reason to suggest this that didn't risk exposing me as a double agent. I finally decided to appeal to her vanity by arguing that the Stephen revelations might prove so explosive as to monopolize public discourse about the book, siphoning the spotlight from Lily to her already overhyped nephew. Did she really want to risk being upstaged in her own memoir?

Alas, in attempting to exploit Lily's vanity I'd underestimated its staggering magnitude. To Lily, the idea that any hullabaloo about Stephen might eclipse interest in herself was absurd, resting as it did on the altogether spurious premise that Stephen was more interesting than she was.

"He's only in a few chapters! The rest of the book's all me and far more compelling. Let's not forget I reveal some pretty juicy secrets! That affair I had with the boy who played my student on *Sorry, Miss Murgatroyd!?* We'd best brace ourselves for *that* tempest! No, I don't think there's any danger of people forgetting who the real star of the book is. By the way, I *adored* the new scenes for *Amelia*. At this rate we'll be ready to shop it in time to take advantage of all the heat I'll be getting."

"Heat?" I asked, mystified.

"When my picture opens—*Guess What, I'm Not Dead.* I met Shawna, our wardrobe girl, at the Liquor Locker yesterday. She'd seen a rough cut and raved about my performance, especially my death scene. 'Awesome,' she called it! Mark my words, Glen, this picture will open a lot of doors for me! So who should we send it to first? Spielberg or Scott Rudin?"

"IS SHE OUT OF her fucking mind?" howled Stephen when I reported this exchange to him.

"I'm sorry. I really thought that argument might work."

"Hey, it was only your first try. Just keep at it, wear her down. I'm counting on you, Phil."

"I know. And I won't let you down, Stephen."

"I know you won't," he said, his voice a caress. "Smooth guy like you can find a way to get anything he wants."

"Anything?" I asked, weak-kneed.

"Anything," he replied, his tone so lubricious as to pass beyond the realm of innuendo into that of contract law.

IT WAS MID-DECEMBER by this point, the holidays fast approaching. Stephen got his Christmas gift a week early when the Hollywood Foreign Press, that bafflingly respected assemblage, bestowed a Golden Globe nomination on him for his performance in *Lothario*. I longed to congratulate him in person but he and Gina had flown off to spend the holidays in Aspen. I knew I would not see him again until the New Year, by which time I hoped to have bent Lily to his will.

I've always been a bit of a sap for Christmas and looked forward each year to celebrating the season with my cheery if perennially cash-strapped circle of friends. I never minded, in fact rather sentimentalized, our meager traditions—the cheerfully tacky decorations, the thrift-store presents, the disgracefully affordable "champagnes." Though I still look back on those customs with a misty eye, I can tell you flat out that nothing spells "holiday cheer" like a whopping paycheck and a spendthrift mogul for a host. The holidays passed in a pleasant blur of pricey gifts and Dom Pérignon and my only care in that festive week was that my hard-won progress at the gym would be undone by Maddie and Max's overabundant buffets.

On the afternoon of their hot-ticket New Year's Eve party, Claire arrived late for our writing session. It was clear from her elegant new coiffure that she'd come straight from the salon and clearer still that she had fresh gossip to share. Her eyes glinted and her smile was the twisty one she only wears when savoring the taste of a secret.

"Gosh, ma'am," I said, "you want some fries with that canary?"

"Sit down, boys. You're going to love this! I was just at Umberto getting a new do—"

"And quite a fetching one."

"Yes," concurred Gilbert. *"Très quelque chose."*

"I thought so. Anyway, I'm sitting bored to tears under the dryer when I pick up this Beverly Hills newspaper—just some society rag for the plucked and privileged set. But I'm leafing through it and just guess, me laddies, whose picture jumps out at me?"

"Stephen's?" I said, having him much in my thoughts.

"Nooooooo," she teased. "Not Stephen . . ."

"Who?" pleaded Gilbert, who can dish out the suspense when delivering gossip but can't bear it when anyone else does.

Claire paused for effect, then adopting an arch, clipped Bette-Davis-when-crossed voice, said, "Little. Miss. *Moira. Finch!!"*

"No!" I said, my stomach lurching like an old washing machine.

"Yes! She's *living* here!"

"Moira?" gasped Gilbert.

"In LA?" I exclaimed, all but slapping my cheeks in an effort to feign surprise.

"Yes! And get this—she's just opened some posh new spa!"

"Wow!" marveled Gilbert. "Who'd have thought it?!"

"Not me!"

"There was a whole article about it," said Claire, breathlessly summarizing the basics regarding Moira's tragically brief marriage, her failed attempt to launch a film career, and her subsequent decision (shaming in Claire's eyes) to become a full-time star-pamperer.

"So," she concluded with a diabolical smirk, "when shall we go?"

"Go?" I repeated, my tummy now well into the spin cycle. "Go where?!"

"To her spa of course."

"Why would we do that!" yelped Gilbert.

"Well I grant you it's a bit small, but isn't there a part of you that would love to pop by and let the little minx know how well we're doing?"

"No!" I replied.

"No part at all!"

"And you're right—it *is* small."

"Childish," agreed Gilbert.

"Prancing in there just to gloat!"

"I've never seen this side of you, Claire. I can't say I like it."

"Success," I declared loftily, "is its own reward."

"*Excuse* me?" said Claire, no doubt recalling the many parties we'd attended of late wearing our "Ask-me-what-I-do" buttons.

"Anyway," I said, switching tactics, "it's not as if she'll give you any satisfaction. You'll say, 'Nyah, nyah, we have a cool job' and she'll say, 'Nyah, nyah, I have a cool spa.'"

"A total wash!"

"And you're out the cost of a facial."

"If you even trust her to give you one."

"Good point!"

"Probably use napalm."

"Yeesh!" said Claire. "All right! It was just a thought."

It was not often Claire found herself peering up at the high ground to see us waving down at her, and the experience was clearly disorienting to her. She asserted primly that if we could rise above the impulse to taunt an old foe with new fame she could certainly do so as well. Gilbert and I exchanged a furtive glance of relief and the workday commenced.

We'd just begun the screenplay's third act and hoped to be finished by the time Stephen returned home for the Globes in two weeks. Our hopes of managing this were given a boost by Lily, who announced she'd be taking the second week off to embark on a press tour for *Guess What, I'm Not Dead*. This struck me as odd since the film didn't open till February and, given Lily's less than scorching celebrity, it was hard to imagine Miramax shelling out for premiere tickets, let alone a junket. I suspected that Monty, in his infinite benevolence, had engaged a publicist and was discreetly footing the bill.

Claire was delighted when I suggested we start working mornings as well, sans Gilbert. This greatly enhanced our productivity and we finished a day ahead of schedule at around noon. Gilbert stirred himself an hour later and feigned pique at finding there was nothing left for him to do. But when he read the final pages he offered his customary benediction:

"Perfect. Just what I was going to suggest."

It may seem odd to you, given our scorn for the source material, but we were actually quite proud of our adaptation. We considered the structure solid and the pacing brisk, and were especially pleased with the dialogue, not a line of which was borrowed from Ms. Gamache. True, the plot retained a certain core gooeyness we could not have expunged without exceeding our mandate. But we knew the key roles would be played by Stephen and Diana, and if anyone could spin goo into gold they could.

Stephen returned the next day. We knew he wouldn't read it that weekend as the Globes would be monopolizing his attention. We held a little viewing party and invited a few friends, including Billy, who screamed the place down when Stephen won. We were pretty delighted ourselves. It not only cemented his shoo-in status for an Oscar nod nine days hence but also ensured that he'd be sitting down to read our script in that sunny, all's-right-with-the-world mood an actor only feels when he's just basked in the spotlight while crushing four fellow thespians' dreams. This expectation was borne out on Tuesday when he called to offer his verdict.

"*Incredible* job, guys," he said warmly. "Really, really great."

For the next five minutes he showered us in superlatives, citing favorite lines and scenes he couldn't wait to play. While Gilbert and I writhed joyfully on the couch like dogs having their tummies rubbed, Claire wore the more tentative smile of a girl waiting for the other shoe to drop. When it did, it landed with the softness of a slipper.

"There are a few places where things could be a little sharper. I see some trims too. But we're talking minor stuff. By and large it's fantastic and I want to give you guys a reward for doing such a great job."

"A reward?" said Gilbert, with unseemly eagerness.

"Here's the deal. Gina and I are going nuts with all this craziness lately—"

"You mean with the Globes and Oscars and all?" I asked.

"Right. Fucking relentless. So we decided to get the hell away. Just Friday through Monday. And we'd like you guys to come too. We can relax, have some laughs, and find a few hours to talk about the next draft. Sound good?"

"Sounds great!" I said, my mind percolating with images of Stephen and me lying side by side on a tropical beach, his eyes boring into mine with a look that says "Ever do it under a waterfall?"

Gilbert boisterously echoed my enthusiasm and even Claire seemed giddy at the prospect of flying off to some jet-setter's paradise with movie stars for hosts.

"So," asked Gilbert, "where are we going? Cabos? Your place in Hawaii?"

"No. We're not actually leaving town. We're just checking into Les Étoiles for a few days. Friday at four, okay?"

Fourteen

★

"CALM DOWN!" SAID MOIRA, with a maddeningly carefree laugh. "What a pair of sissies!"

"It's important!" barked Gilbert into the phone.

"Claire would *kill* us!" I chimed in from the kitchen extension.

"Gawd! I have never understood why you two let that sanctimonious cow intimidate you. But, if you don't want her to know you've been here, fine, I won't mention it."

"Or any of it!"

"Especially *Casablanca!!*"

Moira's laugh was even more abrasively merry.

"So she doesn't know I tumbled to that?"

"No, and if she found out she'd quit on us!" I said.

"So promise you won't say anything!"

"Okaaay! Gawd! I won't squeal on you to Mommy."

As we hung up it struck me that Stephen or Gina might just as easily mention our prior visit. How could we ask them not to without confessing our reason for doing so? Gilbert, displaying once more his flair for impromptu deceit, suggested we say that we felt guilty for not having invited Claire to join us and feared she'd be hurt if she found out.

This seemed a serviceable ruse and I left a message on Stephen's voice mail begging his and Gina's discretion.

THREE DAYS LATER AS we barreled down Sunset toward Bel-Air, I struggled to maintain a calm, chatty demeanor even as my emotions teetered wildly between girlish exhilaration and icy dread.

The exhilaration stemmed from the prospect of spending three nights under the same luxurious roof as Stephen. How I wished Lily hadn't left for her damned press junket! Had she stayed I might have found some means to sway her so that I could now declare my victory to Stephen and claim my rapturous reward. But though I'd not yet earned the full tumescent measure of his gratitude, I had hopes nonetheless of wangling some small down payment.

These thrilling thoughts of stolen kisses kept getting elbowed roughly aside by more worrisome ones concerning Claire and her old nemesis. What possible good could come of their meeting, especially when Claire had no idea what awful power Moira wielded over us? We'd done what we could to ensure her continued ignorance, but three days was a long time and I was much troubled by the smile Claire wore as she gazed dreamily out her window. It was a cool smile and more than a touch smug and I knew that Moira, on beholding it, would feel a powerful impulse to erase it. I resolved to seek Moira out as soon as we arrived to remind her of her promise and beseech her not to be goaded.

As we pulled up to the spa's imposing facade, a broad-shouldered bellman wearing a Les Étoiles–logo polo shirt hastened to greet us. While another linebacker took charge of our bags, he escorted us into the majesty of the lobby.

I hoped at first that Moira's sudden and daunting prosperity might quell Claire's impulse to swank her. Why attempt one-upmanship against so extravagantly armed a foe? Claire, alas, did not see things this way.

"Wow!" said Gilbert, gaping at a vast floral arrangement crammed with blooms so exotic as to still be awaiting classification. "Nice little place she's got here."

"Yes," I agreed heartily. "Sure puts our digs to shame."

"She married it," sniffed Claire, "and the husband kicked off eight months later. I'm guessing strychnine."

"Well," I said, "however she got it, you have to admit she's done well for herself."

"If you ask me," replied Claire, and there was that damn smile again, "doing well for herself would have meant snagging a place like this, then being able to keep it up without asking the public in for back rubs."

We signed in and followed our smiling escort to the adjoining second-floor rooms Moira had arranged for us. I barely set foot in my own before wheeling round and peering down the hall to make sure Claire had entered hers. The hall was empty so I sprinted back down to the front desk and, finding it momentarily deserted, nipped behind it and through a door marked PRIVATE.

I found myself in a small office with three desks, its cramped untidiness strikingly at odds with the splendor of the lobby. At one of the desks a frowsy woman with a nimbus of blond hair and two raccoons' worth of mascara was on the phone, reciting room rates in an improbably posh accent. I saw that a door behind her was marked M. FINCH and informed her of my need to speak to Moira immediately. She said that Moira had stepped out. Doubting her veracity, I said, "I'll wait," and hustled past her before she could stop me.

It appeared she had not misled me. The cluttered office was unoccupied. There was, however, a door in the rear corner. Conjecturing that this might be a bathroom and that Moira might even now be in there, I approached it and knocked gently. I was much surprised when the door immediately flew open without apparent human assistance. But then, gazing down, I beheld a short curly haired woman. Her physique called to mind a dorm room refrigerator, as did her correspondingly chilly demeanor.

"Who the fuck are you?"

"Sorry! Friend of Moira's."

Her diminutive stature afforded me a clear view of the room, which appeared to house an impressively high-tech security system, a mandatory feature, I supposed, in a spa with such an elite clientele. It was dark and narrow, with banks of video monitors such as one glimpses behind guards' desks in office towers. The irate and armed munchkin scowling up at me was, I presumed, Moira's security chief, and there was no mistaking her views on unescorted guests who dared invade her sanctum.

"Moira's not here."

"So sorry, Kim!" came a voice behind me. Turning, I saw that Raccoon Girl had entered and was eyeing me even less warmly than the wee sheriff was.

"I told you she wasn't in!"

"Sorry," I said, smiling inanely. "Do you know where I might find her?"

"She's showing a guest the grounds," said Blondie. "It's a VIP so please don't interrupt them."

"Wouldn't dream of it," I replied and bolted straight for the grounds. For the next ten minutes I searched the lawn, pool, garden, tennis court, hiking path, gazebo, and duck pond but saw no trace of Moira or her VIP guest. I'd wended my way round to the side of the house when I heard Gilbert cheerfully call out to me.

"Philip! There you are. Come join us!"

He'd called from the bar, which, like the salon, opened onto a terrace with tables. Entering, I saw that he was having a drink with Claire, Stephen, and Gina, who were seated by a crackling fire in a cozy grouping of two sofas and a wing chair. Stephen looked dashing in faded jeans and a navy silk shirt. Gina, by contrast, looked downright sluttish in a pink leather mini and a low-cut peasant blouse. She could not have flaunted her breasts more showily had she encased them in a well-lit vitrine.

"Hey, Phil!" she twanged. "We were just talking about your swell script."

I gave her a big extravagant hug. I did so, of course, not from any real affection but so she wouldn't find it odd when I embraced Stephen with equal ardor. Alas, the delicious tingle I felt as his manly arms encircled me was swiftly replaced by a shiver of dread at the sight I glimpsed over his shoulder. Moira, her eyes wide with counterfeit surprise, stood in the entrance to the bar. Next to her, warily scanning the place for hoi polloi, was her VIP guest, Diana Malenfant.

This was unwelcome on several grounds. First, when you're hoping to seduce an image-conscious megastar at a luxury resort it is impediment enough that both his wife and sundry members of the glamorati will be lurking in inconvenient proximity. Toss Mother in and the odds of furtive nooky decline further still. Even more dismaying was the thought that Claire would now be confronting Moira before I'd had a chance to pull the latter aside and broker a nonaggression pact. Factor in Claire's eagerness to brandish her new success and unawareness that Moira knew about what Robert Ludlum might have dubbed *The Casablanca Deception,* and you had a situation that seethed with the promise of disaster.

"Gilbert!" cried Moira ecstatically. "And Philip too! God, it's been ages! When the reservation said 'Donato plus guests' I had no idea it was you! Massimo!" she called to the barman. "Champagne!"

"Wow, Moy!" said Gilbert, planting a loud smacker on each cheek. "Is this a small world or what?"

"Shame on you, Stephen!" said Moira, wagging a finger at our host. "You never told me these guys were working with you!"

"I didn't know you knew them," said Stephen, flashing me a conspiratorial smile.

"Hello, Moira," cooed Claire, rising from the sofa.

"*Claaaairrre!*" sang Moira. "It is *so* good to see you!"

"The pleasure's entirely mine," replied Claire with dangerous warmth.

"And look at you! So svelte! You must have lost a *ton.* Not," she added to Gina, "that Claire was ever really *fat* but—"

"Diana!" I yelped, heading this off. "Where are my manners? This is our partner, Claire Simmons. You remember she was ill when we first met."

"Of course," said Diana. She was in her Lady Highborn mode and the hand she extended to Claire was so limp and regal as to beg a curtsy. "How lovely to meet you at lahst."

"Well, it's an honor to meet you," said Claire. "I'm a huge admirer of your work."

"Thenk you," said Diana, adding that Claire could consider the admiration mutual, as she'd read our script.

"Well, I'm not surprised the script's so good," said Moira, passing round the champagne. "These guys are *so* talented. Is it a musical then?"

"Not exactly," laughed Stephen.

Moira said she'd only asked because Claire was best known to her as a composer. "So you've given up on the music then?" She asked this with just the faintest hint of relief, adroitly suggesting that Claire, given the limitations of her gift, had been wise to do so.

"No, just branching out," replied Claire, who proceeded to lavish compliments on the spa. I wondered where she was going but not for long.

"How on earth did you find it, dear?"

"It was my husband's."

"You've remarried?" exclaimed Claire, all innocence. "Congratulations! When do we meet him?"

"I'm afraid he's passed away."

"Oh," said Claire, stricken. "I *am* sorry."

"He was Albert Schimmel, wasn't he?" queried Diana.

"Yes," said Moira wistfully. "I miss him every day."

"*The* Albert Schimmel?" asked Claire. "Didn't he produce all those wonderful films back in the forties and fifties?"

"Classics," said Moira proudly. She knew though that Claire's intent had not been to praise Albert's oeuvre but to emphasize his advanced years. This was lost on no one, not even Gina, who, with characteristic tact, said, "Wow. He must have been like way older than you."

"But so young at heart."

"Now that I think of it," said Claire, "I recall reading his obituary. It said he'd been battling lung disease for years. How long were you married?"

"Eight months."

Moira said this with just the right note of stoic regret, but her eyes were now boring lethally into Claire's.

"How *awful* for you," gasped Claire, "to have lost him so soon. But at least you have this gorgeous house to remember him by."

"Thank you, Claire. It is a comfort."

Gilbert and I exchanged a glance. I could see from his eyes that we shared the same anxiety, an ominous sense that, though things had not yet gone irrevocably downhill, we'd clearly boarded the toboggan.

Stephen asked Moira why she'd decided to turn the house into a spa. Moira, mercifully removing her gimlet gaze from Claire, said it was partly because she'd felt it a shame not to share its beauty with others, but mainly because she'd craved some stimulating project to ease the loneliness of widowhood.

"I know just how you felt," said Diana. "When Stephen's father died I completely plunged myself into work!"

Diana, to my relief, soon monopolized the conversation with tales of her fantastically productive widowhood. I prayed that Claire, having exposed Moira as a gold-digging hearse-chaser, would consider the skirmish won and withdraw from the field. Alas, she did not but instead found in Diana's stories an ideal springboard to mount a fresh, far riskier attack.

"Now correct me if I'm wrong, love," she said to Moira, "but weren't you also dabbling in films for a while?"

"Who told you that, dearest?"

"Your chum Vulpina. Back in New York. She said it was why you came out here."

"Well," allowed Moira, "I did sort of test the waters."

Stephen said, "When we met you mentioned some projects you were developing?"

"Just a few things," she said airily. "Very back burner just now. You know how long things can take."

"Tell me!" sighed Gina. "When I was starting out it took, like, forever to get anything off the ground."

Claire nodded, her face aglow with infuriating sympathy.

"Yes, *terribly* hard," she clucked. "Believe me there's not a day I don't thank God things came together so *quickly* for us. But I know the average person—not that you're remotely average, dear—can hammer away for years and get absolutely nowhere."

"SHUT UP! SHUT UP! PLEASE, *PLEASE* SHUT UP!!" cried the voice in my head. But Claire, oblivious to her peril, forged implacably on.

"And I'm sure things must have been doubly difficult for you, what with nursing your poor ailing husband, then turning your home into a spa. But if movies really are your first love, then I say keep at it, dear. Things are bound to turn around eventually."

Well, that pretty well tore it. Claire had crossed the line separating casual sniping from Extreme Provocation. It was one thing to imply Moira was a mercenary vixen. Moira saw no shame in this and could usually be seen toward the front of the parade on Mercenary Vixen Pride Day. It was another matter entirely to call attention to her thwarted ambitions, then compound the taunt with condescending sympathy. This Moira would not countenance. Glancing apprehensively toward her, I saw that her eyes were again fixed on Claire. Her smile had grown steelier and one could all but hear the low, metallic hum of silos opening.

"How kind of you, Claire," she said, patting the condemned's knee. "Yes, it was *horribly* difficult getting started. It's so hard to find decent scripts—not just commercial fluff but the sort of things that really, you know, *spoke* to me."

"What sort do you mean?" asked Gina.

"Call me Miss Retro," she said with a girlish laugh, "but I just love a good old-fashioned romance. The sort they used to make years ago. Things like *Casablanca*." Her eyes swiveled back to Claire. "You know that one, dear? *Casablanca?* An old favorite of yours, I believe? I swear, I'd do anything—beg, borrow, or *steal*—to make a picture like that today. But there just aren't scripts like that floating around anymore. Or maybe there are and people just don't *know* about them yet. More champagne anyone?"

I have spoken before of the remarkable sangfroid Claire displays at moments that would make lesser women fall to their knees and ululate in despair. But not even Claire could entirely maintain her composure in the wake of so savage and unforeseen an ambush. Her face turned pale and her eyes took on that wide slightly glazed look one sees in the recently guillotined. I thanked God Moira had offered champagne, as the stars' sudden focus on the waiter was all that kept them from noting Claire's devastation.

"More champagne, Claire?" asked Moira.

"No thank you, dear," said Claire, snapping out of it and plucking her head from the basket. "Goodness — I can't think when I've seen a lovelier sunset."

The Malenfants gazed out the window, allowing Claire to turn and face me and Gilbert. I braced myself for the eyebrow-singeing glare we had coming, but the look she gave us wasn't angry. It was wounded and baffled and it pierced me more deeply than the blackest scowl could have.

It was hardly the first time that cowardice had led me to withhold some crucial bit of information from Claire only to have said info spring without warning from the shrubbery and seize her in its slavering jaws. But by failing to warn her about Moira I'd sunk to a whole new level of heinousness. Her stare reflected this. It was a look such as a lady gladiator might give her trusted comrade-in-arms upon discovering, in the heat of battle, that the new bronze shield he'd given her was in fact foil-wrapped milk chocolate.

"How lovely," said Diana, admiring the sunset.

Claire rose and addressed me and Gilbert. "I'd love to see the grounds before it's dark. Perhaps you boys will join me on a little tour?"

"Sorry! Can't!" said Gilbert. "Massage," he explained, then exited the bar, apparently via catapult.

"Philip?" said Claire.

My first impulse was to follow Gilbert's lead by briskly dismounting the couch and diving through the Gilbert-shaped hole he'd left in the wall on departing. I knew though that the reckoning would have to come eventually and that forestalling it would only anger her further. I rose and, bravely forgoing the blindfold and cigarette, said that a tour sounded delightful. We bade farewell to our hosts and left via the terrace.

We strolled for a bit in less than companionable silence, Claire gazing stonily ahead until we came to the little duck pond. Claire, with an assassin's natural craving for privacy, scanned the area to make sure it was witness free. Then, satisfied that it was just us and the ducks, she pivoted sharply and slugged my shoulder with enough force to send me sprawling over a stone bench.

"How COULD you!" she roared. "How on earth could you do this to me?!"

"Ow!" I whined, rubbing my shoulder in a ludicrous attempt to prompt remorse. "That hurt!"

"So will this!" she advised, smartly kicking my left shin.

"OW! Cut it out!"

"This is *unforgivable!* You SWINE! You treacherous BASTARD! You have wronged me before, Philip, but this is beyond the fucking pale! To let me just traipse in here without warning me that Moira knew about the *Casablanca* business—!"

"I'm sorry! I didn't want to upset you! I didn't know Moira was going to go rubbing it in your face. But then you started goading her and—"

"Do not attempt to blame ANY of this on me!" she roared in a voice so blistering that I cringed like a frequently whipped hunchback.

"How did this *happen?* Tell me, please, because I cannot begin to fathom your motives! Why you would tell *anyone* about that damn script, let alone Moira—"

"We didn't tell her! She found out!"

"*How?!* Nobody knew but us!"

I told her we'd run into Moira at a restaurant and that Gilbert, no less eager to flaunt our success than Claire herself had been, had asked her by for a drink. I outlined the night's ruinous events, laying appropriate emphasis on Gilbert's culpability.

"So you see, we had no choice but to deliver Stephen."

"Then you've been here before?"

"Just once. And Stephen loved it! He's practically a regular. So he's happy, Moira's happy. There's nothing to be upset about!"

"Oh, no!" said Claire corrosively. "Everything's *dandy!* We've won a high-profile job through plagiarism, but hey, that's all right 'cause no one knows about it except a *satanic blackmailing bitch!*"

"She's already gotten what she wants!"

"And you think she'll stop there? She's *MOIRA*, you dolt! She'll be beating us to death with this for the rest of our lives!"

"Calm down," I whispered. "There are people on the terrace now."

"God!" she moaned, plopping miserably onto the bench. "I can't believe I've let this happen to me. Any of it!!"

"Shhh!" I said, for we were no longer alone. A masseur clad in a tight Les Étoiles T-shirt had emerged from a cottage some twenty yards away and was advancing toward us en route to the main house. He carried some used towels and a bottle of massage oil. As he drew closer I realized I knew him, though from where I couldn't say. The man, blond and quite sexy in a boyish Abercrombie & Fitch sort of way, recognized me too and smiled in greeting.

"Hey! How you doing?"

"Great," I said. "And you?"

"Same old, same old," he said with a wink and proceeded on his way. As I watched his well-sculpted fanny retreat, it suddenly hit me.

He was Buster.

Monty's hustler.

And he was working at Les Étoiles, performing chores he characterized as the "same old, same old."

"Who was that?" asked Claire.

A while back, you may recall, I spoke of how hard it is to maintain your equanimity while reeling inwardly from the discovery that the screenplay for which you've been taking bows is, in fact, *Casablanca*. That challenge, I now saw, was mere child's play compared to the task of preserving a poker face while digesting the news that the luxury spa to which you've lured your dream man is, in fact, a discreet, high-end male brothel.

"Who was it?" she repeated, suspicious now.

"No one. Guy from the gym."

"You seem upset."

"Of course I'm upset! Moira's got us by the short ones, you're furious at me, I have a cold coming on—"

She seized my wrist and stared at me so intently her eyes seemed, like a lobster's, to protrude on stalks.

"Is there anything, Philip—*anything*—you're not telling me about?"

"You're hurting my arm!"

"Anything?"

"Look, I know you're ticked off, and I don't blame you, but the truth is—oh, damn!" I rejoiced, for sauntering toward us in her debut performance as a Welcome Sight was Gina. She waved cheerily and Claire, seething, waved back.

"Do you guys have a minute?" she asked. "I had this question about my character."

"Actually," I said, "I was just heading back to my room. Tummy trouble. I'm sure Claire can answer better than I could."

It was a low maneuver but one that would not, I reasoned, make Claire any madder at me since this was, at present, impossible. I hastened toward the terrace, determined to find Moira and demand to know what Buster was doing on her payroll and how many of his ilk could be counted among the spa's amenities. I proceeded to the lobby, where the desk clerk (Harlot? Dominatrix?) told me that Moira was in the lounge. I found her sitting at the end of the bar, inspecting page proofs for an elegant new brochure. The Malenfants had left but there were ten or so patrons scattered about, including Sir Hugo Bunting, the much-lauded English actor whose fondness for Shakespeare was subsidized by hammy stints as villains in big effects-laden comic-book movies. His presence at Les Étoiles did little to contradict my theory.

Moira smirked at me as I took the stool next to hers.

"Someone looks cranky. Claire haul you out to the woodshed?"

"What the hell kind of place are you running here?" I hissed.

"What are you talking about?" Her tone was bland but she'd lowered her voice.

"I'm talking about Buster."

"Who's Buster?" she asked. Her bewilderment seemed genuine, though, being Moira, this did not mean that it was.

"He *works* for you. The blond with the muscles."

Her eyes darted to the barkeep, who was serving a newcomer two stools away. Her expression remained cordial even as she angrily muttered, "There's no one working here named Buster."

"Call him what you want but I've met him and I know he's a goddamn hustler. *Ow!*" I added, as she'd just grabbed my hand and dug her nails into my palm so deeply that I could now add stigmata to my woes.

"Keep your voice down. You want the bartender to hear?"

"He doesn't know?"

She shook her head, then snatched her cigarettes from the bar and lit one.

"Does *Stephen* know?"

She made no answer nor did she need to, her eyebrows conveying more eloquently than words how amusingly obtuse she found the question. A sudden burst of laughter turned our attention to the bar's entrance, where a high-spirited trio of gentlemen, fresh, no doubt, from their happy-hour blow jobs, was ambling in.

"I am not having this conversation here," said Moira, rising and leading me out to the bar terrace. We had it to ourselves, the post-sundown chill having driven her guests indoors. Moira's manner was cooler still as she seated herself at a table and took an exasperated drag off her cigarette.

"Gawd, what is *wrong* with you! Asking about these things right in the middle of my damn bar! You haven't told Claire, have you?"

"God, no!"

"Well, see you don't. That self-righteous cow's just the one who'd blow the whistle on me."

"So you admit it then? That this whole place is nothing but a posh boy brothel?"

"Les Étoiles," she said icily, "is *not* a brothel."

Her eyes darted inside, where the threesome had seated themselves at a window table a few feet away from us. Moira, leery, I supposed, of lip-readers, rose and led me around the side of the building past the dining room to the larger south terrace. This was deserted and the salon overlooking it more comfortably distant. We took a table on the outer edge by the stone balustrade.

"Les Étoiles," she resumed petulantly, "is not a *brothel*. It is a full-service luxury spa. Certain of my clients demand fuller service than others and we're happy to provide it. Top quality, total discretion. Ninety percent of my guests have no idea what the other ten percent are getting and that's just the way my Diamond Plan clients want it. They come here because they feel safe, and they adore me because I'm the first hotelier they've ever met who understands what they *really* want. Sir Hugo called this place paradise on earth, which I found very touching."

"Have you lost your fucking mind?! What happens to you, not to mention *them*, when this all gets out? And you know it will! You can't keep a thing like this under wraps forever!"

"So far, so good," she said blithely. "My boys will never squeal. They're making more money than they ever dreamed of. Besides, they're scared."

"Scared?"

"I told them all my backers are the Russian Mafia and if anyone kills the golden goose I can't be responsible for what happens to him. A complete lie but it keeps them quiet. As for the clients, my God, who are *they* going to tell? I choose them very carefully and they're all very big names. So even when they see some other bigwig they suspect might also be here for the deluxe package—and who might have a good hunch why *they're* here—well, they just smile because they know the other guy's not going to blab any more than they are. These men didn't get where they are by not knowing how to keep a secret. It's very Skull and Bones."

"So to speak."

I did not share her confidence that all squealing would be confined to the massage rooms and I said as much. She replied that it was my timidity that had held me back in life and that I should take a page from Gilbert, who, though indisputably the product of a butter-fingered wet nurse, at least had a certain audacity.

"Tell me! What do you think got us into this mess? God," I said, my mind reeling, "how do you even rope them in? Goddamn movie stars! Do you just say, 'Have a nice massage, and, oh, if you like dick, ask for Buster'?"

Moira conceded that this had been the trickiest part of the enterprise and one she'd pondered at length while honing her business plan.

Her first task, she said, had been to hire a crackerjack staff of real massage therapists, for most of her guests would expect nothing less (nor, indeed, more). Then, after extensive research and interviews, she'd recruited a small but skilled stable of red-hot hunkadoodles who were, she boasted, the cream of LA's beeper-boy set. She promised them she'd more than double their incomes while providing a glamorous working environment plus benefits. She then provided them expert training in various massage techniques so that they'd blend in with the other staff and pass when necessary for the real thing.

"You're right, though—the tricky part was the first approach. It couldn't seem forward or tacky or we'd just scare people off. But we worked out a pretty good system."

Whenever a suspected candidate for Deluxe Treatment was reeled in, he'd be assigned an appropriately pec-tacular full-service masseur. The Adonis, clad in a spandex T and linen drawstring pants, would pop a Viagra beforehand so that by midmassage the client would find looming mere inches from his face what the client, if a studio prexy, might call a "major tentpole event." One of three scenarios would then play out. The client, embarrassed or timid, would ignore it, in which case the masseur would do the same. The client would complain and the masseur would apologize abjectly for his unbidden arousal, then offer to have someone else finish the massage. Or, as happened most often, the client would say, "My, my—whatcha got there?" and voilà, another satisfied customer.

The initial tryst would be followed by a private consultation with Moira. She'd tell the client that she'd heard his massage had grown somewhat exuberant. The extra attention, she'd assure the blushing patron, was on the house, but if he was interested, similar forms of "Stress-Reduction Massage" were discreetly available to those members of the Les Étoiles family who desired them. Such members, she'd assure him, represented a mere fraction of her clientele, most of whom were unaware that such services were on offer to a pampered few. Her regular masseurs and all nonessential staff were equally oblivious to these favors, the fees for which were tallied quarterly and discreetly billed as "membership dues." Often the clients, mostly closeted and/or married, would ask either shrewdly or snippily how Moira had surmised they'd rise to the bait in the first place. Her reply never varied.

"At Les Étoiles we pride ourselves on anticipating our patrons' needs."

"So there you are," she concluded proudly. "Not bad for a little girl from the Upper West Side."

"Oh, yes," I sneered. "From small-time scam artist to Hollywood whoremonger. It's a fucking Hallmark Hall of Fame movie!"

"Prude," she said flatly, then her face suddenly lit up in a welcoming smile. She waved to a newcomer in the salon and held up a finger to promise prompt attention.

"I have to go. Dame Judi's here." She started off toward the salon but after she'd gone a few steps turned back and said, "Not a word about this to anyone, you hear? *Anyone.* Don't forget, dear—you're working for me now."

She left and a familiar voice behind me chirped, "Are you *really?*"

I prayed this was merely a stress-induced auditory hallucination, but when I turned, there, dapper as ever in a blazer and maroon silk ascot, stood Monty Malenfant.

"Glen, you scamp! You're just full of surprises!"

Fifteen

★

MONTY!" I CRIED, CLUTCHING THE BALUSTRADE, the shock
having gelatinized my knees.

"Has anyone ever told you you're adorable when startled?"

"What are you doing here!"

"Surely I needn't tell *you* that," he said with a saucy wink. "I'd
heard the most intriguing things about the place from sweet little
Buster—who goes, can you believe it, by 'Adrian' here!—and simply
had to try it. Makes a nice change, I must say, from ordering in. Rex,
you'll be thrilled to know, is here as well. It's his birthday so I thought
I'd treat him to a boy who wouldn't rob him and then beat him up as
those in his price range are regrettably wont to do."

"But you said you were joining Lily on her press junket."

"Ah, the junket!" he said, laughing heartily. "I'd forgotten you'd
swallowed that one. No, Lily is not on a press junket. The last time
Lily had a press junket the preferred mode of transport was stage-
coach. Junkets are what Lily *claims* to have when she needs to hide out
and heal after making yet another assault on time's ravages. I tried like
hell to talk her out of this one. 'Lily,' I said, 'pull that mug of yours any

tighter and you'll look like a bongo with lips.' But no, she's determined to look her best for the floods of attention she poignantly expects to receive when her next picture escapes quarantine. So, *this,*" he said, gesturing toward the salon, "is where you do your—cough, cough—'physical training'? Well done, I say. A boy couldn't ask for a swankier workplace."

"What do you—?" I began, then stopped, gleaning his drift. "Oh, no, Monty, please! You don't think I *work* here?"

"Now, now," he clucked tenderly. "No need to be embarrassed—not with me of all people."

"Monty, I swear! I'm here as a guest."

"On what Lily pays you? Which, if I'm not mistaken, is thus far nothing? And did I not just hear Miss Finch remind you quite firmly that you were in her employ?"

"Actually—" I began, then paused, stymied.

Actually *what?*

Actually, Moira was not my employer, merely my blackmailer?

Actually, I *could* afford to come here as I'd been paid handsomely to write a screenplay for his estranged sister and nephew?

Actually, I was here as their *guest?*

No, I decided—better Monty should think I was a *garçon de joie* than start to question how I could afford such luxe accommodations or why I happened to be here on the same weekend as Stephen and Diana, whose presence he could not fail to note as they were even now parading into the salon.

"There, there, Glen," said Monty, copping a benevolent feel of my biceps. "You mustn't be embarrassed. I don't think one bit less of you. Why if not for you and your selfless brethren this world would be a far duller place and yours truly a bitter old queen incapable of spreading sunshine. Have you known Moira long?"

I replied ruefully that we went way back.

"Remarkable girl, Moira. Like all true entrepreneurs she has perceived a need others have not and rushed to fill it. For decades gay film stars have scratched their heads and asked, 'When will someone open a top-notch boy brothel I can bring the wife and kiddies to?' Thanks to

Moira, their cries have been heard. Oh dear lord!" he said, glancing into the salon. "Have you a feather handy? Because now would be an excellent time to knock me over with it."

Turning, I saw Stephen, Diana, and Gina sitting in a corner, cozily chatting with Sir Hugo, who'd appeared in the third Caliber picture as Sergei, a sinister Russian who, like most Caliber villains, was stubbornly bent on having the planet to himself.

"Well, there you have it, Glen—exhibit A! My world-famous nephew, sitting there, brazen as you please. No question what he's here for. We both know it—know it, hell, you *are* it. But does he skulk? Does he blush? Does he don false mustache and hooded parka? No, he just waltzes right in, head high, one arm round the missus, t'other round his sweet old mum. Let's go vex them, shall we?"

"No! I shouldn't!"

"Come now. You've been hearing about them for weeks. You can't pass up the chance to finally meet them."

"I can't!" I said with a damp shiver, panic having transformed my armpits into powerful twin showerheads. "I'm not supposed to fraternize with the patrons!"

"A rather silly policy given your other duties. The customer's always right, dear, and that would be me, so let's go!" Seizing my wrist, he dragged me into the salon and we soon stood looming behind his unsuspecting kin. They appeared to be gossiping. They were leaning in very close toward one another, grinning wickedly as they poked the ashes of God only knew whose reputation.

"My, my!" boomed Monty. "This *is* a small world!"

Four heads swiveled and three jaws dropped as they beheld him leering down at them, his arm draped over the shoulder of their once indispensable, now apparently compromised young mole.

"How well you all look! Hugo, my love, it's been ages! Haven't seen you since—dear lord, Thailand, was it? And Diana, radiant as always."

"Monty," she sighed. Her expression could not have been bleaker had she just been asked to sit down by a frowning oncologist.

"Allow me to introduce a delightful young friend of mine, Mr.

Glen DeWitt. Glen, this is my sister Diana, my nephew, Stephen, his wife, Gina, and Sir Hugo Bunting, whom you may already have met."

On hearing me introduced as Glen, Stephen visibly relaxed and flashed me a knowing smile. Monty, he knew, would read this smile as meaning, "So you're Uncle's latest, are you?" but I knew it in fact meant, "Well done, you dashing young master spy—let's get naked later!"

What had I been worried about?! My cover was intact and the situation, though tricky, offered a splendid opportunity to display my skills as a double agent. How impressed Stephen would be by my suavity under pressure, how dazzled by my inspired decision to pose as a spa employee.

"Gosh!" I exclaimed, extending a hand to Diana. "It's such an honor to meet you. I'm a huge fan."

"Thank you, uh . . . *Glen,* was it?"

Stephen took my hand and gave it a firm, deliciously prolonged squeeze.

"Nice to meet you, Glen."

"The pleasure's all mine, Mr. Donato."

"Please, Stephen."

"Charmed," said Gina, her performance, as always, painfully stilted. "How lovely to meet you, Philip."

"*Glen,*" corrected Stephen.

Sir Hugo extended a languorous hand and asked rather pointedly how I knew Monty.

"He's my part-time secretary," said Monty, chivalrously sparing me the ire he knew I'd reap if he exposed me as Lily's coauthor. "He'd told me he had another job but I had no idea till just now that it was here."

Stephen blinked.

"So you *work* here?"

"Yes."

"Doing what?" Sir Hugo asked eagerly. It bears mentioning at this juncture that Sir Hugo had recently triumphed on the London stage as Falstaff and had required no padding. As he was now eyeing me like I was a pastry cart, I decided it might be prudent to bill myself as the spa's bookkeeper.

"Actually—"

"Glen's a very gifted masseur."

"*Really?*" said Sir Hugo, tucking the bib into his collar.

"Lovely seeing you, Monty," said Diana, her magisterial little wave a signal that our audience was over. Monty eyed her in puckish amazement as if to say, "Come, love—you can't think you'll get rid of me *that* easily?"

"So, Stephen," he said, impudently perching on the arm of Diana's chair, "first visit here?"

"More like his seventh," said Gina. "Stephen just *loves* it here. Me too. It is so hard for people like us to find a place that just *gets* it. Where we can come and know we won't be mobbed and photographed 'cause they *get* it and don't let just *anyone* in."

"So one had thought," remarked Diana to her martini.

"And the treatments are *fantastic*. Stephen's had this shoulder problem for years from this stunt he did. He says the people here are the first ones who've really been able to help him."

"Get right in there, do they?" asked Monty. "Deep tissue?"

"They're good," nodded Stephen.

"Glad to hear it," said Monty. "Nothing like finding a masseur who can knead away all your nasty stiffness, leaving you limp and contented."

Stephen, far from seeming rattled by Monty's innuendos, just took them in with a resigned smile that afforded me new insight into their peculiar relationship. Stephen, I now saw, knew he could hide nothing from Monty. He knew equally well though that Monty, however much he teased, would never expose him. That would take Spite, a quality Monty did not possess, his sisters having appropriated the family's full allotment. The weary smile he offered in response to his uncle's sly digs was like that which a Mercedes, if it could, might bestow on a dog that had given chase and caught the bumper in its teeth. "Okay, you've got me," it said. "Now what?"

"Tell me, Glen," said Gina, padding her role, "did you have to study for a long time to be a masseur?"

"Oh, yes, I've trained quite extensively," I said, deadpanning that I'd just completed a three-year course at the West Hollywood Institute for Advanced Relaxation. Gina nodded earnestly as Stephen squelched a giggle.

It suddenly occurred to me that Stephen not only knew firsthand what went on here — he assumed I knew as well and had from the start. I found this disconcerting. I wanted him to see me as a confidant and potential paramour, not as some lowly panderer. On the other hand, he had taken quite a shine to the place. If I confessed I'd had no idea it was Boys R Us when I brought him, might I seem naive to him, a mere dupe? Was I better off playing the worldly young sophisticate whose sexual mores, like his own, bordered on the Parisian? It was all a bit dizzying, though not half so dizzying as it would shortly become.

"So, Glen," said Sir Hugo, "might I engage you for a massage later this evening? After dinner say?"

As I was replying that my dance card was regrettably full, Stephen's eyes widened and he rose abruptly from his seat. Diana, gazing at something behind me, looked similarly distraught. Turning to see what had occasioned their alarm, I found myself standing nose to nose with Claire.

"Hello, Ph—" she began.

"NicetomeetyouGlenDeWitt!" I said with frantic geniality.

"Sorry?"

"DeWitt."

"Claire," said Stephen, darting between us, "I'd like you to meet my uncle Monty. Monty, this is Claire Simmons, a very gifted writer who's working on a script for us."

"Pleasure to meet you."

"Likewise," she said. "I've seen some of your movies."

"Then accept please my profound apologies."

"Monty," continued Stephen, "was just introducing us to his secretary. Glen . . . DeWitt, is it?"

"Yes. DeWitt."

Claire's nothing if not a quick study, and the merest glance at our anxious smiles conveyed to her all she needed to know. Monty, for reasons yet to be strangled out of me, knew me as Glen DeWitt, and all present were keen that he should continue to do so.

"Nice to meet you, Glen," she said, offering her hand. I took it and for the second time in less than an hour an irate female sank her fingernails into my palm.

"Glen also works here," said Gina.

"Really?" she said pleasantly. "And what do you do here, Glen?"

"I'm a massage therapist," I said, forcing myself to meet her ominously cordial gaze. I recalled with a pang her earlier demand to know if there was *anything* (italics hers) I'd omitted to tell her and my assurance that there was not. This was not a point she would fail to press when next I took the witness stand.

"A masseur!" she exclaimed, enchanted. "This *is* my lucky day. I have the most unimaginable pain in my neck. Perhaps you could pop up to my room and work your magic on it?"

You'll remember that the last time Claire made such a request I submitted to the interview, manfully resisting the impulse to flee. This, however, was before she'd walloped my shoulder, kicked my shin, and dug her nails into my palm. I sensed that were I now to explain my alternate identity as Glen, not to mention Glen's dual career as biographer and courtesan, her response would be even more pugilistic. This I refused to submit to; I was a male prostitute now and had a duty to protect the merchandise.

"Sorry," I said. "All booked up."

"Are you sure?" She frowned, rubbing her neck. "You know how these things only get worse if you put off dealing with them."

"Can't be helped. Monty has dibs on me." I clapped him on the shoulder. "Shall we get started?"

"Oh, yes, let's!" he replied with the simple delight of a child accepting a lollipop.

"Nice meeting you all," I said, waving and backing away.

"We'll see you about," purred Hugo.

"Count on it," said Claire.

I scooted across the salon as Monty trotted behind, wagging his tail. We passed through the etched-glass double doors into the hushed, dimly lit treatment center.

It had a spare Zenlike oval foyer with a curved glass reception desk and lit shelves displaying the spa's pricey product line. Three corridors, radiating diagonally like rays of a sunbeam, led to the spa's gym and treatment rooms. The reception desk was unmanned but I saw a comely, tunic-clad attendant approaching via the left corridor. Since sex worker Glen would obviously have known this woman and I did not, I promptly banged a right down the opposite corridor. I turned a corner, then another, and found I'd reached a cul-de-sac, a short hall with doors on either side and an upholstered bench set into the wall where it dead-ended. I slumped onto it and gazed fretfully up at Monty's beaming face, wondering how one tactfully rescinds an offer of paid nooky.

"About that massage—" I began delicately.

"Oh, dear," said Monty. "Don't like the sound of that."

"I'm sorry. It's just . . ." I fell silent, inspiration failing me.

"No need to explain, dear," he said, sitting next to me. "I had my hopes, of course. But I suspected you were just using me as cover to get away from that Claire girl. Can't say I blame you."

"Oh?"

"She obviously wanted more than a neck rub. That look she gave you—pure female rapaciousness. It's a look I've often seen Lily give to Italian waiters and, on our last vacation, to numerous gondoliers. You had to save yourself and I'm glad to have been of assistance."

"Thanks, Monty."

"I don't suppose you'd care to express your gratitude more acrobatically?"

"Gosh, Monty," I blushed, "it would just seem kinda—"

"Say no more." He gave my knee a chaste pat. "You're quite right. We know each other too well. We've reached the point where the attraction is not, alas, mutual and commerce is unseemly. Luckily for me we're in a place that teems with mouthwatering alternatives." He rose.

"Now if you'll excuse me, Lily will be wondering where I've gotten to."

"Lily's here too?"

"Yes and quite unfit for human eyes. She's skulking in our cottage, sucking back the gimlets through a hole in her veil."

He started down the hall and I called after him. "Careful who sees you. Claire thinks you're with me."

He adopted a comical Prussian accent and said, "I vill be stealthy as a cat!" before tiptoeing away. I watched him go, then slumped, exhausted, against the wall. Some weekend in the country this was turning out to be! We'd barely been here an hour and were already up to our necks in pity and terror. "What next!" I thought.

Just then the door to my right opened and a young man wearing a turban and white terry robe poked his head out. His face was concealed beneath a thick mask of beauty goop, its hue a bilious aquamarine.

"Philip! I thought that was you I heard."

"Gilbert!"

"Hon, you have *got* to get a massage here!" He peered down the hall, making sure we were alone, then turned back to me and whispered in naughty glee.

"The masseurs put out!"

Sixteen

★

WE RETREATED TO THE SAFETY OF Gilbert's massage room, a spare, serene chamber with a cool slate floor, dove-gray walls, and cove lighting. I swiftly related the harrowing events that had transpired since his cowardly flight from the bar, getting as far as Moira's proud performance in *Call Me Madam* before pausing to catch my breath. Gilbert was, as usual, slow to grasp the broader implications of the situation.

"Well," he said after a pensive silence, "she's nuts if she thinks I'm paying for that blow job."

"That is not the issue!"

"You think Stephen will cover it, being host and all?"

"Gilbert," I snapped, "we're talking about a criminal enterprise here—and we're practically accomplices! She forced us to shill for the place, and now you're a goddamn customer."

"You're only a customer if you *pay*, which as I made quite clear—"

"Wake up, you brain-dead slut! What if Moira gets busted? What's to keep her from dragging us into it?"

I cannot say if he rolled his eyes, as they were under cucumber slices, but he waved a dismissive hand.

"You worry about *everything*."

"Well, one of us had better 'cause that's only half of it! Monty's here!"

Gilbert frowned. "Has he seen you?"

"Yes. He still thinks I'm Glen. But he also thinks this place is the second job I've been telling him about. He thinks I'm one of Moira's rent boys!"

Gilbert sat up and removed the cukes.

"You *told* him that?"

"I had to!"

"And he *bought* it?" he asked with more astonishment than I felt was warranted.

"He *assumed* it, thank you very much!"

"Well, no offense, hon, but you've seen Moira's boys. We're talking USDA prime. You're more like a nice Salisbury steak."

"I seem to recall being good enough for you for six months!"

"True. But you weren't *charging* me."

I replied with some asperity that there were more pressing issues at hand than my credibility as a top-shelf courtesan. For starters there was Claire, to whom I'd been introduced only moments ago as Glen.

"Ouch! How'd that happen?"

I described the scene in all its horror, ending with my flight to the shelter of the spa.

"Well, guess that cat's out of the bag," said Gilbert. "I mean, once you and Monty took off you just know Claire must have asked Stephen or Diana what the hell was going on."

I replied that at this point my secret career as a ghostwriter seemed the merest triviality compared to what was going on in the treatment rooms of Les Étoiles. What would Claire do when she found out about that?

"You're not thinking of *telling* her?"

"I might as well. You know she'll find out."

"How's she gonna find out?"

"She'll find out! Claire *always* finds out!"

"*Damn right I do!*" snarled Claire from the other side of the door.

Gilbert flinched so violently he fell off the table even as I shrieked like a smoke alarm and lunged for the door, unsure if we'd locked it. Luckily we had and the knob twisted in impotent fury.

"Open the damn door!" hollered Claire.

"Far whom, please, var you luke-ing?" said Gilbert in a ludicrous attempt to sound Swedish.

"I know it's you, you nancy jackass! Let me in!"

Gilbert clambered to his feet. "Follow me!" he mouthed and scuttled over to the room's other door, which I'd taken for a closet but which apparently wasn't if he was proposing we escape through it. He tried the knob and found it locked.

"Shit!"

He spun around, stamped a slippered foot in fury, and slumped, thwarted, against the door, which promptly opened into the room, sending him sprawling once again to the floor. His facialist was not, I presumed, the same staffer who'd been on fellatio duty earlier. This one was a formidable woman who reminded me of the late Lotte Lenya if Miss Lenya had abandoned the musical stage to seek fame as a competitive weight lifter.

"Sorry!" she exclaimed, helping Gilbert up. Riveted briefly by this spectacle, I almost failed to notice that the door to deliverance was even now swinging shut. I saw it in time though and, leaping balletically across the room, grabbed the handle.

"You can't go out that way!" said Lotte sternly. "That's for staff only!"

"First day!" I said and zipped through, locking it behind me. She'd have keys I knew, but it would take her a moment to fish them out and by then I intended to be as far away as possible. I skedaddled down a narrow, dimly lit hall, rounding corners twice before pausing to take in my surroundings.

I appeared to be in some sort of "backstage" area, a drably utilitarian warren of halls and cupboards. Doors to my left led, I presumed, to more treatment rooms; doors to my right might have been storage closets or God only knew what. I tried a few of these and all were locked save one holding towels and sheets.

"Mister!" called the disgruntled facialist, and I resumed my sprint, advancing through the maze till I came to a dead end at a door marked VIP ROOMS—AUTHORIZED PERSONNEL ONLY. I tried the door, which, not surprisingly, was locked. I doubled back, hoping to find a treatment room to escape through without bursting in on some poor überagent who wished only to be spanked in peace. I'd just pressed my ear to a door and was listening for voices when a door on the opposite side of the hall suddenly banged open.

Turning, I saw a fetching young man with short hair and very important biceps enter the hall carrying a garment bag. Both literally and figuratively dashing, he hurtled past me like a chorus boy late for a curtain. On reaching the VIP door, he waved a small card at a wall sensor. There was a click and he hurried through it into another hallway.

"Mister!" called Lotte, angrier now. I sprinted madly toward the VIP door, thrust my arm out to keep it from shutting, and hurried through it just in time to see Biceps disappear into what looked like a small dressing room. Seconds later the handle of the VIP door clacked up and down a few times but Lotte, as I'd suspected, lacked clearance for this area and could chivy me no further.

Glancing about, I found that I liked this hall much better than the last one. Apart from its welcome shortage of marauding facialists, it was sleeker, more like the spa's Zen-chic public spaces. Assuming still that the treatment rooms were to my left, I went to the first door and listened a moment to see if it was occupied. Hearing nothing, I opened the door and immediately received a valuable reminder that sex is not invariably noisy. I don't know if you've seen that famous statue of Romulus and Remus, the mythological founders of Rome, suckling a wolf who represents the city. The sight I now beheld resembled a living sculpture based on it with Rex Bajour as either Remus or Romulus and a nude, broad-shouldered café-au-lait youth in the role of the wolf.

"Sorry!" I said as politely as one could in such a circumstance. "Carry on!" I closed the door swiftly but not before Rex had recognized me and shot me an understandably disgruntled look.

I moved on to the next door, listened at it, and again heard nothing. I opened it the merest crack, peered in, and, finding no tryst in progress, entered.

The room was similar to Gilbert's but larger and with more amenities. There was a leather sofa against one wall and the opposite wall had a counter with a sink and a glass shower stall. The wall between them had a large floor-to-ceiling mirror and in the center of the room stood a sturdy massage table draped in white sheets.

I crossed to the door that led to the public hall and opened it, cocking an ear for predators. I had no plan at this point but to make it back to my room without meeting anyone intent on either pummeling or purchasing me. I'd then barricade myself within, granting admittance to no one save Stephen till I'd figured out my next move.

I listened a moment. Hearing nothing, I set foot gingerly into the hall. The minute I did I heard approaching footsteps and retreated at once, closing the door. I pressed an ear to it and heard the footsteps draw near, then stop directly in front of it. Fearing it might be Claire, I raced over to the door I'd come in through and found it locked. Grasping at once my striking paucity of alternatives, I dove under the massage table, praying the long, draped sheets would serve to conceal me.

The door opened and two people entered.

"How are you this evening, sir?" said a low pleasant voice with a hint of an accent. Spanish? Italian?

"Tense, Ricky. Really, really tense!"

Stephen!

"Well," said Ricky sexily, "we'll see what we can do about that."

It dawned on me that there was no further need to conceal myself. Stephen would have nothing but sympathy for my decision to flee from Claire and would, if anything, be amused by the misadventures that had brought me to my current absurd position. I shifted my weight, preparing to pop out with an impish "Surprise!" when a second more powerful thought struck me.

Stephen was about to have sex with this man.

Right on this table perhaps.

And I was *leaving?*

For leave I certainly would if I revealed myself, the odds of Stephen saying, "Hey, we were just about to fuck—pull up a chair!" being remote at best. Why choose exile when I could crouch here in thrilling proximity as the monarch of my fantasies surrendered to carnal bliss? There was, after all, no guarantee I'd ever win him for myself. This could, I reasoned, be as close to actual sex with him as I'd ever get.

"Crazy fucking day," sighed Stephen as his exquisite ankles swam into view inches from my face. "We barely get here when who walks in but my batty old uncle. He's harmless but my mom hates him. Now she's all, 'I thought you said this was a nice place. They let anyone in!'"

Ricky laughed at Stephen's Diana impression, which was quite good. His ankles suddenly disappeared, obscured behind a heap of fallen terry cloth. I leaned forward, kneeling now in a cat stretch position, and lowered my face to the floor. I found that if I carefully adjusted the crumpled robe I created a thin space between it and the dangling sheet through which I could peer out at the mirrored wall.

There sat Stephen, wearing only a pair of white silk boxers, his godlike physique gloriously backlit by a pin spot over the table. Behind him, gently massaging his shoulders, stood Ricky, quite an eyeful himself, with auburn hair, sensuous cheekbones, and lips like two lovely little flotation devices.

"My uncle's pretty damn nosy," said Stephen, "so if he should, you know, ask you about me—"

"He won't hear a thing from me, sir," vowed Ricky with becoming solemnity.

"Great. Did you remember the, uh—?"

"Right here."

Stephen swung his legs around and sat facing the other way. I could only see his back now though I had no complaint about that. I heard the click of a cigarette lighter and soon the pungent aroma of marijuana filled the air. "Stephen smokes weed!" I thought, delighted to find he indulged in a habit well known to sharpen the libido while hampering judgment.

"Want some?" asked Stephen, holding his breath.

"I'm good."

Stephen took a few more drags, then lay down on his stomach, his face toward the mirror. He seemed to be watching the scene as if it were a movie, smiling at the tableau they presented. Ricky, aware of this, peeled off his T-shirt, proudly displaying what a few thousand hours at a good gym can do for a boy. Stephen's smile crinkled into a loopy grin that was equal parts contentment, anticipation, and pot. I was thrilled to be witnessing the scene even as I wished I could do so in a posture less reminiscent of a Muslim at prayer. I am, alas, tall, and didn't dare lie flat lest my legs protrude.

Ricky removed his pants, revealing a tight pair of briefs. He strad-dled Stephen on the table and began massaging his neck and shoul-ders. This went on for two minutes, then five, then ten. My right thumb began twitching uncontrollably, a reflex that puzzled me till I realized that my brain, acting from long force of habit, was instructing the scene to fast-forward. Ricky finally leaned down and lightly kissed Stephen's neck.

"You are so hot, sir."

Stephen grunted in pleasure as Ricky teasingly worked his hands down Stephen's spine till he reached the top of his boxers. He gently tugged them down, exposing Stephen's bum, which was even more magnificent than I remembered it from its brief but oft-downloaded appearance in the first Caliber movie. Ricky massaged Stephen's butt, kneading the cheeks in slow circular moves. After a moment, he gently parted them.

THOSE OF YOU READING this aloud to small children might find this a good time to tell them that the big strong masseur rubbed the hand-some actor till he felt all better and who wants ice cream? Likewise, those of you whose appetite for hot masseur-on-film-star action is lim-ited or nonexistent may want to start skimming now, as things are about to get pretty racy. I'm aware that certain of my readers (and you know who you are, Aunt Leslie) feel strongly that gay sexual encoun-ters, when regrettably necessary to move the story along, should be de-scribed with all possible decorum, succinctly outlining the essentials before panning across to the fluttering curtains. I remind those who take this view that many others among my readership approach such scenes with positive eagerness, muttering, "Finally!" under their breath and complaining only when they feel the author has stinted on details. It is for their sake (and that of young Amos, who has to learn somewhere) that I relate what follows.

RICKY SLATHERED A GENEROUS amount of massage oil on his right hand and, with little fanfare, poked a finger into Stephen's bottom. Stephen gasped, which was a damn good thing, as it kept him from hearing my own. This was not the sort of incursion one expected a rugged, humanity-saving action hero to countenance and I wondered if Stephen would turn to face his invader with a stern glare and a cry of "You go too far, sir!"

But Stephen did not protest. He groaned softly and wagged his bottom from side to side, a gesture Ricky correctly interpreted to mean, "More fingers, please." He obliged with a second, then a third, performing this chore, I felt, in an oddly dispassionate, businesslike way, as though he were looking for his keys in there.

Some verbal foreplay ensued, Ricky drawing his inspiration from the screenplays of his favorite adult films. Rubbing himself through his briefs, he asked Stephen if he wanted his big nasty cock up his butt. Stephen replied that, yes, he wanted that big nasty cock real bad, lust wreaking its usual havoc on grammar. Ricky repeated the question and Stephen replied once more in the affirmative. "You like a big fat cock, don't you?" asked Ricky, as though Stephen hadn't made himself quite clear on the point. Stephen, polite to a fault, said yes, he did very much. "You want this big boy up your ass?" inquired Ricky, and by then I was ready to spring from under the table and shout, "He wants to get fucked! What do you need? A UN interpreter?!"

Ricky finally decided to oblige, ripping off his tear-away undies and exposing their impressive cargo, a sight that left me feeling both aroused and daunted; it was one thing for Stephen to be a bottom but did he have to be spoiled? Ricky sheathed it in a silvery condom that made it gleam like a hood ornament and I wondered frankly how

Stephen's garage was going to accommodate it. Ricky parked it though and with an ungentle velocity that caused Stephen to arch his back and bury his face in the massage table's doughnut hole, a feature I hadn't even noticed till I felt hot breath on my neck and gazed up to see Stephen's face framed in it mere inches from my own. The eyes, thank God, were tightly closed, his lovely features contorted in a lip-biting wince. The thought bubble, had there been one, would have read, "Remind me again why I like this."

I stared up at him, my emotions whipsawing between terror of being caught and the natural fascination one feels on beholding the face of a penetrated action star. Ricky delivered a second salvo that caused the table to shake and Stephen to whip his head up out of the doughnut. I ducked down and peered out from under the sheet again. There was Ricky, looking less lustful than diligent as he plied his trade, the strokes slow and regular as though quality control were timing him. But the sight of Stephen squirming in bliss was one I found overwhelmingly stimulating and soon old faithful was indignantly battering the walls of my trousers as if to say, "I'm here too, y'know!" I reached for my zipper then stopped, realizing how drastically this would compound my embarrassment were Stephen to peer through the doughnut and discover me. A moment later Ricky, bless him, growled, "Turn over, I want to see you!" and Stephen promptly obliged. Free now from fear of exposure, I exposed myself and soon they were at it again with yours truly downstairs playing the home version.

I could see Stephen's face in the mirror through the whole thing. His eyes never left it, so transfixed was he by the view. There are those who might have called this narcissism, but I was inclined to take a more charitable view. There was, after all, not a gay man alive who wouldn't have been utterly mesmerized by the sight. Why should Stephen himself find it any less engrossing?

This portion of the festivities went on for about five more minutes, Stephen's low moans softly punctuating the hush, the erotic spell marred only once when Ricky, without missing a thrust, remarked, "You know, I'm an actor too." But just when things seemed to be speeding toward the finish, Ricky abruptly withdrew and hopped off the table.

"What'd you stop for?" whined Stephen.

"I'm bringing in reinforcements," teased Ricky.

"Huh?"

"I have a friend," said Ricky. "Someone you know. I'm pretty sure you'll be glad to see him."

"Whizzy?" asked Stephen, sounding more out of it than I'd realized he was.

There was a knock at the door to the back hall.

"That's him now," said Ricky with a smirk. He scooped up his clothes and, fishing a key from his pants, opened the door and said, "Stephen, meet Oscar." And in walked Oscar.

Or rather in walked *the* Oscar.

Or, more precisely, in walked a well-muscled young man costumed quite skillfully as a life-size replica of an Academy Award. The outfit subtly combined gold body paint with some skintight fabric, like spandex but thinner and with a metallic sheen. His face was masked, the features, like the statuette's, barely suggested, and he held the requisite two-edged sword. There was one noteworthy departure from verisimilitude. Real Oscars lack genitalia and this one quite markedly did not, sporting a large gilded erection that jutted out from the costume just to the right of the sword. Ricky cast his eyes on it, his exaggerated double take a clear sign that he'd do well to keep his day job.

"Whoa! I think he likes you!"

Stephen just stared for a long moment, then burst into a bizarre honking laugh that made me wonder again just how strong the pot had been.

"Hey, Oscar," giggled Stephen, "nice to see ya, buddy. Watcha got for me there?"

Ricky, content now that introductions had been made and the new friends had found a mutual interest, bade them farewell and departed. Oscar advanced toward the table with small geishalike steps, as his legs were meshed together to enhance his resemblance to the statuette.

On reaching the table he tossed aside his sword and hoisted himself up to join Stephen, who wasted little time in demonstrating that his own legs were not similarly encumbered.

They soon found their rhythm and Stephen, who'd stared so intently into the mirror before, barely glanced at it now. He only had eyes for Oscar, gazing raptly into the inscrutable gilded face with a look unlike any Ricky had garnered from him. That, it appeared, had merely been lust. This was the Real Thing.

I asked myself, "Would he ever look at me with such rapture, such unalloyed adoration?" It seemed doubtful. It seemed more doubtful still that my plan to seduce him this weekend had even the paltriest hope of success. What would he want with the likes of me when his needs had already been amply met by a studly masseur and a famous award? It was a bitter pill to swallow but one tries to be philosophical about these things, so I just shrugged and resumed masturbating.

"Yeah, big guy!" cried Stephen ecstatically. "Yeah! Just like that, Oscar! Come to Poppa!"

Oscar picked up the pace and they began galloping toward the finish line with self barely a furlong behind. But just when Stephen seemed only seconds from shouting, "You like me! You really really like me!" the mood was shattered by a loud knock on the door.

"Stephen!" came Gina's voice, muffled but unmistakable. "Stephen! I need to talk to you."

"Shit!" he hissed as Oscar hastily disengaged from his flustered recipient and jumped off the table.

"We need to talk! I know you're in there. The woman at the desk said so."

"I'm—having—a—*massage!*" yelled Stephen, his voice choked with terror and frustration.

"You can't give me one minute? What's going on in there?" she added, suspicion darkening her tone.

This was not good. A refusal to open the door now would prompt the most dire conclusions and spell an end to Stephen's freedom to frequent the spa with impunity.

"Nothing! Jeez!" he said indignantly. "Get out!" he whispered frantically, a needless command as Oscar had already hopped to the back exit and was madly twisting the knob on the locked door. He turned to Stephen, flinging his arms wide in panic. I could only imagine his face beneath the impassive mask but Stephen was in the grip of a complete stoned freak-out, his expression calling to mind the one Janet Leigh had worn in *Psycho* shortly after meeting Mrs. Bates. Beholding it, I knew at once what had to be done.

"Fear not," I said, rolling out and springing gracefully to my feet. "Cavanaugh's here!" I felt I'd executed this maneuver with the same manly élan the superheroes of my youth always displayed when swooping in for last-minute rescues. Glancing down, I saw that the effect might have been more suave had I remembered to do up my pants.

I addressed Oscar, my voice soft but commanding.

"Under the table!"

He hastily complied as I handed the stunned and speechless Stephen his boxers. "Put these on."

"How did you . . . ?" he began, then trailed off, just staring at me with a look some might have characterized as zonked but which I preferred to see as worshipful.

"Shh," I said, boldly stroking his cheek. "All will be well. Lie down."

He obeyed as I refastened my belt and opened the door.

"Gina!" I said, my tone brisk and assured. "Come in."

"What are you doing here? I thought Stephen was getting a massage."

"He is. From me."

"But you're not a masseur."

"Ah," I replied smoothly, "but Monty *thinks* I am. If I don't follow through and massage a few people he'll know I'm lying and then where are we?"

"But weren't you giving Monty a massage?"

"There's the rub, so to speak. I'm not, as you pointed out, an actual masseur, something I feared Monty would detect unless I got some practice in first. Stephen graciously volunteered to be my guinea pig. We've only been at it half an hour but I'm making great strides, wouldn't you say, Stephen?"

"Uh . . . yeah?" came Stephen's rapier reply. I saw that the cannabis had done little to enhance his improvisatory skills and that this would not be a good time to name a famous person, a household object, and a literary genre, then shout, "Go!"

"So, whassup?" he mumbled.

"Your mother is totally out of control! She's going to get us kicked out of here!"

Gina explained that after Stephen had left for his massage Diana had withdrawn from the salon to the terrace.

"I went with her and right away she orders another martini. It's what she always does when we're alone—like she can't endure my company unless she's smashed. I think it's a bad idea and I say so, very tactfully, but she has it anyway and then she wants a *third* so she calls the waiter. And this bizarre woman at the next table—she's wearing this huge hat with, like, netting covering her face—"

"Lily!" I said, remembering her gardening hat from my first visit.

"Exactly! And she's even more crocked than Diana! She starts making this huge stink about how she was there first and how the whole world doesn't bow to Diana the Great. And by now we realize who it is and Diana lays into her, calling her a washed-up old drunk, and Lily's all, 'Wait till my book comes out! We'll see who's washed-up then!' And you know me, Miss Peacemaker, I'm doing my best to—"

She paused abruptly and wrinkled her nose.

"Do I smell pot?"

Knowing Stephen to be hobbled in the quick-answer department, I jumped in.

"I smelled that too. Some sort of incense, I think, piped in through the air vents."

"It's pot," said Gina, an accusing eye on Stephen. "You're stoned, aren't you?"

"I'm under a lot of stress, okay?" managed Stephen. "Monty showing up, now all this with my mother . . ."

Gina, in a rare display of lucidity, pointed out that Stephen had gotten stoned before she'd told him about Diana. Then, softening, she said, "It's this whole Oscar business, isn't it?"

Stephen stared at her in frozen horror before catching her drift and replying uneasily in the negative.

"Oh, *please,*" she said, tousling his hair. "It's all I've heard about for weeks. You're *going* to be nominated, hon." She turned to me. "He is *obsessed* with the Oscar. It's this whole mother-son thing. Y'know, 'Mom's got an Oscar so I've gotta have one too.' "

"Gina . . ." he pleaded weakly.

"I tease him all the time. I say, 'Oscar or me—if you could only have one which would it be?' I hope he never has to choose though 'cause I think Oscar would win! *Kidding!*"

I thought of shooting Stephen a wry look to comment on the irony but sensed he wasn't ready to see the humor yet.

"Look," he said, his voice quavering, "we came here to relax, which I am *trying* to do. Let me finish my massage and I'll talk to Mom before dinner."

He would in fact talk to Mom a good deal sooner for she was even now staggering indignantly into the room.

"There you are!" she declared with that majestic exasperation only a drunken thespian can summon. "Will you kindly inform your friend Moira that if she does not evict my sister immediately we're leaving this place!"

"*Maaaaaa!*" wailed Stephen, now officially in hell. He shot me a look of aggrieved disbelief. You couldn't blame him. Moira's brochures, while stressing the advantages of a family friendly brothel, had mentioned none of its potential pitfalls, which clearly were numerous. "I am trying to have a massage here!"

"She struck me!" thundered Diana, then, registering my presence with a woozy double take, asked what I was doing there.

"Giving Stephen a massage."

"You're a masseur now?"

"I'm learning."

"I see," Diana said vaguely, then returned her attention to Stephen.

"Your aunt has gone quite mad! If you could see the hat she was wearing!"

Her harangue continued and Stephen listened in helpless misery. There is no overstating the dismay of a man who must mollify an irate wife and mother even as he contemplates the catastrophe that awaits should either of them peer beneath his massage table and notice the nude, gilded man there. It was a daunting dilemma for a man in peak form and more harrowing still for one on whom pot had conferred the mental acuity of a bivalve. I resolved to rescue him as swiftly as I could.

"Look," I said, my tone calm and reassuring, "I've known Moira for years and I know how much she values your patronage. I'm sure if I explain the situation she'll rectify it immediately."

Stephen shot me a grateful look, which made me glad I'd spoken up. Then Claire walked in, which made me rather wish I hadn't.

"I thought that was you, Philip. Or is it Glen still? Or perhaps some third identity I haven't met, in which case hello, I'm Claire."

Stephen, unable to believe yet a third female had invaded his sex den, blurted, "Jesus!" and buried his face in the doughnut. Diana imperiously informed Claire that they were having a private discussion and Claire sweetly replied that she hadn't meant to intrude; she'd just grab me and be off.

"Sorry," I said, "I haven't finished Stephen's massage."

"Excuse me?" said Claire. Gina helpfully explained that I was practicing and, by all reports, getting quite good.

It was at this unfortunate juncture that I chanced to notice that Oscar's large golden sword was still sitting where he'd thrown it, leaning against the sofa. I gave a little gasp and my eyes ricocheted involuntarily to the base of the massage table, a serious blunder as the eagle-eyed Claire noticed it and began eyeing the same region with regrettably keen curiosity.

"Sorry about the whole Glen thing," I said, babbling in a futile attempt to distract her. "I had to pretend, you see, because Monty—"

"Yes, I know," said Claire. "Gina was kind enough to explain your extracurricular chores to me."

"Does everyone need to know our business?" wailed Diana as Claire discreetly yanked a button from her blouse and let it drop to the floor by the table.

"Oops, lost a button!"

She knelt to retrieve it and, pretending it had gone under the table, lifted the sheet slightly and peered in as Stephen looked on in stoned agony. It was clear that the day's events had done much to inure Claire to bizarre surprises and restore her native aplomb.

"Found it," she said airily, then rose. "I'm off. I'm absolutely desperate for a drink. You look like you could use one too, Diana."

"You know, ashually I could," replied the star.

Claire then told Gina that when she had a moment she'd like to discuss the script, particularly several scenes that did not currently feature Gina's character and which Claire felt suffered from the omission. Gina said there was no time like the present, then turned to us.

"You guys finish your massage."

"That shoulder's still tight," I said, kneading it lightly, the thrill of my first touch of his bare torso shamefully undiminished by the presence of his wife.

"You'll talk to Moira?" asked Diana.

"Soon as we're done," I vowed.

"Bye, hon," said Gina to Stephen.

"See ya."

Claire shepherded her charges out the door. The look she shot us as she closed it contained volumes, none of which I looked forward to reading.

Seventeen

★

THOUGH IT WOULD HAVE BEEN DIFFICULT to imagine a more shattering ordeal, there was no topping it as a bonding experience for Stephen and me. When the ladies had finally gone the look that passed between us was one such as two World War I doughboys might have exchanged after passing a long night in their foxhole, staring death in the face while dodging their less fortunate comrades' flying viscera.

"Jeez," said Stephen with a shudder.

"Yikes," I concurred.

The door to the back hall opened and Ricky entered, clearly agog with curiosity.

"I was going to check on you but I heard all these voices! Was that your mom?"

Stephen nodded darkly.

"I thought so! What was she so pissed about?" asked Ricky, apparently laboring under the misapprehension that his brief residency in Stephen's bottom entitled him to hear family secrets.

"Please," sighed Stephen, "just go."

"Okay," he said, a bit stung. "I was just—" He paused and looked around, puzzled. "Where'd Oscar go?"

Oscar crawled sheepishly from his hiding place, his previous allure now dimmed by the flaccidity of his gilded cock and the charley horse he'd acquired while crouching down there.

"So," inquired Ricky, "would you like to reschedule for maybe—"

"Just go," repeated Stephen. Ricky nodded, chastened, then helped his limp and limping colleague from the room.

You might suppose that such a debacle, offering as it did the clearest possible warning on the dangers of extramarital spa nooky, would have banished all lewd thoughts from my head. You would, however, suppose wrong. The instant the door closed I became powerfully aware that Stephen and I were truly alone for the first time ever and that he was nude save for boxers. I also realized that although two skilled sex workers had escorted him briskly around the sexual bases, his cleats had yet to touch home. I scurried to the hall door to make sure it was locked, then returned to Stephen's side. I perched subserviently on the edge of the table and eyed him with tender concern.

For a while he said nothing but just lay staring ahead with the air of a man waiting for the hearse. Then he turned to me, his eyes boring into mine.

"If you tell one single person what happened here—!"

"Stephen!" I said with a maidenly gasp. "Never! No one!" I touched his shoulder and gave him my most soulful gaze. "I'm on *your* side. Always. Don't you know that by now?"

"I guess so," he conceded with a sigh. "But what about Claire?"

"Oh, don't worry about Claire," I said lightly. I was eager to dismiss the whole topic of Claire, which I deemed dangerous and inconducive to erections. "She's the soul of tact. I mean, you saw her peek under the table. Did she cry 'Aha!' or even bat an eye? No, she just stood up, realized this was no place for ladies, and hustled your mom and Gina out. You've nothing to fear from Claire. God, you're so tense!" I observed, tentatively kneading his upper back. "Allow me."

Holding my breath, I began to gently massage the area, fully expecting that any second he'd ask what the fuck I thought I was doing. His muscles *were* tight though and he accepted my ministrations without protest. Emboldened, I began kneading the area harder, concentrating on my technique even as I marveled that I was fondling the screen's most legendary trapezius.

"So," he asked dreamily, his eyes closed now, "where the hell'd you come from? What were you doing in here?"

Having just extolied Claire's benevolence it seemed imprudent to admit I'd been running for my life from her. I said that, in order to avoid an unwelcome pass from Monty, I'd claimed to be double booked then taken refuge in here, hiding beneath the table when I'd heard footsteps approaching.

"Once I realized it was you I was going to come out but . . . well, things had kinda heated up by then. One hates to kill the mood."

"Liar," he said with a stoned smirk. "You just wanted to listen in."

"And watch," I conceded boldly.

"You could see?" he asked, more intrigued than offended.

"A little. In the mirror."

"Slut," he said companionably. "Played with yourself too, I'll bet."

"Oh," I deadpanned, "like that was the dirtiest thing going on in here."

He laughed softly. Silence fell. It lengthened and I grew concerned. Had I overstepped? Or worse, put him to sleep? But then he gave a little sigh and without opening his eyes asked, "So, wudja think?"

A part of me couldn't help thinking "Actors! Can't they do *any-thing* without wanting a review?" But a far shrewder part of me realized that there's nothing like boffo press to raise an actor's spirits and in this case perhaps more. So I launched into a rhapsodic appraisal of Stephen's performance, leaning heavily on words like "stunning" and "godlike" plus several metaphors drawn equally from the worlds of ballet and rodeo. I hoped my lascivious praise joined with my increasingly visible excitement would reignite Stephen's libido. He shifted onto his side and I stole a glance at his boxers.

Success!

Rubbing his neck now, I lowered my face to his ear.

"You," I growled huskily, "are the sexiest man of all time." This phrase proved the sexual equivalent of open sesame. He grabbed the back of my head and gave me a kiss so electrifying it damn near finished the job it was meant to begin. When our lips parted I squatted there, nose to nose with him. I gazed into those perfect eyes, waiting breathlessly to hear the words that had echoed in my fantasies since the moment we'd met. And though I'd been hoping for "I want you, Philip, I always have!" or "Take me, my love!" I settled quite happily for "Get busy. You're batting cleanup."

WHEN THE DAY COMES that I lay wizened on my deathbed, preparing to breathe my last, should those in attendance note that I am smiling more lewdly than is quite decorous during extreme unction, they may confidently assume that I'm recalling the eight and a half minutes that followed Stephen's invitation. It is a memory I've revisited times without number and one that has never, even in the darkest hours, failed to divert.

The question most often put to us members of the Fucked-a-Megastar Club by the frustrated applicants who crowd its waiting list is, "Was it all you dreamed it would be?" In strict honesty I must say not entirely, if only because my dreams were more romantic in nature and ran toward sleigh beds, roaring fires, and perhaps dinner. But these are mere quibbles. When you're making love and the face you're gazing down upon (or, by midpoint, up at) is that of Stephen Donato, matters of venue pale into insignificance.

True, if I wanted to cavil, I might have preferred it if he'd have spent as much time gazing raptly at me as he did at the mirror, this previously mentioned predilection of his having reasserted itself rather vigorously. Again, some might have seen this as narcissism. I preferred to think it was his scrupulous devotion to craft and that he watched his performance much as he might the dailies of a new film, searching for ways to better his technique. How thrilling for me though to gaze into, or at least at, those beautiful azure eyes. How much more gratifying still to see them widen in ecstasy at the jubilant finish. Hey, Stevie fans! Think you've seen all his major releases? I can name one you missed!

When it was over we lay there panting. Then Stephen pecked me lightly on the cheek (this being, after all, our first date) and said, "Thanks, I needed that."

"Oh, anytime."

He sat on the edge of the table, still a bit foggy. He remarked on the unusual strength of the pot and said he'd need some coffee in his room before dinner. I offered to walk him out.

As we promenaded past the unsuspecting guests in the spa foyer and main salon, a wave of euphoria stole over me as I savored the delicious secret we now shared. It was something I hadn't felt since Gilbert and I, at the age of fifteen, lost our virginity to each other, then proceeded directly to a rehearsal of *You're a Good Man, Charlie Brown.* Our covertly exchanged smiles flooded my heart with happiness, erasing the pique I felt over playing the thankless role of Schroeder.

Stephen and I were adults, not schoolboys. We exchanged no telltale grins but ambled through the salon and into the foyer with that studied nonchalance illicit lovers have cultivated from time immemorial. But beneath my placid exterior I was already reliving our torrid antics and happily imagining even steamier assignations to come. Could I lure him over to my place some night when Gilbert was out? Was my bedroom nice enough? Would I need a bigger mirror?

The problem with euphoria, of course, is that it lowers your defenses, leaving you vulnerable to predators lurking in the underbrush, which is why I gave no thought whatsoever to Claire until she fell on me from behind as we strolled down the upstairs hall. Seizing me by my collar and belt, she frog-marched me back to her room. Stephen, so recently assured by me of her benign placidity, watched in pardonable confusion. "You too!" she barked, motioning for him to join the party. When he failed to do so immediately she stomped over, grabbed him by the sleeve, and dragged him to her door.

"What do you think you're doing?!"

"Just get in!" she snapped and shoved us both inside, slamming the door behind her. The room was all but identical to my own, the sole addition to the decor being Gilbert, who sat at the foot of the bed and wore the dazed, beleaguered look of a suspect hauled in for questioning on a day when the good cop has phoned in sick.

"Watch who you're shoving!" scolded Stephen.

"Excuse me, Your Highness," said Claire, offering a sarcastic curtsy. "Just sit."

"I don't know what your problem is but I don't take orders from—!"

"Sit!"

Stephen scowled but some instinct told him to obey and he parked himself resentfully on a love seat. I sat next to him, bracing for the worst, which Claire wasted no time in dispensing.

"Your friend under the table—did you have sex with him?"

Stephen just stared, aghast at the impertinence of the question.

"*Did you?*"

"What are you talking about?" he replied with the knee-jerk outrage such calumnies invariably provoked from him.

"Your little chum," prompted Claire. "Golden boy. What were you doing before Mum and the missus crashed the party?"

"I have no idea what you're talking about! There was no one under that table," he declared so forcefully even I almost bought it. "Philip will back me up, won't you?"

"Oh, absolutely."

"I *saw* him, you idiots!" said Claire. "And what's more I saw you see me see him, so do not please imagine you can act your way out of this. I know all about what goes on in Moira's VIP rooms. This one told me everything."

She indicated Gilbert, whose fascination with his lap remained undiminished.

"Nice going!" I sniped. Unfair of me, I know, since I'd have sung like a drunk show queen had Claire worked me over. It was vital though that Stephen view me as a stalwart confidant who'd never crack under pressure.

"Look," said Stephen, rising to face her, "if you think you can shake me down here—!"

"Oh, sit, you stoned jackass. I'm not trying to shake you down. I'm trying to save your sorry ass, though I'm guessing it's too late for that."

Stephen, accustomed to a touch more obeisance from his employees, said, "Hey! There's no need for name-calling!"

"Oh, I'm sorry. Hurt your feelings, love? I have not begun to name-call, you conceited, overprivileged oaf! You dick-brained, Oscar-fucking imbecile!"

Stephen turned to me with a flustered, betrayed look that broke my so recently euphoric heart.

"You told me she wouldn't be a problem!"

"Trust me," said Claire, "I am the least of your problems! Do you even begin to realize the magnitude of the blunder you've made in delivering yourself into the hands of Moira Finch? Do you have the first idea whom you're dealing with?"

"Claire," I explained weakly, "has never liked Moira."

"No, I never have, Stephen. Neither have these two. And do you know why? Let me spell it out for you. Moira," she said, jabbing a finger into his chest, "is not a *nice lady!* She is a thief, a liar, and a grifter par excellence. She is a backstabbing con artist who would sell her own mother for a Tic Tac, and if a vampire bit her, the vampire would die. *That,* my friend, is the woman you have so shrewdly entrusted with your most incendiary sexual secrets!"

"What are you talking about?" exclaimed Stephen, eyes bulging. "Philip said she was great!"

"He had to. She was blackmailing him!"

"What?" yelped Stephen, recoiling at his least favorite word.

"It was hardly blackmail," I said, rising, alarmed, to my feet. "More an exchange of favors."

"It's why they brought you here in the first place," said Claire. "Because Moira made them. She threatened to spill our dirty little secret, which is that our spec script, the one that made Bobby recommend us, was this one's"—she thrust a finger at Gilbert—"clever little rewrite of *Casablanca.*"

"I don't think it matters how we got the job!" said Gilbert. "What counts is the bang-up job we've done on the new one, which is completely our own work and—"

"Shut up about the fucking script!" snarled Stephen. He sprang to his feet and began pacing frantically about the room.

"Is this true, Philip?" he demanded. "She *blackmailed* you into bringing me here?"

I said she had not done so explicitly, but conceded that we'd sensed a certain danger in saying no.

"She wanted a big fish," said Claire, "and thanks to these two she got one. Which brings us back to Oscar—was that your idea or Moira's?"

"Of course it wasn't my idea! He just walked in!"

"And you were stoned?"

"It relaxes me!"

"A bit stronger than usual, was it?" asked Claire.

Stephen gaped at her as if she'd guessed the name of his fifth-grade crush.

"How the hell'd you know that?"

"Then one thing led to another?" pressed Claire.

"None of your damn business!"

She stared at him in amazement and something like pity, which unnerved me more than her wrath.

"And it never occurred to you she might be *filming* it?"

It clearly had not. The suggestion literally floored Stephen, making him stagger backward and trip over an ottoman. As he lay there, his face a rictus of horror, I wondered briefly if he'd had an actual coronary, his body making the snap decision that death would be preferable to life in a world where such footage existed and was easily downloadable.

"You think she *filmed it?!*" said Gilbert, sounding less alarmed than eager to secure premiere tickets.

"If I know Moira," sighed Claire, "that's exactly what she did, what she's been doing from the start. Roping in the suckers, pinhole cameras in every room, biding her time till she can name her price."

"*Fuck!*" The expletive did not spring from Stephen's lips but rather rocketed from the back of his throat like a forcefully Heimliched olive pit.

"*Fuck, fuck, FUCK!!*"

"Now let's not panic!" I said, rushing to help him up.

"Don't touch me!" he growled. "You're the asshole who set me up for this!"

His words were like daggers and I brimmed suddenly not with guilt but anger at Claire, whose alarmist theory had turned my beloved against me. I wheeled on her. "Well, thanks a lot for getting him all freaked out! For all we know it's never even occurred to Moira that she could—*oh, shit!*"

For an image had just detonated in my head. It was of the small security room located off Moira's office. I recalled the locked door, the pugnacious little guard, the computer equipment. Mostly though I remembered the rows of flickering video monitors. Hadn't one displayed a room much like that in which our recent sexcapades had unfolded?

"What?" demanded Claire.

I described my discovery, which did little to lessen Stephen's hysteria. He was pacing now like a caged puma, his thoughts no doubt centering on Oscar and his own regrettably abandoned calls for brisker fucking.

"Don't worry, Stephen! I'm going to fix this!" I vowed.

"Oh, really, Phil?" he said with venomous sarcasm. "And just how are you gonna do that?"

"Yes," chimed Gilbert snidely, as if he bore no responsibility for our present dilemma. "Do tell us your master plan!"

The desire to regain lost love is a powerful spur to invention and I swiftly hit on a strategy. I outlined it in broad strokes. Stephen seemed cautiously hopeful, Claire offered astute embellishments, and Gilbert said he'd been about to suggest it himself.

Stephen called downstairs and asked for Moira. He told her there was a matter of some delicacy he wished to discuss but could not do so in his suite as Gina was there. Could she meet him in Philip's room? Moira consented and we hastened next door to my room, where Claire, Gilbert, and I secreted ourselves in the closet. Moira arrived and when she'd advanced far enough into the room we pounced and tackled her to the floor.

"Get your goddamned hands off me!"

She struggled, demonic and wild-eyed as though fearing an unsolicited exorcism, but Claire and Gilbert held her down while I frisked her and found the prize I was after—her key ring. I smiled, dangling it before her in triumph.

"How *dare* you assault me! You give those back right now or I'll say something you'll wish I hadn't!"

"You mean the *Casablanca* business?" said Claire. "Sorry, love, those beans are all spilled. Now it's your turn to come clean."

"Have you been filming me?" demanded Stephen.

"What?" replied Moira, doe-eyed and bewildered.

"My massages!" he snapped. "Have you been filming them?"

"Of course not!" she exclaimed, scandalized. "The very idea! You know I treat my clients' privacy with the utmost respect!" She jerked her head toward Claire. "I suppose *she's* the one who's been filling your head with this rubbish?"

"If it's rubbish," said Claire, "then you won't mind waiting here while we pop downstairs and check out your little video room."

Moira heaved an irate sigh and shook her head, marveling at our paranoia.

"Fine. You've got the keys. Knock yourselves out."

She sank into a chair and gazed out the window with the bored superior look young poetesses wear in algebra class. This was not the response we'd anticipated and the four of us exchanged a puzzled glance. Moira, taking advantage of our momentary inattention, sprang from the chair and flew toward the door. She managed to open it and very nearly got out but Stephen, making good on his boast that he does his own stunts, gave chase, dove to the ground, and grabbed her ankle, causing her to fall. He dragged her caveman style back into the room, ignoring her shrill threats of legal action, which Claire promptly silenced with the aid of a rolled-up pillowcase. We then secured her hands and feet with neckties and deposited her, bound, gagged, and furious, back into the chair.

We agreed it would take two of us to guard Moira and prevent her, if possible, from turning into a wolf and leaping out the window. Claire and Stephen agreed to stay with her while Gilbert and I plundered her sanctum.

As we raced down the hall I stopped suddenly, struck by a disquieting thought.

"What?" said Gilbert.

"The guard," I said, describing the malevolent Kewpie doll who'd barred my way earlier.

"You say she's tiny?"

"Yes, but her gun's not."

"Ah." Gilbert frowned. "We'll have to distract her then."

"How?"

Gilbert pondered the matter for all of three seconds, then darted back down the hall to where a fire alarm was mounted next to an extinguisher. He triggered it and the tranquility of the spa was instantly shattered by a clangorous din. Doors flew open and startled guests, Claire among them, popped their heads out. I rushed back, told her to sit tight, then rejoined Gilbert, who was standing at the top of the stairs, smiling proudly down at the chaos he'd wrought.

As anxious guests streamed into the lobby from the bar and salon, our eyes remained fixed on the door behind the reception desk. In due course it opened and out came the receptionist along with slutty raccoon girl. Seconds ticked by and I began to wonder if Kim's dedication was such that she'd sooner face incineration than abandon her post but she finally emerged, scowling, from her den.

"Yeesh!" said Gilbert. "Who put a dress on Danny DeVito?"

As Kim busied herself herding patrons out to the lawn it was simplicity itself to dash down the stairs, nip behind the desk, drop to a crouch, and waddle into the office. As we'd expected, the door to the security room was locked, but the fourth key we tried opened it.

Once inside, we closed the door and inspected the bank of video monitors. There were twelve in all, displaying four different treatment rooms from three angles each. Two of the rooms were now empty. In the other two rooms buff young men were struggling hastily into their clothes while their clients, gentlemen of middle years, huddled in robes, looking fretful and thwarted.

Beneath the monitors was a counter on which sat an Apple laptop with a large screen. I hit COMMAND-F for "find" and typed in "Donato." This led me to a folder that bore his name and contained thirty-two items, the icons for which were little filmstrips, suggesting video files. Each was labeled by date, the most recent being today's. I clicked on it and the screen filled suddenly with remarkably crisp footage of Stephen sitting on the massage table, smoking the joint as Ricky kneaded his neck. I pressed COMMAND-QUIT and the scene disappeared.

"Watcha do that for?" squawked Gilbert. "They weren't even naked yet!"

"There's no time, you horny idiot! Check the drawers and cabinets!"

A hasty search yielded a Lucite box containing twelve shiny disks like DVDs. They were in paper sleeves on each of which was scrawled some famous name, Stephen's among them.

"You take these, I'll get the laptop!" I said, disconnecting the cables but keeping the power cord. Satisfied we'd confiscated all we could, we exited through Moira's lair to the outer office, entering it at the precise moment that wee Kim barreled in from the lobby.

"*You!* What the fuck do you think you're doing?" she inquired, reaching for her gun.

My usual strategy in moments of such dire peril is to freeze in horror and pray to wake up. But I had a megastar to save and wasn't about to let this surly Cerberus stand between me and his tender gratitude. Noting that she was standing on a beige carpet runner and that we were not, I dropped to a squat and gave it a brisk yank, causing her to plummet the relatively short distance to the floor.

"C'mon!" I yelled and we fled, Gilbert taking care to stomp on her kidneys so as to extract still more wind from her sails. We sped through the lobby and out to the driveway, where the confused guests milled about, anxiously speculating on the whereabouts of the fire.

"Shit!" cried Gilbert, frantically patting his pockets.

230 | *Joe Keenan*

"What?"

"We valeted!"

The LA custom of valeting—leaving one's keys and car with a fellow who parks it for you then retrieves it when needed—is normally a welcome convenience. There is nothing like it, however, to put a crimp in a getaway, which is why your savvier burglar eschews the practice entirely, preferring to keep a driver waiting or, at the very least, self-park. There was no chance that even the speediest valet could retrieve Gilbert's car before Moira's enraged sentinel emerged from the spa, pistols blazing.

"Moira's keys!" said Gilbert. "Is her car on there?"

I whipped the ring from my pocket and saw that it indeed held a key to her Porsche. This was a timely stroke of luck as the enraged thuglet had just exited the lobby and was letting rip some full-throated war cries.

"Stop! Thief! *Stop them!!*"

We sprinted madly toward the parking area in search of Moira's Porsche. It would not, we promptly realized, be easy to find, since, owing to the affluence of her clientele, the lot looked pretty much like a dealership. Fortunately for us, Moira liked her boss lady perks and the RESERVED FOR M. FINCH sign led us swiftly to her gleaming black Carrera.

Gilbert took the wheel. We peeled out, tires screaming, and roared down the driveway at a speed that brought loud rebukes from guests near its edges. We barely heard one last furious cry of "Stop them!" before we passed through the gate.

After we'd traveled a safe distance, taking many an arbitrary turn to foil pursuers, I borrowed Gilbert's cell, having left mine at the hotel, and called Claire. I informed her of our success and asked if she'd retrieve Gilbert's and my luggage as we'd not be returning to Les Étoiles anytime soon. I asked to speak to Stephen. I told him what we'd found, laying it on pretty thick in the derring-do department, then asked if he wished to rendezvous later for a handoff. This drew a howl of protest from Gilbert, who saw no reason to relinquish the disks before we'd had a proper screening.

Stephen said he was bursting to take possession but couldn't meet us tonight owing to Gina, whom he'd just glimpsed from the window. She was wandering the grounds, searching hysterically for him, convinced, despite the conspicuous absence of fire, that he lay trapped in some smoldering corner of the spa. She'd be hurt and wonder why he hadn't sought her out during the scare to make sure she was safe. To abandon her again for some mysterious nocturnal errand would only further inflame her suspicions.

"Can't you just tell her you're antsy and want to go for a drive?"

"Uh, she's kinda heard that one a lot."

He said he'd call me first thing come morning to arrange a hand-off. Then Claire took the phone and urged us not to return home as Moira knew where we lived and was not above dispatching ungentle emissaries to reclaim her prize. We agreed this was prudent and arrived some twenty minutes later at the Chateau Marmont, having stopped just once, at Gilbert's request, for popcorn.

Eighteen

★

I WOKE THE NEXT MORNING AT NINE. For perhaps ten blessedly confused seconds I peered, groggy yet untroubled, at my unfamiliar surroundings. I even wondered, having just dreamed of him, if the mound of bedclothes snoring gently beside me might be Stephen. Then Gilbert rolled over and sleepily deposited a bit of drool on my pillowcase and I remembered all. With memory came a galloping herd of emotions, Regret leading the pack by a comfortable margin. I regretted acquiescing to plagiarism; I regretted luring Stephen into Moira's clutches; I regretted stealing a car in front of seventy witnesses; and, having seen the film of me and Stephen, I regretted not having worked harder on my abs.

I sort of regretted having sex with Gilbert, though reproached myself less for this, such an outcome being all but inevitable when two former boyfriends check into a hotel together, order up wine, and watch three hours of celebrity porn.

Gilbert stirred. He did not seem at all disoriented to be waking in a strange bed, the experience having long been drained of novelty for him.

"Mornin'," he yawned.

"Morning."

He peered under the sheet and, finding us naked, smirked like a naughty choirboy.

"Well, weren't we silly?"

"Very."

"Still, it's nice now and then for old times' sake." He raised himself up on one elbow and regarded me with a look of amused wonder.

"What?" I asked.

"Do you have any idea how *famous* you'd be if that film of you and Stevie ever got out?"

"Well, it's not going to," I said emphatically.

"I'm just saying. I mean, Gawd—you would *rule* West Hollywood."

"Gilbert—"

"*Parades.*"

I reminded him that we'd promised Stephen we'd surrender everything we'd taken to him so that he could destroy it.

"You're such a Boy Scout. If it were me shtupping Stephen Donato I'd want the whole world to see."

"Well it's not you. And I don't want anyone to see it."

He considered this a moment.

"I see what you mean. The tummy and all."

"It's not my stomach! I'm thinking of Stephen. If this got out he'd be completely humiliated."

"Don't run yourself down, hon, it's just a little *pouche*. A few more crunches and—"

"I'm not talking about me! I mean Oscar!"

"Oh, right." He giggled at the memory and agreed that it would be a dark day indeed for Stephen if the public at large ever got a good gander at him thanking the Academy.

The day ahead certainly looked like a dark one for us; there was poor, disastrously compromised Stephen to deal with, not to mention Claire, plus God only knew what fresh machinations from Moira, with whom we were now officially on a war footing. Gilbert, true to form, suggested we hole up at the Chateau for a few days so as to give all con-

234 | Joe Keenan

cerned time to calm down. I replied that our disappearance would do little to calm Stephen. An action star who has giddily flown the flag of surrender to not one but three butt pirates does not breathe easily till all evidence of this has been seized and deposited with care in the nearest furnace.

We breakfasted in the room, then checked out and drove warily home. When we got there I remained in the car, motor running, while Gilbert courageously checked the house for lurking assailants. When he returned and pronounced it ninja free, I retrieved the laptop and disks from the trunk and scurried inside with them. I entered the living room, and the first thing I noticed was our answering machine. Before leaving I'd cleared it of old messages but now the number "thirteen" was blinking unpropitiously up at us.

"I don't know about you," frowned Gilbert, "but I'll definitely need a Bloody before I hear those."

I seconded the motion and moments later, after we'd each taken a fortifying gulp, I hit the play button. The first call was from Moira, who informed us that if we did not return everything we'd taken immediately, she would swear out a warrant for our arrest on charges of grand theft auto.

"Oh, please!" snorted Gilbert. "Like she wants the police dragged into this!" I saw his logic but was still uneasy, feeling it was never wise to underestimate Moira's chutzpah.

Stephen had called next, urgently demanding I phone him. Ditto Claire. The fourth call, logged at one a.m., was from one Brandon, a recent acquaintance of Gilbert's offering to drop by if Gilbert were in the mood for company. "Damn! Why'd I have to miss that?" lamented Gilbert, then, remembering he'd been sleeping with me at the time, took an embarrassed sip of his Bloody. The next call, which came in just after two, was from Sonia Powers. She excoriated us at length for the irreparable damage we'd done to her trusting client, demanded that we immediately hand over any and all items we'd taken from Les Étoiles, and vowed that vengeance against us would be, from this moment to that of our demise, her highest priority. Of the eight remaining calls one was from Claire again and the rest were increasingly rabid follow-ups from Sonia.

If the messages offered little to cheer us, they did provide a window into Stephen's thoughts and actions in the hours since we'd spoken. If he'd departed the spa not long after us, he'd have gotten home by nine, giving him three or four hours to sit and contemplate the dilemma in which he now found himself.

It is, as he already knew, bad.

But it is only now, as the marijuana haze that so disastrously clouded his judgment lifts, that he begins to grasp the full, catastrophic dimensions of what awaits him should his most recent film achieve wide distribution. His downfall, he now sees, will make all previous scandals, no matter how explosive in their day, seem mere faux pas — bloopers! — when measured against his towering shame. His mind clear (unaffected as yet by the scotch he sips to still his trembling hands), he sees it all: the worldwide ignominy; the ceaseless screaming headlines as the jackals of the press feast on the carrion of his career; the public's quenchless appetite for new, more shocking revelations, true or otherwise; the emergence from the woodwork of every man he's ever touched, eager to vend his heavily embroidered recollections; the articles bursting with sympathy for Gina, mining every last nugget of her pain and betrayal; the jeremiads from the right proclaiming him the new poster boy for Hollywood depravity.

Mostly though he sees the jokes, the unbridled public hilarity, the giddy national mirthquake that will ensue as the late-night wags milk his plight for every chuckle it's worth.

"Stephen Donato vowed today that he'll win the Oscar, no ifs, ands, or buts. He later amended the statement, ruling out only ifs and ands."

"Stephen Donato can't wait for Oscar night. He heard that if his wife goes to the ladies' room they'll replace her with a good-looking seat-filler."

It is a bleak vision, made bleaker still by his grim certainty that his fevered mind is not exaggerating a whit, that he is, if anything, overlooking humiliations beyond his present ability to imagine. As the hours tick by he stares deeper into the abyss. Who, he asks, will save him? To whom can he turn to smite the villainess who holds his future captive? The answer, he knows, has always known, is Sonia. It is only his fear of her wrath (for we all have our Claires) that forestalls his cry for help till past midnight.

Imagining that call, I felt a bizarre flicker of sympathy for Sonia. When one thinks of the things that make publicists lie awake at night nibbling antacids, one pictures the usual potholes on fame's highway: the drunk-driving arrests, the colorful relapses into addiction, the hookers stubbornly unresponsive to resuscitation efforts. Publicists brace themselves for these things. They make contingency plans and fortify their Rolodexes with the numbers of those who Know a Guy. But not even the most battle-hardened flack is ever quite prepared to hear that her most famous client, on the eve of his all but certain nomination for Best Actor in a Motion Picture, has taken one up the keister from a life-size Oscar and yes, there were cameras.

Let us not speculate on their discussion; we have seen Stephen suffer enough. It's clear though that when he informed her we'd made off with the evidence, her policy had been to take possession immediately. Hence her two a.m. shot across our bow and many strident follow-ups. Hence too the call she made now as Gilbert and I drained the dregs of our Bloodies.

"It's Sonia," growled the voice on the machine. "Pick up the damn phone!"

"I wouldn't," counseled Gilbert.

"I know you're there, assholes! I've got a guy across the street and he saw you come home. SO ANSWER THE GODDAMN FUCK-ING PHONE!"

Gilbert assured me he'd get the next one, so I took a deep breath and raised the receiver to my face.

"Hey, Sonia!" I said, perhaps a shade too cheerfully.

"Don't 'Hey, Sonia' me, you miserable ass-wipe! You plagiarist! You low-life pimp!"

"Well, good morning to you too."

"Where the fuck have you been?"

"At a hotel. Moira knows where we live so we didn't want to come home, the theory being—"

"Yeah, whatever. You still have the stuff? The computer, the disks?"

"Right here, safe and sound."

"I'll be there to collect in forty minutes."

"Oh?"

"And don't even *think* of going anywhere. My guy's watching you and he's got orders to do what he needs to to make sure you stay put."

"Now really, Sonia," I chided, "I know you're upset but I'd think we could resolve matters without recourse to hired goons."

Her response was brief and devoid of warmth. I hung up and told Gilbert that Sonia was en route and expected us to hand over the purloined materials *in toto*. Gilbert frowned thoughtfully.

"I wouldn't," he advised.

"What?"

"Hand it over. Not all of it anyway. I'd hang on to the Stephen Oscar stuff."

"Are you serious?"

"We have to think of ourselves, Philip. Things have gotten pretty nasty—threats, thugs on our doorstep! What if they get worse? Who knows what they may try to do to us? If we have the film we can say, 'Back off, or else.' Without it we're totally at their mercy!"

I conceded there was some validity to this but felt it would be unforgivably disloyal to Stephen to hang on to evidence he wished dearly to see obliterated.

"You have to understand, he trusts me *completely* and I'd hate to—"

"Oh, Stephen, Stephen, Stephen!" brayed Gilbert. "Get over it, hon! This fantasy of yours that you two are some sort of couple is the most pathetic delusion you've had since you thought the mustache worked. Wake up!"

He grabbed my ears, pulled my face to his, and bellowed into it.

"He's a *MOVIE STAR!* He's not like you or me! Stephen loves Stephen and good luck breaking up that little romance! You're not his boyfriend. You're not even his friend. You're someone who was useful to him. He knew you'd do anything he asked if he just let you moon over him and flirted back once in a while."

"Flirted!" I bristled. "You saw the movie, you jealous boob! Is that what you call flirting?"

"Oh, please! You were hardly his first choice for costar, were you? Or his second. They both fell out, then you got called in like some sexual understudy. Trust me, that was the first and last time you're ever getting yourself some Stephen and I can't believe you're even thinking of giving away your only souvenir! Gawd, if I had film of me doing the nasty with Stevie do you think I'd hand it over to some pushy dyke battle-ax? Hell, no! I'd make myself a nice digital copy, keep it for the rest of my life, and watch it more often than *All About Eve!*"

I mulled this option for roughly half the time it has taken you to read this sentence, then asked, "How do you make a copy?"

As it turned out, rather easily.

I'd told Stephen we'd taken the laptop and some DVDs, three of which bore his name. Since I hadn't specified the number of non-Stephen disks there was no way Sonia could know if one was missing. I inserted one such disk into the drive, erased its contents, then copied the files with me and Stephen onto it. It pricked my conscience that by doing so I was also creating copies of the more explosive Oscar footage, but Sonia was due in half an hour, hardly enough time to master the laptop's complex editing software and copy only such portions of the files as were indispensable to the Cavanaugh Archive.

"There you go," said Gilbert as I ejected the disk. "Now hide it."

I did so and smiled, knowing Sonia would never find it on the bookshelf, tucked imperceptibly into our landlord's apparently unread copy of Uta Hagen's *Respect for Acting*.

It occurred to me that with Sonia even now exceeding the speed limit for broomsticks in her haste to reach us, it might be wise to ask Claire over. Angry as she was at us, I knew that Sonia's vulgar belligerence would push all her buttons, making her rise instinctively to our defense. I phoned her and she arrived twenty minutes later, bearing the suitcases Gilbert and I had left at the spa. On entering she delivered her most scathing philippic to date, the details of which I'll spare you as they did not differ in substance from her previous tributes to our intelligence and integrity. She then demanded a full précis of what had transpired in the massage room, and I obliged with a terse, PG-13 summary, i.e., Pot, Ricky sex, Oscar sex, Family Hour, Me sex.

"So," she said when I'd finished, "is that Moira's laptop?"

I nodded.

"And the copy you made? Well hidden, I hope?"

"What copy?" I asked, thrown, not for the first time, by her perspicacity.

She heaved an annoyed sigh. "You have a laptop containing footage of you making whoopee with Stephen. You also have a stack of rewritable DVDs. Do you expect me to believe you didn't make a copy?"

"It never even occurred to me!"

"Is it well hidden?"

"Yes, very."

"Good. We may need it if the going gets rough."

"Just what I said!" crowed Gilbert, pleasantly astonished to be vindicated by Claire of all people.

Claire advised us not to mention the copy to Sonia, prompting hoots of derision from Gilbert and me.

"Well, duh!"

"What are we, *idiots?*" I asked, realizing at once that I'd rather lobbed it up there for Claire, who responded with a solid triple.

A car pulled up outside. Peering through the blinds, I saw a large black sedan in our driveway. I was suddenly grateful that Claire had rallied to our defense and told her so.

"I'm not here to defend you, you half-wit. I'm just here to keep that vindictive harpy from demolishing our careers."

"How do you plan to do that?" asked Gilbert.

"Wouldn't it be lovely if I knew?"

I opened the door and was much taken aback to find Sonia accompanied not only by Stephen but Diana as well. Sonia's expression would have had to brighten considerably to achieve mere malevolence. Diana looked only slightly less murderous while Stephen resembled a morose somnambulist.

Stress has a way of bringing out my perky side and I chirped, "Come in!" as though they were my book group and we were reading Patrick Dennis. "Can I offer you something to drink?"

Stephen and Sonia declined but Diana growled a request for a vodka rocks as Sonia steered her into the living room.

"You told your mom?!" I whispered to Stephen.

"Sonia thought we might need her help," he said, his glazed, "Do not resuscitate" stare suggesting just how merry that mother-son chat had been.

We entered the living room, where Gilbert had mixed himself a second Bloody, which, from its watermelon hue, looked to be 90 percent Stoli. I fixed Diana's drink and was rewarded with a glare of unbridled abhorrence; she couldn't have hated me more if I'd been a fluorescent light.

"I'm guessing you're Claire," sneered Sonia.

"Yes. Nice to meet you."

"Oh, yeah, it's a real pleasure! Makes my whole fucking morning." She jabbed a finger at the table where we'd gathered our plunder. "Is this all of it?"

"That's everything," I said.

She squinted mistrustfully.

"You sure about that, Daisy?"

"Oh, quite."

"Because if you assholes are holding out on me—"

Claire said, "They obtained this material at considerable personal risk for the sole purpose of protecting your client. You might show a little less rudeness and a little more gratitude."

"*GRATITUDE!*" roared Sonia. "Oh forgive me, Missy! *Thank you* for luring my client into a gay sex ring! *Thank you* for telling him to trust a woman you knew was a blackmailing bitch! *Thank you* for possibly making the most successful actor of his generation a washed-up fucking punchline! Scumbags! You make me puke!"

She seized the computer and disks, marched out to her car, hurled them into her trunk, and rejoined us. She appeared to feel that, with the evidence now secured, she could safely abandon the bonhomie she'd displayed thus far.

"You miserable little shits! I told you what would happen if you messed with my clients, but you didn't believe me, did you? Well, you're going to find out how wrong you were! For starters, don't think you can tell *anyone* about this and be believed because you will have *zero* credibility in this town. The minute I leave here I'm sending Bobby Spellman a DVD of *Casablanca*. Then I'll make sure there are stories in *Variety*, the *LA Times*, and the AP about how you sleazebags conned your way into a job with my clients—which you can consider terminated as of now. Then you will drag your sorry asses back to whatever fucking hole you crawled out of and never come near this town or my clients again!!"

Harsh stuff, you'll agree, and Gilbert and I regarded each other with suitably bug-eyed distress. But Claire rose and faced the ogress with an assured, commanding look such as Joan of Arc might have worn after a fortifying breakfast.

"I don't think so."

"Oh, you don't, huh?"

"No, 'fraid not. We have an agent here and other job offers and we mean to take them."

"Oh, trust me, hon," said Sonia with a vinegary snicker, "those offers are gonna go away real fast."

"Are they?" Claire turned to Stephen. "I notice Gina didn't come along today."

"Leave Gina out of this," he said sharply.

"It seems to me you're the one leaving her out. She doesn't know, does she?"

"Of course, she knows," said Diana a shade too quickly. "She was too upset to come with us."

Claire said, "Then you won't mind my calling her to offer my con-

242 | Joe Keenan

dolences? She gave me her cell number so we could share thoughts about the script."

"You keep away from her!" warned Stephen.

"You haven't told her. And you don't intend to. She's a bit of a loose cannon, your Gina. Not the brightest bulb on the marquee and not exactly the soul of discretion. She told me all about your aunt's memoir and her fear that Lily might rehash the malicious, 'completely unfounded' rumor that you've slept with men. You're terrified that if she finds out she'll divorce you and tell anyone who asks why. She might even write a book of her own."

Sonia was incredulous to the point of apoplexy.

"Are you *threatening* my client?!"

"Sorry, love, was I not being clear? Yes, I'm threatening your client and frankly, you truculent toad, I have every right to. How dare you presume it's our duty to safeguard your reputations even as you blacken ours, firing us and telling the whole town we're plagiarists!"

"But you *are* plagiarists!" said Sonia triumphantly.

"And your client *did* fuck an Oscar! And if you smear us, his wife will hear about it."

"That's telling 'em, Claire!" shouted Gilbert.

Stephen shot me a look of pleading disbelief as though he were being mugged and I was a nearby patrolman tending to my nails with an emery board.

"Believe me, Stephen, this wasn't my idea! Claire's her own woman!"

He wheeled on her, his face a mask of aggrieved astonishment.

"So you're just going to destroy my marriage?!"

"No, *you* are," parried Claire, "if you don't call off your pit bull and let us finish our work."

"Right!" said Gilbert. "It's time you people stopped blaming your problems on us. It's not our fault!"

"Fuck you!" spat Stephen. "It was you two that dragged me to the damn spa!"

"For a massage! You're the one who decided to throw an open house in his ass!"

"And just what," added Claire, "were you planning to do about 'Glen' here? Do you really want to pull your spy out now, just when Lily's getting to the good stuff? Or do you have the Olympian gall to imagine Philip will go on doing your dirty work after you've dragged him through the mud? Honestly, have you people thought this through at all?"

It was clear from Stephen's and Diana's expressions that they had not, recent events having consigned Lily's memoir to the back burner. I sensed too from the vexed glance Diana gave Stephen that she saw Claire's point. They could hardly fire me off Project A, permit Sonia to skip rope with my entrails, and still expect me to provide cheerful service on Project B. And while Cavanaugh the Screenwriter could be liquidated without consequence, Cavanaugh the Mole remained a crucial asset.

"Look, Sonia," sighed Stephen, "maybe we're letting our emotions get the better of us."

"*YOU DO NOT NEED THESE PEOPLE!*" shouted Sonia, beside herself at the thought that her scimitar might rust, unused. "We can get someone else to ghost Lily's book!"

"Not if we warn her, you can't," said Claire.

"*More threats!!* Jesus, Stephen, are you gonna let these traitors, these *nobodies*, blackmail you?"

"There's a difference," said Claire, "between blackmail and self-defense. Which, I believe," she added, glancing toward the foyer, "we're about to see illustrated."

A throat cleared and the rest of us, startled, turned toward the foyer.

"I'm glad everyone's here," said Moira with a placid smile. "Saves *so* much trouble."

I SUSPECT MOST OF you will concur by this point that a little Sonia goes a long way, so I'll spare you the volcano of vitriol she disgorged on learning that our visitor was the proprietress of Les Étoiles. Moira did not interrupt or try to defend herself. She listened with the patience of a lass who has long known that one's victims like to get these things off their chests and the experienced villainess does not take them personally. When Sonia had finally barked herself hoarse, the rest of us agreed it might be best to hear what Moira had to say.

Moira rose and addressed us with infuriating warmth, as though she were not the depraved architect of our misery but some benevolent grief counselor to whom we'd turned for succor.

"First I want you all to know . . . I *get* it. You're angry, you're scared, you're freaked out. All totally valid emotions. You feel like your whole world's coming to an end. But, here's the headline—it's not. So lighten up! I don't blame you for what you've done—"

"Blame *us?!*" Diana snorted incredulously.

"I'm talking now. I mean, assaulting me in my own hotel, stealing my car. I was plenty mad about that. But, hell, you were mad at me too, and if we can't put all that behind us and move on, then where are we? I'll be taking my car back of course. As for the laptop"—she chuckled, ever the good sport—"I don't expect you'll be handing *that* over. Or the disks. You're not idiots. But neither am I.

"Did you really think those were my *only* copies—just what was on the laptop and those disks? Or that I kept everything I had in the office where Kim could steal them if she got greedy, leaving me with *nothing?* Trust me, kids, I have backups of everything. Or don't trust me."

She reached into her Hermès bag, removed a DVD, and tossed it to Stephen.

"Take a look at that, then ask yourself if I'd be giving it to you if it were my only copy. And in case you're wondering, yes, Oscar's on there. So, nice try, kids," she said, lighting a cigarette, "but I'm still driving the car."

Stephen, who, from his expression, wouldn't have cared at this point if the car were being driven by Thelma and Louise, stared bleakly at the disk on his lap. Sonia, her spent bile duct having replenished itself, lumbered to her feet and began frothing in injudicious proximity to Moira's face.

"You snotty bitch! You will hand over EVERY COPY or I will rip your FUCKING HEART right out of your chest! ARRGH!" she added, for Moira had just pepper-sprayed her.

"I'll *KILL* you for that!" roared Sonia. She lunged blindly at Moira, who calmly sidestepped her, then, applying the sole of her Manolo to Sonia's ample fanny, sent her crashing chins first into a Bang & Olufsen subwoofer.

"Honestly, Stephen," sighed Moira, distastefully eyeing her crumpled foe. "You should really consider hiring someone who can calm down and just take a damn meeting."

"You vile woman!" wailed Diana. "How can you do this to my son?"

"I haven't done *anything* yet. And forgive my frankness, but you of all people should know what a woman has to do to get ahead in this town."

Diana, stiffening at the suggestion that her success could be ascribed to anything save diligence and prayer, glared at Moira, then helped Sonia to her feet.

"So," said Claire, "is that what this was all about? The spa, the boys, the blackmail? All just your slimy little way of jump-starting your film career?"

"Sorry, I missed that. Did the plagiarist say something?"

Claire glowered briefly at Moira, then shot me her "Have-I-thanked-you-today?" look. Meanwhile Moira, back in therapist mode, sat beside Stephen, her manner earnest and comforting.

"I know how painful this is for you. You think your whole career is ruined. But it's *not*. It's going to go on, stronger than ever. And I'm going to be part of it. That's been my whole purpose, my dream from the beginning—to be in business with you."

"Dream is right!" said Diana with woozy hauteur. "My Stephen would never make a picture for the likes of you!"

"He already has, dear," noted Moira.

"If you show a single person one *frame* of that defamatory—!"

"Let her talk, Ma!" snapped Stephen.

"Thank you, Stephen," Moira said and proceeded to outline the future they would share.

They would become partners. They would, effective immediately, form a company called Finch/Donato Productions. It would be headquartered at Pinnacle, which, at Stephen's insistence, would permit them to greenlight at least three pictures a year with Stephen starring in at least one every other year. The partnership would be totally equal profitwise, Moira not being the least bit greedy. And, as it was already in preproduction, the company's first feature would be *The Heart in Hiding*.

"So, what do you say, partner?" Moira smiled, extending a hand to shake. Stephen just stared at it, aghast at the thought of forming a public alliance with this grinning pathogen.

"I *have* a production company."

"Dissolve it."

"If you think for one goddamn INSTANT—!"

"Oh, shut up, Sonia!" said Moira. "If you want Stephen to keep you on you'd better learn a little respect for his partners. Because he is going to say yes." She returned her high beams to Stephen. "We both know it. I mean, ask yourself, where do you want me? Outside looking in, or working beside you, totally invested in your success? Think how much easier you'll sleep knowing I'd never do a thing to harm you since your loss would be mine. That's called security, Stephen, and it is my gift to you. Trust me, in six months you'll be *glad* this happened— I plan to be one hell of a partner! You have to admit I'm pretty darn resourceful. What I want I get. And now all that skill, all that drive, will be working for you—so smile already!"

She extended her hand again and this time Stephen meekly shook it. Moira, beaming like a pageant winner, exuberantly embraced her prey, who numbly addressed Gilbert and me over her shoulder.

"Thanks for the introduction, guys."

"Don't mention it," chirped Gilbert, the second Bloody having dulled his ear for subtext.

"This is so wonderful!" gushed Moira, as though the deal had been struck with the utmost mutual delight. She then pulled a document from her bag and gave it to Sonia. "Here's the press release. Oh, and if any of you have plans for Thursday, cancel 'em—I'm throwing a launch party at the spa!" She then produced a star-studded guest list, saying she felt confident that despite the short notice, most of those on it would not miss the chance to wish Stephen good luck on his exciting new venture. She bade us farewell and practically skipped out to the foyer, turning at the door.

"Please have the script for *The Heart in Hiding* messengered to me. Oh, and Claire, love—you and the boys should call me Monday. Say threeish?"

"What on earth for?" snarled Claire.

Moira bared her teeth in a smile.

"My *notes*, silly."

Nineteen

★

THREE DAYS LATER THE ACADEMY AWARD nominations were announced and Stephen, as had been universally predicted, scored a Best Actor nod for his performance in *Lothario*. I did not speak to my beloved, who failed, to my chagrin if not surprise, to return my congratulatory call. Even had we spoken I wouldn't have dared ask to what extent his happiness over the honor had been blighted by the irony recent events had bestowed on it, or by the article that graced the front page of *Variety* the very same morning.

Titled "Finch Perches on Donato's Shoulder," it ran as follows:

> Stephen Donato, widely seen as a shoo-in for an Oscar nom, announced plans today to shutter his successful production company, Monogram, and form a new company in partnership with Moira Finch, widow of the legendary producer Albert Schimmel.
>
> Finch, who has no producing credits, is best known as the proprietress of Les Étoiles, the Bel-Air spa that has found favor with some of the town's biggest names, Donato among them. "The minute I met Moira I knew she was an

extraordinary person," said Donato. "We got to talking and it was obvious Albert had taught her everything he knew about filmmaking. I was blown away."

Finch said she'd coaxed Schimmel out of retirement and the pair were developing several projects at the time of his death. Stunned by her loss, she shelved the projects and opened Les Étoiles. "Then one night Stephen asked me what Albert and I had been working on and he just immediately connected with the material." The clincher for Donato came when he attempted to option a novel he'd admired, only to find Finch had recently acquired the rights. "That's when I said, 'Whoa, this is fate! We are totally meant to be in business together.' "

"Stephen has an amazing eye for talent and Moira Finch is a true visionary," added Donato's publicist, Sonia Powers.

Finch/Donato's maiden effort will be *The Heart in Hiding*. The World War II drama, which also stars Donato's mother, Diana Malenfant, and wife, Gina Beach, will be a coproduction with Pinnacle Pictures and Bobby Spellman's My Way Productions.

THE PREVIOUS MORNING MOIRA had messengered hundreds of invitations to her impromptu launch party and, thanks to Stephen's nomination, nary a single available star declined to attend. Given the place we now occupied in Stephen's affections I was initially surprised that our lowly trio was invited as well. Then I realized it was Moira's party, not Stephen's, and that in her view nothing perked up a coronation so much as having one's subjugated foes on hand to bear witness.

Claire, unsurprisingly, declined to attend. Claire, in fact, wanted nothing further to do with the lot of us or *The Heart in Hiding*, condemning me to write the second draft with only Gilbert's "assistance." I begged her to reconsider but her rebuff was blunt and withering.

"Are you *mad?*" she asked hotly. "Work for *Moira?* Take her notes? 'Yass, Miss Finch, no, Miss Finch'? I'd sooner seek work as a carnival geek! I'd sooner emcee cockfights! I'd sooner clean toilets—nay, *portable* toilets!—or apprentice myself to a rat catcher before I'd spend one minute answering to that gloating succubus! Do not, please, ask me again!"

It was just as well for Claire that she skipped the party since she'd have ground her teeth to powder watching Moira's elaborately stage-managed apotheosis. For starters there was the guest list, which was hardly less glittering than the Oscars themselves. The decor too would have given her ample cause to wish she'd worn her night guard. How it must have maddened Stephen to see that Moira had already designed their company's logo and had it reproduced on napkins, bunting, and a huge bas-relief wall plaque. The lead time required to fabricate these items served as a constant galling reminder of how long and confidently Moira had presumed she'd come to own him.

One of the things that most vexes us bitter alumni of Moira University is the depressing fact that those whose pelts she has not yet harvested invariably find her delightful. She's quite pretty in a peppy young Mary Tyler Moore sort of way and, when she chooses to be, re-lentlessly charming. She's a diligent researcher and expert flatterer; her praise never sounds like the star-struck effusions of a mere fan but the carefully weighed opinion of a savvy insider. (When extolling a per-formance she always speaks gravely of its "layers.")

I'd once watched her turn a roomful of cold-blooded mafiosi into fawning admirers but I'd never seen her play a crowd as adroitly as she did on the night Les Étoiles lived so gloriously up to its name. She re-alized early on that the best way to meet Everyone was to lasso herself to Stephen. Then as each grandee approached to offer congratulations, he was compelled to introduce her, citing again the high esteem for her that had prompted their partnership. Moira, who can blush at will (and has never done so any other way), would then make droll, self-deprecatory jokes before lavishing praise on the Star, placing special emphasis on abilities or past projects the Star felt had been unjustly neglected. Minutes later the Star would walk away, marveling at the acuity and sweetness of the woman who'd just filed him away in her Potential Victims pool.

My invitation had said "plus guest" and it had occurred to me what a treat it would be for Billy Grimes. To actually hobnob with Stephen was his highest aspiration, and when I invited him over the incline press he shrieked and kissed me in a manner that raised eyebrows even in a West Hollywood gymnasium.

Not having spoken to Stephen since Saturday's debacle, I was understandably nervous about how he'd receive me. I spent my first hour there ogling the celebs and sipping champagne to bolster my courage. Finally, at what seemed a good moment, I dragged Billy over to Stephen and Moira, who'd just bade farewell to Dustin Hoffman.

"Phil-ip!" sang Moira. "So glad you could come! Mwah! Who's your friend?"

I introduced Billy, who promptly began babbling to Stephen in exactly the manner I'd prayed he wouldn't. To make matters worse, he produced a camera from his jacket and asked if he could have a picture with him.

"Have we met?" asked Stephen, dimly recognizing him.

"I tend bar at your mom's restaurant. Gosh, I'm so sorry my dad was such a dickhead that day!"

"Oh, right," said Stephen, his smile looking genuine for the first time all evening. "You're Rusty's son."

"Guilty as charged!" replied Billy with a honking laugh.

Stephen patted the sofa next to him. Billy gave me the camera, then sat beside his dream man, who draped an arm suggestively around his shoulder and abruptly kissed his cheek on "Cheese!"

"Wow! Thanks!" gushed Billy, who suddenly had cause to wish he'd worn baggier pants. "I think I've got next year's Christmas card!"

Stephen grinned. "Be sure you send one to your dad."

I smiled too even as I wondered if it was quite wise for Stephen to be goading the DA just as he'd acquired a partner of more than passing interest to the vice squad. I shot him a wry yet cautionary look. The gaze he returned was crushingly aloof and I shuffled morosely away like a puppy that's just soiled the sisal.

Max and Maddie arrived to the delight of Gilbert, who, aping Moira's strategy vis-à-vis Stephen, pinned himself to Max like a wrist corsage. He then passed the night happily chatting up the A-list, all of whom were duly apprised of his pivotal role in bringing the happy honorees together.

If Max was disgruntled at having been strong-armed into a deal permitting Stephen and his newbie partner to greenlight three pictures a year, he betrayed no sign of it. And Maddie was even more ebullient than usual, delighted by her former daughter-in-law's sudden but no doubt well-deserved success. I overheard her gushing to Stephen, who was standing with his new Siamese twin in a group that included his mom, Bobby, and George Clooney.

"Boy, ain't life something! First my Gilbert comes out here and writes a script so good Bobby Spellman hires him to write one for you guys. Then he introduces you to Moira and bang, just like that you're partners!"

"Astounding," agreed Stephen.

"I'm so happy Moira and Gilbert have stayed friends. They used to be married, you know. They were nuts about each other but one day Gilbert woke up and realized he was gay. Kinda sticky, ain't it, when the man doesn't figure that out till after he's married?"

Diana turned her sympathetic gaze to Moira.

"How immensely trying that must have been."

"It was, Diana," said Moira, with a stoic little smile. "But all that really mattered to me was that Gilbert be happy."

"How teddibly generous of you."

I have in the course of this account displayed a certain cattiness regarding Diana's dramatic abilities. But her performance at the Finch/Donato launch party convinced me that, the occasional flight of hamminess aside, she is the greatest American actress of her generation. Stephen, faced with a similar challenge, acquitted himself competently but could not entirely subdue a certain manic quality that those who noted it ascribed (accurately enough) to Oscar jitters. But Diana's fears for her son and passionate loathing of Moira were completely undetectable beneath her amiable and gracious veneer. It is no small task to clutch a viper to your bosom all night while pretending it's a puppy, but Diana pulled it off with remarkable aplomb.

BENEATH THE WAVES OF admiration on which Moira happily surfed that evening there ran an undercurrent of gossipy speculation as to why Stephen had hitched his wagon to a woman of such limited experience. Some smelled an affair, a theory bolstered by Gina, whose anxious glances at the new partners inspired many a whispered comment. There were, however, a number of gentlemen present who more accurately surmised why Stephen now found himself yoked to Moira. These men, many with wives in tow, had been to Les Étoiles before and sampled its more furtive pleasures. They gathered in corners, exchanging looks both knowing and leery, for if Moira had stung Stephen, might she not do the same to them? In the days that followed, most of these skittish fellows wisely kept their counsel. A few though could not resist airing their suspicions, and when word of this reached Moira they received photographic reminders that discretion was its own reward.

MONTY, OF COURSE, knew what was what the instant he read the *LA Times'* coverage of the party.

"Blackmail, plain and simple," he declared as we waited for Lily to stir herself. "My emotions, I confess, are mixed. On the one hand it saddens me to see that a woman I'd admired and trusted to uphold the madam's sacred code has betrayed it so basely. And for what? A movie deal! Common, I call it.

"On the other hand, it couldn't have happened to a nicer fellow. Don't mistake me—I love Stephen as a dutiful uncle should, but his ego's gotten quite out of hand lately. His head, always a tad swollen, has taken on the proportions of a zeppelin. It's good to see him brought to heel now and then. Builds his character. Be frank, Glen—did Moira confide her nefarious scheme to you?"

"No! Never! And I don't work for her anymore. She fired me."

"Ah," he said, eyebrows levitating. "So the rumors are true?"

"Rumors?"

He explained that an acquaintance of his had recently visited Les Étoiles and requested the services of Hans. He was informed that Hans no longer worked there. Requests for Adrian, Rudolfo, Sven, and Horst met with the same response.

"She's fired the lot of you. She's gotten what she wanted and now she's gone respectable."

It was the first I'd heard that cock was off the menu at Les Étoiles, but it certainly made sense. Having achieved her dream of mogulhood, why would Moira jeopardize it by continuing to peddle boys on the side, risking arrest while giving new customers cause to intuit the roots of her partnership with Stephen? Far better to close shop and let the whole enterprise fade into oblivion. Tongues might wag for a while, but the story would eventually recede into legend. In time it would be just another showbiz myth, one laughed away as easily as that of the gerbil once said to have met its maker in Richard Gere's bottom.

"Hang on," said Monty, suddenly brightening. "If Moira's let you go, mightn't that free you up to spend more time on Lily's book?"

"Uh, perhaps," I said.

There was, in fact, no reason I could not now devote myself full-time to Lily, Moira having informed me and Gilbert that we weren't to start our next draft till she'd hired a director and received his input. I'd looked forward to having my afternoons free, but I realized that more time with Lily meant more time to convince her not to expose Stephen. As success in this seemed my sole hope of regaining his affection, I leaped at the chance.

Lily was elated to hear she could henceforth have me all to herself and even cheerily consented to my proviso that we limit ourselves to one glass of wine with lunch so as not to impede our afternoon progress. "Elated" seemed, in fact, to be Lily's default mood during those brief tranquil days before the Showbiz Gods, reviewing my case file, returned it to the Downfall Department with a Post-it attached reading, "Sad, yes, but tragic? Try again. Cf. Oedipus."

She was delighted with the results of her face-lift, chemical peel, and Botox injections, which had indeed shaved a decade off her appearance.

They'd done so, unfortunately, at the cost of permanently raised eyebrows and badly decreased lip mobility, the combined effect suggesting a startled ventriloquist. She was atwitter too over the forthcoming release of *Guess What, I'm Not Dead* and the critical bouquets she felt certain it would win her. The only thing that marred her consistently fizzy mood was my persistent harping over the question of outing Stephen.

Having failed with the argument that to do so risked eclipsing her own story, I changed tactics, saying it risked making her seem cruel and spiteful.

"Spiteful? Oh, no, I don't think so, Glen. If anyone comes off as spiteful, it's Diana. She's the one who hit the ceiling when she found out about Stephen and his friend. She's the one who said, 'You get over this gay business right now, young man, if you want any sort of career!' I was the one who accepted him as he was and bought him Bette Midler tickets."

I next tried arguing that the gay stories would not be worth the legal fracas they'd inevitably provoke.

"You know he'll claim its libel," I said as we diced avocados for our lunchtime Cobb. "What if he gets an injunction to keep you from publishing? The book could wind up in limbo for years. Think of your fans!"

I'd felt certain this would unnerve her, but her response was well to the left of fiddle-dee-dee.

"It's not libel if it's *true*, Glen. And it is. I can prove it. It's all in here," she said, lovingly patting the diary she'd kept twenty years ago. "All written down long before he was a big star. Let him argue with that! Now set the table, dear, while I pour my one glass of wine. What a taskmaster you are!" she said, emptying half a bottle of Chablis into a soda tumbler.

That afternoon we reached the point in her memoir where she discovers Stephen in flagrante with his tennis coach, the aptly named Randy. Lily recounted it with gusto, throwing in juicy details I hadn't heard before. My stomach churned like a LAVA lamp as I typed up the results and e-mailed them to Stephen, asking whether I should send the day's output, per usual, to Sonia and Diana or provide them a doctored version. He phoned almost immediately. His tone frosty and commanding, he instructed me to inform Sonia that Lily had the flu and we wouldn't be working this week. He then asked me to meet him at midnight on a scenic outlook on Mulholland Drive.

I arrived early to find him already there. I parked, then joined him in the front seat of his Lamborghini. At first he said nothing. He just stared into the Valley with the tight-lipped brooding air one would expect to see in an action star whose aunt has just laid bare the full scope and tumult of his first gay affair. ("He didn't molest me! He's my boyfriend! *Will you close the damn door?!*") The acrid silence lengthened uncomfortably, then he finally spoke.

"You've let me down, Phil," he said, not looking at me. "I was counting on you to take care of this."

"I'm so sorry," I bleated, then outlined the strategies I'd employed, including the threat of legal action. "She says it's not libel, that she can back it all up with this damn diary she kept back then."

He turned to me, his gaze icy and penetrating.

"Steal it."

My eyes bugged like those of a Tex Avery wolf who's just spotted a pinup girl.

"Her *diary?*"

"All of it. You can still fix this, Phil. Just take her diary, every copy of what you've written so far, plus the notes, scrapbooks, photos — everything. I want her back to square one with nothing to back up a word she says. Then Glen will disappear. With any luck she'll be so discouraged she'll quit. But if she doesn't I'll sue her ass off and she'll have nothing to fight back with."

I could only stare openmouthed, stunned by the enormity of what he was proposing. I had, in the pursuit of romance, pulled some pretty low stunts before, but nothing like this, an act of such black treachery that Moira herself, hearing of it, would shed proud tears like a parent on graduation day. Stephen, sensing my reluctance, put his hand on my thigh and stared even more deeply into my eyes.

"I'm fighting for my life here, Phil. You're the only one who can help me."

"Gosh, Stephen, I know how you feel about her writing this, and how you'd prefer to come out someday in your own book—"

"Hmm? Oh, right. That too."

"But to steal an old woman's memories—!"

His hand tightened its grip on my thigh and inched north toward the capitol.

"It's the only way. Be a buddy, Phil. I need a buddy right now."

As I stared, torn, into his sad, beautiful face, a single tear welled in the corner of his left eye. Seeing it, I winced in gentle sympathy and he kissed me. The kiss tasted lightly of scotch and I knew even as his lips pressed against mine that he was performing a sort of reverse resuscitation, not forcing air in through the mouth but sucking scruples out through it.

"Mmm . . . nice," he murmured, savoring the taste of my last qualm. "So you'll do it?"

"Absolutely!"

"Tomorrow?"

"*Tomorrow?!*"

"I'll come by your place about seven. I'll bring a joint. We'll celebrate."

"Tomorrow it is!" I said and, grabbing his crotch, greedily kissed him again. In the language of Hollywood contracts, this is known as a signing bonus.

NOTHING IN THIS ACCOUNT pains me as much to confess to you as the cold-bloodedness with which I perpetrated my despicable crime against Lily. Following a cheerful and productive morning, I suggested that in lieu of our usual positively Mormon glass of Chablis, we toast our progress with a pitcher of that yummy lemonade she so favored.

Lily thought this a capital idea and whipped one up. We enjoyed it with our salads as Lily chatted away about the dress she'd bought for her premiere and the state of Martin Scorsese's health, the latter concern prompted by his failure to get back to her about the *Amelia* script.

"That was refreshing," I said as we finished the pitcher. "Another?"

Lily said, "Aren't we naughty!" and something else I didn't catch as she was already in the kitchen. Two hours later Lily, having consumed most of the third pitcher, fell into a doze on the living room sofa. Tiptoeing about like her personal Grinch, I packed up my laptop, then collected her notes, diaries, and scrapbooks, the printed copy with her scrawled revisions, and a photo album with pictures of young Stephen and Randy. I loaded it all into a shopping bag and, casting a final pained glance at my slumbering victim, crept perfidiously away.

I SPOKE A WHILE back about lust's efficacy as a guilt suppressant. At the time I'd had only my dirty daydreams of Stephen to distract me. Now I had actual porn, which, as studies have shown, is 80 percent more effective. As soon as I'd stashed the shopping bag in the kitchen closet, I hastened to fetch my precious DVD from its hiding place and popped it into my laptop.

Though I'd played it dozens of times and never tired of it, I'd always felt a twinge of melancholy when watching my own scene, since the encounter, however sizzling, seemed to represent both the beginning and end of my romance with Stephen. How thrilling it was to view it now as more of a trailer — coming attractions, so to speak, for delights still to be savored. Somewhere in my third viewing I was startled to hear a knock on the door. I checked my watch and saw that it was six forty-five. My beloved was early! It would not, of course, have done for him to see what I'd been watching, so I hastily closed the laptop and stowed it on the coffee table's lower shelf. I primped briefly in the foyer mirror, then, flinging open the door, saw that my caller was not Stephen at all.

"Monty!"

"What the hell, please, happened today?" he demanded hotly. "I just left Lily, who's in a state of complete hysteria!"

"Over what?" I asked, opting for confused innocence with Gilbertian swiftness.

"The book's gone! Her only copy! Not to mention her notes, her diaries, everything!"

I gasped like a Wes Craven heroine. "My God! Who could have taken them?!"

"I was hoping you'd know. You were there today."

"I don't know a thing! Lily dozed off so I went home. When I left it was all still on the—wait a minute!"

"What?!"

I said that on leaving I'd noticed a black sedan parked across the street with a man at the wheel, reading a newspaper. "Gosh, you don't suppose Sonia sent her goons in!"

"Well someone's goons were certainly there! Poor Lily's sobbing her eyes out and I'm not feeling too well myself. My tummy's in a dreadful uproar. I don't suppose you have any antacids about?"

"Sure," I said, glancing anxiously at the hall clock. It was imperative that Monty leave before Stephen arrived. "Hang on," I said and dashed upstairs to the master bath.

It is, of course, axiomatic that the more urgently one needs to complete a task swiftly the more circumstances and one's own nervous fumbling conspire to draw things out. It took me two minutes to locate a linty roll of Tums and convey it to Monty. I found the poor old boy sitting on the foyer bench, literally panting with anxiety. It pained me to see him in such a state, know that I was the cause of it, and still have to give him the bum's rush. But what's a treacherous mole to do?

"Here you go. Look, I'm really sorry about this but I've got a . . . well, a client due really soon, so—"

"Yes, of course. I should be getting back to Lily as it is."

Stephen arrived five minutes later, displaying a promptness rare among megastars and unheard of in the nominee class. He'd clearly popped an extra sexy pill that morning. He wore snug jeans, a black leather jacket, plus a two-day growth of beard and, had he brought a stethoscope along, would have found my heartbeat indistinguishable from Gene Krupa's drum solo in "Sing, Sing, Sing."

"So you do it, big guy?"

I smiled roguishly. "I don't let a man down when he asks me so nicely."

We retired to the kitchen, where he inspected the merchandise, lingering over the photos of him and Randy.

"You sure this is all of it?"

I said I was and that Monty's visit had confirmed it. For a moment I feared that, having gotten what he wanted, he'd renege on his promised tryst. Fortunately for me, recent events had made him risk-averse and hustlers were the new carbohydrates. His needs had gone unmet for several weeks and he was disinclined as such to pass up any trustworthy penis on offer. He asked me for a shoulder rub and as I obliged, he lit a joint, took a long drag, and passed it to me.

Having already yodeled at length over our first dalliance I'll refrain from any chest-thumping over the second, which did not differ greatly. True, it was nice having an actual bed and Stephen seemed a bit bossier this time, but I didn't mind as I was eager to prove I could take direction.

The only thing that marred my complete bliss (excepting, of course, the treachery that had secured it) was Stephen's firm insistence that it remain entirely our secret. When one has the good fortune to bed a megastar, one's natural impulse is to tell people afterward. Hell, had Stephen permitted me I'd have told people *during* it, phoning friends at random to say, "Hey, guess where my penis is!" Still, forfeiting bragging rights is a small price to pay to have a stunning Best Actor nominee writhe beneath you, loudly insisting you play with his nipples.

When we'd finished, Stephen, pot-parched, asked for water, and I padded downstairs to fetch some. As I passed through the living room I felt a sudden prickle of paranoia over my failure to return the DVD to its hiding place. I squatted to retrieve my laptop from the lower level of the coffee table where I'd stowed it when Monty arrived.

It was gone.

I tried for a few desperate moments to persuade myself that I'd put it somewhere else or that Gilbert had come home unexpectedly and moved it. But the hideous truth was clear even to a stoned idiot like myself.

Monty had taken it.

He'd seen through my feigned innocence, then spied the computer, which he knew contained a full draft of Lily's memoir. He'd shrewdly asked me to fetch something he knew would be upstairs, then seized the laptop and ran it out to his car. That's why he'd seemed winded when I returned. I sank dizzily onto the sofa, hyperventilating as I contemplated the terrible power that now rested in that aging delinquent's hands.

"I thought you were getting water," said Stephen, standing nude on the stair landing.

"Sorry. I just, uh . . . misplaced something."

"Are you okay?"

The phone rang. I let the machine answer and Monty's ebullient voice filled the room.

"Glen, you naughty boy! Or is it Philip, as Stephen calls you in that utterly *captivating* video? Pick up, my love! Pick up! We have much to discuss!"

Twenty

★

WHENEVER I LOOK BACK ON MY brief affair with
Stephen—for, make no mistake, Monty's call ended it
with thudding finality—what saddens me most is that
Cupid, while generously granting me two rapturous trysts with my
dream guy, stinted appallingly in the afterglow department. After
our first date I was granted a mere ten minutes in which to sigh and
ponder china patterns before our idyll was shattered. The fat boy was
stingier still after round two, letting disaster pounce a mere forty seconds after the Kleenex hit the carpet. I had thought I'd return to bed
with our waters and we'd lie there awhile, limbs lightly entwined,
telling each other secrets. But it was clear from Stephen's growing
alarm as I pleaded for Monty's mercy that, while secrets would doubt-
less be spilled, cuddling was pretty well off the agenda.

"Oh, splendid!" said Monty after I'd snatched the phone up. "I
was hoping you were still there. I just saw your debut feature, dear,
and I must say, I can't think when I've enjoyed a film more. It has
everything—drama, comedy, suspense, dazzling plot twists, and
Stephen Donato in the role he was born to play."

"Look, Monty—!"

"Between us, I've never cared for his Caliber pictures. Too slick and noisy for my taste. No quibbles with this one though. In fact, I'd say it's his first truly *Oscar Caliber* performance."

"Monty, *please*—"

"You hear the pun? 'Oscar' and 'Caliber'?"

"I get it! You have to give it back!"

"Do I?" he said quizzically. "No, dear, I don't believe I do."

"Give what back?" demanded Stephen.

"We'll do a swap, okay?! I'll return everything I took from Lily and you give back the DVD."

"What DVD?!" asked Stephen, though I sensed from the way his hair sprang straight up like quills that he had a fair inkling. I covered the phone.

"The one Moira made! You and me at the spa!"

"You made a copy?!!"

"Ah! So Stephen's there, is he?" chirped Monty. "I thought he might swing by to collect your plunder. Put him on, would you? Uncle wants to chat."

"YOU MADE A FUCKING COPY?!!"

"Just one! Purely as a memento."

"AND YOU GAVE IT TO MONTY?!!"

"Well, no, Stephen. I would hardly do that. Monty stole my laptop when he came by earlier. The DVD just happened to be in the hard drive. He wants to talk to you," I added, hoping this might divert at least some of his anger from me to Monty.

Stephen grabbed the phone and snarled into it.

"You fucking thief! I want that DVD back and I want it now!" He listened a moment, then screamed, "HOW DARE YOU TALK TO ME THAT WAY!" (Monty, as he later informed me, had replied, "Well, aren't you the bossy bottom?")

Of the ensuing discussion I heard only Stephen's side, which began with demands and threats, segued into appeals to family feeling, and ended in escalating offers of financial compensation. But Monty had no intention of surrendering his prize. Stephen closed negotiations with a curt "Fuck you," then turned back to me. It shattered me to see the man who'd so recently gazed on me, if not adoringly, at least *approvingly*, glare at me now with undisguised loathing.

"Here," he sneered, hurling the phone at me. "He wants to talk to you."

Monty's tone was soothing and cheerful. "I just want you to know, Glen, that I entirely forgive your recent misdeeds. I'd be the last to blame an impressionable youth for succumbing to the wiles of a skilled temptress like Stephen. When he found out you had access to our home and Lily's memoir, he won your heart and bent you to his evil will. But that's all over now. You're fatally compromised as a spy. And as for your romance with Stephen, it's time, you must sadly agree, for a quick chorus of 'Goodbye, Little Dream, Goodbye.'

"My advice to you is throw in the towel and join Team Monty! See you in the morning, dear, and I trust you and Lily will continue making splendid progress."

I replied that I doubted Lily would care to speak to me after what I'd done.

"Not to worry. I told her that after she dozed off you'd noticed a prowler in the shrubbery. Fearing the dark hand of Diana, you collected all key documents and spirited them away for safekeeping. She applauds your vigilance. Nighty-night."

"Wait! The DVD! What are you going to do with it?"

He emitted a short, sharp laugh like the bark of a seal.

"Why, what I always do, child! Good deeds!"

And with that he hung up.

I followed Stephen, who'd stormed upstairs to dress. He had no one to spend his fury on now but me, and spend it he did in a long profanity-strewn tirade I have no intention of reproducing here. At core I'm a pretty positive person. When a romance ends I try not to dwell on the bitter breakup but focus instead on the good times. When I think now of Stephen I like to recall the thrilling intimacy of our tête-à-tête at the bar, his romantic knee squeeze under the table, the laughs, the hugs, the nipples. Likewise with the things he said to me. I'd much rather recall him saying, "Wow, I play a spy on the screen, but you, you're the real thing!" or "Ooh, yeah, big guy, just like that!" as opposed to "You fucking incompetent shithead!" or "I wish to God I'd never laid eyes on you!"

I especially wish I could expunge from memory the scabrous exchange that made it finally and devastatingly clear to me how fine and powdery was the sand on which I'd built my dream castle.

"I'm sorry!" I mewled as he struggled into his boots. "I fucked up! I wouldn't blame you if you fired us off the picture!"

"Fire you!" He snorted. "That's a laugh! How can we fire you when you were never hired in the first place?"

"What?"

"The script job—it was never *yours*, jackass! Not from day one. We just let you think you were hired 'cause we needed you for the other job—the one you fucked up so royally!"

"But . . . but you paid us!" I stammered, my mind reeling.

"Which means what?" he replied with a nasty laugh.

"It was in *Variety!*" I exclaimed, as though citing scripture.

"Oh, wow! So it must be true, huh? Wake the fuck up! We can announce anything we like. We just put out that release so you idiots would believe the job was yours. The next week we signed Ted Schramm to write the *real* script and asked him to keep quiet while we waited for you to finish with Lily."

"No, Stephen!" I wailed, battling tears now. "You're just saying this because you're upset!"

"Do the math, bozo! Why do you think you only dealt with us? Why do you think you never got notes from Bobby or one fucking person from the studio? I'll tell you why—'cause *it wasn't real!*"

The tears declared victory, cascading down my cheeks in a maudlin, hiccupping torrent. Ashamed, I averted my face, staring bleakly down at the carpet and my widely scattered smithereens.

"Hell, none of us even *read* your dumb script through except Gina! We didn't tell her 'cause she can't keep a damn thing to herself. Yeah, go on—*cry*, Phil! That's gonna make me feel real bad for you after you've ruined my whole goddamn life!"

He stomped down the stairs to the foyer and, reaching the door, turned to deliver his coup de grâce.

"Oh, and from the coverage I did read of your draft, it totally *sucked!* I mean, Jesus, you cut the kid's ghost! That's the best fucking part!"

MY REMEMBER-THE-GOOD-TIMES approach to soured affairs is, of course, more of a long-term strategy and impossible to implement in the immediate aftermath of a rancorous split. My short-term approach can be summarized as follows:

a. Sob hysterically.
b. Rock back and forth, hugging self while exclaiming, "Why, [name], why?!"
c. Pour and consume a large scotch on the rocks.
d. Repeat as needed.

At such times a boy both needs and expects his closest friends to rally round and sit shivah for the relationship. Gilbert didn't come home that night but I reached his cell the next morning and asked him to meet me for breakfast at the Chateau. I then called Claire and told her that recent developments merited her attention.

It was, I suppose, foolish of me to expect much sympathy over my split-up with Stephen, but I was not prepared for the raucous indifference with which they greeted my heartbreak.

"Excuse me," asked Claire, "but for a relationship to end doesn't it technically have to *begin* first?"

"*Thank* you!" said Gilbert, slapping the table like a parliamentarian seconding a motion.

"We were very close!" I retorted angrily. "He used to phone me late at night for long intimate chats! And we had fantastic sex!"

Claire tartly replied that to the best of her recall my tryst with Stephen had been only one part of an extended sexual repast in which I had been the cheese course.

"Well, guess what? We had sex again last night and it was amazing! He was sweet and tender and couldn't get enough of me!"

"Was this before or after he dumped you?"

I frowned sheepishly at my corned beef hash (the impulse to diet having understandably fled). "That happened afterward."

I told them the whole shameful tale, from my film noir rendezvous with Stephen where he'd Stanwycked me into double-crossing Lily to my horrified discovery that Monty had made off with my laptop. This last item prompted a loud, extravagant groan from Gilbert even as Claire, her appetite laid to rest, pushed her frittata away.

"You *lost* the DVD?!" cried Gilbert, burying his face in his hands.

"I did not *lose* it. It was *stolen*."

"And you never made a backup?" asked Claire incredulously.

I replied indignantly that I had of course made a backup, conceding that this did us little good as I'd backed it up on my laptop.

"Well, good news, boys," she sighed. "We're officially defenseless."

"Of all the dim-witted, imbecilic—!"

"Oh, *thank* you, Gilbert!" I said acidly. "Maybe someday *you'll* do something stupid, then you'll know what it feels like!"

Claire asked if I had any idea what Monty planned to do with his new toy. I said it was anyone's guess but he was already having a grand time making Stephen squirm.

"No wonder he dumped you!" said Gilbert. "He must've gone ape shit!"

I replied that Stephen had indeed taken it badly and had said several things he was no doubt already wishing he could take back.

"So what does this mean for us?" demanded Gilbert, his tone suddenly accusatory. "Has your bungling gotten us fired off the picture?"

"If we were ever on it," muttered Claire.

I could only stare, startled afresh at her Holmesian perspicacity.

"How'd you know that!"

"So, it's true then?" she asked. "He admitted it?"

"With bells on."

"Admitted what?" said Gilbert, annoyed as always when the grown-ups talked over his head.

Claire said, "When I found out the only reason we were hired was that Philip agreed to play spy, I started to wonder how 'hired' we ever really were—if the whole job wasn't just a charade they'd maintain till Philip's work was done."

I asked her why she hadn't voiced this suspicion earlier.

"I only learned about your cloak-and-dagger chores at the spa. The next day Moira took over and I quit. I figured you'd be wretched enough writing the next draft with just this one without my suggesting it might be a mere fool's errand."

Claire, having already surmised it, took the news of our nonstarter status in stride. Our typist, by contrast, was devastated to learn that his work would not reach the wide audience it deserved.

"This is total bullshit! Are we going to let them just *use* us like that!"

Claire gave his arm a maternal pat. "Just walk away, dear. I did and it felt lovely. We made some money, got decent agents and a little name recognition. If I were you I'd use all that to get the next thing going. Now if you'll excuse me, I need to get home and start packing."

"Packing?" I said, alarmed. "Where are you going?"

"On a well-deserved vacation."

She said that tomorrow morning she planned to drive up the coast with only a guidebook for a companion. She would drink in the beauty of Big Sur and wine country and hopefully meet a few Californians capable of sustaining a five-minute conversation that involved neither the weekend grosses nor pilot season. She'd then finish up in San Francisco, where she planned to look up one Henry Baumbach, a nice-looking Berkeley professor whom she'd met when he guest lectured at UCLA. They'd lunched twice and dined once.

"You have a new beau?" I asked.

"Possibly."

"Why didn't you tell us?"

"Gosh," she said dryly, "I had this strange feeling that dragging you two in might jinx it somehow. Odd superstition. Can't think how I came by it."

She rose and, the thought of leaving LA having restored her appetite, plucked a muffin from the pastry basket.

"You have my cell number," she said. "Please don't use it."

"Well, I'm sorry!" fumed Gilbert when she'd gone. "Why should we just roll over like good little lackeys? I mean, Gawd, with everything we've got on them?"

I pointed out that we could no longer prove any of it.

"We could still raise a nice little stink! There are enough tongues wagging already about why Stephen's in bed with Moira. I say we let the scheming bitch know who's boss!"

I said I saw little hope of wringing concessions from Moira, who'd be mad enough at me for letting the disk fall into Monty's hands. Gilbert didn't care, contending that Moira's fury could not begin to match his own. When I saw there was no hope of dissuading him, I decided to tag along so as to limit the carnage and glean what, if anything, was new on the Monty front.

We approached in stealth, obtaining our studio drive-on through Max. We easily located the offices of Finch/Donato Productions and Gilbert led the charge into its serene blond wood antechamber. He gave our names and demanded to see Moira immediately, adding that if she refused our next stop would be the *LA Times*. The receptionist was a slender young Asian queen whose languorous hauteur could not conceal the raging curiosity Gilbert's ultimatum had stirred in his breast. He pressed a button and murmured into his headset.

"Miss Finch will see you shortly," he said, using only his eyes to direct us to the sofa.

"Oh, right," scoffed Gilbert. "Like we're going to sit here while she slips out the back. Fat chance, Madame Butterfly!"

He barged down the hall toward the door that bore Moira's name in raised brass letters. I trotted behind while the gatekeeper, who had much to learn about sanctum guarding, struggled to extricate himself from his headset.

When Gilbert burst in, Moira, who was seated in a rich brown suede chair, leaped up, a radiant smile of welcome on her face.

"Well, look who it is! What a nice surprise!"

We were thrown by her cordiality until we realized that her performance was purely for the benefit of her illustrious guest, who rose now from the matching sofa.

"I'd like you to meet two dear old friends of mine, Philip Cavanaugh and Gilbert Selwyn. We go back ages! Guys, this is Harrison Ford."

We didn't chat very long with Harrison, but he struck me as a very polite, genial, and, I hasten for clear reasons to add, non-male-bordello-patronizing sort of fellow.

"Nice to meet you, Harrison," I said, moving toward him and extending my hand. As I was congratulating myself for having struck just the right warm-but-not-fawning note, my shin collided with the coffee table, striking it so hard that Harrison's coffee sloshed over.

"You all right there?"

"Ow! Yes, fine! Hope we're not interrupting?"

Harrison said they'd just been discussing a "little project" but were pretty much done. He bade us farewell and Moira saw him out, asking him to think it over and call her. When she'd closed the door she walked calmly to her desk, picked up a lovely Montblanc pen, and stabbed Gilbert in the neck with it.

"OWW!"

"You miserable fuckers! If you EVER try to threaten your way in here again I'll have your damn legs broken! I mean it! And *you*—!" She jabbed a red-lacquered nail at me. "You starfucking jackass! I've been on the phone all morning trying to calm Stephen down and convince him I can handle this mess you've made! I don't know what the old queen wants but it better be reasonable or I swear to God I'll whack him!"

"I'm bleeding, you crazy bitch!" cried Gilbert, dabbing his neck with a hankie.

"Baby."

She sat behind her desk, its chair imperially high, and glared across at us.

"If you're looking for your final script payment, have your agent call. If you're looking for anything else, fuck off."

Gilbert, his attempt to project manly menace badly undercut by his canary yellow Miyake T, demanded that we be reinstated as the sole authors of *The Heart in Hiding*.

"We worked our asses off on that script and it's a damn good one!"

"Sorry. I disagree." She said this while initialing some papers, having already acquired the mogul's knack of compounding an insult by multitasking while delivering it. "I read it and frankly I thought it lacked pathos."

"*Pathos!*" roared Gilbert. "You wouldn't know pathos if pathos threw a bar mitzvah in your vagina!"

"So we disagree," yawned Moira. "And I'm the producer."

"Fine then! We'll just go to the *LA Times* and tell them what kind of hotel you were running!"

"Ooh! I'm so scared!" exclaimed Moira, waving her hands with annoying vigor like Mandy Patinkin performing a minstrel song. Then she relaxed and leaned back in her chair.

"Fine. Go to the papers. They won't print what they can't prove. I'll deny it and let them know my accusers are two writers I fired off a project when I found out their spec was *stolen*. I'll make sure the whole town knows what you idiots did. Trust me, you'll never make the word 'madam' stick to me but 'plagiarist' will dog you to your graves. So," she said brightly, "anything else, kids? Or was that your best shot?"

Sadly it was, Gilbert being the impetuous sort of warrior who rushes into battle with scant regard for the contents of his quiver. Moira rose, signaling that we were dismissed. But just as I stood, bitterly regretting that we had no means to wipe the triumphant smirk off her face, a lovely thing happened. Her phone buzzed, she answered it, and, whatever she heard, her smile vanished so abruptly she might have been a doorman on December twenty-sixth.

"Just send him in," she said testily, then told us to beat it. Gilbert and I exchanged a pointed glance and defiantly resumed our seats. We'd surmised from her sudden dyspepsia that her surprise visitor was none other than Monty and this was not a skirmish we intended to miss. I only prayed the old scamp had brought along his squirting boutonniere.

Alas, Moira's visitor was not Monty but a man whose arrival curdled my own smile as swiftly as it had Moira's.

"Thanks for seeing me on such short notice, Miss Finch," said District Attorney Rusty Grimes.

He glanced my way and I waved a limp hand in greeting.

"Hello, again."

"Have we met?"

"Yes. At the bar at Vici. Phil Cavanaugh."

He squinted in confusion.

"I was with Stephen Donato?"

He squinted again and I realized we had not in fact met because he was not in fact Rusty Grimes. The resemblance, however, was uncanny.

"Sorry. I thought you were the DA."

"S'okay. I get that a lot. I'm his brother, Hank Grimes."

I soon discovered that in addition to sharing Rusty's unfortunately bulbous features, he also had his brother's off-putting cockiness and snide machismo.

"Now that I think of it, I remember runnin' into Rusty that night. He told me he'd stopped by to see his kid and had a run-in with Stevie and a little *friend* of his."

He gave the word "friend" about four extra "n"s and, lest his innuendo be missed, added an extra "s" or two to "his."

"Gosh, Hank," I said, "I'm kinda missing your inference here. Perhaps if you put on a dress and sang 'Over the Rainbow.'"

There it was again, that fatal impulse of mine to twit the constabulary. It had not been wise at Vici with Rusty and was even less wise here in the midst of what, unless I missed my guess, was an actual criminal investigation. Foolish, yes, but what can I say? Show me a surly soldier and right away I'm Eve Arden.

"They were just going," said Moira.

"Wait, you say your name's Cavanaugh?" he asked, pulling a notebook from his pocket and checking a page. "Stick around, pal. I got some questions for you too."

He asked Gilbert his name, then consulted his list again.

"Bingo. Trifecta," he said and, seating himself, commenced his interrogation.

His performance, in less dire circumstances, would have struck me as an amusingly clichéd rendition of the old-school tough cop. The body language was insolently relaxed as though he owned the joint and the voice suggested extensive elocution lessons from Mickey Spillane. Every gesture and inflection was calculated to convey that he was The Law, that we had run afoul of it, and that when the state finally slapped numbers on our chests the brewskis would be on him.

"Just correct me, Miss Finch," he said, his tone sarcastically deferential, "if I'm wrong on any of my facts here. You are the owner and former full-time proprietor of Les Étoiles, a spa and resort hotel in Bel-Air?"

"Yes."

"You recently formed this production company in partnership with Stephen Donato?"

"Yes," she repeated, her tone flatter this time to convey impatience.

"Prior to forming this company you had no previous producing experience?"

Moira's lengthy response touched on the many projects she and Albert had been developing before his untimely death, but boiled down to no.

"You met Mr. Donato through these gentlemen here some eight weeks ago?"

"That's correct."

"One of them, Mr. Selwyn I believe, is your ex-husband?"

"Correct," came Gilbert's arch reply.

"Gee," said Hank, cocking an eye at Gilbert's yellow Miyake T, "I wonder what broke that little romance up. Wouldn't you say, Miss Finch, that eight weeks is an awfully short time to know someone before starting a business together?"

"Not if you click, which Stephen and I did immediately. He found me very creative."

"Makes two of us. Let's cut to the chase, okay? We have a suspect in custody, we'll call him Kenneth. Good-looking kid, midtwenties. Male prostitute. Last week a john of his dropped dead while Kenny was with him. Heart attack. Drugs were involved and we're pretty sure Kenny supplied 'em. We hauled him in after he went on a shopping spree with the old guy's MasterCard. Not a bright boy, Kenny. His lawyers said if we went easy on him he could deliver a big fish. That fish was you."

No one does bewildered innocence better than Moira. She regarded him with the guileless stare of a little match girl accused of arson.

"What on earth did he say I've done? I've never broken the law in my life!"

"Not to hear Kenny tell it. He says he worked at your spa for three months as a 'massage therapist.' He says that during that time he had sex over fifty times with sixteen different men, most of them prominent in the entertainment field. He says he did so with your full knowledge and that both he and the spa were well paid for his services. He says there were seven other hustlers working there as well and that three of them claimed to have had sex with Stephen Donato. He also believes but can't prove that the sex was filmed."

To quote a recent screenplay of ours, Moira was "shocked— shocked!" at these accusations, which she declared utterly groundless and libelous to boot.

Hank grinned. "Maybe so. But they go a long way toward explaining how you got yourself such a sweet deal with Stephen—which means you can throw in extortion too."

"First pandering, now extortion!" huffed Moira. "What are you going to charge me with next? Arms trafficking?!"

"No one's charged you with anything, Miss Finch. Yet. We're just asking questions."

Moira, speaking with glacial disdain, said that if this Kenny had ever in fact worked at her spa he was clearly someone she'd fired for drug use who was now paying her back by concocting this spiteful fiction.

"If I may be frank, Mr. Grimes, it both wounds and disgusts me that you've fallen for such a tale. I can't believe you'd take the word of a self-admitted thief, dope-dealer, and prostitute over that of a hard-working Christian businesswoman and grieving widow! Please leave my office this instant!"

But Grimes wasn't done. He had several questions for Gilbert and me, most of which hinted disconcertingly at collusion in Moira's enterprise. Why had we brought Stephen to Les Étoiles? Had we been compensated in any way? Could we describe our visits there? Had we observed any activities consistent with Kenny's accusations? We perjured ourselves as vigorously as Moira had, for we knew beyond question that if she went down she'd find a way to take us with her.

"I mean, c'mon!" I said with a desperate chuckle. "If a guy wants to have illicit gay sex, does he really invite his wife and mom to tag along?"

Hank leered knowingly. "Maybe that's the part he gets off on. Makes it dirtier."

Moira, refusing to brook such vile aspersions against her partner, strode angrily to the door. Before hurling it open, she crossed her arms sternly and said, "Don't think I don't know what this is about. Your brother's had a personal vendetta against Stephen for years. He's also running for governor this fall and could use another sensational case to whip up his homophobic supporters. You tell him for me that Stephen and I will not be scapegoated! And if he leaks one word of these malicious lies to the press I will sue him into the ground for libel!"

Hank just laughed, tickled by her pique. "I'll be in touch, Miss Finch," he said as he ambled past her.

"And by the way," he added, his words a disquieting echo of Lily's, "it's not libel if you prove it."

Twenty-one

★

I ONCE READ AN ARTICLE ABOUT the unanimity with which de-
pressed San Franciscans agree that, if you're going to off yourself,
the Golden Gate Bridge is absolutely *the* only place to do so, all
lesser bridges being poor substitutes, resort to which risks exposing
oneself to comment at the memorial. One fellow who miraculously
survived his plunge said that the instant he'd leaped he realized there
was no problem in his life he could not solve save the one he'd just created for himself by stepping off the Golden Gate Bridge. As we pulled
out of the Pinnacle lot I felt a pang of empathy for that poor jumper,
for I too could now see how laughably trivial were the concerns that
had consumed me only an hour ago.

You've been fired off a movie? Big deal! It was a crappy story anyway! Stop whining! Write a new one!

Your closeted megastar boyfriend has dumped you? Boo hoo! Is he
the *only* closeted megastar in town? Hardly! Get out there! Become a
Scientologist! Meet people!

The DA wants to nail you on charges ranging from pandering and
extortion to conspiracy and obstruction of justice? Okay—*that's* a

problem! That, my friend, is the difference between inconvenience and actual Peril. And the peril, it grieves me to report, only deepened once Hank left Moira's office.

The moment she slammed the door she stridently informed us what revenge she'd exact if we were so foolhardy as to cooperate with the police. She'd say we were full-blown accomplices who'd lured Stephen to Les Étoiles with full knowledge of her intentions. She also told us that, were we to check our most recent bank statements, we'd find that ten thousand dollars had been deposited into our accounts the day after we'd delivered Stephen to her.

"That was you!" I said, recalling the delightful discrepancy, which I'd assumed, in my general flightiness with all matters financial, to be some sort of script payment.

She would also claim that the price we'd demanded for luring Stephen to the spa included sexual favors from her staff and that she had film of Gilbert to prove it (this, of course, being the sole reason she'd arranged for his massage to end happily). This last calumny seemed especially foul, and my head swam at the thought of *National Enquirer* headlines screaming, "Madam Moira: 'Stevie's "Pals" Betrayed Him for Sex Freebies!' "

As we drove through the Pinnacle gates, I wanted desperately to go straight to Claire and seek her counsel, but I was due at Lily's and felt too guilty over yesterday's heinousness to keep her waiting. I arrived in Los Feliz at noon, returning everything I'd taken from Lily, who greeted me with shaming effusiveness.

"Glen, my angel! How good to see you! Mwah! How clever you were to take this all away when you saw that man in the bushes! But do leave a note next time! I was beside myself and the fear gave me a splitting headache! Didn't I warn you there were those who'd try to stop us? You didn't believe me, but now you know!"

It wasn't easy to concentrate on Lily's ramblings that day, what with dark visions of prison life flitting like bats through my tortured imagination. I was also bursting to pull Monty aside and ask what havoc he planned to wreak with his new arsenal. I didn't get him alone till six-thirty, when Lily withdrew to dress for her weekly night out with the girls. I decided to come clean about everything, starting with my real name and my history with Stephen and Diana.

"Good lord," he said, flabbergasted, "you were in cahoots with them before we even met?"

I apologized abjectly for my duplicity, laying great emphasis on how desperate we were not to lose our first screenwriting gig.

"And, of course," I confessed, "there was Stephen."

"Gave you the look, did he?"

"Huh?"

"The look," he repeated. "That languid, smoldering, surrender-your-genitals stare. I know it well, having watched him devise and perfect it in this very house the summer he turned sixteen."

"Yes, he did. But still, I can imagine what you must think of me."

"Don't be silly! If anything it makes me fonder of you."

"Huh?" I said, flummoxed.

"Before this," he explained, "I'd assumed you'd turned on us after you'd already known us for weeks. I understood and forgave. Were Stephen not kin I'd betray any number of old ladies for him, but I can tell you, it stung. But now I find you'd signed on to do us dirty before we'd even met, back when you assumed us to be the baby-munching grave robbers my loved ones no doubt painted us as. It was only after you'd pledged your fealty to them that you came to see what splendid creatures we really are."

"Exactly!" I said, grateful for this magnanimously proffered loophole. "And once I did, I felt *awful*. But what could I do? I'd given my word! It seemed dishonorable to renege."

"And you wanted to screw Stephen."

"Well, that too, of course."

"And you did," he laughed, slapping my knee. "And with cameras, yet, which was good news for me. So there, you see, Glen—Philip?—what *are* we to call you?—all's well that ends well!"

I said that all had not yet ended and the odds of it doing so well were growing remoter by the hour. I breathlessly described our run-in with Hank, a tale which, to my surprise, did not alarm Monty in the least.

"Mere saber rattling. If they had any proof they'd file charges. Besides, Moira's far too clever to get herself caught. She thinks things through, that girl. She anticipates contingencies. Well, look who I'm telling—she stapled your lips well in advance of need. Buck up, dear. Have faith as I do in her evil genius."

I asked what he planned to do with the DVD.

"Fear not," he said cryptically. "All will be revealed shortly. And I promise you a front-row seat for the proceedings."

"Proceedings?" I said, not liking the word one bit. But then the doorbell rang and Monty sprang limberly to his feet.

"That will be Rex. We're painting the town pink if you care to join us."

I said I doubted Rex would relish my company as the last time I'd seen him he'd been using a strapping black youth as a pacifier. I contemplated a swift retreat through the French doors but then Rex's belly entered the room followed shortly by Rex.

"Well, look who's here," he said with a dainty sneer. "It's the *voyeur!*"

I rose with the serene smile of a boy who has his exit line.

"*Former* voyeur, Rex. You've cured me."

MY MOOD AS I departed Lily and Monty's was at least a shade less funereal than it had been on arrival. Though I could not share Monty's hey-diddle-diddle outlook on the Grimes menace, I did feel that doom was, perhaps, not quite so inevitable as I'd feared. Hell, even the jumper had survived.

But the lightening of my mood was mainly the result of having finally laid Glen to rest. The ongoing deception had weighed increasingly on my conscience and as I drove west I felt that proud glow that only steals over me when the better angels of my nature have scored one of their rare victories.

*   *   *

THAT NIGHT GILBERT AND I dined at Orso with Claire, who strongly urged us to lawyer up and tell all in exchange for immunity.

"For God's sake," she whispered, "save yourselves while you can! Trust me, it's all *going* to come out. Too many people know about it. The first ones to cooperate will get immunity and everyone else will be thrown to the wolves!"

"But we haven't done anything wrong!" protested Gilbert.

"That's not what Moira will say. Just play ball. Tell them the truth—she was blackmailing you over the screenplay."

"*What?*" I said, choking on my carpaccio.

"You want us to ruin our careers?!"

"And what sort of careers do you think you'll have in *prison?!* Wake up! This isn't *The Producers!* They don't do musicals in there!"

I said that while I valued her advice, she was, I feared, underestimating the harm that could be inflicted on us by an enraged and vindictive Moira, whom I frankly feared more than the police. I also pointed out that the Grimes brothers had formed robust dislikes for me, and their bona fides in any negotiation could not be assumed. Besides, there was no guarantee anyone else would come forward. The clients had much to hide and the working boys, fearing for their safety, had largely dispersed to other cities. By talking we might be *creating* a case that could have been avoided had we just kept our mouths shut. Gilbert declared my logic impeccable, which, needless to say, troubled me deeply.

Truth to tell, my main reason for rejecting Claire's advice was one I left unspoken so as to spare myself the howls of ridicule it would have prompted from both my companions. That reason was Stephen.

Granted things hadn't ended well between us and his behavior toward me had fallen short of the highest standards of chivalry. But did I really want to be the cause of his downfall? To deliberately drag him into the mire of scandal and global mockery? I recalled our first meeting with the bully Grimes, how bravely we'd stood shoulder to shoulder and crossed swords with the foe. How could I now deliver him to that gay-baiting plug-ugly? No, I could bear to be Stephen's lovestruck pawn, his ill-used ex-squeeze, but I would not be his Judas.

*　　*　　*

THE NEXT FEW DAYS proceeded without incident. Claire lit out for parts north while Lily and I did our best to spice up the details of her threadbare midlife career. Then Friday morning Monty phoned to inform me there'd be no work that day as he was treating us to a festive lunch. He told me to don my spiffiest suit and meet them at twelve sharp at the Beverly Hilton.

"Can I come?" whined Gilbert as I jotted down the address. I asked Monty, who said, "By all means! The more the merrier!"

On reaching the Hilton we found ourselves trapped in a long caravan of limos at the end of which was a red carpet. The carpet was lined with a great noisy rabble of reporters, all shouting and elbowing one another aside in their frenzy to get a glance, a smile, a comment from the arriving luminaries. A large banner over the press line read FILM-FEST LA and I suddenly recalled that Stephen had mentioned the event some weeks ago, saying he was to be honored as the Entertainer of the Decade. My heart fibrillated even as my breakfast petitioned for early release, for I realized at once that Monty had chosen this diabolical moment to pounce.

For those of you unfamiliar with it, FilmFest LA is an annual confab of producers, distributors, and deal makers who gather to flog their wares and bestow a dozen or so spectacularly ugly trophies. Unlike the Oscars, which ostensibly celebrate excellence, or the Golden Globes, which, whatever their stated mandate, celebrate Heat, the FilmFest unabashedly honors commercial success.

Back in the seventies they started giving an Entertainer of the Year Award to add more star power to the proceedings. It worked so well they began offering an Entertainer of the Decade Award every five years, justifying the double-dipping by alternating male and female performers. The Decade Awards draw the starriest crowds, and the red carpet along which we made our unhectored way seemed thronged with every actor who'd ever worked with Stephen or hoped to. We jostled past them, soon reaching a checkpoint where we were mercifully refused entrance owing to our lack of tickets. I was trying to convince Gilbert that we'd be better off heading home and donning our Hazmat suits when I heard Monty shouting my name.

Turning, I saw that he and Lily were making their way down the carpet. Monty sported a stylish pin-striped suit and carried a leather shoulder bag the contents of which I could only surmise with dread. Lily, her face's taut translucence concealed beneath a thick coat of maquillage, wore a chic green Chanel suit and looked happier than I'd ever seen her, vamping and posing up a storm for the stymied paparazzi, some of whom took her picture anyway, figuring they'd sort it out later.

"Isn't it exciting, Glen!" she twittered on reaching us. "Oh, forgive me. I keep forgetting you've taken Philip as your nom de plume."

"Gilbert, I presume," said Monty, pumping his hand. "Are you two an item?"

"Ages ago," said Gilbert. "Now we're just collaborators."

"I see—though not right together, nonetheless you write together." He addressed the gatekeeper. "Hello, Monty Malenfant here."

She asked to see tickets and he explained that they were the aunt and uncle of the honoree.

"Well, she knows *that!*" laughed Lily, shooting the bewildered ticket taker her "Yes-dear-it's-me" smile. Monty, doubting if the lass had sufficient clout to assist us, asked to speak to her superior or anyone able to establish contact with Stephen. At length an officious fellow with a clipboard appeared and curtly informed us that Stephen was upstairs in a hospitality suite and could not be disturbed. Monty politely insisted that a message be conveyed to him, assuring Clipboard that Stephen was waiting for it and his failure to deliver it would earn him the star's lasting ire. The message was that his uncle Monty and dear friend Oscar were there, as arranged, to see him. Were Stephen too busy to see us just now, Monty would happily wait, passing the time by introducing Oscar to the many charming people on hand. Clipboard scowled and bustled away, dialing his cell phone. When he returned shortly, the medic tending to his ear with a fire extinguisher made clear the message's impact on its recipient. "He asked to speak to you," he said, handing Monty the still-smoldering cell phone.

"Stephen, my darling! So sorry I'm late. Should Oscar and I just pop up with the material? . . . Splendid! Oh and could you arrange seating please for Lily and a young friend? . . . How terribly kind of you."

Clipboard escorted us up to the penthouse. He rang the bell and we were promptly admitted to a large, elegant suite packed to the rafters with Entourage.

Owing to the highly secretive nature of our work with Stephen, we'd been granted the exceedingly rare privilege of dealing with him one-on-one, all handlers save Sonia being banned from our meetings. This then was my first glimpse of the army of courtiers who daily danced attendance on him and whose ranks only swelled on such august occasions as this. There was Sonia, of course, her girth encased in a pin-striped black pantsuit that made her look like one of the gangsters in an all-lesbian *Kiss Me, Kate*. Joining her was a babbling swarm of publicists, agents, studio reps, stylists, hair and makeup artists, bodyguards, sundry friends, and a masseur of the conventional variety. They fluttered and swooped around Stephen, anticipating his every need. When not genuflecting they jabbered into cell phones with the staccato self-importance that invariably infects those who've been granted that most glittering coin of the Hollywood realm—Access.

At the center of it all, like a child with thirty nannies, sat Stephen. He was having a neck rub while smoking a cigarette that trembled slightly in his hand. I didn't see Gina or Diana and wondered if they were off in other suites with minions of their own. At this level of fame were entourages something one didn't share, even with family? Like toothbrushes?

"Stephen!" cried Monty exuberantly, capturing every eye in the place. "Do forgive my tardiness. Not to worry though—I've made all the changes you asked for. Give your old uncle a hug!"

Stephen, I knew, was as thrown as I was by Monty's brash ebullience and puzzling reference to requested changes. But as discretion forbade his replying, "What do you mean, you blackmailing scum?" he summoned a wary half smile and said, "Hey, Monty." He gave him a perfunctory hug, stiffening slightly when Monty kissed him loudly on both cheeks.

"Mwah! How nice you smell. New cologne? Hello. Monty Malenfant," he said to the masseur. "Stephen's uncle and head speechwriter. And you are?"

"Julio."

"A pleasure to meet you, Julio. My, what a firm grip! Sonia, my angel! It's been ages. What a pretty frock you're wearing. Hello, hello!" he said, waggling his fingers at a nearby haggle of agents. "My goodness!" he chortled, surveying Stephen's retinue. "You should've told me you were low on help today. I'd have brought another regiment. Ha ha!"

He opened his satchel and removed a manila folder containing several typed pages.

"Now per our discussion I've made the alterations you requested, and if I may say so, the whole thing just sparkles. You'll no doubt want to read it over and—might I ask your cupbearer for some of that wine? And for Philip?—if you think any last-minute tweaks are called for I'll be happy to make them. Thanks, Ganymede, aren't you a darling? Cheers!"

Sonia, tight-lipped with rage, stepped forward. Mindful of the onlookers, she attempted a smile, the result suggesting a constipated gargoyle.

"Maybe we could all talk about this somewhere more private?"

"Of course! Mustn't spoil the element of surprise! Lead the way, my pretty."

We followed Sonia down a short hall to the suite's large bedroom. As soon as she'd closed the door, she wheeled on us with a look that made me know how the matador feels.

"How dare you show your miserable faces here!"

"Now there's a silly question," said Monty. "You know perfectly well *how* I dare. The question for you is *what* I dare and trust me, it's a doozy, though in light of your disgraceful treatment of Lily I find it eminently fair. Your views may vary. How are you coming with that?"

he asked Stephen, who was staring goggle-eyed at the pages Monty had given him.

"What the hell is this?!"

"I should think that was obvious. It's your acceptance speech, love."

"Are you fucking kidding me?!" said Stephen, aghast. "I can't say this crap!"

"Of course you can," said Monty. "Been doing it all your life. Speaking words written by others as though they were your own, lending them force and the bracing tang of reality. Do try to keep your voice down when you reach page two, as the impulse to howl will be a strong one."

Stephen turned the page, read a bit, then leaped like a man who's just peed on the third rail.

"Have you lost your fucking mind!"

"Give me that!" growled Sonia, grabbing the pages.

Alarmed to think Stephen might assume me a witting accomplice, I fervently assured him I had no idea what the speech even said. It was hard to make myself heard though, as he was rhythmically pounding the arms of his chair while repeating the word "no."

"Jesus fucking Christ!" exclaimed Sonia, reaching page two. "You're fucking nuts! I'm calling security!"

Monty retorted that the only security Stephen could hope for lay in delivering the speech verbatim.

"How can you do this to me!" raged Stephen. "You're my goddamned uncle!"

"And entitled, as such, to administer discipline when called for. Come along, Philip."

"No!" cried Stephen, bounding past us to block the door. "I'm calling your bluff! I know you, Monty! You can threaten me all you like but you'd never send that film to the media!"

Monty gently patted his nephew's cheek and spoke, as they say, more in sorrow than anger.

"Once, Stephen. Once I wouldn't have. But that was before you bewitched this one into stealing your poor aunt's diaries. Bad form, love. Very bad form. It made me quite angry at you, which is why I've posted clips of your little Oscar party on a website."

Stephen blanched and Sonia grabbed Monty roughly by the shoulder.

"You put them on the fucking Web?!"

"Unhand me, sir. Yes, on a site the domain name of which is known only to me. I see, Sonia, by the fur that's just sprouted on your forehead that you're contemplating doing me an injury. Don't. I've already e-mailed links to ten publications. I've done so on a time delay so the message will go out at five today unless I return safely home and cancel it. So you see, there's no wriggling out of this one."

Stephen stepped away from the door but kept his imploring eyes on Monty. I must say that for all the fierce and genuine emotions he must have been feeling, his gaze had a whiff of the stage about it. He was feeling pain but playing it too in a last-ditch attempt to shame his uncle into mercy.

"This was supposed to be *my* day, Monty. The biggest damn day of my life."

"And so it will be. One way or another."

AS WE LEFT THE SUITE I begged Monty to tell me what he'd written for Stephen. He declined, puckishly maintaining that he didn't want to spoil the surprise. His real reason, as he later conceded, was his well-grounded fear that if he told me I'd have bolted from the hotel, leaped into a cab, and screamed, "Airport!"

We returned to the lobby and relocated Clipboard. Monty informed him that Stephen had requested we be seated backstage to serve as prompters. Could two chairs be placed in the wings? This clearly struck Clipboard as an odd request, but as Monty had proven himself an authority on Stephen's wishes, he acquiesced and led us into the ballroom.

I saw that Gilbert had been squeezed into a table on the other side of the room. Lily sat opposite him, chattering away to Quentin Tarantino, whose eyes darted madly in search of rescue. Moira was

there too, of course, at a front center table well larded with A-list stars,
plus Bobby, Max, and Maddie.

Clipboard led us down the side of the ballroom and up three stairs
to the wing space, which was just two curtains with logos flanking the
low stage. He informed a fellow with a headset that Stephen wanted us
seated there as prompters. This greatly flustered Headset, who seemed
to have a lot on his plate just now, but one doesn't flout the Entertainer
of the Decade's will, so chairs were produced and we sat down to await
the festivities.

Stephen's award was, of course, the last on the program, and the
hour leading up to it seemed the longest of my life. The suspense alone
was torment enough, but it was even worse having to endure it while
listening to a ponytailed producer tearily extol the "courage, tenacity,
and vision" he'd displayed in shepherding *Whoa, You're No Chick!* to
the screen. Finally after much boasting and bathos, Bobby Spellman,
Stephen's introducer, took the stage. He did a little double take when
he spotted Monty and me in the wings, then launched into his remarks, which for sheer bombast left his predecessors entirely in the
dust.

I've never understood why speakers at award shows insist on making it sound as though movie stardom is not merely a swell job offering fame, fun, glamour, and a heck of a nice salary. No, it is rather a
great and selfless service to humanity, ranking on the nobility scale
somewhere between cancer research and famine relief. In Bobby's
intro, which ran an exhausting ten minutes, he praised Stephen's high
principles, uncompromising integrity, and countless good works on
behalf of the less fortunate. As an actor Stephen was a "visionary"
whose boldness, versatility, and artistic daring would influence screen
acting for centuries to come. He dwelled at length on the Caliber films,
the grosses for which were the real reason Stephen was being honored.
To Bobby these were not just well-crafted escapist entertainments —
they were "modern retellings of sacred myth," soaring testaments to
the human spirit and man's unconquerable heroism in the face of evil.

When he'd finally run out of blather, a screen was lowered and
highlights of Stephen's career were shown. It's no small comment on

my vanity that even in my agonized suspense I felt a frisson of pride to see that gorgeous kisser fill the screen and think, "Yeah, I know that guy. Did him."

The screen was raised and Bobby proclaimed, "Ladies and gentlemen—Stephen Donato!" We heard the audience applaud wildly and presumed from the scraping of chairs that they'd offered the de rigueur standing ovation. Stephen took his place behind the podium and Monty waved to catch his attention. He hadn't expected to see us there and, should he ever tackle the role of Macbeth, the moment will make a good sense memory for the scene with Banquo's ghost. He was not carrying any pages, but when Monty shook an admonitory finger he removed them from his jacket and spread them on the podium. He took a breath so deep it drew chuckles from the house—how charming that he's nervous!—then began to read.

"I'd like to thank my great and wise old chum Bobby Spellman for that generous introduction. We go way back, Bobby and me. Sterling fellow. Don't be fooled by the scary eyebrows and Prince of Darkness goatee. True, he may look like something red-hooded young ladies would do well to avoid en route to Grandma's, but beneath that carnivorous exterior beats a showman's tender heart. Splendid filmmaker too, if a mite too fond of explosions, but we all have our little foibles, so I say why cavil?

"Thanks too to the good folk of FilmFest LA, not only for this curiously designed trophy but for the invaluable service they perform. Especially now during awards season when the whole town's gone gaga over 'Quality' and 'Artistic Merit' it's nice to see someone give a well-deserved pat on the head to those savvy producers who've kept a keen eye on the bottom line and shrewdly gauged the public's often baffling appetites. I'd also like to thank my new partner, Moira Finch. Most of you have met her by now—she's seen to that!—and I'm sure you'll agree she's quite a gal—smart, charming, and, as those of you who've visited her spa can attest, one hell of a hostess.

"Most of all I want to thank my family—my indomitable mother, Diana, for everything she's taught me and for always accepting me just as I am. Gina, my supertalented wife who looks after me and forgives my little quirks and habits. And I especially want to thank my aunt Lily . . ."

His voice caught as he said "Lily." He paused and glanced down, massaging his forehead like an overcome eulogist. Monty though knew that his inability to continue stemmed not from teary sentiment but from the most profound reluctance. Monty had anticipated just such a contingency and prepared for it shrewdly.

Reaching into his shoulder bag, he removed two small male figures. One appeared to be a nude G.I. Joe. The other was an Oscar. Coughing lightly to catch Stephen's attention, he positioned the two figures horizontally, Oscar on top, then commenced grinding them together while fluttering his eyelids in mock ecstasy. This gentle reminder served its purpose admirably. Stephen promptly recommitted to his text, bringing to it a fervor and conviction his performance had thus far lacked.

"I want to thank my *wonderful* aunt Lily, who always looked after me whenever Mom was away on location or hospitalized. Lily was my first real acting coach and I will always be grateful to her for that gift.

"I'm grateful too for a more recent gift she gave me, one I hadn't been expecting. You see, I always knew Lily was a fantastic actress but never dreamed she was an amazing writer as well. But then I read her screenplay, *Amelia Flies Again!,* a gripping tale that dares to imagine what fate may have befallen Amelia Earhart after her disappearance in 1937. I'm thrilled to announce that I've acquired the rights for Finch/Donato Productions and will be starting preproduction immediately."

On hearing this, Lily (reports Gilbert) shrieked in astonished glee and squeezed his arm so tightly it bruised.

"That's me!" she announced to her luncheon companions. "That's my screenplay! I'm his aunt Lily!" she added as if she hadn't made this abundantly clear to the whole table and several adjoining ones as well.

Stephen, real tears now dampening his cheeks, thanked her as well for writing a nice juicy role for him. "But mostly," he concluded, taking his deepest breath yet, "I want to thank her for agreeing to play the rich and complex role of Amelia herself. Lily, take a bow!"

Lily did not need to be asked twice. She sprang immediately to her feet, a good thing, noted Gilbert, as it kept her from hearing Tarantino exclaim, "He's shitting us, right?!" Advancing to a clearing between tables, she executed a series of elaborate curtsies while blowing kisses to her suddenly beloved nephew. The crowd applauded madly if only to drown out the wild, gossipy buzz that greeted this jaw-dropping announcement.

His *aunt?*

She's still *alive?*

Were they even on *speaking* terms?

Could she *ever* act?

Amelia Earhart?!

The applause went on at length, only tapering off when it became clear that Lily would not stop bowing as long as she could hear a single pair of hands colliding. As Lily milked her ovation Stephen cast a glance at us and pointedly returned the pages to his jacket. It was a token gesture of defiance. He'd done Monty's bidding and would not demean himself further by spouting more of his folderol. When the applause finally subsided Stephen closed with a portion of the remarks he'd originally planned. He spoke of the Healing Power of Art and Giving Back, ending with a million-dollar pledge to build an Arts Center for inner-city youth. All very laudable, of course, but not half so scintillating as his bizarre promise to costar in a period epic with his washed-up aunt.

As Stephen stepped offstage into an ocean of hugs and handshakes, Monty rose and clapped me heartily on the shoulder.

"Congratulations, dear! You're back in showbiz!"

"Thanks a lot! Jesus, Monty, have you *read* that script?"

"Yes, and, if I may be frank, it needs work. The plot's far-fetched, and the Hitler stuff's a bit of a giggle. Still, nothing a talented fellow like you can't set right. Lily's happy and that's the main thing. I've done my good deed."

Lily was a damn sight more than happy. She was wafting deliriously through the party in a spot well north of cloud nine, hobnobbing with the stars who'd been transformed by a wave of her fairy godfather's wand into peers. When we caught up with her and Gilbert, she was accepting polite congratulations from her new pal Meryl Streep.

"Glen! There you are! We must talk soon, Meryl, there's a part you'd be divine for! Glen—sorry, Philip—isn't it marvelous? Monty, you devil! Keeping it all from me like that! But what a way to find out! *Everyone's* talking about it. Mr. Tarantino was full of questions. He didn't say as much but I can tell he wants to direct. Philip, I'm so sorry Stephen forgot to say you were my coauthor. Don't worry, though— I'm telling everyone."

"*No!* I mean, it's okay. It's your script! I just did a polish!"

"Nonsense!" tutted Lily. "You were indispensable. Why without your help who knows if—oh, look! It's that Scorsese man. Methinks *he's* learned a thing or two about striking while the iron's hot!"

"You know," said Gilbert generously, "if you'd like a fresh eye to help with the rewrite—"

"Stephen!" cried Lily, waving to where he stood receiving congratulations and no doubt a query or two from Max and Maddie. "Gracious me, we haven't even thanked him!" she said, grabbing my arm and hastening toward her benefactor. Monty and Gilbert scampered after us, determined to witness firsthand this moment in cinematic history.

"You darling man!" she shrieked, throwing her arms around him. "I can't tell you how thrilled I am that you liked my little script and want to bring it to the screen! I should actually say *our* script since Philip here had quite a hand in it!"

"You don't say?" replied Stephen. His tone was flat and unsurprised, things having reached a stage where, when catastrophe struck, my involvement could safely be taken as a given.

"Good for you, hon!" said Maddie, pinching my cheek. "Good things just keep coming your way, don't they?"

"Why hello, dear! You must be Moira!" said Lily to the enraged yet smiling vixen who'd just materialized at Stephen's elbow. "How lovely to meet you," said Lily, pumping her hand. "I've heard you have the most marvelous taste—and now I know it's true! Ha-ha! I must say, Stephen, when Monty told me you'd invited us and to expect a surprise I never dreamed it would be anything so wonderful as this! I had no idea he'd even sent you the script!"

"So, it's a good one?" Max asked anxiously and Moira replied truthfully enough that she'd never read anything like it. Max then scrutinized Lily, his brow understandably furrowed.

"And you play Amelia Earhart?"

"Yes. The story takes place later in her life."

"Well, it would have to," said Maddie.

Lily clasped Stephen's hands and gazed adoringly at him, her eyes welling up with gratitude. "Thank you *so* much, my dear. What a marvelous Henri you'll make! What fun we'll have finally working together!"

Stephen just stared at her, speechless, and the smile he wore for the benefit of gawkers had a distinctly befuddled edge. His confusion was pardonable. Though etiquette authorities from Emily Post to Miss Manners have done their best to prepare us for every conceivable form of human interaction, none has yet addressed the question of how to behave toward a person who is ruthlessly blackmailing you but does not appear to know it.

"Well," he stammered at length, "I'm, uh, looking forward to it."

Our little group was joined by Diana and Gina. Diana managed with her customary aplomb to cloak her outrage and was betrayed only by her nostrils, which flared uncontrollably at Lily's galling magnanimity.

"Diana, my dear! I adore what you're wearing! So slimming. I don't know if Stephen's told you but there's a part in our picture you'd be perfect for. Not large, mind you, but terribly effective."

"How kind of you," replied Diana, her pitch several ledger lines below the bass clef.

Gina was, as usual, an open wound. "He never tells me anything!" she complained to no one in particular, and Stephen remarked that the deal had come together rather quickly.

"Yes, very," grinned Monty. "I asked Stephen if he wanted more time to think, but Moira counseled against it. She said, 'When a script like this comes along, you snap it up. Don't wait for a bidding war.'"

"Most wise of you, Moira," said Lily, citing Scorsese's imminent offer.

Diana announced that she had a headache and was going. Stephen, who had no stomach to face the inquisitive well-wishers pressing in from all sides, offered to see her out. The rest of us followed, Lily Velcroing herself to Stephen in the hope there'd still be press outside.

The preshow throng had thinned but there were still plenty awaiting us, and at the sight of Stephen and Lily they went wild, furiously snapping the photos that would appear the next day in newspapers round the world. They shouted questions to Stephen, who, smiling grimly, said he had nothing to add to his speech. Lily, of course, could not shut up and burbled away about this grand opportunity to costar with the man she'd known since he was a little boy staging plays in her backyard.

"Kept all the best parts for himself of course. Male and female. My shoes were forever going missing. Oh, before I forget, this is Philip Cavanaugh. He's the brilliant young man who cowrote *Amelia Flies Again!*, though the idea for it was totally mine."

"Totally!"

When Stephen's limo pulled up he eyed it without relief, no doubt contemplating the discussions still to come with Gina and Diana, not to mention the script he'd just agreed to produce and star in, sight unseen. For now he could only imagine what horrors lurked there, but I'll never forget his ashen expression when he received his first dark inkling of what he'd signed on for.

"Just so I'm clear," said Max to Lily as Stephen's driver opened his door. "You play Amelia but the story takes place long after she disappeared in 'thirty-seven?"

"Yes, of course! *Years* later! World War II! Oh, look, Philip! There's Tom and Rita! Let's say hello!"

Twenty-two

★

"Comeback?"

Lily Malenfant repeats the word with a sly smile as she gazes dreamily out at the small lovely garden where she grows her award-winning roses. "I'm not sure I'd call it a comeback, *dear. The truth is, I never left!" she says with a girlish laugh as she refreshes her lemonade. The multitalented actress who has wowed audiences in everything from film noir to sitcom says she's been happy to spend her life in the shadow of her more famous sister and nephew, a guy you may know as Stephen Donato.*

"I'm not like Diana—you know, someone who's miserable if she's not the center of attention and having all her affairs and drunken fights written up in the papers. That's not what acting's about. Not to me. To me it's all about the craft."

For the last thirty or so years Lily has chosen to display her craft mostly onstage, spurning all but a few of the many film offers she's received. "It's so much more fun acting for people, not just cameras!" she says, her ageless face aglow. "To know they're out there and hear them all laughing, sometimes in

places you never imagined they would." Unfortunately for
Lily, her cozy life in the shadows is about to come to an end.
Starting this weekend audiences will thrill to her riveting per-
formance as Miss Hepps, Drew Barrymore's *sinister landlady*
in the taut new thriller Guess What, I'm Not Dead. *Though*
on-screen for less than seven minutes, Malenfant dominates
the movie, creating an indelible portrait of bitterness and lu-
nacy that reverberates long after the character's grisly death.
Lily will follow this bravura performance by costarring with
her famous nephew in the historical epic Amelia Flies Again!,
the screenplay for which the versatile Miss Malenfant coau-
thored with Frederick Kavanaugh.

The above article, excerpted from *People,* was but one of scores of
fawning profiles of Lily that appeared in the wake of Stephen's announcement and the modestly successful release of *Guess What, I'm
Not Dead.* These puff pieces, along with numerous talk show appearances, were engineered by Sonia, who'd checked out the contents of
stephendonatogoesoscarwild.com and capitulated instantly to Monty's
demand that she place her vast media clout in the service of Lily's
greater glory. Favors were called in, threats made, and access to bigger
stars denied to any media outlet that refused to feed the public's nonexistent appetite for all things Lily.

What amazed me most about Lily's comeback was how little it
amazed her. It did not strike her as remotely miraculous that the press
to whom she'd long been dead should now clamor for interviews. Nor
did she for a moment ascribe this sudden avalanche of attention to
anything save the public's entirely sensible, if belated, recognition of
her genius. Not once during her long winter of obscurity had she
doubted that her stardom would return and now it had, both as welcome and inevitable as the spring.

"What did I tell you, Philip? Fame's a fickle mistress but true
Talent always wins out in the end. I don't know how we'll get a lick of
work done today! I have a *Vanity Fair* shoot, then I have to find a dress
for tonight's museum gala. They're screening *Shame Is for Rich Girls*

and then I'm supposed to get up and speak. Heaven knows what I'll think of to say!"

On that score Lily needn't have worried, for she was never at a loss for words. Stories, aperçus, and bracingly frank opinions came bubbling out of her in a ceaseless, sparsely punctuated torrent that leaped madly from topic to topic. It wasn't long before Sonia no longer needed to browbeat people into covering her, so charmed was the press by Lily's infectious delight in celebrity and remarkable candor. She was especially forthcoming about Diana, whom, despite frequent disclaimers of familial devotion, she would skewer remorselessly at the mildest prompting.

"Monty and I were so thrilled when Stephen was born. Neither of us thought Diana could still have children since she'd had so many—well, I adore her, so I won't say the word. We'll call them *procedures*, shall we? . . . 'Shame about his father dying'? No, not really, dear. Certainly not to Diana. . . . Well, of course she says that *now*. She's loved him dearly since he died, but not a moment sooner. The fights they had! Had Roberto lived poor Stephen wouldn't have made it to three without being killed by a flying decanter!"

STEPHEN OF COURSE IMMEDIATELY demanded a copy of *Amelia Flies Again!* and, on finishing it, was understandably perturbed.

"Is this a fucking JOKE?!" he roared at me over the phone. "You expect us to MAKE this piece of shit!"

"Stephen," I said in the penitent whimper that had come to mark all our discourse of late, "you don't think I know how bad it is? I barely gave the damn thing a polish. I thought, 'Why bother, who's going to make it?'"

"I AM, THAT'S WHO! This is a total fucking disaster! The script sucks, it'll cost a fortune, she can't act, and she's TWENTY-FIVE YEARS TOO OLD FOR THE PART!!"

I pointed out that there was at least one frail sunbeam poking through the clouds. Just that day Lily had decided to heed my advice and leave Stephen's youthful liaisons out of her memoir. They were, after all, colleagues now and it seemed bad form to tattle on one's costar.

"Oh, gee, THANK you, Phil! I'm so RELIEVED!! That'll be such a COMFORT to me after her brother turns me into a FUCK-ING GAY PORN STAR! What the hell am I supposed to do with this script? I've got people all over me asking to read it—Max, Gina, my agents! I can't show them this turd and tell 'em I paid half a million for it!"

"Half a million?" I repeated, stunned.

"Yeah, right," he sneered. "Like you didn't know that!"

"I didn't!"

"Half to Lily's agent, half to yours, just like your pal Monty ordered. Enjoy your blood money, you miserable leech!" he said and hung up.

I immediately phoned Monty to protest that his negotiations had dragooned me into the role of extortionist.

"Nonsense," replied Monty. "You wrote a script and he purchased it. Surely you're entitled to compensation. It's a pittance next to the five million he's paying Lily to star in it."

"Five million! You've got to be kidding!"

"Odd, that's just what Stephen said."

Stephen, once he'd recovered from the sticker shock, had desperately offered to pay all requested fees, plus a million under the table to Monty, if Monty would only withdraw his demand that he make the damned movie. Monty had held firm though, vowing not to surrender his nukes till the picture had been filmed and released. Stephen could hire anyone he liked to doctor the script so long as Lily's premise remained intact and Lily and I received at least shared credit for the screenplay.

IT IS NO SMALL MEASURE of Stephen's woes during what should have been his joyous reign as a Heavily Favored Nominee that *Amelia* was not his biggest headache. It was not even his second biggest. Those honors went to the ongoing criminal probe into Les Étoiles and Gina's

298 | Joe Keenan

mounting suspicions, two problems that now collided with disastrous results.

I was, of course, no longer Stephen's late-night phone pal. What follows represents the clearest picture I can deduce from subsequent reports, gossip, and reasonable conjecture.

Stephen and Gina were questioned by Hank Grimes, who minced no words about Stephen's alleged escapades at the spa. Grimes also voiced his extortion theory, which had now broadened to include Lily and me as the most recent recipients of Stephen's unlikely largesse. Though both Gina and Stephen vehemently refuted the vile slander, the allegations prompted Gina to ponder with fresh unease the events of that tumultuous day at the spa.

She remembered how flustered Stephen had appeared when she'd interrupted his massage and how long I'd taken to answer the door. She recalled too that he'd been smoking pot, a drug she knew he favored mainly for its aphrodisiac effect. She remembered Claire peering under the table, then whisking her and Diana from the room.

And what of Stephen's odd remarks on accepting his award and still odder decision to produce *Amelia?* She asked him again if she could read the script. His pleas that she wait for the next draft only sharpened her suspicions and she demanded that he surrender it. By page seven it was obvious even to Gina that he'd been strong-armed into producing it. Stephen, cornered, laid bare his dilemma. He portrayed himself as a pitiable victim lured into a sexual sting by the evil Moira and us—her treacherous henchmen—who'd plied him with drugs to mar his judgment, filmed everything, and used the footage to hijack his career.

But Gina didn't buy it. Hadn't the snitch claimed that not one but several men had sold their favors to Stephen? And wouldn't such doings help explain why Stephen, who'd always insisted that such folk as trainers and masseurs pay house calls, had become such a devoted patron of a day spa? Stephen denied it but the panic in his eyes told another story and soon Gina Knew All.

Yet she did not leave him.

I can only imagine what combination of tears, pleas, and pledges quelled her impulse to engage the firm of Mulct & Pillage to strip-mine Stephen's assets, leaving him only bus fare to and from the studio. If I had to guess though, I'd say that she simply liked being Mrs. Stephen Donato. She liked it a great deal. Her celebrity pre-Stephen had been minor indeed and, while her ego might have liked to believe her present luster would not be dimmed by divorce, some small core of common sense told her this would not be the case. She liked Stephen's company. He was lovely to look at and capable, when prodded, of putting himself through the paces of heterosexual passion. God knew he was charming—and how much more charming would he be, how much sweeter and more accommodating, now that he was absolutely scared to death of her? It must have been torture for Stephen to have a blabbermouth like Gina be the custodian of his deepest secret. But for once Gina wasn't talking and would, in time, prove just how far she would go to preserve her imperfect but picturesque marriage.

GIVEN MOIRA'S FLAIR FOR the wrathful gesture, I spent most of the days following Monty's *Amelia* gambit glancing fretfully over my shoulder and flinching at sudden noises. But I soon realized that Moira had urgent matters to contend with and these left her little time for pulling the wings off the likes of me.

Grimes and his minions had by now questioned every employee of Les Étoiles as well as several patrons with whom Kenny claimed to have dallied. They'd learned that six former masseurs at the spa, Adonises all, had ceased working there almost immediately after the formation of Finch/Donato Productions. None of these men could now be located.

Not one of the spa's extravagantly paid massage therapists admitted knowing a thing about sex on the premises. As for the patrons Kenny had fingered, each staunchly maintained that this was the only manner in which he'd ever done so. Prominent men all, they had no choice but to dissemble. They knew Moira had the goods on them and would, if they talked, make certain that whistles weren't all they'd be famous for blowing.

Moira did not rely on threats alone to shield her from exposure.

She and Stephen became avid supporters of Congresswoman Brooks Almy, Rusty's likely democratic opponent for governor. They threw Ms. Almy a star-studded fund-raiser at Les Étoiles, thus assuring that any public allegations from Grimes would now be tainted not only by his well-known loathing of Stephen but by the stench of political payback as well.

As adept as Moira was at staving off formal charges, there was one adversary against whom even she was powerless—Dame Rumor. Hollywood has always been a place where gossip spreads with near telepathic speed, and if its tongues could have been harnessed for energy, the wagging produced by Grimes's probe into Les Étoiles could have powered the town through Labor Day.

It began with a few panicked whispers wafting from the Palladian homes of Moira's VIP victims, then spread like a Malibu wildfire once Grimes began interviewing Moira's less discreet bellmen and chambermaids. As with most such scandals the rumors were right on the gist of things, though wildly off on the details. The more lurid gossips confidently described ballroom-size orgies, though none ever breathed the name Oscar. The town seemed evenly divided between those who believed the rumor unshakably (as they'd believed every such rumor they'd ever heard) and those who found it either too far-fetched or too delicious to be true.

Stephen, who'd been through similar squalls, if none of this magnitude, knew that the best course was to brazen it out, maintaining a crowded social calendar lest he appear to be hiding. He knew too that bold flippant jokes were a useful badge of unflustered innocence. At one pre-Oscar soiree when his agent rose from their crowded table and asked if he could get him something from the bar, Stephen breezily replied, "Sure, how about a masseur with a big dick?" This convulsed those present and made clear the Olympian insouciance with which he viewed the gossips' prattling. This, the partygoers agreed, was not a worried man. And why, they asked, should he be? If the vengeance-bent Mr. Grimes had even a shred of evidence wouldn't he have arrested someone by now?

My own view of Rusty's presently insufficient case was less sanguine. I knew the proof was out there and so long as it was it might fall into the wrong hands. I'd already demonstrated this with Monty and it was now Monty's turn to prove it again with even more catastrophic results.

ONE EVENING THE WEDNESDAY before the Oscars, Gilbert and I were sitting at home watching the Academy screeners Gilbert had filched from Max's house. We were surprised when the phone rang at quarter to one and the glance we exchanged conveyed our mutual suspicion that this was unlikely to be good news.

"Philip, are you there?" called a voice on the machine. "It's Billy. If you're there, pick up! Quick or you'll miss it!"

I answered and asked what I was missing.

"Rex Bajour! Channel fifty-three! Hurry!" he said and hung up.

I did as he asked but couldn't fathom at first what had so excited him. Rex's guest was Jason Mulvaney, writer and star of the one-man autobiographical show *I Was a Male Prom Queen*. A hit off Broadway, it was now playing in West Hollywood. Gilbert and I had seen it last summer and enjoyed it both for Jason's humorous portrayals of multiple characters and for the refreshing absence of his shirt through much of act two.

Rex, however, had no desire to discuss Jason's play. He wished only to laud the young actor's candor about his sexuality, the better to mock the cowardice of a certain closeted Oscar nominee.

"Well," said Jason modestly, "I'm not sure I'd use the word 'courageous.' I mean there are lots of out actors and writers—"

"Not in this town, sweetie!" brayed Rex. "Especially not if you're a big moooovie star who always has to play the hero like Miss Stephen Donato!"

"So you were saying," sighed Jason.

"You've heard the rumors, haven't you? You haven't been living in a *cave?*"

"Yeah, a few. But to get back to my play—"

"*ALL TRUE!* I have seen the proof with my own little peepers, and let me tell you, it was quite a peep show!" said Rex, guffawing at what he appeared to regard as wordplay. He then produced his trusty pocket recorder and, holding it up to his mike, purred, "You know what Stevie's going to say if he wins Best Actor this Sunday?"

"Uh, no, what?" asked his hostage.

Rex pressed play and out came Stephen's voice, clear as a bell.

"Oh, yeah, Oscar! Come to Stephen! Just like that! Urgh!"

Rex erupted into evil high-pitched giggles and clicked off the machine.

"Was that really him?" asked Jason.

"You bet your sweet ass! And there's plenty more where that came from. But I'm not going to play it all on one show. Oh no—gotta keep people tuning in! So let's get back to your wonderful movie."

"It's a play."

"I've done lots of plays. I remember back in 'sixty-two—was I a cutie-pie then!—I appeared onstage with Miss Martha Raye in, oh shoot, what was it called . . . ?"

The minute the show ended the phone rang again.

"So was it real?" Billy asked breathlessly. "C'mon! You know! Admit it!"

"I know nothing about it! It's a complete forgery! Just don't tell your dad or your uncle about this!"

"*Oh my Gawwwd!* It *is* real!"

"Just don't say anything!"

Billy assured me he wouldn't dream of telling Dad or Uncle Hank anything that might harm Stephen. This was scant comfort since, knowing Billy, they were the only people he wouldn't tell.

"This," said Gilbert sagely, "is bad."

"Gee, you *think?*"

"How do you suppose he got hold of it?"

I said he'd obviously gotten it from Monty, for whom I'd have some choice words come morning. The more pressing question was not how Rex had obtained it but how he could be kept from broadcasting further snippets.

"God," I groaned, sinking wretchedly onto the couch. "If only Claire were here!"

"Really, Philip," said Gilbert peevishly. "Why do you always make out that we're helpless without Claire to ride to our rescue? I can deal with Rex every bit as effectively as she could!"

"Really?" I said archly. "And what do you suggest?"

"Well, let me at least *think* about it for Chrissake! I'll come up with something in the morning."

I did not see him in the morning, which dawned appropriately bleak and drizzly. He was still asleep when I left for the gym, which, thanks to Billy, was abuzz about Stephen and the sex tape. I declined Billy's invitation to the Rex Bajour viewing party he was hosting that night and drove through the now torrential rain to Los Feliz, where Lily's mood was as buoyant as mine was disconsolate.

"Philip! I knew there was someone I was supposed to phone! I can't work today. Too many appointments! Cheiko dear, please make a note that I must call Philip early when things are this hectic."

She addressed this to a slim Japanese lass who sat ramrod straight on an ottoman, exuding competence. She plucked her PDA from her lap and began poking at it with a stylus.

"Cheiko's my new assistant! So efficient! If things work out she'll be vice president of my production company."

"Production company?"

"All the stars have one. Don't look so stricken, dear—there'll be a post for you as well."

She introduced us, then Cheiko told Lily it was time to leave for their pitch meeting at New Line.

"My new screenplay," said Lily excitedly. "Female musketeers! I only started it last night but the first fifty pages are heaven!"

As soon as they left I confronted Monty. He hadn't seen the show and was outraged when I told him what Rex had shared with his viewers.

"Why that pudgy little viper!" he fumed. "After all the meals he's cadged off me!"

He explained that Lily had gone out the evening before last so he'd invited Rex over for dinner. Rex, he found, had recently asked for and received a copy of *Amelia Flies Again!* from its proud authoress. He'd surmised instantly that Stephen had been coerced into buying it and was bursting to know what they had on him. It was something that happened at the spa, wasn't it? Monty declined to comment but Rex's pleas were unrelenting and after much wine he finally fessed up and agreed to show him the DVD on the firm condition that Rex not breathe a word to anyone, as to do so would risk derailing Lily's comeback.

It was clear that at some point in the viewing Rex had realized he had his recorder in his pocket and that, though Monty would never consent to loan him the disk, he could at least make an audio copy. Having done so, he'd waited less than a day to betray his oath of silence.

"You do an old dwarf an act of kindness and this is how he repays you! I mean, I expected he'd tell people! I saw little harm in that. There's no lack of tall tales going around already and with all the whoppers Rex has told in his day I figured who'd believe him? But to record the damn thing and broadcast it, with no regard for the consequences to Lily! I never want to see that bloated homunculus again! He is dead to me!"

"He's not the only one who'll be dead if he doesn't shut up! What if the police get wind of it?"

As if on cue there came a disconcertingly authoritative knock on the door. Monty proceeded to the foyer, a puzzled frown on his face, and I followed at a timid distance. He opened the door and his frown deepened, for standing on the mat was a uniformed LAPD officer. He was looking down at his feet so all that was visible of his head was the crown and bill of his navy police hat. His head slowly lifted, revealing a familiar face smirking impishly at our surprise.

"Howdy, boys!" said Gilbert, saluting smartly. "Officer Selwyn reporting for duty!"

Twenty-three

★

W HY IT'S ABSOLUTELY BRILLIANT!" exclaimed Monty.
        "*I* thought so," preened Gilbert.
        "I don't know when I've heard a plan so simple yet in-
genious. And the uniform!"

"You like it?" he asked, executing a spokesmodel twirl.

"Perfection. It brings back tender memories of a strip search long
ago. How on earth did you find it?"

Gilbert said he'd told his mother he'd been invited to a costume
party. She in turn had spoken to Max, who'd placed the whole Pinnacle
wardrobe department at his disposal.

"That's what I call using the old cabbage," said Monty. "Philip,
where have you been hiding this resourceful fellow?"

The plan, I grudgingly conceded, did indeed sound pretty fool-
proof and I cursed myself for not having thought of it first. The idea,
as my shrewder readers have no doubt surmised, was to call on Rex
and, masquerading as a police officer, scare the bejesus out of him and
confiscate his recorder as evidence.

Monty gave us his address, warning us to hurry as he'd be leaving
soon to tape that evening's show. It took us twenty minutes to reach

West Hollywood and locate Rex's building on North Flores Street. It was one of those unsightly motel-like apartment complexes with three two-story wings forming a U around a barren cement courtyard and a swimming pool only marginally more hygienic than the Grand Canal. We rang Rex's bell and a full minute passed before he opened the door. He had a towel tucked into his shirt collar and wore the impatient frown of a man interrupted while putting his face on.

"You!" he said sourly to me. "What do you want?" Then he saw Gilbert and his brow crinkled in concern.

"Good afternoon, Mr. Bajour," said Gilbert, speaking in his lowest register. His intent, I supposed, was to convey masculine authority but it just made him sound like Bea Arthur. "Officer Hank Grimes, LAPD here. If you don't mind I have a few questions for you."

"It's not a good time," said Rex as dismissively as an empress. "I have a show to tape."

"I'm afraid I must insist," said Gilbert. "We won't take much of your time."

Rex frowned and said we'd better not, as one did not keep Joanne Worley waiting.

"I think you should know, Mr. Bajour, that—"

"Wait!" said Rex, casting a wary sidelong glance. Following it, we saw that a potato-faced Russian crone, complete with babushka, had emerged from the next unit and was watering her window box with unpersuasive nonchalance.

"Old bitch probably saw you from her window," muttered Rex. "Now the whole building will hear about this!" He pivoted with an annoyed flounce and disappeared into his apartment.

We followed him into the small, fusty flat, an experience unpleasantly akin to entering the very mind of its tenant. It was airless and cluttered with heavy drapes that kept out all natural light. The furniture was upholstered in threadbare gold velvet and every surface was cluttered with newspapers, kitschy mementos, and dirty dishes. Scores of framed photos featuring Rex and the formerly acclaimed blanketed the cracked, water-damaged walls, which, if they could talk, would have screamed, "Fame is fleeting! Save every penny!"

We seated ourselves on the sofa, prompting the plump ginger cat who'd been lolling there to rise, offended, and stalk off to find something it hadn't peed on yet.

"I think you should know," said Gilbert, "that my brother the district attorney is thinking of filing charges against you."

"Charges?!" yelped Rex. "What are you talking about? What sort of charges?"

Gilbert turned solemnly to me. "Is this the man you observed at Les Étoiles performing a sex act with the youth in question?"

"Yes, it is."

"Are you positive? Take your time, Mr. Cavanaugh. This is a serious matter."

"No, it's him all right."

"What youth?" said Rex, now thoroughly rattled. "I didn't have sex with anyone at that spa! I had a shiatsu and a seaweed wrap!"

"You can claim what you like, Mr. Bajour. We have our witness."

"Okay, I fooled around with my masseur! But he was no kid! He was twenty-five if he was a day!"

Gilbert assured him he had irrefutable proof that the young man was even now three weeks shy of his eighteenth birthday.

"Well, he didn't look it!" said Rex. "I didn't ask to see his birth certificate!"

"And that," said Gilbert gravely, "is where you made your mistake. I'd like to turn now to the contents of your broadcast last night."

"You saw my show?" he asked, and it says much about Rex that even in these circumstances he sounded pleased.

"Of course. We on the force seldom miss it. You displayed a small recorder and played a voice you purported to be that of Stephen Donato. I'll take that recorder now."

"*What?!*" shrieked Rex. "That's private property! Very valuable property!"

"It's key evidence in a criminal investigation. Produce it please."

"Don't you need a warrant or a subpoena or something?" asked Rex, drawing a patronizing smile from Gilbert.

"You obviously watch a lot of television, which is forever getting these points of procedure all wrong. You should know that I have my brother's full authority to arrest and book you should you fail to cooperate. If you'd rather sort this out at the county jail—"

"No! I'm not going back there! I'll get it!"

He skittered away and returned shortly with the recorder in his outstretched palm.

"Have you made any copies from this?" asked Gilbert, pocketing the device. Rex assured him he had not.

"I must advise you, Mr. Bajour, to make no further public statements on this matter. Your reckless remarks are hampering our investigation by alerting the suspects, rendering them flight risks." Rex, now perspiring heavily, vowed not to say another word about it.

"I should warn you that my brother has only hesitated to charge you because he enjoys your program and would hate to put an end to your piquant conversations with the beloved stars of yesteryear. Your continued cooperation will factor heavily in his ultimate decision. Good day, Mr. Bajour."

WE GIGGLED ALL THE WAY back to Los Feliz, giddy with triumph. Monty greeted us as conquering heroes, heaping praise on our boldness and cunning. Curious to see how much audio Rex had captured, we rewound to the beginning and pressed play. We heard a slight hissing sound followed by Rex's high, petulant voice.

"Note on Brad Pitt—if he doesn't return my calls by next week start show with 'I just saw Brad Pitt's new movie. That's Pitt as in PITIFUL!'" he added with a loud cackle. This was followed by several memos in a similar vein and a reminder to thank Ruta Lee for the fudge. Finally we heard a series of low moans followed by Stephen saying, "Oh, man. That's great. Yeah, just like that."

Rex had remembered his recorder toward the end of the first leg of Stephen's sexual triathlon. At least he hadn't captured the verbal foreplay that preceded it with poor horny Stephen's repeated petitions for cock. But he had captured the whole Oscar scene as well as the arrivals of Gina, Diana, and Claire. The recording ended just after the ladies'

departure, when Lily had returned home, forcing an abrupt end to the
screening.

"Bravo, you young Lochinvars!" said Monty, clapping our shoulders. "But we must not ignore the sobering lesson this episode has
taught us. We've been far too lax in the security department.
Henceforth I'll share my prize with no one."

"And you'll hide it *really* well?"

"It will, I assure you, be harder to lay hands on than the queen's
pussy. Now where may I take you boys for our victory dinner?"

Gilbert suggested Vici since the crowd was starry, the food improving, and Billy could always be relied upon for a free round. I
phoned him and arranged a table, not letting on, of course, that I had
just canceled his favorite show.

IT WAS, UP TO A POINT, a jolly little evening. Gilbert, still elated by his
triumph, repeatedly rehashed the routing of Rex, convulsing Monty
with comic embellishments I was too happy to contradict. Monty in
turn regaled us with stories of the gay Hollywood demimonde of his
youth, and with each drink his roster of purported conquests grew
more dubiously impressive. The wine was superb and my salmon with
fried leeks beyond reproach. As we perused dessert menus in search of
the one sweet our figure-conscious trio could agree to share, an emotion crept over me so unfamiliar of late that it took me a moment to
identify it as hope.

Was it possible, I wondered, that the worst was really behind us?
It was certainly starting to look that way. The police were proving no
match for so wily an adversary as Moira. The Stephen rumors seemed
more of a joke every day and the one pustule who could prove them
had been cowed into silence. True, Monty's unyielding insistence that
Stephen produce *Amelia* still posed troubling challenges, as the screenplay, in its present form, screamed "blackmail" to anyone who read it.
But the script, though ailing, was surely not inoperable, and once the
town's leading surgeons had worked their magic, it might emerge as
spry and refreshed as Lily herself after one of her periodic resurfac-

ings. Perhaps when that happy day arrived I'd blow some *Amelia* dollars on a vacation. It seemed the least I deserved for having braved so many tempests with such pluck and fortitude.

As I sat pondering the relative merits of Paris and St. Barts, I felt a hand land heavily on my shoulder. Gazing up, I saw the mottled face of a Grimes brother peering down at me, though which I couldn't say as the abrupt widening of my eyes had caused a lens to slip.

"Well," observed Rusty, "you boys look like you're having fun."

"We *were*," sniffed Gilbert, who shares my knee-jerk impudence toward swaggering lawmen.

Blinking to right my lens, I examined Rusty's face and did not like what I saw. I'd hoped that if I ever encountered him again he'd be wearing the sour, thwarted look of a lawman whose leads are not panning out and whose case has reduced him to a diet of bourbon and Maalox. But Rusty wasn't scowling. His lips bloomed with the self-satisfied smile of a man about to cry, "Checkmate!" or, in Rusty's case, "King me!"

"Hi. Rusty Grimes," he said, nodding to Gilbert and Monty.

"We gathered," said Monty.

Rusty pulled up a chair.

"Champagne, huh? You guys must be celebrating something. Good day?"

"Yes," replied Monty, "and in the interest of keeping it that way—"

"I won't be long. I just stopped in 'cause I'm celebrating myself. I thought a twelve-year-old Macallan might go down pretty nice."

"Well, don't keep him waiting," said Gilbert.

Rusty just chuckled, another ominous sign.

"I can see you're a sassy one. Kind of like this guy I met today." He turned to Monty. "Friend of yours. Rex Bajour?"

"Oh?" said Monty.

"Don't know him from Adam but he phones, all eager to see me. Says it's about what he told my brother today at his place. Now I know for a fact my brother didn't see him today 'cause he's in Palm Springs trying to track down one of Moira's 'masseurs.' But this Rex, he says he didn't tell my brother everything. He'll tell me though if I promise not to press charges. I figure what the heck and tell him to come on in."

He paused here to savor our discomfort, then leaned back in his chair, hands behind his head, clearly having a ball.

"Rex shows up and he's this weird little guy who seems to think I'm some kinda fan of his. Keeps going on about Moira's spa and some black kid and how old he looked for his age. 'Course, by now it's obvious he knows something and that he has—or had—some kind of proof someone scared him into giving up. So I ask him to describe his talk with my 'brother.' And what do you know—my 'brother' didn't visit Rex alone." He turned his flinty smile on me. "He brought you."

"That's ridiculous!" I protested once the coughing fit had subsided. "I was nowhere near your brother today!"

"It wasn't my brother. Just some guy who said he was. And you were with him."

"Really, my good man," tutted Monty. "A little rigor, please. If, as you say, Rex was gulled by a Grimes impersonator mightn't his accomplice merely have claimed to be Philip?"

Grimes pointed out that Rex actually *knew* me and would not have been fooled by a substitute.

"Nonsense. You forget this is Hollywood, a town awash in actors and skilled makeup artists. No criminal mastermind would have the slightest trouble recruiting a skilled Cavanaugh impersonator."

Rusty, not troubling to dignify this theory with a response, said he'd told Rex he had two brothers on the force. Could he describe the one who'd questioned him? Turning now to Gilbert, he said Rex had described a slim, blond, blue-eyed man of about thirty.

"Thirty!" said Gilbert indignantly, not much helping matters.

Rex had then described the confiscated sound track and the DVD from which he'd recorded it, not skimping on a single X-rated detail. Rex said it had been screened for him by Monty, who was using it to compel Stephen to produce *Amelia Flies Again!*

"So let's see," concluded Rusty, counting off the charges on his fingers, "we've got extortion, conspiracy, obstruction of justice, and impersonating an officer. . . . Do you fuckers have any idea how much trouble you're in?"

"Now really," said Monty with a condescending laugh. "I ask you, sir—when a ludicrous gnome like Rex Bajour romps into your office spinning tales of megastars cavorting with gilded statuettes does no part of you pause to question the veracity of your witness or his fantastic account? Would any jury the foreman of which was neither Dopey, Sneezy, nor Doc find him a credible witness? No, to answer your question, we do not consider ourselves in any peril whatsoever. Not if Rex is all you've got."

"He's not all I've got."

"You refer, I presume, to your other witness, Kenny the freelance proctologist?"

"Him too. But also the tape."

"Tape?"

"Rex made a copy."

It's not easy to maintain an air of bland insouciance when you've just received a tomahawk to the forehead, but Monty kept his cool, refusing to give Grimes the satisfaction of a gasp.

"You don't say?"

"I do." Rusty turned to Gilbert. "When he told you he had no copies he was lying. He felt real bad about that so he came clean. I gave it a listen and it's Stevie all right. Not to mention his wife and mom. You're on there too, cupcake," he said, patting my cheek. "We'll see what a jury thinks when they hear, 'Oh, yeah, Oscar, fuck me. Fuck me harder.' "

"Dessert?" asked our blushing waitress.

"Not now," said Monty. "Our friend's reminiscing."

Not even that could wipe the smirk off Grimes's face.

"Toodle-oo, boys," he said, jauntily rising. "We'll be talkin' again real soon. Oh, and Monty—I'm sorry if your place is a little messed up when you get home tonight. I got a warrant and my guys are searching it right now, looking for that DVD. So feel free to dawdle over dessert."

His cell phone rang. He answered it and as he strutted away toward the bar his voice boomed with jubilant malice.

"Stevie, my man! Thanks for gettin' back to me. You sittin' down, sweetie?"

GILBERT AND I SLEPT together that night though we did not, as you might suppose, seek comfort or oblivion in sex. It was now impossible for us to contemplate let alone commit a sexual act without imagining what it would be like performing the same act in prison with the three-hundred-pound skinheads to whom we'd find ourselves affianced.

On reaching home we'd found our machine predictably crowded with messages. Peppered among the expected eruptions from Stephen, Moira, and Sonia were several calls from high-powered attorneys, household names all, cursing our names and demanding we come to Diana's the next morning to debrief them on our disastrous dealings with Rex and Rusty.

The sole welcome call that night came from Monty, who informed us that the police had failed to find the DVD. They had, however, seized a sizable stash of male erotica and an address book containing a three-page addendum embarrassingly headed "Monty's Joy Boys." They'd also taken Lily's memoirs and our script for *Amelia,* which meant that in addition to pandering and extortion I could now be charged with impersonating a screenwriter.

THE NEXT MORNING GILBERT, Monty, and I traveled to Diana's to meet with her, Stephen, Moira, Sonia, and the august array of legal piranhas they'd retained for their defense. I'll spare you a lengthy account of that heated conclave. You know the aggrieved parties well by now. You've seen them in similar circumstances and observed their grace and good humor under pressure. You can readily imagine their response to our trio's story, especially Monty's confession that he'd screened his prize disk for a petulant gossip with a lifelong hatred of Stephen and his own talk show.

I'd presumed going in that my many previous excoriations had inured me to their invective, but the severity of this latest crisis was such that even their most vicious past reprimands seemed by comparison like coy rebukes delivered in baby talk. They rabidly demanded that Monty surrender his disk to them, as the police knew he had it and he'd proved himself too blithering a dolt to be entrusted with its safekeeping. Monty refused, prompting such frenzied vituperation that I was relieved when we were interrupted by a call from the DA.

Stephen's lawyer took the call. Grimes informed him that he wanted all of us who'd been at the spa that fateful day to report to his office tomorrow at noon. The lawyer naturally protested. Stephen and his family had been charged with no crime and would only answer questions in the privacy of their homes. Grimes said he understood the family's shyness but would be most grateful if they'd attend anyway. He would show his thanks by keeping the meeting strictly "hush-hush" and by doing all within his power to ensure that no one in his office leaked the contents of Rex's tape to the media. The threat could not have been plainer; either Stephen would acquiesce or news of his tryst with Oscar would be broadcast from here to Micronesia.

This ploy prompted several thousand dollars' worth of bluster from the attorneys, and Moira, with staggering chutzpah, decried it as "nothing short of blackmail!" There was much talk about strategy and gag orders, but judging from Stephen's thousand-yard stare the only gag orders he was thinking of were the ones Leno and Jon Stewart would shortly be issuing to their writing staffs. His voice cracking, he said he'd do as Grimes asked, then fled before his humiliating tears could commence flowing. We were dismissed shortly thereafter, the assembled agreeing that there were no names left to call us.

There's no more joyless way to spend a morning than to sit contemplating jail while being energetically reviled by men who'd had no trouble finding nice things to say about O. J. Simpson. By the time Gilbert and I reached home we felt like two hydrants in unfortunate proximity to a kennel, and the messages waiting on our machine did little to cheer us. The first was from Hank, offering directions to his brother's office and advising promptness. The second was from Billy.

"If you're there, pick up! Please, please pick up! How come Rex showed an old rerun last night? Who the hell's Tippi Hedren? And what happened with you guys and my dad at Vici? He won't tell me a thing! Please call me! I really want to know what's going on."

"Don't we all?" came a voice behind us.

We turned, startled, and there in the doorway stood Claire, bathed in radiant sunlight, her simple white blouse perfectly setting off her newly acquired coat of bronze. Gilbert and I, like that fellow in *Angels in America,* were caught completely off guard by this unscheduled manifestation and could only stand dumbstruck, gaping at her effulgence.

She repeated the question, raising her voice slightly so as to be heard over the heavenly trumpets.

"What on earth is going on?"

"Claire!"

"Thank God you're here!"

"We need you!"

"We're in terrible terrible trouble!"

She said she'd gathered as much from the message on her machine ordering her to appear at the DA's office tomorrow.

"He wants you too?" I said, elated. "That's fantastic!"

"Oh, yes! Just peachy!"

I explained I was merely glad she'd be there, batting for the home team. I assured her she had nothing personally to fear and had only been summoned because she was on the sex tape.

"Yikes! Don't tell me the DA's gotten hold of *that?!*"

"No," said Gilbert, "but it's almost as bad. He got an audio copy from Rex Bajour."

"Rex Bajour?"

"Tiny fellow? Talk show host?"

"You're losing me."

Wearily seating herself, she called for strong tea and a comprehensive summary of all that had occurred in her absence, plus anything prior that we'd kept from her. She stressed that we were to omit no detail, however insignificant we deemed it.

"Right-o!" I said, thrilled to think that peerless brain would soon be exerting itself in service to our salvation. As I hastened to the kitchen to put the kettle on, I could just barely hear Gilbert's low confidential murmur as he started in without me.

"It was all going along just fine . . . then Philip had this *asinine* idea that I dress up as a cop!"

Twenty-four

★

W E TOLD HER EVERYTHING. It took a while but when we'd
finished there was no detail recorded in these pages of
which Claire was not now cognizant. She tried at first to
listen with a calm nonjudgmental expression but this soon gave way to
a wince of pained astonishment such as an unworldly village priest
might wear while hearing Mick Jagger's confession.

"So?" I asked meekly when I'd reached the shaming conclusion.

"So *what?*"

"What do you think?" said Gilbert.

"What does it matter what I think? The only person whose opinion counts now is the DA and he thinks you're guilty as sin. Not that
you've given him much cause to doubt it."

"I know," I groveled. "We just thought that, y'know, seeing as
you've helped us out of jams before, you might—"

"Jams?!" she repeated incredulously. "*Jams?* I have news for you,
me boyo—this is not a JAM! Nor is it a scrape, a spot, or a pickle! This
is doom, you idiot! This is game over! This is orange fucking jumpsuits! How could you possibly have been so stupid as to take money for
the *Amelia* script when you knew Stephen was blackmailed into buy-

ing it?! And YOU!" she roared at Gilbert. "It wasn't witless enough to go impersonating an officer? You had to use the DA's brother's actual name?!"

"It was my whole way into the character!"

"Look, we fucked up. We *know* that. We're just looking for a little advice 'cause we thought—"

"I know what you thought," snapped Claire. "You thought I was going to waltz in, wave my wand, and make everything right—and after all you've put me through! Well, I'm sorry—I haven't the tiniest idea how to help you out of this mess! I'd advise you to hire the best lawyers in town but they've already been hired by Moira and Stephen to save their asses while no doubt selling yours up the river. I'll vouch for you in court, though God knows what my word will be worth once the *Casablanca* business comes out. And thank you, by the way, for ensuring that the word 'plagiarist' will be manacled to my name for the rest of my miserable life! Thank you for that!"

"I'm sorry," I sniveled and my lower lip began to tremble, a sign that a full-blown Cowardly Lion blubberfest was mere seconds away. Seeing this, Claire rolled her eyes but softened her tone.

"Calm down, you big baby. You're not the ones Moira and Stephen's attack dogs will be ripping apart tomorrow."

"We're not?" Gilbert said hopefully.

"I doubt it. They'll be too busy demolishing Rex. They'll claim his tape's a forgery. They'll say there was no prostitution, no Oscar, and no extortion—Rex made it all up because he hates Stephen. Or for publicity. If I know Moira she'll claim Rex tried to blackmail *them* with his 'fake' tape, then when they refused to pay he ran to the police out of spite."

"But what if Grimes doesn't buy it?" I asked. "What if he knows they're lying and goes public with the tape?"

"Well," said Claire, sighing mightily, "then all bets are off. When this thing breaks there'll be a media circus like none you've ever seen. People crawling out of the woodwork to cop pleas or make a quick buck on their stories. I mean, God, think how Oscar will clean up if he can avoid jail while doing it. Do you know who he is?"

I said that according to Moira he was a young beauty named Kurt who was now, thank God, residing in Paris, having met a French banker and traded his gilded costume in for an even more impressively gilded cage.

"And you think they won't hear about this in France?" She finished her tea and rose. "Well, isn't this the perfect end to a lovely vacation?"

We followed her to the door like anxious toddlers fretful over Mother's departure.

"Any thoughts?" pleaded Gilbert.

"Yes, but they all involve return flights to San Francisco."

"But you'll think about it?" I asked plaintively.

"Do you imagine I'll be able to think of anything else? Just don't, please, count on me to get your necks out of the noose this time, because at the moment I don't even know where to start."

"But you'll think about it?" I bleated.

"Yes! And for God's sake, get some lawyers!"

"Right," said Gilbert.

"And you'll think about it?"

"Goodbye!"

She left and the fragile glow of hope she'd brought with her vanished as well. At this point our rescue did seem a tall order even for a girl of Claire's prodigious intellect. And did we even deserve her help after the grief we'd caused her? I realized with a stab of shame that we hadn't even thought to ask how things had gone with her new beau. I bemoaned this lapse to Gilbert, who couldn't hear me over the blender.

The afternoon yawned unpleasantly ahead and I couldn't imagine how to fill it. Gilbert, as is his custom in times of great turmoil, suggested we go shopping, and this was how we came to find ourselves at the bar at Neiman Marcus, sipping martinis while wistfully ogling the neckwear salesman. We each bought two pairs of Italian loafers that we agreed would make us the envy of the cell block. Then we drove home, Gilbert's silence en route that of a man realizing for the first time that there are some problems in life even Prada can't solve.

* * *

NOT ALL OF US SUMMONED to face the DA passed the wait as Gilbert and I did, paralyzed with dread. Stephen surely did, as well as his family, and even Moira, I'm sure, passed the time chain-smoking while rereading her copy of *Absconding Made Simple*. Lily, by contrast, felt only the highest dudgeon that Grimes had forced her to fly home in the middle of her East Coast press tour, canceling three talk show appearances.

"The nerve of the man!" she fumed, sweeping grandly in as Monty, Gilbert, and I were finishing a last supper of Chinese takeout. "Who does he think he is?! Ordering people about with no regard whatsoever for Regis or Kelly, not to mention their poor disappointed audience! And what's all this nonsense about criminal charges!"

"Well," Monty said gingerly, "the police seem to think that the time we all collided at the spa—here, have some wine, love—that Stephen got a bit frisky with a masseur and Moira got it on tape and that's why they're partners."

"*No!*" said Lily, agog. Her fascination gave way to a puzzled frown. "But what on earth has that to do with us?!"

Monty outlined the DA's curious theory that he and Lily had somehow obtained this compromising footage and used it to compel Stephen to make *Amelia*. Lily stared a moment, aghast, then threw back her head and howled with mirth.

"Dear lord! I've never heard anything so absurd in my life! As if we'd need to *force* anyone to buy a script that brilliant! It's just too ridiculous! Though offensive too, when you think of it. Mrs. Clinton will hear about this! We met in the *Today* show greenroom and we're very close now."

Lily, exhausted from her flight, retired. The rest of us were less eager for sleep, which would only hasten the arrival of morning. We stayed up till past three watching old movies, drinking far too much wine, and wondering how we'd come to so desolate a pass.

"Funny thing," sighed Monty. "You try to do a good turn for your big sister and look what it gets you."

"Your heart was inna right place," consoled Gilbert.

"It generally is," said Monty. "It was nice to want to give her something. Where I went wrong was trying to make it a career."

"Zackly."

"I should have stayed more in the scarf area."

"There's still Claire," I said, though when I'd last spoken to her at ten she'd declared herself still stymied.

"This Claire," inquired Monty, "she has a hat, you say, and is skilled at the timely production of rabbits?"

"Not this time," prophesied Gilbert. "We're doomed."

I declared my staunch faith in Claire, and Monty suggested we drink to her, which we concurred was an excellent idea.

"To Claire," said Monty, reaching for the wine bottle.

"To Claire!"

"Oops. Sorry, lads, I'll open another."

GILBERT AND I PASSED out on the couch, which was a good thing as neither of us was in any shape to drive. When we awoke, limbs sore and heads throbbing, it was already past nine. We staggered to the kitchen, found coffee, and started a pot brewing. Monty sauntered in, dapperly dressed and annoyingly hearty for a gentleman of advanced years who'd matched us drink for drink only hours ago. He suggested that a spot of breakfast might revive us. We requested Advil omelets, then I phoned Claire. She didn't answer her home or cell phone and I left suitably frantic messages on each. As Monty whisked the eggs Lily joined us, pert as a pixie and ready for battle. Although our appetites were much reduced by dread, hangovers, and the alarming shortness of Lily's peignoir, we managed to choke down a few forkfuls and some toast. We were just heading home to spruce up for the beheading when my cell rang.

"Good, you're up," said Claire briskly.

"I've been calling all morning! Where have you been?"

"Chez Moira," she replied.

"The spa?!" I exclaimed. "What were you doing there?"

"Gathering ammo. Where are you now?"

"We're at Lily and Monty's. We were just heading home."

"Don't. Stay there."

She asked for the address and said she'd swing by as soon as possible.

"Why here?" I asked as the connection began to crackle. "Can't we talk at our place?"

"Just stay there!" she commanded and was gone.

"That was Claire!" I said, grinning insanely, for the last barely smoldering ember of hope was once more a cheery little flame. "She's coming over! It sounds like she has a plan!"

"A plan for what?" asked Lily.

We menfolk exchanged a stealthy glance. We'd agreed that Lily's complete ignorance of her career in extortion was one of the few advantages we possessed heading into this showdown and that we'd do well to preserve it.

"Just a plan for dealing with the DA," murmured Monty.

Lily laughed feistily. "You leave the DA to me! I'll settle *his* hash!"

It occurred to me that we didn't know how long Claire might take to reach Los Feliz. It was possible that by the time she'd arrived and briefed us it might be too late for Gilbert and me to go home and change our clothes, which were badly stained with duck sauce, the wine having demolished our chopstick skills. Our hosts offered their showers, and Monty, who seemed roughly our size, placed his wardrobe at our disposal. We hastened upstairs, chose shirts and slacks, and I claimed dibs on the steam shower in Monty's master. No sooner had I disrobed and lathered up than Monty burst in on me without knocking.

"Jeez, Monty!" I blurted, modestly covering myself.

"Oh please, dear, I've seen the movie. Claire's here."

"Tell her I'll be right down!"

"She says she can't stay. She just came by to borrow the DVD."

"The *sex* one?"

"Yes! She says she needs it immediately. Says Moira couldn't give her a copy—she's moved all hers to an offshore safe-deposit. So she needs mine!"

"What for?"

"She didn't say. Just said she needs it and if I wasn't sure whether to give it to her I should ask you."

"Give it to her! Do whatever she says! Just tell her to wait till I get down there!"

But Claire did not wait. By the time I'd dressed and raced downstairs she'd driven off, Monty tagging along to ensure his property's safe return. I scowled at the empty driveway, cursing myself for having conditioned as well as shampooed. It was nice to know Claire had a plan but maddening to have no idea what it was. What had she been doing with Moira? And why on earth did she need the disk? She *couldn't* be thinking of bringing it to the DA, could she?

I asked Lily if Monty had said when he'd be back. She said he wasn't sure but that if he hadn't returned by eleven-thirty we should just meet him downtown. Gilbert joined us and threw a minor hissy fit when he found we'd missed Claire and might now learn nothing of her strategy till we were in the DA's presence or, worse, custody.

"Such drama!" chirped Lily, wafting up the stairs to dress. "Strange young ladies babbling about mystery disks! Dire last-minute errands! Sometimes I think you keep things from me."

When she descended at exactly eleven-thirty, she appeared, from her costume, to be laboring under the misapprehension that we would shortly be boarding the Orient Express. She wore a vivid scarlet suit, its dramatic chinchilla-trimmed jacket more like a cape with sleeves. Her makeup was liberally applied for daylight and the matching pill-box hat with faux ruby starburst beyond camp. But the confidence she exuded was that of a True Star, one who knows beyond doubt that no harm can ever befall her since the Almighty is a Fan.

"Not back yet, are they? Ah well, much better this way. Just me and a handsome young escort on each arm. That's how you make an entrance!"

Gilbert and I insisted on giving Claire and Monty ten more minutes, but when they didn't show we had no choice but to set off alone, still writhing in suspense.

As a general rule we felons, when compelled to surrender ourselves to the authorities, hope that any persons accompanying us on our grim journey will comport themselves with appropriate tact and solemnity. Lily, oblivious to the gravity of our situation, joked and jabbered without cease the whole way. By the time we arrived I felt like a death-row convict who, having steeled himself to walk the last mile with dignity, finds that the chaplain is Robin Williams. But even Lily fell silent when we rounded the corner onto Temple Street and beheld the monstrous snare into which we'd been lured.

"*Sweet Jesus!*" I yelped.

"That *asshole!*" exclaimed Gilbert, for it was clear now how base and treacherous an opponent we faced in Rusty.

A police barricade lined the entire block on which stood the Clara Shortridge Foltz Criminal Justice Center. Behind this barricade there seethed a frenzied swarm of reporters and camera crews at least two hundred strong with more crowding in by the minute. Four news choppers circled overhead and the attention of the whole furious phalanx was riveted on a black BMW sedan that stood idling in the middle of the block. The driver of this sedan, which, I presumed, contained Stephen, was honking madly while trying to flee this vile ambush. He was impeded in this goal by three police cars that had neatly boxed him in. There were a dozen or so officers keeping order and two of these were standing next to Stephen's car in conference with one of his famed lawyers, who was no doubt taking issue with the DA's somewhat lax definition of "hush-hush."

I stared, tremulous, at the press gauntlet through which we would now have to pass. Though they bore a superficial resemblance to the loud fawning horde who'd lined the carpet at the FilmFest, their character and mission could not have been more different. Courtiers no more, they'd come today as inquisitors, bloodthirsty hellhounds who'd gathered in hopes of witnessing the most thrilling spectacle our culture has to offer—that of an actual, still-reigning megastar being roasted alive in the public square. A bonfire of the *Vanity Fair* set! A Starbecue! They'd seen such immolations before and knew their power to enthrall the populace. But when had a star ever toppled so abruptly or from so dizzy a height? When had the whispered details been so deliciously sordid or the timing so flawlessly ironic? The tabloid perfection of the event had driven the press to complete, unashamed hysteria. They shrieked like bacchantes and seemed ready to fall upon Stephen's car and chew their way through to him.

"Look at them!" squeaked Gilbert, clutching my hand. "They're like wolves!"

"Vultures!"

"Jackals!" agreed Lily, freshening her lipstick.

A loud rapping caused us to jump in our seats and we turned to see a policeman gesturing for me to roll down my window. I obeyed and he told us we were blocking traffic. I explained our situation and he generously volunteered to valet the car himself so we wouldn't be late for our mug shots.

Gilbert and I took Lily's arms and began steering her through the jammed traffic toward the center of the barricade, where a small gap allowed access to the building. Less than a month ago she'd vamped her way past many of the same reporters without exciting a ripple of interest. Thanks though to her recent ubiquity she was recognized the instant we squeezed through the space between Stephen's sedan and the squad car blocking its escape.

"Hey!" someone shouted. "It's the aunt!"

"Lily! Over here!"

"Lookin' good, Lily!"

"Yo, Amelia!"

Flashbulbs exploded and Lily, unable to discern the crucial difference between a fan club and a lynch mob, waved coquettishly and began tottering toward them as fast as her dangerously high heels could carry her. I gasped, for I'd suddenly realized that the instant she reached a microphone she would angrily deny that we'd blackmailed Stephen into buying *Amelia*. I didn't want her to say this because a.) it was doubtful the press had even *heard* this charge yet and b.) it was true.

An intrepid Hispanic go-getter, camera crew in tow, beat her colleagues to the punch and said, "Lily, do you have anything to say about your nephew and these sex-spa rumors?"

"I most certainly do!" huffed Lily, turning to give the camera her good side. "But first let me say that I've never in my life heard any-

326 | *Joe Keenan*

thing so preposterous as the DA's libelous claim that my partner, Philip Cavanaugh, and I resorted to—put me down!"

She made this request because Gilbert and I had just thrust a hand under each of her armpits, scooped her up, and were now sprinting toward the entrance with her dangling indignantly between us.

"No comment!" we shouted to the outraged mob whose first morsel of red meat we'd rudely snatched away. "No comment!" we screeched over the uproar and kept shouting it till we'd entered the lobby, from which the media had been barred.

"What on earth did you do that for!" asked Lily irately.

"Just keeping you safe," said Gilbert. "You might have been trampled."

"I saw no danger!"

Turning, I saw that Stephen had taken advantage of the distraction we'd provided. He'd bolted from his trapped sedan and, flanked by four attorneys, was barreling toward the entrance, Gina and Diana scrambling behind. He was soon spotted and the press went berserk, screaming his name and pelting him with the sort of questions journalists pose on these occasions less in hope of an actual response than as a means to broadcast unsubstantiated rumors and generally spice up the festivities.

"Stephen! What sex were the hookers?!"

"Has Gina forgiven you?"

"Is it true there are pictures?!"

"Are you a sex addict?!"

Stephen paid them no heed, but just kept charging toward the door, barely visible beneath his thick parka of lawyers. To his credit he held his head high and his chin tilted defiantly, though a redness around his eyes bespoke a nice little cry in the car.

Once they'd escaped into the building his look of noble defiance was replaced by one of black outrage.

"*That fucker!* He is so going to pay for this!"

"How dare he do this to you!" I said supportively.

"Fuck you!"

"Right."

We were squired through metal detectors, then whisked upstairs to Rusty's office. We entered through an antechamber where his secretary, a chubby and, given the circumstances, offensively cheerful woman, greeted us. Her name, she informed us, was Dorothy but we could call her Dottie. She ushered us into the lair of our captor, where Moira stood by the window, staring down at our well-wishers.

"Rusty's running a little behind today," said Dottie, "so just make yourselves comfy and he'll be with you in a jiff!"

"Thank you," replied a lawyer. His tone was curt and clearly dismissive but Dottie felt chatty and was not so easily dislodged.

"Wow! You people sure drew us a heck of a crowd!"

We eyed her balefully as Stephen icily replied that this had not been our intention.

"Well, I just *love* your movies!" gushed Dottie.

"Thank you, dear," said Lily.

"Can I get you guys anything? Water, coffee, soda?"

Stephen's lawyer said we were fine and would she please just leave us the hell alone. Dottie, adopting a droll look of contrition, mimed zipping her lip before tiptoeing hilariously from the room.

The office was a large corner one with tall windows that enabled us to gaze below and monitor the progress on our pyre. In addition to Grimes's imposing mahogany desk there was a sitting area with a badly scuffed leather couch, two armchairs, and a poker table in the corner with seating for eight. The side tables and shelves were crammed with photos, law tomes, and the sort of books publishers promote heavily in the weeks prior to Father's Day. The decorative accents reflected Rusty's keen interest in the Wild West and combat aviation while the walls bore many proud plaques and citations from groups whose names contained various combinations of the words "Police," "Republican," "Christian," and "Family." It was not, in short, a room designed to make a nervous homosexual feel any less so.

We sat awhile in a fraught silence that was finally broken by Lily, who waspishly inquired what precisely Diana was staring at.

"Well, forgive me, Lily, but that suit! You must have bought it forty years ago! You wouldn't catch me wearing my old things from the sixties!"

"As if they'd fit!" laughed Lily, winking saucily at a lawyer.

"Well, we can't all stay as young as you, dear," cooed Diana. "I really should see your cosmetic surgeon. Perhaps he can give me that lovely, trapped-in-a-wind-tunnel look that suits you so well!"

"Oh," riposted Lily, "I think you've had quite enough work for now, love. I mean be frank with me—is your hair in a bun or is that skin?"

"*Catfight!*" I thought to myself. "At last *something* in this office a gay man can relate to." But then the door opened, the ladies retired to their corners, and the Grimes boys were upon us.

Twenty-five

★

THEY DID NOT ARRIVE ALONE BUT were attended by six co-
horts, an assortment of dark-suited men so stern and judg-
mental of mien as to resemble the male ensemble from a
musical version of *The Crucible*. Rusty swaggered to his desk and
seated himself. Hank took a chair next to it and the Menfolk of Salem
clustered grimly around the poker table.

"For those of you I haven't met, I'm Rusty Grimes. I believe most
of you have spoken to my brother, Detective Hank Grimes, LAPD."
He introduced his deputies, whose names and titles need not concern
us, then asked us to state our names and occupations for the record. As
we did he tried to project a solemnity appropriate to his office and the
occasion, but his glee at having us at his mercy was uncontainable and
a bratty half smile kept leaking through the gravitas.

These preliminaries concluded, Stephen and Moira unmuzzled
their lawyers, who bayed at length over Rusty's scandalous mistreat-
ment of their clients. He had, they hotly maintained, blackmailed
them into coming here, promising discretion only to orchestrate a
media ambush in a deliberate and malicious attempt to damage their
reputations and scar their fragile psyches. They demanded that

Grimes apologize at once, then see them safely out through some secure and private exit. Should he fail to do so they would sue him into the ground, dig him up, burn the remains, and sue the ashes.

Grimes took this all in with a smug patient air, being, like Moira, long inured to his victims' impotent bluster. When their wrath was spent he declared coyly that he had no idea who'd alerted the press and that the tattletale, when found, would be properly spanked. His eyes scanned the room, then he turned to me.

"Where's your pal Monty? And what's her name"—he consulted a paper—"Claire Simmons?"

As I was saying I didn't know, the door opened and Claire and Monty were escorted in by a fish-faced functionary who briefly ogled Gina's cleavage, then withdrew.

"You're late," scolded Rusty.

"Sorry, milady," said Monty. "We had trouble getting past the welcoming committee you so thoughtfully arranged."

"Are you sure you called everyone?" asked Claire. "Because I didn't see Al-Jazeera down there."

It was hard for me to read this salvo. While her cheekiness suggested confidence and was thus a hopeful sign, her expression was more grim than cocky, which was not. I shot her an imploring look, hoping for some heartening sign, a discreet thumbs-up perhaps or an ace poking cheerfully from her sleeve. All I got was a maddeningly inscrutable nod. They found seats and Rusty resumed.

"I don't need to tell you people why you're here. It's our intention to question you separately and alone about charges ranging from pandering to extortion. But before we split up there are a few things I'd like to say to all of you.

"For a while now we've been asking you about all this and you've been lying to us. Stonewalling." He smiled and shrugged. "It's understandable. People who break the law or hire hustlers aren't in any rush to admit it. But playtime's over, kids. We have two witnesses who say they either paid or were paid for gay sex in the treatment rooms at Ms. Finch's spa."

"Witnesses!" scoffed Moira's lawyer. "Do you really think a jury's going to believe a Z-list talk show host and an employee Miss Finch fired for drug use?"

Rusty smirked and shrugged again. "Who knows? People like a good story. And stories don't come any better than Rex's." He proceeded to outline Rex's woefully accurate account of Monty's porno disk, who'd filmed it and why, and how it had fallen into Monty's hands. He then produced a document bound with brass brads and tossed it to Monty, who failed to catch it, prompting manly chuckles from Hank and the Salem Six.

"Rex also told us how you used that disk to make Stephen cough up half a million bucks for that."

"What is it?" inquired Lily.

"It's your screenplay, dear."

"What's *he* doing with it?" she demanded haughtily.

"He wanted to read it."

Lily addressed Rusty. "I'll have you know that screenplay's copyrighted so if you were thinking of stealing my idea you can just think again!"

"Steal it?" snorted Grimes. "That's a good one. Who'd even want to sit through a moldy, stupid piece of crap like—"

"How *dare* you!" roared Lily, rising in majestic indignation. "So, now you're a film critic, are you? *Amelia Flies Again!* is a soulful and thrilling work of cinematic art! Philip and I can see that, as can my nephew, who knows a damned sight more about movies than you do! I'm not surprised that its poetry eluded a philistine like you, but that hardly means Stephen was forced to buy it!"

"Well said, my dear."

"Thank you, Monty. The very idea!"

Grimes turned to Moira with a skeptical smile. "So you liked the script?"

"*Adored* it. I mean Stephen and I felt it could use a wee polish, but the story was just gripping."

Stephen emphatically seconded this opinion. "You don't like it, that's your privilege, but no one here's blackmailing anyone!"

This assertion led to an even pricklier discussion of Stephen's de-

cision to cast his seventy-five-year-old aunt as the film's heroine at a
salary of five million dollars. Stephen's slightly red-faced contention
that his aunt's "ageless beauty" would make her fully credible as a
woman of forty-seven drew rude sniggers from the lawmen, which
sent Lily into a sputtering rage.

"Get up, Monty! We're leaving! I refuse to spend one more minute
being insulted by this cherry-faced fool! So now you're a beauty expert
too? Buy yourself a mirror why don't you and take a good look at that
beet-stained lump of cauliflower you call a nose! And shave your ears
while you're at it, you insufferable gargoyle!"

Eventually Monty succeeded in calming Lily and persuaded her to
stay if only to help defend her costar against still more grievous accusations.

"So," said Grimes, "where were we before I offended Miss Teen
America here? Oh, right, Rex. As all of you know, Rex didn't just
watch Monty's home movie. No, he's a resourceful guy, Rex, and he
secretly recorded it so he could break the story on his show. Let's give
that tape a listen, shall we?"

Noting that it was pretty raw stuff, he gallantly offered the ladies
the option of sitting out the risqué portion in the anteroom with
Dottie. Sophie's choice if you asked me, but Gina promptly took him
up on it and flounced melodramatically out of the room.

"Mom . . . ?" hinted Stephen, his eyes pleading.

"I want to know what we're facing," replied Diana, every inch the
tragedienne. He didn't even bother asking Lily, whose wide eager eyes
made clear her determination to hear every racy minute.

Having watched the film some nine thousand times I knew the dialogue by heart and could understand why Stephen was writhing at the
thought of the assembled hearing the sweet nothings he'd cooed to
Oscar. He'd have writhed even more had he known as I did that this
furtively recorded version included Rex's ribald running commentary,
making it sound like the director's track on the Criterion Collection
edition of *Assbusters III*.

Rusty produced a Walkman and pressed play. An electronic hiss filled the room, followed by some slapping noises and moans. After a moment we heard a giggle and Rex's high, inebriated voice.

"Ooh—Miss Stephen likes that! Miss Stephen likes that a lot!"

This and many similar remarks from Rex may actually have helped Stephen, who, determined to declare the recording a forgery, was striving to maintain a look at once outraged and mystified as though to say, "Who can this skilled impersonator be?" Every time Rex piped in with a "Lordy, lordy!" or "Ain't she in heaven!" this outrage came more easily to him. When we reached the point where Stephen was loudly exhorting Oscar not to stint on the pistons, he decided mere grimaces weren't enough to sell his innocence and began exclaiming, "Who the fuck is this guy?! 'Cause it sure ain't me!"

"If you say so," stage-whispered Lily, "but you must admit it sounds awfully like you."

"Quiet!" snapped Diana. "It's clearly not Stephen!"

"Harder! Yeah, pound that ass, gold boy! *Yeah!!*"

"My mistake, dear. Nothing like him!"

After a few more excruciating minutes we heard the knock on the door and Gina calling, "Stephen?" This prompted drunken gales of laughter from Rex.

"Oops!! Oscar *interruptus!*"

Grimes paused the tape and asked that Gina be brought back in.

"I'm sorry, Miss Beach, but I'll have to ask you to listen to this next portion."

You may recall that most of the après-Oscar conversation had centered on Diana's boozy skirmish with Lily, who was venomously disparaged by both her niece and sister. Lily's response to these calumnies did little to bolster claims that the recording was fraudulent.

"Lies! All lies!!" cried Lily, rehearsing for the courtroom. "I was sober as a judge that night!"

"Be quiet!" pleaded Diana. "That's not even us!"

"Don't play innocent! I remember it clear as a bell. You were drunk and belligerent! Caused a hideous scene!"

"Shut the fuck up!" suggested an attorney.

Grimes was naturally quick to pounce on this. If the tape was a malicious fiction, why did Lily recall its events so clearly? There was a brief flummoxed silence, then Gilbert, that prince of prevaricators, leaped into the fray.

"Honestly! You call yourselves detectives? You couldn't detect a skunk in a perfume shop!" He pointed out that Diana and Lily's spat at the spa had been no whispered exchange of hostilities but a noisy, flat-out brawl that could easily have been overheard by any number of guests. And who happened to be on hand that very night?

"Rex Bajour!" I exclaimed.

"Precisely!" cried Gilbert, all but tucking his thumbs into imaginary suspenders. "When Rex came to make his defamatory tape he decided to incorporate the squabble, knowing that adding the expertly mimicked voices of Diana and Gina would help him pass it off as authentic. We don't, of course, know who Rex hired to portray the stars or what has since become of them. We can only speculate on the fate of those who've outlived their usefulness to Rex Bajour."

This last flourish was a bit over the top but Stephen and Gina endorsed the theory and their lawyers vowed to produce experts who'd testify that the tape was a sham. Rusty, unfazed, said he'd match them expert for expert, and lest we forget, Rex had not merely heard Monty's sex disk, he'd seen it. He then poked his intercom and said, "Send Rex in."

The office had a second door that gave onto a conference room. This door now opened and Rex entered. I had never in my twenty-nine years as a gay man seen someone actually sashay. I did now as Rex paraded in, employing the sort of gait one only excuses in tall, strikingly beautiful women wearing large feathered headdresses. It was clear from his face that our day of dark reckoning was for him some combination of Mardi Gras and Christmas morning. How it must have thrilled him to see the clamoring press outside and know he'd soon bask in its full ravenous attention. Never a Star, he would finally find glory as a Star Witness, all thanks to Stephen, on whom he bestowed a curdled smile of triumph.

Grimes asked if he could identify the man he'd seen on film having sex with a Les Étoiles masseur and a man costumed to resemble an Oscar.

"It was him! *Stephen Donato!*" he cried, thrusting a righteous finger at the accused.

"Oh, dial it down, Tallulah," said Monty.

At Rusty's prompting Rex proceeded to identify me, Gina, Diana, and Claire as the other players in the film Monty had shown him.

"Before you go, Mr. Bajour, tell us—did a man dressed as a police officer and claiming to be Detective Hank Grimes visit your apartment this week and confiscate a voice recorder from you?"

"He most certainly did!" harrumphed Rex.

"Is that man in this room?" asked Rusty, and Rex, still miffed at having been duped, gloatingly fingered Gilbert, adding that I'd served as his accomplice.

"What utter rubbish!" cried Gilbert. "I've never laid eyes on this man! And as we've established that he's a liar and expert forger—"

"Let's have Mrs. Popov," said Grimes to his intercom.

A lumpy beak-nosed woman in a floral housedress was escorted in. I stared a moment, bewildered. Then I placed her and blanched, overcome by that abrupt chagrin Wile E. Coyote feels when he glances down and finds that he parted company with the mesa several strides ago.

Rex giggled. "I see you remember my neighbor."

She identified Gilbert and me as the faux Hank and his confederate. Then she and Rex were thanked and escorted out, Rex blowing a kiss to Stephen as his witty parting gesture.

"Two witnesses, boys. Looks like you'll be bunking with us tonight."

"WHAT!!" shrieked Gilbert, who could at least find speech. The best I could manage was a high-pitched wheeze like an off-key concertina. I turned frantically to Claire, whose eyes met mine. They brimmed with sympathy, but sympathy was not what I wanted. I wanted a chopper on the roof and a suitcase full of Krugerrands and I wanted them now.

Grimes, his smile broadening, turned to Moira.

"I think we'll be making room for you too, Miss Finch."

"Oh?" said Moira blandly.

"On what charge?" howled her outraged counsel.

"Well, we got two witnesses who say she's the new Hollywood madam, so I guess we'll start there."

Moira yawned showily. "Do you honestly think you can win this on what you've got?"

"Maybe, maybe not. But we will on what we'll *get*. This case has been a tough one to crack 'cause your staff and la-di-da customers have kept their traps shut. But once they see people going down they'll get nervous. And when people get nervous they talk. Just ask Rex.

"So," he concluded, leering in triumph, "I guess we're about done here. But before we split up I'm gonna give you folks one last chance to come clean. Stevie, old pal, level with me—is that your voice on that tape?"

His lawyers strongly advised Stephen to answer no further questions. Ignoring them, he shot Grimes a contemptuous look and said, "Absolutely not." Grimes went down the line, asking us if we'd admit those were our voices, and we all denied it, clinging to our tattered forgery defense. All, that is, except Claire, the last in order of appearance and the last to be asked.

"How about you, Miss Simmons?" he asked, his tone pro forma, expecting another frosty denial.

"You really want to know?" asked Claire.

Grimes, thrown, regarded her quizzically.

"Since you ask, yeah, I kinda would."

"Well, then," said Claire, "I'll tell you. On one condition."

"You're giving *me* conditions?" asked Grimes with a snide laugh.

"Yes, I am. You can take them or leave them but I won't answer your question unless they're met."

The lawyers leaped frantically to their feet.

"I must advise Miss Simmons that—!"

"Shut up! She's not your client. What do you want, Claire? Because if it's immunity, I'll tell you right now—"

"No, nothing like that. All I ask is that there be no officers present except you and your brother. No lawyers either. Send them away, then we'll talk."

The lawyers, of course, argued vociferously against this. But Rusty, though clearly loath to take orders from a pushy lady screenwriter, did seem intrigued.

"Any particular reason?" he asked.

"If you agree my reasons will be clear soon enough. And of course nothing will prevent you or anyone here from sharing my comments with your colleagues or attorneys later."

Rusty seemed literally to chew on this, twisting his lips like a stumped sommelier.

"What the hell," he said finally. "I'm willing to humor her. If the rest of you don't mind."

Moira said she had no objection, then stared pointedly at Stephen, clearly advising him to agree. Stephen, thoroughly confused, looked to Claire.

"You know it's for the best," she said earnestly. Stephen, who knew nothing of the sort, turned his questioning gaze to me. I nodded vigorously, my imploring eyes conveying that, if there was to be any hope for us at all, it was time to let Claire be Claire. He hesitated briefly, then asked his counsel to leave.

"That way, please," said Claire, indicating the conference room from which Rex had entered. There was much balking and stern admonitions, but eventually the disgruntled lawyers and lawmen filed out, heads cocked defiantly with the frayed dignity of the banished.

When they'd gone Grimes made a mock courtly gesture and said, "I believe the floor is yours, Miss Simmons."

"Thank you," said Claire, rising. "To begin with the obvious, you have absolutely no case."

"I'm not interested in your legal analysis."

"Well, you're going to get it. You have no case whatsoever against Moira, Monty, or Lily. You have, alas, an excellent case against these two," she added, indicating me and Officer Selwyn. "They did something extraordinarily foolish and illegal. But they did it for a good cause and when we're done I don't think you'll care to press charges."

This gave the Grimes boys their heartiest laugh so far.

"Oh, you don't?" hooted Hank.

"No," she replied serenely, "I don't. But we'll get back to that. Let's start with Moira. You have two witnesses against her—a drug-abusing hustler and Rex. You have his tape too, of course, but you fail to see how worthless it is."

"Worthless, is it? If you're still peddling that forgery line—"

"What I mean," said Claire, "is that all you have is the audio and no one's word save Rex's for what's actually going on. As his slurred diction makes amply clear, the man's blind drunk start to finish. How can a jury possibly credit his subsequent claims of what he *thinks* he remembers seeing?"

"Good point!" said Stephen.

Rusty replied that though Rex's recall might not be 100 percent accurate, Stephen's pillow talk left few doubts as to what he and Oscar were up to. He also noted that we were trying to have it both ways, arguing on the one hand that Rex had forged the tape and on the other that he'd drunkenly imagined what he'd seen. Which was it?

Claire, unruffled, said she preferred to focus for now on the charge that Moira was running a brothel.

"Is there any point on the tape where the subject of money or payment is broached, even obliquely?"

"No," conceded Grimes, "but the tape starts with Stephen getting it on with a Les Étoiles masseur."

"Does it? We only have Rex's word for that. I didn't hear anything but a lot of moaning and grunting—noises perfectly consistent with a man getting a deep-tissue massage."

"You're forgetting we have Rex's confession that he himself purchased sex at the spa."

"Ah," said Monty, "but he didn't."

"Okay," snapped Rusty, getting testy. "Technically he says *you* picked up the tab as a birthday gift."

"Balderdash!" said Monty, who then turned to Claire. "May I?"

"Please."

"I paid for Rex to have a massage. Nothing less and certainly nothing more. It so happened the masseur, an aspiring actor, recognized Rex from his show and, hoping to further his career, offered his favors. Rex told me all about it, boasting in the most nauseating manner about his ageless sex appeal. Finally, to shut him up, I told him that the spa was a discreet brothel, that I'd arranged and paid for the sex as a surprise gift, and that when the masseur had laid eyes on Rex he'd doubled his fee. A bit mean of me perhaps, but you'd have done the same if you'd just spent an hour watching Rex fluff his curls and admire his shapely ankles."

Monty then faced Moira, his manner abashed and contrite. "I should have realized a gossip like Rex would repeat my cruel fib to others. I never dreamed though that it would gain such wide currency. Forgive me, Miss Finch, for giving birth to the scurrilous rumors that have plagued your fine establishment."

"Apology accepted," said Moira magnanimously.

"So," continued Claire, "I'd guess your other star witness, the junkie, got wind of the rumors and, when he landed in hot water, decided to exploit them to save his skin. Still think you have enough to charge Moira?"

"Damn right I do!" snarled Rusty, but his assurance seemed more forced now and his cocksure grin had vanished. "If you don't mind, Miss Simmons, this whole damn sideshow began with my asking you a simple yes-or-no question. Is that your voice on the tape or not?"

"Oh, yes, of course it's me," said Claire lightly. "It's all of us."

"You *traitor!*" howled Diana, rising in fury. "How DARE you suggest such a thing!"

Stephen too sprang to his feet, stunned by his savior's apparent betrayal.

"This is *bullshit!*" he shouted. "I want my lawyers back in here!"

"No! Just hear her out!" I beseeched him, tugging pathetically at his sleeve. To be honest, I was miffed at Claire myself for doing such a bang-up job of exonerating Moira while merely complimenting Rusty on the excellence of his case against Gilbert and me. But surely she was going *someplace* with this bold admission.

Claire approached Stephen, placed her hands on his shoulders, and gazed intently into his eyes. Her voice was firm yet soothing, as though she'd had years of experience as a star whisperer.

"I know this is hard for you, Stephen, but he's forced our hand. *Trust me.* This is the only way we can put this whole affair behind us once and for all. Now sit down please and let me finish."

Stephen obeyed but his hollow eyes suggested that he did so less out of any real faith in Claire than from a bitter conviction that all was lost and there was no sense struggling while they fastened the electrodes. Claire then turned to Grimes, her gaze crisp yet courageous like Emma Thompson playing Portia.

"It's clear to me that from the beginning this whole case has not been about pandering or extortion, neither of which crime occurred. It's been about your hatred of Stephen and determination to ruin his life and career."

"Like hell!"

"It never occurred to you that by pursuing your vendetta you might bring great harm and embarrassment to others as well, people who'd done nothing to warrant your scorn or to suffer from your obsession. We've done everything in our power to protect these people. But we can do so no longer.

"Yes, your so-called evidence captures Stephen in the throes of passion with another man. But the man was not a prostitute, nor was he unknown to Stephen. What you have on that tape is a simple massage interrupted by a surprise romantic tryst, abetted by Moira, who, like hoteliers the world over, was discreetly catering to the romantic needs of a VIP guest. Excuse me please."

She exited to the outer office, where we heard her ask Dottie to fetch Grimes a cup of coffee. "Don't bring it in though. He'll come out for it."

We heard the door to the hallway open and close. Then Claire returned. She gave Stephen a strange smile, at once wry and compassionate, then, looking back to the outer office, beckoned for someone to enter.

Into the room walked Oscar.

Or, at least, Oscar from the neck up. The expressionless gold mask completely covered his head but beneath it he was clad in a navy turtleneck and jeans. But as soon as the door closed behind him he swiftly peeled off the turtleneck, revealing his magnificent gilded torso.

It was an electric moment and one that triggered a wide range of responses, from Stephen and Gina's saucer-eyed horror to the Grimes boys' irate confusion. Diana teetered on the brink of a picturesque swoon while Lily clapped her hands like a little girl who's seen a magic trick. Monty and Gilbert just stared transfixed at the golden pectorals, their faces ablaze with curiosity as though wondering, "Do the pants come off too? Will he *dance?*"

"What kind of cheap fucking stunt is this?" bellowed Rusty, red-faced and truculent.

"This 'stunt,'" replied Claire, "is the person we've been trying to protect—Stephen's former lover. I think it's time he introduced himself."

She nodded to Oscar, who whipped off the mask, revealing the freckled, defiantly smiling face of Billy Grimes.

"WHAT THE FUCK!" remarked Dad.

Stephen stared a moment, vaguely recognizing him but unable at first to place him. Then it hit him and a smile exploded on his face, for he'd instantly grasped the simplicity and genius of Claire's plan to save him.

"Stephen!" cried Billy.

"Darling!" throbbed Stephen, who'd never been good with names.

"Billy!" I exclaimed for Stephen's benefit. Gilbert and I exchanged a euphoric glance, for we too saw in a flash how masterfully Claire had checkmated the enemy.

At last all the morning's mysteries were rendered clear. Claire had gone to Moira to get the costume and she'd needed the disk to show Billy. She'd known the steamy footage would stir him profoundly. She'd known too that it would illustrate the peril his hero now faced, a peril from which Billy alone could save him. How noble of Billy, how selfless to fall on the grenade of his father's wrath in order to rescue his unworthy idol!

"Who the fuck is this?" asked Gina with understandable pique.

"It's my goddamn son, that's who!" hollered Rusty, who now resembled an enraged tomato.

Stephen, bashfully facing Gina, said, "This is Billy. He and I had . . . we were—"

"Boyfriends," said Billy with a dash more pride than was quite seemly when informing the missus.

"What kind of bullshit is this?!" demanded Hank.

"It's the truth," said Claire. "What we've been trying to keep quiet for both Stephen and Billy's sake while you've been trying to splash it all over the front page."

On hearing the words "Billy," "Stephen," and "front page" so alarmingly juxtaposed Rusty recoiled and sat as though suddenly dizzy. Spinning his chair, he cast an anxious eye out the window at the street below where the ever-growing press mob was clamoring for news and filling the airwaves with greasy conjecture. He shut his eyes tightly like a toddler about to throw a tantrum.

"NO! *NO WAY!* I'M NOT FUCKING BUYING THIS!"

"It's the truth!" proclaimed Billy, throwing a gilded arm around Stephen. Again, an understandable impulse, but bad form in front of the wife.

"Show him the picture," said Claire and Billy produced a laminated photo and presented it proudly to his father. I caught a glimpse and saw that it was the photo I'd taken at the Finch/Donato launch party. There they were, the picture of young love, with Billy grinning up a storm as Stephen planted a big smooch on his cheek. It was a good thing Billy had laminated his keepsake, as Dad's first impulse after wincing in disgust was to tear it up. He clawed helplessly at the plastic and Billy snatched it away.

"That's my property!"

"Take it! And put your damn shirt back on!"

Rusty wheeled menacingly on Stephen, who regarded his nemesis with manly defiance but seemed nonetheless eager to keep the desk between them.

"You sick fuck, Donato! You did this just to get back at me!"

Stephen, who'd never had more riding on a performance, threw himself into his role with passionate intensity.

"You think everything's about you, don't you, Rusty? Well it's not! This was about Billy and me finding each other!"

"You tell him, Stephen!"

"I could have cleared this all up weeks ago but I didn't 'cause I was determined to protect Billy from you, you smug, self-righteous bigot!"

You may recall that when Billy first poured Stephen and me drinks at Vici I remarked on his uncanny ability to teleport himself across the bar in his eagerness to serve his idol. This gift clearly ran in the family because Rusty now popped across the room like a bad edit and decked Stephen with a right hook that sent him careening onto the coffee table, landing painfully on a small replica of a Sopwith Camel.

"Assault!" shouted Lily.

"More like attempted murder!" cried Gilbert.

"You all saw that!" declaimed Diana, and Moira said she'd gotten a picture on her camera phone.

"You keep your filthy hands off him!" said Billy, fearlessly leaping between his father and the fallen star.

As he knelt and helped Stephen to his feet, Gina, who'd been looking a tad bilious since Stephen had addressed Billy as "darling," rose and announced she was going to be sick. Grimes, remarking that she wasn't the only one, said that Dottie would see her to the ladies' room. Diana volunteered to accompany her, though I sensed from the leery glance she and Stephen exchanged that she was less concerned about Gina's well-being than the risk of her buttonholing the first stranger she met and wailing, "My husband cheated on me! WITH A MAN!"

With the ladies now gone Stephen and Billy sat boldly together on the couch, Stephen rubbing his jaw as Billy rested a comforting hand on his knee.

"I know you're upset about this, Dad, but you have no one to blame but yourself! You're the one who brought us together!"

"You're blaming this on *me*?!"

Billy explained that they'd met at the bar the night that Rusty had traded barbs with us. Billy, embarrassed by his father's rudeness, had introduced himself and apologized. Then, said Billy, I'd left and he and Stephen had talked more.

"We felt this immediate attraction."

"Instant!" agreed Stephen. "Which was really weird for me 'cause I'd never been with a guy before—"

"Phmph!" said Lily, covering her mouth. "Sorry. Go on."

Billy, his powers of invention honed by years of Stephen-themed fantasies, sweetly unfolded the tale of their brief, idyllic romance. He spoke of their great love, their unquenchable physical passion, and many shared interests and beliefs. The need for secrecy had, of course, been paramount, and they'd had trouble at first finding safe places to meet. This problem was solved by the genially discreet Moira, whose spa's treatment rooms provided ideal trysting spots.

As Billy spoke we all listened with gently sympathetic smiles, save, of course, for the Grimes boys, who could not have looked queasier had they been watching a male-to-female sex change on the Surgery Channel. But their disgust didn't faze Billy. Nothing could mar his rapture at sitting thigh to thigh with his dream man, spinning stories of their love and hearing each detail tenderly corroborated.

"I was so excited for Stephen 'cause I was sure he was going to win an Oscar for *Lothario*. Remember?"

"You always believed in me, Billy."

"Whenever I'd tell him that, he'd just look at me and say, 'You're my Oscar, Billy. You're the only prize I want.'"

It was this remark that had inspired Billy's idea to surprise Stephen by showing up for a tryst costumed as an Oscar. Knowing that Moira had security cameras, he'd asked her to film this encounter, claiming he wanted to present it to Stephen as a keepsake. The truth, he sheepishly conceded, was that he'd wanted it for himself.

"You see," he confessed, eyes misting at the memory, "we knew by then we'd have to end it soon. Stephen was married. The scandal could've ruined his whole career and I loved him too much to let that happen. We finally said goodbye after he got nominated. The attention was so crazy by then we'd have been nuts to think we could keep going and not be found out."

Not long after they'd parted, explained Billy, he and I had met for drinks. He'd talked about the affair (which I, of course, knew of, having been under the table) and unwisely mentioned his filmed memento. Agog, I'd begged to see it until Billy, less wisely still, relented. We watched it on my laptop, and unbeknownst to Billy, I'd copied the file onto my hard drive.

"So you could blackmail Stephen!" accused Rusty.

I maintained, blushing prettily, that my motives had been purely recreational. I then confessed that I'd later loaned my copy to Monty, who, most foolishly of all, had screened it for Rex.

"So there you have it," said Claire, summing up for the jury. "No prostitution, no extortion—just a star-crossed romance and a very personal keepsake passed around a damn sight too freely."

"Chin up, old man!" said Monty, giving Rusty's shoulder an avuncular pat. "We know this is quite vexing for you, as witness your face, which resembles a bowl of steaming borscht. But do try, if you can, to learn from your error. This all might have been avoided if you'd been less hidebound on matters of sex and raised your son in a loving, broad-minded home—one in which, if asked how his weekend had gone, he'd not have hesitated to reply that his tips had been sluggish but, on the bright side, he'd done it with a movie star. I hope this experience will open a dialogue that in time may—"

"Fuck off, you snotty old queen!"

"Ah, well. Baby steps."

"So that's it, huh?!" sneered Rusty, his jowls gratifyingly aquiver. "You think I'm just going to buy all this crap and let you waltz out of here?"

"You'd better," warned Billy. "Because if you arrest *any* of my friends I'll go downstairs and tell that whole mob how you squandered thousands in taxpayer money in a dumb-ass effort to frame my boyfriend!"

"And we don't want that!" yiped Stephen.

"No," Claire said to Rusty. "No one does, least of all you. If this comes out you can kiss the governor's mansion goodbye. The last thing your party wants is a candidate mired in scandal—or a bumptious oaf who set out to uncover a crime ring and found nothing but his own son in a gay love nest. Which is why I doubt you'll be charging these two for their little caper with Rex. Not when they'll be forced to defend themselves by explaining they were trying to keep him from exposing your son's affair with Stephen."

"You've got it all worked out, don't you, Missy!" said Rusty, spittle flying, as Prudence Gamache would have observed, from his enraged, incensed, livid, furious, unhappy lips. "Well, what if I just don't buy it? Huh? What if I think the whole story's one big fat lie?"

"Well, in that case," Claire said blandly, "we'll show you the DVD."

I gasped and my eyes swiveled to Stephen.

Speaking strictly as Cavanaugh the historian, I confess that the greatest challenge I've faced in recounting this tale is that, in the course of it, both I and the other dramatis personae suffered so many abrupt and hair-raising reversals of fortune that the further along I get the more I fear I've exhausted the vocabulary of rude surprise. I assure you though that at no point in the whole harrowing journey was anyone quite so unhappily startled as Stephen was by Claire's breathtakingly casual offer. He rocketed from his chair like a pilot from an ejector seat and his face was that of a man struck by lightning while eating a bad oyster.

"*WHAT?* HAVE YOU LOST YOUR FUCKING MIND?!"

"I know you'd prefer not to, Stephen, but if it's the only way to convince them—"

"You can't!" thundered Diana. "The film doesn't exist! The copies have all been destroyed!"

"Not mine," said Monty, winning a fond look from sis.

"It's not like they'll show it to anyone," argued Billy, the complete altruism of whose motives I was beginning to question.

"You brought it *with* you?" marveled Hank.

Monty explained that no, we did not have a copy immediately at hand. Billy, determined to protect Stephen, had destroyed his own. The sole remaining disk was the one he'd borrowed from me and he'd sent it to a friend in Key West for safekeeping. He could have it

Express Mailed back today and have it on Rusty's desk by noon tomorrow. Would that be satisfactory?

Rusty, who'd sooner have identified his son in a morgue than in a skin flick devoid of ladies, just glowered murderously at the grinning dandy. His brother placed a hand on his shoulder and said, "You don't have to watch it, Russ. I'll check it out."

"How will you even know it's my kid under that kinky fucking mask?!"

"Oh, don't worry about that," said Billy. "I only had the mask on when I first walked in. I pulled it off right away so Stephen would know it was me. From then on I had it off the whole time."

Billy turned and beamed at his once and future lover.

"Right, hon?"

"Of course, dear," muttered Stephen, somehow managing a wan smile. Gilbert, Monty, and I discreetly exchanged a wry glance, for we knew that beneath the smile he was positively seething with resentment.

One understood, of course. If there's one thing self-important film stars loathe it's reshoots.

Epilogue

★

THOUGH I HAVE SPARED FEW KIND words in this account for my rival Gina, I must concede that at close of day, when there was nary a centimeter between our backs and the wall, she proved herself one heck of a good sport. She did, of course, display a pardonable lack of enthusiasm when first asked to wait patiently in the wings while her husband was humped to a fare-thee-well by a gilded bartender, then enter on cue to reprise her role as a clueless cuckold. But once Claire had helped her grasp the full ghastliness of the alternatives, she relented and signed on for the remake. She did, however, inform Stephen that the magnificent diamond-and-sapphire choker she'd been loaned for the Oscars would not see the inside of Buccellati again.

Securing Gina's cooperation was but one of several hurdles that faced Finch/Donato Productions' freshman effort. Ricky the masseur had to be located and bribed handsomely to reprise his role, sans the sex this time. The most daunting challenge though was the one posed by Rusty's unfortunate possession of an audio copy of the original. It meant that the new production had to be lip-synched to Monty's copy, and lip-synched flawlessly, as any mistake would expose it as a redo. So our little band of players had to speedily memorize not only the dialogue but the precise timing of it as well.

Stephen and Diana, seasoned pros that they were, rose masterfully to the challenge, and Claire and I, after much rehearsal, acquitted ourselves competently. Gina, by contrast, was quite undone by the whole lurid undertaking and teetered constantly on the brink of maudlin hysterics. The lip-synching defeated her entirely, especially at the point where she had to banter lightheartedly about Stephen's keen longing for an Oscar. Claire finally solved the problem by blocking the scene with Gina's back to the camera.

There was concern as well over Billy. We'd scripted a brief coda for him and Stephen in which they ruefully acknowledged the madness of their affair and vowed to break it off. Billy had only acted once before when, as a sophomore in high school, he'd assayed the role of Bud Frump in the musical *How to Succeed in Business Without Really Trying*, delivering a performance that landed him firmly in the chorus for the remainder of his career there. We took heart though from his more nuanced work in Rusty's office and hoped that the presence of cameras would not unnerve him.

OUR SHOOT BEGAN AT two a.m. Saturday on what was arguably the most closed set in film history. We rolled sound and began with Ricky's now PG-rated massage. Stephen's moans sounded less libidinous when heard against the visual of Ricky digging an elbow into his shoulder blade. Ricky backed off on cue, teasingly informing Stephen that someone he'd be "glad to see" would be taking over. He then opened the door to Oscar, whose costume was now accessorized with little gold shorts. His predecessor, you may recall, had entered exposed and ready for immediate boarding. We felt this priapic approach was out of keeping with the remake's more romantic tone and, worse, made Ricky look like a pimp and not, as we preferred, like some discreet and worldly sexual concierge. We carefully timed Stephen's stoned burst of laughter to come immediately after Oscar removed his mask, revealing Billy's smiling face. Ricky withdrew with a continental wink and only then did the shorts come off.

Though Stephen had to stay in sync with the sound track, Billy's lack of dialogue permitted him more leeway to reinterpret the role. The first Oscar, in keeping with his featureless mask, had performed like some exotic sexbot. Billy was more tender, kissing Stephen as often as the sound track allowed. The most crucial difference though was that Billy, unlike his forerunner, knew he had exactly six minutes and twenty-two seconds before pencils down and if he meant to finish he'd better bear this in mind. Finish he did, bringing Stephen to climax as well, as he has since remarked on times without number.

"Fear not! Cavanaugh's here!" I mouthed, bounding up from below stairs and tossing a towel to the panting and red-faced Stephen. Billy took his place under the table, Stephen rolled tactfully onto his stomach, and I admitted Gina. Her performance, seen only from behind, required little of her beyond some appropriate hand gestures; her face, unseen by the camera, scowled ferociously at Stephen even as she uttered endearments to him on the sound track. Diana entered and flawlessly re-created her drunken outburst; Claire arrived next, discovered Oscar, and escorted the ladies out.

That was where Grimes's audio ended. I stayed behind to apologize to Stephen and Billy for my unseemly presence, explaining that I'd been hiding from the libidinous Monty. I left and then Stephen and Billy played their brief touching farewell, a scene for which Billy had no problem summoning real tears.

Moira yelled, "Cut!" then retired to her sanctum to view the results and mix the sound. Stephen and his kin fled the spa with nary a goodbye, a move that was highly if absurdly disappointing to Billy and me.

"What were you expecting?" Claire asked incredulously. "A *wrap* party?"

The three of us and Gilbert retired to the bar for a much-needed drink while Moira burned a DVD for us (no doubt making several backups for personal use). Gilbert and I delivered the disk to Monty just after five a.m. We screened it and agreed the performances and timing were first-rate. Though I, for understandable reasons, will al-

ways prefer the original version, I could not deny that the new finish
gave it a poignancy the Cavanaugh ending had lacked.

Monty had instructed an old friend in Key West to FedEx him a
note reading:

> Dear Monty,
> Thanks again for loaning me this *very* special movie! I part
> with it most reluctantly and only wish I had the technology to
> make a copy for my personal library. What a cutie little Oscar
> is! Do you know him? Do visit soon.
> Love,
> Trevor

This arrived in Los Feliz shortly after ten a.m. Monty barely had
time to open the FedEx pouch and insert the disk before Hank
Grimes, who'd been watching the house, barged in to seize it. Hank,
we presume, then screened it, comparing the audio to Rex's tape, and
reported to his brother.

That afternoon Rusty held a press conference. He began by apol-
ogizing to Stephen, his family, and colleagues for any embarrassment
they'd suffered during yesterday's "deplorable circus," vowing again
to find and discipline the tipster who'd alerted the media. He said that
Stephen and Moira, far from being targets of a criminal investigation,
were the innocent victims of an extortionist who'd spread false and
malicious rumors about them and Miss Finch's spa. The extortionist
had then fabricated "evidence" to support these rumors and mailed it
to Stephen with a demand for thirty million dollars. Rusty's office had
examined this so-called evidence and determined it beyond doubt to
be a computer-generated forgery, which would not be released to the
press out of respect for its intended victims. In closing he vowed to
spare no effort in finding and prosecuting the still-anonymous blackmailer who had, it was feared, fled the country.

Come Oscar morning the story completely dominated the headlines and Sunday chat shows. Stephen declined all interview requests,

saying he'd been advised not to discuss details of the case as to do so might impede the investigation. He would, he vowed, have plenty to say once the perpetrator was apprehended and tried. Until then he hoped his fans and the media would respect his family's privacy.

That night when he and Gina walked down the aisle of the Kodak Theatre, the audience rose as one in thunderous support for this great and greatly maligned star. For Billy and me, watching at home with Gilbert and Claire, it was a bit of a *Stella Dallas* moment—you know, the classic weeper that ends with poor selfless Stella standing outside the party in the rain, nose pressed to the glass, watching proudly as the daughter for whom she has sacrificed so nobly basks in the admiration of the beau monde.

"What is she *wearing?*" asked Gilbert of Gina. She was sporting one of those gowns where the breasts are barely concealed by criss-crossing satin panels only slightly wider than suspenders.

"Tramp," I said flatly.

"Go on," sneered Billy. "Flaunt your gazongas. You'll never make him as happy as I did!"

"As *we* did," I corrected.

"Well," drawled Billy with the off-putting smugness that had crept into his tone of late, "I think I made him a *little* happier."

"Do you?"

"He *looked* at me."

"How could he not with you slobbering over him like a border collie?"

"You want to talk tummies?"

"You will cease this conversation immediately," demanded Claire, "or I'll hurl this bottle through the screen."

I was happy, at least, for Stephen. How glorious he looked and how much more glorious he must have felt bathing in that Niagara of applause. He had sojourned in purgatory, clutching a boarding pass for points south, but now he'd been welcomed once more into this celestial assemblage, yea, even seated at the right hand of Spielberg. Had the balloting for Best Actor taken place that night his rivals wouldn't have mustered a single vote between them. Unfortunately for Stephen, the ballots had been mailed in some days ago when he was still under a cloud and the Academy had felt a soupçon more love for Laurence Osgood Fenton, the brilliant newcomer who'd portrayed a traumatized Iraq war vet in the searing drama *Anthem*. Laurence, only twenty-four, stumbled, disbelieving, to the stage and gave an eloquent speech, declaring himself unworthy to share the category with the likes of Nicholas Cage, Al Pacino, Liam Neeson, and, most of all, his hero Stephen Donato. The screen filled with Stephen's face as he applauded and brushed aside a grateful tear.

IF THE OSCARS BROUGHT little joy to Stephen, they did provide a welcome distraction from the blackmail story, which was bumped off the front page by the usual coverage of winners and losers, gowns, gripes, and gaffes. This was a relief as our cover story with its murky details and mystery villain had been hastily concocted and would not bear undue scrutiny. People still gossiped about it but conventional wisdom deemed Stephen innocent of any same-sex shenanigans. How could he be otherwise when even his bitterest enemy was forced to declare him the blameless victim of a conspiracy? A few naysayers, Rex among them, continued to cry cover-up, but their crackpot theories won little attention and the public, starved of fresh developments, soon lost interest.

STEPHEN WAS NOT ENTIRELY out of the woods. There remained the nettlesome matter of *Amelia Flies Again!* Monty still had his disk and refused to return it till Stephen made good on his promise. Stephen pointed out that he could no longer disseminate it without revealing to Rusty that our alibi was a hoax. True, countered Monty, but what of Lily? She now knew all about Stephen's "romance" with Billy. Though she was disinclined to tattle on her costar, if Stephen reneged she would not hesitate to include every succulent detail in her memoir. This left Stephen in a pickle. He could, of course, call in the script doctors but was loath to let anyone read it since not even Gina had failed to discern that he'd bought it with a gun to his head.

It was, of course, Claire who finally proposed a compromise ac-

354 | Joe Keenan

ceptable to all parties. And, as it happened, her neat solution dove-
tailed happily with another development in the Donato household.

In an exclusive cover interview for the May *Vanity Fair* (timed to
coincide with the release of *Caliber IV: Who'll Save the Sun?*), Stephen
announced that he and Gina were expecting their first child. Thanks to
this joyous event, production on *The Heart in Hiding* would be accel-
erated so that Gina could film her scenes before her pregnancy became
apparent. This rescheduling, alas, meant that his mother, who had a
conflict, would no longer be able to play the heroic housekeeper Greta.
Fortunately his aunt had graciously consented to step into her sister's
shoes. This would, alas, compel Lily to put her Amelia Earhart project
on hold but family was family and one sacrificed for them as needed.

GILBERT, HAVING EMERGED UNSCATHED yet again from a disaster of
his own making, was, as always, maddeningly blasé, claiming he'd
never doubted it would all work out in the end. This greatly annoyed
our rescuer, Claire, who brusquely remarked that the only reason he'd
escaped arrest was that he was in the "witless protection program."

I'd feared he'd be hurt when I told him we would not be collabo-
rating with him on any future projects. He was unfazed though, having recently decided that a lad with his looks and charisma belonged
more properly in front of the camera. He had head shots taken and declared himself an actor, throwing himself into his new métier with the
same commitment and discipline he'd brought to his careers as a novelist and screenwriter.

ANGUS BRODIE RETURNED FROM LOCATION, evicting us from our
movie-star bachelor pad. Gilbert decamped to Max's guesthouse while
I took a one-bedroom apartment in West Hollywood on Fountain and
Hayworth. Though perfectly charming, it was still quite a comedown
from our aerie in the hills, which, sadly, was visible from my bathroom
window.

Claire and I kept plugging away, trudging from one "creative"
meeting to the next. Ironically, we wound up winning an assignment
from Irv Bushnell, the producer I'd last glimpsed taking lachrymose

bows for *Whoa, You're No Chick!* The picture, based on Irv's original concept, was a comedy about an alien running for congress. We'd liked it much better than his time-traveling rap-star pitch.

THE HEART IN HIDING opened in November a week after Rusty lost the governor's race to Ms. Almy and only days before Gina, two weeks overdue, tearfully consented to a cesarean. Gilbert and I attended the premiere as Lily and Monty's guests.

The picture, as most of you save Amos know, turned out rather well. Gilbert and I had to concede that the screenplay was depressingly superior to our own. In Ms. Gamache's novel, Heinrich's transformation from Nazi to saint is preposterously rapid and unconvincing, a problem less than adequately remedied in our script. In Mr. Schramm's version the only reason Heinrich fails to report Greta's family is his lust for Lisabetta, whom he very nearly rapes. His moral awakening comes in agonizing inches and he fights it every step of the way, making it both more plausible and moving. The direction and brooding cinematography were flawless, and Stephen's performance as Heinrich was compelling and, as Moira was heard to remark, "layered."

The revelation, though, was Lily. Both during and after production she'd decried the director, Peter Kistiakowski, as a tyrannical bully, sorely lacking in respect for an artiste some years his senior. But even Lily had to admit his hectoring had paid off. Her performance was unlike any she'd ever given, stripped of her usual mannerisms and excess and steeped in pain, cunning, and fortitude. I can't tell you how strange it felt afterward to compliment her and actually mean it.

I saw Stephen at the party as well. It was the first time we'd seen each other since that bizarre last night at Les Étoiles. Conversations with ex-boyfriends are almost always awkward and never more so than when the ex is standing arm in arm with his massively pregnant wife.

"Really amazing work," I said, daring no more than a handshake. "You must both be very proud."

"We are," said Gina, her tone, like her performance, a bit on the stiff side.

"So, how are you guys doing?" asked Stephen.

"Oh, fine. Claire and I are busy. Gilbert's started acting."

Stephen rolled his eyes. "Has Gilbert ever stopped acting?"

"Good point. Anyway, I was just bowled over. Really. You deserve an Oscar for this."

Gina frowned, the name, I suppose, forever tainted for her. But Stephen smiled and said, "From your mouth to God's ear."

There was something about his smile, something wistful and perhaps a touch nostalgic, that made me realize how much he missed me. He may even have been trying to discreetly signal that he hoped I'd call him again sometime. "But no," I thought to myself, "best not." You have to know when to let these things go. I realized that even if Stephen didn't.

STEPHEN WAS INDEED NOMINATED again for Best Actor. Again he lost. The camera lingered with customary cruelty on his face at the moment of defeat. This time he could not even manage a brave smile, just an odd, faraway look of rueful astonishment. Claire, Gilbert, and I, watching at home, were certain beyond doubt that he was thinking of Lily and recalling what she'd said nearly three hours ago when she'd jubilantly taken the stage to accept her Best Supporting Actress Oscar.

"Thank you! Thank you! Oh, my word, thank you! I won't say I never dreamed this would happen because I did! Dreamed it every damned day! I'm so glad I've put off finishing my memoirs—now they have an ending!

"I want to thank the Academy and all the dear, sweet people who voted for me. I want to thank my brother, Monty, and my many loving friends who never doubted this night would come! I want to thank our brilliant young director for his great kindness to me and our producers Bobby Spellman and Moira Finch for their courage and unwavering integrity. I want to thank my sister, Diana. She turned this role down, you know, so she could make *Who Needs Tomorrow?* The very few of you who saw it know what a mistake *that* was! Bless you, Diana! This should really be yours—*but it's not!*

"Most of all I want to thank my wonderful costar, Stephen! Where is he? Oh, there you are! Don't look so anxious, my dear! You'll be standing up here soon enough! Thank you, my darling, thank you so much! You're more than a nephew to me. Yes, you are! You're my hero, Stephen! My champion! My lucky star!"

Author's Notes and Acknowledgments

★

While most of the Hollywood award rituals depicted in the book are, as even young Seth knows, real events, FilmFest LA is not. It was modeled very loosely on ShoWest, an annual film industry trade show that does indeed bestow an award for Distinguished Decade of Achievement in Film. (As of this writing the latest recipient is Drew Barrymore and I like to think that *Guess What, I'm Not Dead* gave her just the extra boost she needed to outshine the competition.) ShoWest takes place in Las Vegas; I chose to place my ceremony in LA and sprinkled in a few more stars than such an event might normally attract.

In the past I've used these acknowledgments to thank those who've assisted me with my research on previous books. Since my research for this one consisted solely of reading *Vanity Fair* and gossiping at parties, I can't offhand think of anyone who falls into this category. There are, nonetheless, a fair number of people who deserve thanks and perhaps apologies for the role they've played in this book's creation.

Owing to the demands of my second career in series television, which offers handsome remuneration but very little downtime, this book has had an embarrassingly long gestation period. In searching my hard drive I was taken aback to discover that the earliest notes for it were written in the spring of 1995. The first draft was not completed until the summer of 2004. I wrote most of it during vacations, meandering through various world capitals and islands, muttering to myself and scribbling in pocket-size notebooks.

When a writer takes close to a decade to complete a work of light fiction, there are two ways he can choose to behave during its protracted composition. He can be reticent to the point of secrecy, mentioning his pet project so seldom that his friends discover he was writing it only when they receive invitations to the book party. Or he can, like me, prattle endlessly on about it, telling anyone who'll listen about the marvelously fun book he's embarked upon and which he only wishes he had more time to complete.

I don't doubt that a few of those whose ears I've bent about this book have listened with genuine interest. I suspect though that most have endured my effusions with the strained patience of well-wishers too polite to inform an expectant parent that, while they will happily attend the christening once the bundle of joy arrives, they could do without the weekly sonograms. So, whether for their avid interest or tactful forbearance, I thank the following people: my frequent collaborator Chris Lloyd (who got more frequent earfuls than most), plus Rob Greenberg, Rob Hanning, Jeff Richman, Chris Marcil, Sam Johnson, David Lee, Peter (and Rosie) Casey, Bob (and Janet) Daily, and pretty much anyone else who ever wrote for *Frasier;* our incomparable cast, Kelsey Grammer, David Hyde Pierce, Jane Leeves, Peri Gilpin, and John Mahoney; my dear friends Victor Bumbalo, Tom O'Connor, Randy Sturges, Harriet Harris, Matt Sullivan, Crosby Ross, Richard Cassese, Lisa Banes, Jill Young, Edward Hibbert, Jennifer Langham, Brian Hargrove, Albert Mason, Adam Small, Leslie Kolins Small, Arleen Sorkin, Christine Baranski, Maggie Blanc, Roy and Dorothy Christopher, Tony Mclean, John Coughlan, Roger Hedden, Anne Carney, Richard Gray, Maryanne Terrillo, Sal Terrillo, Karen Fausch, Matthew Pym, Elisa Sarno, Lynn Hanks, Reggie Burke, and Brooks Almy; my sister, Geraldine Fennelly; my brother-in-law, Richie; my nephews Michael and Brian; my brother, John; and my mother-in-law, Bruna.

I extend especial apologies to my trainer, Doug MacDonald, and assistant, David Nahmod, who, being in my employ, have served as captive audiences for many a long-winded progress report.

I'd like to thank my extraordinarily patient agent Geri Thoma; Jay Sures; Andrew Canava; my diligent editor, Judy Clain; her assistant, Molly Messick; my eagle-eyed copyeditor, Karen Landry; and my publisher, Michael Pietsch. Twenty years ago he struggled to persuade his superiors at Harmony Books to publish my first novel. When he failed (for philistinism has ever been rampant in the industry) he helped find me my agent, Geri, proving himself as aptly named a fellow as ever I've met.

I'd also like to thank the numerous real-life luminaries I've conscripted to cross paths with my characters. They are all fine actors for whom I have the highest regard, and I have endeavored to depict their actions as at best impeccable and at worst innocuous. (I realize, Drew, that the movie may not sound like a classic but, trust me, you're quite the best thing in it.)

Most of all I'd like to thank my husband, Gerry Bernardi, who has lovingly endured more blather about this book than the above mentioned combined. Were it not for his unwavering support and affection I would be, as Monty puts it, "a bitter old queen incapable of spreading sunshine."

About the Author

JOE KEENAN is the author of two previous novels, *Blue Heaven* and *Putting on the Ritz*. As a playwright and lyricist, he won the Richard Rodgers Development Award from the American Academy and Institute of Arts and Letters for his musical *The Times* and also won the 1993 Kleban Award for the show's lyrics. He served for seven years as a writer/producer for *Frasier*, where he received five Emmy nominations for Outstanding Writing in a Comedy Series, winning once, plus four Emmys for Outstanding Comedy Series and two Writers Guild Awards.

My Lucky Star

★

A novel by

Joe Keenan

A conversation with Joe Keenan

Reviews of your work frequently compare you to P. G. Wodehouse. Were you attempting to update his special kind of farce? If so, what is it about the genre that appeals to you?

Reading Wodehouse was what first made me want to write fiction. Before I discovered him in my early twenties, my only ambition had been to write comedies for the stage. Reading his books, I saw for the first time that not only could a novel be as funny as a good stage farce, but it could be funny in ways that a play couldn't be. His writing brimmed over with wonderful jokes that could be made only in prose, jokes based on narrative tone, witty descriptions, and comic metaphors and similes. In Wodehouse's world butlers "shimmer" into rooms and an annoyingly hearty girl has a laugh "like a squadron of cavalry charging over a tin bridge." I loved his endearing characters and wonderfully twisty plots and wondered why no one bothered to write books like that anymore. A few years later I decided to try my hand at something in a Wodehousian vein and began *Blue Heaven*. In the book's first scene the narrator, Philip, attends a gallery opening of work by a talentless downtown poseur. A friend maliciously informs the pretentious sculptor that Philip's a great admirer of his. Philip reports that the artist then fixed him "with a hungry, expectant look, like a vampire watching a hemophiliac shave." A very Wodehousian joke and the first of many I would make in my books.

As much as I owe to Wodehouse, there are many other writers I read when I was young whose work had a great influence on my writing. Off the top of my head I'd cite Oscar Wilde, Saki, Noel Coward, Kaufman and Hart, Neil Simon, Alan Aykbourn, and Joe Orton.

When you created the characters of Philip, Gilbert, and Claire in Blue Heaven, *did you know then that you would be writing a sort of series about this trio? Did you have a model or plan for this, or did it just happen?*

When I began *Blue Heaven* I actually thought I was writing a short story, but I did imagine even then that—assuming I managed to finish and get it published—I'd write more stories about the same characters. The dynamic between them—the ambitious, insanely impetuous Gilbert, the wry, brainy and scrupulously ethical Claire, and the sweet, ever-seducible Philip—seemed like one that could inspire multiple adventures. And again, too, my model was Wodehouse, who repeatedly returned to his favorite characters (most famously Bertie and Jeeves) throughout his long and prolific career. As a reader I always found it cheering to know when I finished a book I'd especially enjoyed that I hadn't seen the last of its characters and there were further exploits still to be savored.

The Philip in Blue Heaven *and* Putting on the Ritz *is much the same age as the Philip in* My Lucky Star, *even though years have passed and his surroundings have changed. Why did you choose to make your main characters frozen in time?*

Again (yes, *again*) my model was Wodehouse, whose delightful Bertie Wooster remained a deliciously dim young man-about-town for more than half a century. There are plenty of other examples as well, particularly in detective fiction, where characters like Miss Marple and Nero Wolfe seemed to stay about the same age for quite a long time. My main reason, though, for not letting Philip and Gilbert age is that the things that make them funny, their naïveté and rashness, their knack for self-delusion and occasional flat-out stupidity, are qualities one finds more endearing (or at least forgivable) in the young than in men who have reached an age by which they ought really to know better.

Who came first, Joe Keenan the novelist or Joe Keenan the TV script-writer? How have you managed to juggle these two personas? Do you find the writing to be similar in nature, or completely different?

The novelist came first, although curiously it was my fiction that led to my career in television. A wonderful TV writer named David Lloyd happened to read a *Boston Globe* review of *Blue Heaven* that cited its "Wodehousian merriment." David, an ardent Wodehouse devotee who owns first editions, both British and American, of his ninety-something books, read my book and gave copies to many of his friends, including Glen and Les Charles, the team behind *Cheers*. They liked it and asked me if I'd like to create a series for them, so I wrote a pilot called *Gloria Vane,* a comedy which, coincidentally, was also about a movie star, a temperamental actress in thirties Hollywood. The pilot was lavishly produced with a cast that included JoBeth Williams, Nina Foch, Emily Proctor, Jerry Adler, Mark Blum, Carole Cook, and *Frasier*'s Edward Hibbert and Harriet Sansom Harris. It was not ordered to series but it did lead to an offer to join *Frasier* in its second season.

As for how I juggle the two personas . . . well, clearly not all that well, as it took me nine years to write *My Lucky Star.* But the two disciplines do have a fair number of similarities. In each you're trying to come up with a story that's both amusing and at least somewhat unpredictable while crafting dialogue that's heightened and funny without being altogether implausible.

There are, of course, very significant differences between the two disciplines. One is that television writing's highly collaborative. On half-hour comedies the stories are crafted by committee and then, once in production, rewritten daily by the staff with the showrunner serving as final arbiter of both processes. On some shows every script is gang-written, with writing credit being assigned on a rotating basis among the team. On *Frasier* we preferred to let the author (or authors) of record write the first draft alone and only then would it once more become the property of the room. The best and most conscientious writers (and I will not stoop to such patently false humility as to exclude myself from this group) took pride in producing drafts that required as little tweaking as possible to be camera-ready. Another key difference is that, unlike a book, a television or film script is not the final and finished product—the film or episode that will spring from it is. This is why, if forced to state a preference, I would have to come down on the side of fiction.

That's not to say that I don't enjoy writing scripts. It's just that every time I complete one, I'm keenly aware that the job is far from done and that my work won't reach its intended audience until the actors, director, designer, director of photography, and film editor have all had a good whack at it. Most often these are marvelously gifted people who greatly enhance my work and bring it to glorious fruition. There are times, though, when things go less auspiciously and, at close of day, the dear little offspring I nurtured so tenderly lays cold on a gurney and can only be identified through dental records.

When I finish a book, the job's pretty much done. Yes, my editor might have a civilized suggestion or two and a suitable artist must be found to slap an eye-catching cover on the thing, but once these small matters are attended to, my book is ready for its audience. There are no further middlemen, no long casting sessions where my cheeks ache from attentive smiling, no run-throughs attended by studio and network executives bursting with insights, and no fretful debates about whether or not to recast the sexy ingénue whose performance suggests that she's learned the role phonetically. Just my story, my words, and an attentive reader. Heaven.

What, to you, is the biggest challenge of writing a novel? What's the most enjoyable part?

The biggest challenge of writing the sort of novels I write—i.e., farces—is working out the damn plots. How will Gilbert drag Philip into yet another ghastly mess (or, as Philip says in *Putting on the Ritz*, "Disaster, brilliantly disguised as Opportunity")? Who do they become entangled with and why? What complications ensue? How do you keep the situation escalating and make sure that, as in all good farces, the characters' efforts to extricate themselves from an increasingly perilous situation only dig them in deeper? How do you finally bring them to a place where disaster and ruin seem utterly inescapable, then how do you save them?

The hardest part, of course, is making sure that however wild and absurd the plot gets (and you want things to get as outrageous as possible) that it doesn't do so at the expense of logic or credibility. The plot twists, relying at times on unhappy coincidence, may be mildly improbable, but they can never be flat-out unbelievable. (Peter Stone, author of musicals such as *1776* and movies such as *Charade,* was a teacher of mine at NYU and he passed along this sage dictum of storytelling: "You can use coincidence to get your characters into trouble, but never to get them out of it.") Likewise, your characters must always behave in a manner consistent with both their essential natures and best interests. In plotting *My Lucky Star* I was faced with several conundrums of character logic and had to carefully devise credible solutions for each.

The first and perhaps thorniest was that I wanted Claire to be along for the ride, helping Philip and Gilbert write the screenplay. If she weren't, she'd be sidelined for the whole story and then who would save them? My problem, of course, was that the unshakably principled Claire would never agree to accept the job once she learned that it had been secured through plagiarism, and there was no way to prevent her knowing this as she'd never sign on without first demanding to read the spec script to which Gilbert had signed her name. I got around this by using Claire's own ethics to entrap her. Convinced, once Stephen and Diana are on board, that there's no possible way they can keep the assignment, she gives Gilbert her oath that she'll stay if they win the job in exchange for his promise to have Max find her another job in the event, inevitable to her, that they don't. She may bitterly repent having given her oath, but to Claire a promise, however foolish, cannot be reneged on.

Another tricky part was getting our boys involved with Moira again. When Gilbert decided to marry her for the gifts in *Blue Heaven* he knew she was a bit shifty but was blind to the full scope of her cunning and malevolence. By that story's end, though, both he and Philip knew only too well how diabolical a fiend she was. Readers of that book would never have forgiven them for being so brainless as to trust her again, yet my story dictated that she somehow worm her way back into their lives. I decided to use Gilbert's loathing of her and desire to rub his success in her face as a means to get her in their door. Once inside, Moira, being Moira, required no more than an unguarded moment in their office to ferret out the proof of their plagiarism and have them once more at her mercy.

If there's a scene in the book where I feel I may have cheated logic just a tad it's the scene at Vici where Philip reports first to Stephen and then to Diana. In reality Diana (and certainly Sonia) would most likely have preferred to hold so sensitive a meeting in a more private location—her home, say, or Sonia's office. My problem was that I was determined that Philip and Gilbert should first encounter Moira when in the company of their famous new friends. If this did not happen at Vici then I'd have had to invent a whole new scene just for this encounter—and how often would Diana and Stephen socialize publicly with these two nonentities (whose screenplay, lest we forget, they had no intention of ever using)? I massaged the issue as best I could by having Diana own the restaurant and by putting them in a private dining room, but I still felt I was bending things just a bit. (Though I recently read Kurt Wenzel's highly enjoyable *Gotham Tragic* in which one top-secret conversation after another is held in the private dining room of a hot restaurant, in front of waitstaff yet, and this made me feel a little better.)

The most enjoyable part of writing my books is, well, *writing* them—the part after I've figured out the story and can finally start telling it. I love writing sentences and especially love rewriting them, polishing, honing, searching ceaselessly for the wry turn of phrase and *le mot juste* (or at least *le mot* I haven't already used six times.) A big part of the fun is writing in the first person, in Philip's voice. There's a certain fantasy or wish-fulfillment element to it. I get to pretend that I've personally lived through all these fantastic and glamorous events and then relate them to the reader as amusingly as possible. (I've always felt that Philip strives so clearly to amuse because he's embarrassingly aware that his own behavior in the story is pretty boneheaded and he hopes that, by at least telling it well, he'll redeem himself somewhat in the mind of the reader.) And, of course, there are all the other characters I get to give voice to, many of whom I feel enormous affection for. Readers often speak of getting "lost" in a good book, luxuriating in a world far different from their own, one they're sad to leave when the story finally ends. I've often had that feeling while reading a favorite book, but feel it all the more acutely when I'm writing the book.

How do you go about mapping out your elaborate plots? Do you know before you even put pen to paper what's going to happen, or do you let it all unfold as you write?

I tend to outline pretty heavily. I can't imagine how else you'd go about writing such a complicated plot. For the first two years I spent on the book, working only during my vacations from *Frasier*, I concentrated solely on figuring out the plot. (My notes ultimately weighed in at 26,000 words on 84 single-spaced pages.) When I'd reached the point where I had a detailed map of the first half and a somewhat sketchier one of the second, I began chapter one. I wrote seven or eight chapters, then started feeling nervous because I hadn't figured out the ending, so I stopped and concentrated on that. It was a very happy day when it occurred to me that Claire could allege that "Oscar" (whose identity I'd not even thought about) was, in fact, the DA's son and that he'd been having an affair with Stephen. Thus was Billy born and I went back over the outline, finding ways to thread him through so that he'd be there at the end, securely nestled in Claire's top hat at the precise moment that she needed to produce a rabbit.

Are there more adventures ahead for Philip and Gilbert?

I certainly hope so. I already have some preliminary notions of what Gilbert might be up to in a fourth book and, given my druthers, would devote almost all my time to writing novels and the occasional play or musical. We live, alas, in a nation where there's no shorter route to insolvency than a career dedicated primarily to penning Light Comic Fiction Heavily Populated by Homosexuals. And while I'm flattered that many in my small but loyal following have voiced their desire that I write more novels, I fear that, till the day comes when one of them nobly steps forward, checkbook in hand, and says, "You do another book, Joe, I'll handle the mortgage," I'll be forced to toil primarily in the more lucrative field of television.

OK, indulge us: does Stephen Donato have a real-life counterpart?

From what one hears, yes, plenty, and, in creating Stephen, I thought about all of them. I was keen to avoid him seeming like a thinly veiled portrait of any particular actor, mainly because I feared that in many people's minds the book would cease to be a comedy about Hollywood and become a comedy about [famous name here]. Stephen and his behavior are equal parts composite, conjecture, and invention. I took care to introduce aspects into his life (like his equally famous diva mother) that did not dovetail with any of the real-life stars whose sexuality has inspired much fevered speculation. That said, there are several among that notorious bunch whose exploits, if even half the stories I've heard are true, lend credibility to what I'd initially feared might seem an unrealistically reckless streak in Stephen.

Questions and topics for discussion

1. Who is your favorite character in *My Lucky Star*? Do you find yourself drawn to the more conventional characters or the more outlandish ones? Are there any characters in whom you see qualities of your own, however exaggerated?

2. What roles do Philip, Claire, and Gilbert play in their friendship? What does each one add to the trio? Does the way they interact remind you of any of your own friendships?

3. *My Lucky Star* is great fun to read, but it's also a biting social satire. What vices/people/habits is the author commenting on? Which situations or characters did you find the most successful in this respect?

4. When Philip volunteers to write Lily's memoirs, he infiltrates her scheme through the use of his own. When else does this sort of backstabbing happen in the book? What do these situations say about each of the characters involved? Is one motive better or more moral than the other?

5. As the novel's heroes make their way through the maze that is Hollywood, Gilbert manages to get them into one sticky situation after another. Why are Claire and Philip always unable to put their

foot down, no matter how hard they may try? Do you have a friend like this, who always creates trouble and yet whom you can't resist having around?

6. From a faded film star to a backstabbing ex-wife, *My Lucky Star*'s Hollywood is filled with characters out for blood. But how else is one to act in such a dog-eat-dog city? Are there any characters you sympathize with, despite their seemingly evil intentions? Discuss the motives behind each of the key players.

7. Have you been to Hollywood? Do you think Keenan's depiction of the city is accurate?

8. Do you like Keenan's swift and witty voice? What do you think comic novels offer us as readers, besides enjoyment? Do you find comedy to be even more telling than drama, or less?